The
Illustrated
PLANT
LORE

A unique pot-pourri of history,
folklore and practical advice

JOSEPHINE ADDISON

Illustrated by Rosemary Wise
Foreword by David Bellamy

SIDGWICK & JACKSON
LONDON

My thanks to David Bellamy for writing the Foreword; to the Central Libraries in Grimsby and Lincoln for their help with reference books; and to the Botanical Library in London.

First published in Great Britain in 1985
by Sidgwick & Jackson Limited

Copyright © 1985 by Josephine Addison

Line drawings by Rosemary Wise
Designed by Lynda Smith

ISBN 0-283-99134-8

Phototypeset by Falcon Graphic Art Ltd
Wallington, Surrey
Printed in Great Britain
by
Biddles Ltd, Guildford, Surrey
for Sidgwick & Jackson Limited
1 Tavistock Chambers, Bloomsbury Way
London WC1A 2SG

Contents

Note: plants which appear in bold type in the text are those with a plant entry of their own.

For my sons
James and Duncan

Ye botanists, I cannot talk like you
And give to every plant its name and rank,
Taught by Linné, yet I perceive in all,
Known or unknown, in the garden raised,
Or nurtured in the hedge-row or the field,
A secret something that delights my eye
And meliorates my heart.

JAMES HURDIS, 1763–1801

Foreword

I will always remember my Granny warning us never to bring May blossom into the house, 'it's plain back luck' she said. She also extolled the virtues of lavender, pennyroyal, and witch hazel – and she was right. Grannies always are. Born in Hoxton and married in Spurgeons Tabernacle, she lived all her formative years in London's East End which, even in those days, could not have been regarded as a rural environment. Yet she was well versed in what can only be called plantlore.

I knew that the juice of the dock cured the sting of the nettle, that willow trees could provide a cure for headaches, and that the poison in a foxglove was sufficient to kill you many times over. My Dad was a pharmacist and so we were brought up with *materia medica* which gave official recognition to many of Granny's remedies. But why are rowan trees still planted at the gates of many houses – to ward away the witches or to provide sweet jelly for Halloween? Why are lungworts so called, and where did the name selfheal come from? What is the Doctrine of Signature? Read this book and rediscover a wealth of things that we in the twentieth century have begun to forget.

Josephine Addison's book is rich with the knowledge of a mellow past when spring, summer, autumn and winter seasoned all hopes and fears and when a detailed knowledge of plants was the only hope anyone had for a good harvest and a healthy life. The same is of course still true, for we depend on plants for all the food we eat and the oxygen we breathe. What is more, even in this overcrowded, underfed, electronic, space-age world seventy per cent of all primary medicine comes in the form of extracts of plants, and from a knowledge of ethnobotany and homoeopathy – which has its roots firm in plantlore.

Plant breeders work continuously to keep the pampered megacrops on which this hungry world depends one jump ahead of disease and epidemic. To do this they must 'outbreed' with wilder, more ancient genetic stock weeds which hold within their primitive nature unique information from the past. Scientists are also forced to seek out knowledge concerning the more benign gifts of nature.

In recent years, study of extracts of *catharanthus roseus* – a plant from Madagascar, endangered in the wild yet prized in Jamaica as a cure for diabetes – has provided the world with the drug *Vincristine*, which now gives hope to three out of every five victims of leukemia. *D-tubocurarine*, extracted from a forest vine and used by the local Indians to poison their arrows, has helped to make open heart surgery an everyday reality. While the vitamin F, present in the extracts of the wasteland weed, evening primrose, helps prevent arteries from fatty decay and could alleviate the need for surgery.

My Granny was right. The beautiful May petals would soon fall, to litter the linoleum, and the stench of the dying flowers would dent the pride of a dozen amorous tom-cats. Lavender contains oil of lavender, pennyroyal the drug *pulegone*, and witch hazel has a home in many bathroom cabinets. All of these find a use in medicine, provided the dosages and method of administration are correct and the patient is not allergic to the preparation, and here the warnings must be sounded strong and clear.

It grieves me to know that if only we had studied Egyptian papyri in the detail they deserved we might have benefitted from penicillin long before the 1940s, and that only one per cent of the world's flora has been screened for its potential usefulness, while ten per cent of all the world's plants live on the brink of extinction. We still insist that money does not grow on trees and relegate much of what we learn from the past to the realm of Old Wives Tales, and quackery. This book draws together and celebrates much of this learning. Learning which throughout history has enriched prose, poetry and art in all its forms, facts which could so easily have been forgotten.

David Bellamy
Bedburn, 1985

Introduction

I consider myself very fortunate to have spent most of my life living in the country and having the opportunity over the years to make notes and observations on the flowers and trees which we have in abundance. Looking back to my childhood, however, I cannot help but notice that many plants we considered quite commonplace, such as the cowslip, are fast disappearing. The need for more land for agriculture and building development has taken its toll on the woodlands, marshes, hedgerows and pastures which formerly hummed with the sounds of insects and birds and were bright with the movement of colourful butterflies.

There are many books on wild flowers but I felt that if I could write of interesting superstitions, old sayings and history associated with them, and also of their special 'language', it would not only enliven walks in the country but make us look at this very beautiful backdrop to our lives in a totally different way.

Many plants are not indigenous to this country but have travelled from distant empires over the centuries – living reminders of the customs and festivals of the ancient Greeks, the Romans and the Egyptians, for example. There are, however, many contradictions in the customs and superstitions surrounding some plants, mainly due to regional differences in the identity of flowers and their names and to the confusion brought about by the imposition of Christian beliefs on pagan traditions.

For the quotations I have drawn on the work of many poets. The nature poets provided the most valuable sources, in particular John Clare, the Northamptonshire farm labourer who, despite poverty and a limited education, managed to establish himself as a poet whose reputation has survived. Victoria (Vita) Sackville-West, whose living memorial is the garden which she so lovingly created at Sissinghurst Castle, gave me great pleasure with her long poem, 'The Garden'. Many of the older books I used did not always give the source of their quotations or old sayings but I have included them because they were so often appropriate for a particular plant.

One of my oldest sources of information is Pliny (C. Plinius Secunda the Elder), born in Verona in A.D. 23. A very industrious man who wrote a lengthy work on natural history consisting of thirty-seven books, he died ever curious, seeking knowledge viewing Mount Vesuvius! The Tudor era produced a number of botanists and herbalists such as John Gerard, who wrote the *Herball or Historie of Plantes* (1583). He brought together many of the writings of others in this work, and he also made a list of the plants he grew in his own garden, which gives an excellent idea of those being cultivated at the time. Another famous herbalist, Nicholas Culpepper (1616–54), believed that every disease was governed by a planet and could be cured by a herb under the dominion of that planet, or its opposite. Centuries ago, plants were gathered according to astrological rules which, if not observed, were said to make them ineffective. Later, botanists and chemists, whilst dismissing the astrological aspect, claimed that the medicinal properties of plants were more potent at certain times of the day and year. Physicians also used to treat the whole man – soul as well as body. The folklore of medicine is the most ancient aspect of the art of healing. Plants were also thought to cure parts of the body they resembled, and (the basis of modern homoeopathy) could be used to cure something they had caused.

Interest in alternative medicine has increased over the last few years, and particularly in herbal remedies, but they do not have the full approval of the British Medical Association yet and plants and remedies should not be taken without medical advice or consultation with a homoeopathic chemist. For those interested in herbal remedies there is a wealth of information available. I have only touched upon the subject but hope I have whetted the appetite.

In recent years the growing awareness and need for nature conservation has contributed to a revival in craftwork, ranging from the use of various woods in carving and furniture making to dyeing wool for spinning and weaving with vegetable dyes obtained from leaves and flowers or roots. There is also an increasing interest in pressed flowers, pot pourri, and a revival of interest in the use of herbs in cooking. Nurseries selling herb plants are now quite commonplace, although a small number of dedicated growers have always existed:

> From far and near they come, for our quiet fame –
> The men and women who wish for plants to grow –
> Whose gardens harbour herbs without a name
> And those beguiled by the lore, who long to know
> All that they can of the 'mystery and the art'
> (To borrow an ancient phrase); and 'way they go
> With a fragant trophy, an infinitesimal part
> Of the stored ages, the perfumed winds that blow
> Through the long passage of centuries past.
>
> MARGARET BROWNLOW, 'TRADITION' (1956)

It is worth bearing in mind that many plants are now protected and, as a rule, plants should never be dug up in the wild.

It is to Carl Von Linneor (Linnaeus, 1707–78), the Swedish naturalist, that we are indebted for the first comprehensive classification of animals, vegetables, and minerals. His Linnaean System divided each into classes, orders, genera, species, and varieties, according to certain characteristics. In this book I have used the generic and specific names. This charming poem, called 'Those Latin Names' by Reginald Arkell, attempts to explain to a child that English flowers have Latin names!

> *Eranthis* is an aconite
> As everybody knows,
> And *Helleborus Niger* is
> Our friend the Christmas Rose.
> *Galanthus* is a snowdrop,
> *Matthiola* is a stock
> And *Cardmine* the meadow flower
> Which you call lady's smock.
> *Muscari* is a grape hyacinth,
> *Dianthus* is a pink –
> And that's as much as one small head
> Can carry, I should think.
> She listened, very patiently;
> Then turned, when I had done
> To where a fine Forsythia
> Was smiling in the sun.
> Said she: 'I *love* this yellow stuff.'
> And that, somehow, seemed praise enough.

But I have also included a few of the familiar country names for each plant. These vary in different parts of the country but I hope I have put in those generally used. There are bound to be some omissions. My main sources for common and botanical names were *The Wild Flowers of Britain and Northern Europe*, R. Fitter, A. Fitter and M. Blamey (Collins, 1978) and *Sanders' Encyclopaedia of Gardens*, (Collingridge, 1966 edn).

Occasionally I have made reference to the old and new calendar. In 1752 England adopted the new style (Gregorian) calendar which suppressed eleven days, so Wednesday 2 September was followed by 14 September. This gave rise to a double computation: Lady Day, 25 March, Old Lady Day, 6 April; Midsummer Day, 24 June, Old Midsummer Day, 6 July; Michaelmas Day, 29 September, Old Michaelmas Day, 11 October; Christmas Day, 25 December, Old Christmas Day, 6 January.

Lady Day commemorates the Annunciation of Our Lady the Virgin Mary and there are many flowers dedicated to her – mostly white ones, some carrying the prefix 'Lady'. The origins of Midsummer Day, which is also the feast of St John the Baptist, can be traced back to the pagan fire festivals honouring the sun gods. Michaelmas Day, the festival of St Michael and All Angels is a more sober period – the day magistrates are elected. It is also a quarter-day, when rent is due. (Agricultural rents are still paid on quarter-days and the other three are Lady Day, Midsummer Day and Christmas Day.) The Christmas Day celebrations, incomplete without an abundance of evergreen leaves, falls about the time of the great Roman feast of Saturn, Saturnalia, when they too decorated their temples with evergreens. A perfect example of the rituals that have become strongly interwoven during the passage of time.

It was from Gertrude Jobes's *Dictionary of Mythology, Folklore and Symbols* that I took the delightful language of the flowers. This charming custom of sending messages with a simple flower, or even a bouquet, expressing one's thoughts was very popular during the Tudor period. William Shakespeare makes constant reference to it in his plays, hinting at the secret meanings of flowers – with which his audience must have been familiar. In the western world each day is also assigned a flower. However, not all plants have a day as they far exceed the days in number. The selection of flowers and trees for this book does not include all plants either. It is based on the amount of interesting lore I could find and I apologize if a particular favourite has been excluded.

I hope reading my notes gives you as much pleasure as I had collecting them, and that you discover a new countryside as you turn the pages.

March 1985

Acacia   see **False acacia**

Acanthus
Acanthus spinosus

Greek *akanthos*, prickle, is the derivation of the name. Also known as bear's breech, acanthus has handsome, thistle-like leaves and long flower spikes which make excellent large dried flower arrangements in winter. Earlier botanists classified the plant as a thistle, and it was generally agreed that the beauty of the leaves exceeded that of the flowers. Some authorities claim that it was introduced to England during the sixteenth century; however, it may have arrived much earlier for the name appears in *De Naturis Rebus*, *c*. 1200: 'Cucumber, poppy, daffodil and acanthus ought to be grown in a good garden.'

The legend of acanthus is that it sprang up around a basket of trinkets that Callimachus, a Corinthian architect, had placed on his daughter's grave. The leaves, which curved back and around the basket, so impressed him with their shape and beauty that he used them as a design motif in his buildings: the capital of the Corinthian column is decorated with acanthus leaves. Acanthus is often found on ancient Greek temples, probably signifying immortality and a funeral leaf. In early Christian art it is the plant of heaven, typifying the garden of heaven.

Herbalists used a compound of the leaves and roots in the treatment of burns, cramp and gout; also internally and externally for stomach disorders. The leaves, boiled or bruised, were applied as a poultice to heal broken bones.

Acanthus is the birthday flower for 23 December. In the language of the flowers it signifies love of art, and that nothing will separate the giver and the receiver. Astrologically the plant is under the dominion of the moon.

Aconite   see **Monkshood**

Adderstongue
Ophioglossum vulgatum

The generic name *Ophis*, comes from the Greek for serpent, and *glossa*, tongue: in fruit the plant was thought to resemble the tongue of a serpent. Like the reptile, it was believed to have great power for evil, to destroy the grass in which it grew and injure the cattle which grazed there. The plant is also known as adder's spear and Christ's spear. In his play *The Sad Shepherd* the Elizabethan dramatist, Ben Jonson, lists plants favoured by witches for sinister purposes:

> . . .The Venom'd Plants
> Wherewith she kills! where the sad Mandrake grows
> Whose grones are deathful! the dead numming Nightshade!
> The stupifying Hemlock! Adders tongue! and Martagon!

Nevertheless herbalists prized adderstongue as a medicinal herb to cure snakebite:

> For those that are with newts, or snakes, or adders stung,
> He seeketh out an herb that's called adders tongue,
> As nature it ordained, its own like hurt to cure,
> And sportive did herself to niceties inure.

wrote Michael Drayton (1516–1631). Culpepper, the Elizabethan herbalist, favoured adderstongue leaves with 'distilled water of horse-tail' (see **marestail**) as an excellent remedy for internal wounds and sore eyes. Adderstongue ointment was a well-known preparation of plantain and other herbs mixed with the plant to treat a variety of wounds.

Astrologically adderstongue is under the dominion of the moon and the sign of Cancer. In the language of the flowers it signifies jealousy.

Agrimony
Agrimonia eupatoria

The generic name is derived from Greek *agremone*, formerly misinterpreted as meaning a white speck in the eye, for which the plant was said to be a cure. The specific name comes from Eupator, King of Pontus (today, northern Turkey), who is reputed to have used the plant. Country names include rats' tails, salt and pepper, money-in-both-pockets, cockle burr and church steeples; the Anglo-Saxons called it *garclive*, and it was the *egremoine* of Chaucer (*c.* 1340–1400), who recommended it for 'alle woundes and bad back'. In his 'Muse's Elysium' Michael Drayton mentions it with several other supposed herbs of virtue:

> Next these here Egremony is,
> That helps the serpent's biting;
> The blessed Betony by this,
> Whose cures deserving writing;
> This All-heal, and so named of right,
> New wounds so quickly healing;
> A thousand more I could recite
> Most worthy of revealing.

Herbalists used the plant extensively to treat almost all complaints, as well as wounds and dislocations. An infusion of the leaves made an excellent tonic and was used until recent times, particularly for rheumatism and as a gargle for a relaxed throat. The plant was said to have even stronger powers, though this source is unknown:

> If it be leyd under a mann's head,
> He shall sleepyn as he were dead
> He shall never drede ne wakyn,
> Till fro under his head it be taken.

The whole plant, dried naturally and powdered, yields a yellow dye.

In the language of the flowers, agrimony means gratitude. Astrologically it is under the dominion of Jupiter and the sign of Cancer.

Alder   see **Common alder**

Almond
Prunus dulcis

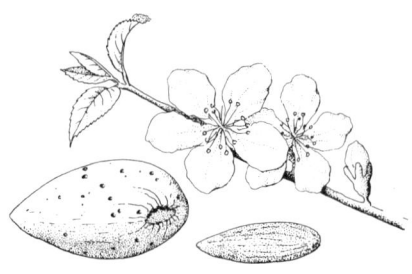

Greek *proune*, plum, is the source of the generic name. Almond derives from a word meaning to hasten or awake early, referring to the growth of the tree. In Hebrew the name signifies a watcher and typifies divine approval. The almond is alleged to be the tree from which Aaron took his magic wand, and in the Christian tradition it is an emblem of the Virgin Mary. *Prunus dulcis* is one of the earliest-flowering almond species, the blossom appearing in February. A classical poet wrote about predicting the quality of the harvest by the blooming of the almond tree:

> Mark well the flowering Almond in the wood;
> If odourous blooms the bearing branches lead,
> The glebe will answer to the sylvan reign,
> Great heats will follow, and large crops of grain;
> But if a wood of leaves o'er shade the tree,
> Such and so barren will the harvest be.

Bitter oil of almonds is well-known as the poison cyanide, but there is only a minute trace of it in the ordinary almond. Confectionery is flavoured with almond; marzipan is probably its best-known form. A butter consisting of almonds, roses and sugar, eaten with violets, 'rejoiceth the heart and comforteth the brain, and qualifieth the heat of the liver', said Culpepper. Sweet almond oil was used as a demulcent for coughs.

Almond is the birthday flower for 8 April, and signifies heedlessness, indiscretion, stupidity; it also means the awakener, the first to life in winter, and is a symbol of self-protection, vigilance and both virginity and fruitfulness. The almond in flower signifies hope. **Mulberry** and almond flowering simultaneously indicates the middle way between hastiness and slowness – the first flowers early, the second late.

Angelica
Angelica

The plant was believed to be of heavenly origin, hence its name. Legend tells us that the wonderful virtues of the plant were revealed to a monk in a dream. Country names for it are Holy Ghost plant and holy plant, and it is said to flower on the Feast of the Apparition of St Michael (8 May old-style calendar).

The wild plant, *Angelica officinalis*, used to grow freely in London, particularly on the slopes surrounding the Tower of London and in Lincoln's Inn Fields, where it was collected for medicinal and culinary purposes. It was cultivated as garden angelica, *A. archangelica*, for its aromatic stem, which was boiled in sugar syrup and used as a sweetmeat and later for cake decoration. The confection was once in great demand for 'wind and strengthening the stomach', and was surpassed only by ginger.

Robert Bulkeley in *His Book*, dated 1641, suggests angelica as being helpful 'in extreme labour and when women have been left for dead'. The recipe consisted of a lapful of angelica and freshly spun **flax**, boiled in water for half an hour and placed, in the pan, under a special delivery stool. Sitting on the stool, the prospective mother had to drink 'stooned horse dung strined in white wine, some three rounds to halfe a pint of wine'. The horse dung had to come from a family animal as a precaution against its having been bewitched. The juice of angelica root was placed on teeth to relieve toothache, and the distilled water from the plant used for eye and ear complaints. Many herbalists used the distilled water from plants for their remedies. The plant, or parts of it, are boiled in water and the distilled vapour provides the required essence.

Angelica is the birthday flower for 11 July, and signifies ecstasy, inspiration and magic. Astrologically it is a herb of the sun and comes under the sign of Leo. Magical properties were attributed to it, such as offering protection against witchcraft. It was also chewed in the vain hope of rendering people immune to the plague (according to a poem quoted by Rev. H. Friend in his *Flowers and Flower Lore*, published in 1883):

> Contagious aire ingendering Pestilence
> Infects not those that in the mouth have ta'en
> Angelica, that happy counterbane
> Sent down from Heav'n by some celestial scout
> As well the name and nature both avout.

Antirrhinum   see **Snapdragon**

Apple
Malus domestica

The generic name is the Latin for apple. Many varieties were propagated from the wild apple or **crab apple** and were cultivated in monastery gardens during the Middle Ages. In his 'Poly-olbion' of 1613, Michael Drayton wrote of the Kentish orchards, listing varieties already familiar at that time:

> The pippen, which we hold of kernel fruits the king;
> The apple orange; then the savoury russetan;
> The permain, which to France long ere to us 'twas known,
> Which careful fruiterers now have denizen'd our own;
> The renat, which though at first it from the pippen came,
> Grown through its pureness nice, assumes that curious name;
> The sweeting, for whose sake the schoolboys oft make war,
> The wilding, costard, then the well-known pomewater,
> And sundry other fruits of good yet several taste,
> And have their sundry names in sundry counties placed.

From early times the apple was regarded as holy or magical and in some districts was thought unsuitable to eat. Ideally the fruit should be blessed by rain on St Peter's Day, or St Swithin's Day. Blossom appearing in the autumn foretold the death of a member of the owner's family especially if the flowers and fruit were on the same branch. An alternative death omen was an apple left to over-winter on the tree after the fruit had been picked. However in some parts of Britain it was considered unlucky to remove all the apples – some should be left for the birds or, in earlier times, as a gift for the fairies and spirits. It is said that if the sun shines through the trees on Christmas morning, although some sources say Easter, it is a sign of a good crop and a prosperous year for the owner. An ancient ceremony to ensure a good apple crop, known as apple-wassailing, was celebrated on Twelfth Night or New Year's Eve. People would assemble in the orchard at dusk, armed with guns, kettles, pans and cider. One tree was chosen and everybody drank to it. Cider was poured over the roots and a piece of cider-soaked toast fastened to it. Guns were discharged through the topmost branches to rouse the sleeping tree spirits and drive away the demons. Extra noise was generated by the beating of trays, pans and kettles. A great deal of singing, shouting and dancing accompanied these rites.

One popular Hallowtide game was really a love divination ceremony. Each person would whirl an apple round on a string in front of the fire. The first apple to fall indicated a marriage, the last that the owner would die unwed. Another form of love divination involved peeling an apple in one long strip and throwing it over the left shoulder: it would form the initials of one's future spouse on the ground where it fell. Apple pips also played their part: girls pressed them on their cheeks, giving a name to each one; the pip that stayed on the longest indicated the future husband. Pips were also arranged on the bars of the fireplace and these words spoken:

> If you love me, bounce and fly,
> If you hate me, lie and die.

If the pip burst noisily the lover was faithful, but not if it burnt quietly away. A variation, however, held that a silent burning foretold a smooth courtship with a happy ending, while a bursting pip meant the break-up of a romance.

Superstitions associated with the medicinal virtues of the apple are very familiar. Apples were recommended for melancholy disorders, and an unusual cure for warts required the fruit to be halved and each portion rubbed on the wart; the halves were tied together again and then buried – as the fruit rotted away the wart would disappear. Eating a large apple at midnight on Halloween would prevent one having a cold for a year. John Gerard (1545–1612), the herbalist, refers to a cosmetic ointment consisting of apple pulp, swine's grease and rosewater, known as pomatum, as being very popular.

Apple blossom is the birthday flower for 31 December, signifying preference. In the language of the flowers it means 'He prefers you', and 'Fame called him great and good'.

Arrowhead
Sagittaria sagittifolia

The botanical name comes from Latin *sagitta*, arrow, referring to the shape of the leaves. Country names for this charming aquatic plant are water archer and Moses in the bulrushes. Charles Bryant, in his *Flora Dietetica* (published in 1783), the object of which was to point out various plants which might be used as food, wrote, 'I cured some of the bulbs of this plant, in the same manner that saloop [a drink prepared from sassafras bark] is cured, when they acquired a sort of pellucidness, and on

boiling afterwards they broke into a gelatinous meal and tasted like old peas boiled,' – hardly culinary praise.

Ash
Fraxinus excelsior

The tree's generic name comes from Latin *frango*, I break, denoting the ease with which it may be split. Because of its toughness it was used for spearshafts, and the Anglo-Saxon *aesc* (ash) came to mean spear, and *aesc-plega*, the game of spears, a battle. Ash is assigned in classical mythology to the bloodthirsty Mars, god of war, but it is perhaps better known in Norse mythology, where it is dedicated to Odin, the chief god, and is called Yggdrasil, the Tree of Life. The legendary ash represented the universe on a small scale. By its roots were the three wells of primitive force, of remembrance and of destruction and rejuvenation. Idun, the goddess of life, lived in the branches. The three weird sisters of fate, the past, present and future, sprinkled the tree with pure water so that it would not wither. An eagle, a squirrel and a hawk lived in the branches and a serpent in the roots; a goat, which fed on the leaves, gave milk to the heroes of Valhalla, the Nordic heaven. Under the tree stood a horn which would one day blow to announce the end of the universe.

In Northern Europe the ash was generally considered sacred and therefore protective. In Scotland a sprig of ash placed over a bed safeguarded the occupants. Like the **rowan**, it was planted around the home for the same reason. In some parts of Europe honey from the sacred ash tree used to be the first food put to the lips of a newborn baby; in Scotland a green ash stick was burnt at one end and the sap that oozed out of the other end was used for the same purpose. On Christmas Eve the burning of the ashen-faggot, ash twigs bound with more ash, was a popular fire charm ceremony in inns and farmhouses; single girls would pick one of the bands, and the first one to burst in the heat indicated a marriage. In Brand's *Popular Antiquities* of 1797 a poem alludes to this old custom:

> . . . nine bandages it bears,
> And as they disjoin (as custom wills),
> A mighty jug of cyder's brought,
> With brandy mixed to elevate the guests.

Mothers would suspend their children in cradles from the ash branches 'that the shadow of the tree might protect them from noxious creatures'. Witches' brooms were said to be made from ash wood to prevent their owners drowning, and generally speaking ash did have a reputation as a charm against such perils: it was used for boat building, by the Vikings in particular. Advice on using ash as fuel is given in a rhyming proverb:

> Burn Ash-wood green
> 'Tis a fire for a queen;
> Burn Ash-wood sear,
> 'Twill make a man swear.

It is usually found growing on good land, which gave rise to an old saying: 'May your footfall be by the root of an Ash tree.'

Ash is well-known throughout Britain as a weather oracle, though the words vary in different counties:

> Oak before ash, only a splash;
> Ash before oak, in for a soak.

Another old saying, 'Oak choke, ash splash', meant that if the oak came into leaf first, dry, dusty weather would follow, but if the ash was first, rainy weather was to come.

A leaf with an even number of leaflets was called an even-ash, and was used in love divination ceremonies:

> The even-Ash-leaf in my hand
> The first I meet shall be my man.

If a Yorkshire girl slept with the leaf under her pillow her future husband would appear, whether he was married at the time or not.

Ash was used in the treatment of a variety of complaints. A country remedy for bedwetting involved sending the afflicted child to select an ash tree. The following day he had to gather ash keys from it, place them with his left hand, in the hollow of his right arm, and carry them home to be burnt on the hearth. If the child then urinated on the ashes he would be cured. Passing a child through a split in an ash sapling was thought to treat hernia and rickets. Whooping cough was cured by pinning a lock of the patient's hair to an ash tree. In some parts of England April and May were considered the best months for curing children's warts. A packet of new pins was carried to an ash tree by one of the parents; a pin was pressed into the bark of the tree and then into the wart until it caused pain, and then back again into the bark. Alternatively one could cross the wart three times with a pin – after each crossing this charm was spoken:

> Ashen tree, Ashen tree,
> Pray buy this wart off me.

A thirteenth-century remedy for ulcerated ears suggested boiling ash keys in the patient's urine, soaking black wool in the liquid and placing it in the ear, with the words 'By God's help, it will cure it.' Animals were also said to benefit from the ash: mice and shrews were holed up in the tree to cure diseased cattle – as soon as the small creatures died, it was believed, the animals would be cured.

Governed by the sign of the sun, ash is the birthday flower for 27 December, and signifies grandeur. In the language of the flowers it means 'With me you are safe'. It is a symbol of adaptability, modesty and nobility.

Asparagus   see **Wild asparagus**

Aspen
Populus tremula

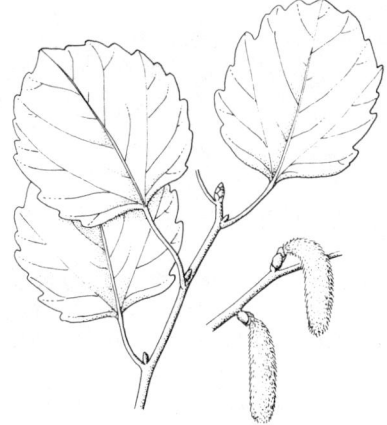

Named from Latin *populus*, the common people, it means tree of the people: '. . . its readily moved and ever-stirring leaves were, like the ever restless multitude, quickened into action by the slightest breath.' The constant movement of the foliage was also 'likened to the unceasing course of time'. Country names include trembling poplar, old wives' tongue, shaking asp and pipple.

In the Christian tradition it is a tree of mourning, pride and sinful arrogance. According to one legend the cross was made of aspen and that is why it trembles with shame and horror at its past:

> Trembles yon towering aspen tree,
> Like one whose bygone deeds of ill
> At hush of night before him sweep,
> To scare his dreams and murder sleep.

Herbalists long regarded it as a cure for ague, and in *Folklore of the Northern Counties* Henderson refers to a girl pinning a lock of hair to the tree and saying:

> Aspen tree, aspen tree
> I prithee to shake and shiver instead of me.

If she returned home in complete silence she was supposed to be cured. Alternatively a piece of fingernail (like hair, used in witchcraft world-wide) was pressed into the bark of the tree; as the bark grew over it the cure would gradually take place.

The bark of the tree, which is somewhat astringent, was used in tanning and powdered as a medicine for domestic animals. In the language of the flowers aspen signifies scandal, lamentation and fear.

Auricula
Primula auricula

The botanical name comes from a diminutive of Latin *primus*, first, and *auricula*, ear-shaped. An old name for the plant is bear's ears, referring to the shape of the leaves; they are also rather leathery and appear to be covered in a white powder, which explains another of its names, dusty miller.

The first auriculas are said to have been brought to England by the Huguenot refugees in about 1570, although they must have been varieties of the wild plant. In the early nineteenth century the auricula was very popular with the miners and silk weavers of Lancashire and Cheshire. New varieties and colours were introduced, societies formed and exhibitions held. A copper kettle was often given as a prize.

In the language of the flowers it signifies 'Wealth is not always happiness', and it is a symbol of avarice.

Autumn crocus   see **Meadow saffron**

Balm
Melissa officinalis

The ancient Greek proper name Melissophyllon, meaning 'beloved by bees', is the source of the generic name and refers to the quantities of nectar in the flowers. According to Alice M. Coates in *Flowers and their Histories*, Pliny the Elder, the first-century Roman naturalist, recorded: 'When they [bees] do strain away, they do finde their way home againe by it.' The plant is also known as bee-herb. Beekeepers valued it as a forage plant and rubbed it on the insides of the skeps. Pliny tells us that 'the hives of bees being rubbed with the leaves of balme, causeth the Bees to keepe together, and causeth others to come unto them'.

Balm is an abbreviation of balsam, whose scent it resembles. During Elizabethan times the delicate, lemon-scented leaves were used in chaplets and garlands, in which connection Michael Drayton refers to it in his *Herbularis*:

> The Balm and Mint help to make up
> My chaplet, and for the trial
> Costmary that so likes the Cup,
> And next is Pennyroyal.

Juice was extracted from the leaves and the stems to make wine, and rubbed into furniture to impart a lemon scent. Shakespeare alludes to this in *The Merry Wives of Windsor*:

> The several chairs of order look you scour
> With juice of balm. . . .

Culpepper wrote that 'it causeth the mind and heart to become merry . . . and driveth away all troublesome cares and thoughts'. Essence of balm was believed to preserve youth, and Llewellyn, a Prince of Glamorgan, was said to have lived to the age of 108 with the assistance of the plant extract. Much earlier, Pliny wrote that if it was tied to a sword that had inflicted a wound the bleeding would stop instantly. Balm was the principal ingredient of *eau des Carmes*, a forerunner of *eau de Cologne*, which was produced by Carmelite monks in Paris during the seventeenth century.

Balm gives a pleasant fragrance to tea, particularly China tea, and summer drinks. The effect, as Culpepper had noted, is to relieve tiredness and headaches, to calm the nervous system and stimulate the heart. Medicinally the plant is a moderate stimulant and diaphoretic – a warm infusion to cause perspiration is a twentieth-century remedy to relieve painful menstruation.

For culinary purposes the fresh or dried leaves give a lemon-mint flavour to any dish. It can be used in soups, stews, sauces, salads, mayonnaise and egg dishes, and is particularly good with fish. Astrologically balm is under the dominion of Jupiter and the sign of Cancer.

Barley
Hordeum sativum

The botanical name is the Latin word for barley, plus *sativum*, cultivated. Its bearded spike gave the plant its common name, in Old English *bearlic*, meaning bearlike or burlike. Most barley in Britain is grown for the brewing industry. Barley bree or barley-broth was a malt liquor brewed from barley; Robert Burns refers to it in his poem 'Willie Brew'd a Peck o'Malt':

> The cock may craw, the day may daw,
> And aye we'll taste the barley-bree.

A heap or stack of barley was known as a barley mow.

In ancient fertility rites barley, regarded as a king, was castrated and ritually murdered at the harvest feast, the end of his reign. Superstition surrounds the sowing of barley seed, for instance, to sow the seed on wet land would ruin the crop:

> Dry your barley land in October,
> Or you'll always be sober.

Advice on the most favourable time to sow is suggested by the size of the leaves on elm trees:

> When the elm leaf is as big as a mouse's ear,
> When you sow your barley never fear
> When the elm leaf is as big as an ox's eye
> Then say I
> Hie, boys hie.

Alternatively 1 March is a possibility:

> Upon St David's Day
> Put oats and barley in the clay.

Also 'Sow Barley when the Sloe is white'. An omen for a bad crop of barley is found in the couplet:

> Bad for barley, good for corn,
> When cuckoo comes to an empty thorn.

Traditionally barley was 'sown' on the Eve of St Agnes (29 January). St Agnes is the patron saint of young virgins, and the 'sowing' was a love divination ceremony which took place in an orchard where a girl would scatter seeds under an **apple** tree, saying:

> Barley, barley I sow there
> That my true love I may see
> Take thy rake and follow me.

Her future husband could be seen behind her, raking up the seed.

Herbalists recommended a variety of poultices consisting mainly of barley meal. One such recipe for inflammations on the body required barley meal to be boiled with vinegar and honey, with a few dried figs added, and applied to the affected area. Water distilled from green barley in May was said to be very good for eye complaints. White bread soaked in this distillation could be bound on the eyes for further treatment.

Astrologically barley is assigned to Saturn.

Barberry
Berberis vulgaris

The generic name is a Latinized form of the Arabic word for the fruit of one of these sharply spined shrubs. Alternative names are jaunders tree and guild tree. Farmers dislike it because it is said to be the alternative host of the wheat rust fungus, which blackens the ears of the wheat.

Herbalists recommended the inner bark of the rind, boiled in wine, as a daily tonic to cleanse the body, relieve itching scalps, and cure ringworm, jaundice and boils. In some countries the bitter roots were used to treat syphilis and complaints involving a discharge of mucus. The stem and root, fresh or dried, produce a yellow dye which was used chiefly on silk, although hair could also be coloured with it. A preserve can be made from the red berries.

Barberry is the birthday flower for 10 April, and signifies ill temper and sourness. Astrologically it is assigned to Mars.

Basil
Ocimum basilicum

The aromatic scent of some of the species is reflected in the generic name: *Ocimum* derived from a Greek word meaning to smell. The name basil is derived from the Greek *basilicon* royal. The ancient Greeks associated the plant with hatred and vituperation; to ensure satisfactory growth the seeds had to be sown with a certain amount of abuse. The pungency of the plant is said to dominate that of garlic. Introduced to England early in the sixteenth century, basil was used as a strewing herb, and, finely powdered, as a snuff. The aroma and sensitivity of the herb were described by Charles Leyland (1824–1903) in 'Sweet Basil':

> I pray your Highness mark this curious herb:
> Touch it but lightly, stroke it softly, Sir
> And it gives forth an odour sweet and rare:
> But crush it harshly and you'll make a scent
> Most disagreeable.

Herbalists used the plant as an expectorant and a laxative, also to expel 'birth and after birth', but is perhaps best known in the kitchen. One of the few herbs that increase in flavour when cooked, it can be used in a variety of egg and cheese dishes and for shellfish, poultry and game. With the addition of parsley it makes an unusual herb butter. It goes particularly well with tomatoes, and is an essential ingredient of the classic Italian sauce, *pesto*.

Basil was regarded by the superstitious as a tell-tale herb because on the delicate question of chastity it died immediately if the wearer was 'light of love'. It is the birthday flower for 12 July, signifying hatred for the other sex, and is symbolic of poverty. Astrologically it is a herb of Mars, under the sign of Scorpio.

Bay
Laurus noblis

The generic name is the Latin for laurel (not to be confused with the larger-leafed laurel popular in Victorian shrubberies) or bay. Alternative common names include Roman laurel and lorer. In classical mythology bay is sacred to Apollo who fell in love with Daphne, the daughter of a river god. As she had sworn to spend her life as a virgin, she rejected him. To escape his advances she asked her father for protection, and he changed her into a bay tree (see also **daphne**). Apollo declared that from then on he would wear bay instead of oak leaves and that all who sought his favour should do likewise. Bay was also used in garlands and crowns awarded for poetic elegance or victory in battle. The Greeks gave a wreath of bay to the victor of the Pythian games and crowned heroes and poets with it. Being the traditional plant of victory and fame, dispatches reporting a battle victory were wrapped in it and it decorated the mail coaches carrying the news of the British success at Waterloo.

Because it was assigned to Apollo, people believed that if it was planted close to the house 'neither witch nor devil, thunder nor lightening will hurt a man where the bay tree is'. A quotation from the Jacobean dramatist Webster advised:

> Reach the bays
> I'll tie a garland here about his head
> I will keep my boy from lightning.

Tiberius and other Roman emperors wore a wreath of bay as an amulet, especially against thunderstorms. During the Saturnalia festival, a pagan forerunner of Christmas, the Romans decorated their homes with bay. The withering of a bay tree in a garden meant disaster, and before the death of Nero all the Roman bay trees are said to have died. Shakespeare refers to this superstition in *Richard III*, when a Welsh captain takes leave of the Earl of Salisbury:

Tis thought the king is dead; we will not stay,
The Bay trees in our country are all withered away. . . .

Bay was hung in English churches as a sign of welcome to elves and
fairies, and used generally as a counter charm against witchcraft. If bay
leaves crackled on the fire, good luck was coming; if the leaf smouldered,
the signs were less favourable.

Girls used the leaves as a love oracle. In parts of England, on the Eve of
St Valentine, a bay leaf was pinned at each corner of a pillow and one in
the centre. Before she fell asleep she had to repeat this rhyme:

Good Valentine, be kind to me,
In dreams let me my true love see.

Attired in a clean nightgown, the girl would then dream of her future
husband or lover – not necessarily the same person.

Medicinally the berries were used as an antidote for snakebite and bee
and wasp stings, and for treating infectious diseases. Seven berries given
to a woman in labour ensured a quick delivery, and the berries could also
be taken to procure an abortion.

Bay has a strong, almost bitter flavour which is more noticeable when
the brittle leaves are crushed. In cooking it is ideal for game, fish and beef
dishes, as well as for sauces.

Astrologically it is a tree of the sun, under the sign of Leo. It is the
birthday flower for 14 July and signifies undying affection. In the
language of the flowers a bay leaf means, 'I change only in death'.

A bay berry means discipline and instruction, a bay wreath reward of
merit.

Beech
Fagus sylvatica

The generic name, *Fagus*, is Latin for beech; *sylvatica* means growing in
woodlands. The earliest runes were written on beech board, and the
Anglo-Saxon word *bece*, meant book and beech. The beech nut or mast
was formerly known as 'buck', from which the county of Buckingham-
shire, famous for its beeches, ultimately derives its name. Beech wood is
hard and was the favourite timber for the keels of wooden sailing ships,
galley oars, piles and floodgates. If a beech tree is felled about midsummer, it is said that the wood will last three times longer than wood felled
in winter. An old saying advises:

> Beech in Summer,
> Oak in Winter.

Large buds on a beech tree foretell a wet summer. Chips of beech wood were used to clarify wine. In the words of the seventeenth-century poet Abraham Cowley:

> He sings to Bacchus, patron of the vine,
> The Beechen bowl foams with a flood of wine.

Herbalists used the boiled leaves as a poultice and an ointment. Because of their coolness, fresh leaves were applied to hot swellings. Water collected from the hollows of the tree soothed sores, scabs and scurf on man and animals. Beech leaves collected in the autumn before the frosts made an excellent stuffing for mattresses, lasting seven or eight years, giving, at least in the early stages, a 'fragrant odour like that of green tea'. The catkins were also used as a stuffing and for packing fruit.

Astrologically the beech is under the dominion of Saturn. It is the birthday flower for 11 April, symbolizing grandeur and prosperity. Beech is a symbol of honour and victory: beech, palm and laurel branches were awarded at ancient Greek games.

Berberis   see **Barberry**

Betony
Stachys officinalis

Stachys is derived from the Greek *stachus*, a spike. Pliny suggests that the Vettones, a people of Spain, were the original discoverers of the plant known as vettonica; the transition to betony was an easy one. In Christian legend it is said to be named after Beronice, the woman healed by Jesus of an issue of blood. The plant is also known as woundwort, because of its healing properties.

Antonius Musa, physician to the Emperor Augustus (63B.C. −A.D.14), is said to have written a long treatise devoted to the virtues of the plant, to which Culpepper, writing in *The English Physician* of 1652, refers. He concludes: 'These are some of the many virtues of Antony Muse, an expert physician – for it was not the practise of Octavius Caesar to keep fools about him – apportions to betony, it is a very precious herb, that is certain, and most fitting to be kept in a man's house, both in syrup, conserve, oil ointment and plaister.' No early physician would be without it. The Italians had such faith in it that 'Sell your coat and buy betony' became a well-known proverb. A person might often be described as having 'more virtues than betony'. Every English herbal sings its praises, and in Scott's *Demonology and Witchcraft* the reader is advised that 'the house where *Herba Betonica* is sown is free from all mischief'. With the possible exception of **vervain**, no herb was more highly valued. The Saxons believed it cured every ill, including nightmares. In the Middle Ages it was held in high repute for both its medicinal and spiritual value, and was cultivated in monastery herb gardens and churchyards. It was worn around the neck as a protection against evil spirits.

Herbalists made a mixture of powdered betony and a plant called colewort, to be taken every morning during periods of fasting. Betony was thought to be beneficial to the digestive system, for insomnia, jaundice, palsy, convulsions, gout, headaches, fatigue and harmorrhaging; mixed with honey, it was used to treat coughs and colds, shortness of breath and consumption, while betony infused in wine was said to ease toothache. Because it was thought to be at enmity with the vine, whose tendrils turn away from it, it became a favourite cure for hangovers.

Betony is the herb of Jupiter, under the sign of Aries. In the language of the flowers it symbolizes surprise.

Bilberry
Vaccinium myrtillus

The Romans called the plant *Vaccinium*, the Latin for blueberry; in Britain it is also known as whortleberry, blaeberry, blackheart and black-wort. The natural habitat of the shrub is moorland and mountain. The poet Samuel Coleridge (1772–1834) recalls,

> At my feet
> The whortleberries are bedew'd with spray,
> Dash'd upwards by the furious waterfall.

The Ancient Britons used the juice to stain their faces; later it was used as a blue dye for linen and paper. The fermented berries yield a highly intoxicating liquor. Herbalists used the juice as a conserve or in the form of a syrup to treat lung diseases, vomiting and stomach upsets. Bilberries can be eaten raw, with cream and sugar, or cooked in pies and puddings which are quite delicious. They also make excellent jams and jellies.

Bilberry is the birthday flower for 17 July, and signifies deceit and treachery. Astrologically the plant is assigned to Jupiter.

Bindweed   see **Hedge bindweed**

Birdsfoot trefoil
Lotus corniculatus

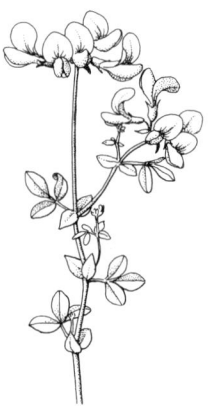

Corniculatus is Latin for horned. *Lotus* is a name adopted by the Greeks for a trefoil-like plant. Alternative common names for the plant are shoes and stockings, boots and shoes, fingers and thumbs, crowsfeet and cross-toes, many alluding to the shape of the pods.

Herbalists knew that the plant was drying and binding by nature, and for this reason it was used, externally, on wounds. A compound was also taken internally to relieve diarrhoea.

Astrologically, birdsfoot trefoil is under the dominion of Saturn. In the language of the flowers it signifies revenge

Biting stonecrop
Sedum acre

The generic name, *Sedum*, is derived from Latin *sedes*, home or habitation. The plant was believed to protect the inhabitants of a house from lightning and was therefore often grown on the roof. The specific name alludes to the pungent taste of the leaves, as does the name Biting stonecrop. It is very bitter and sharp. Country names for the plant include wall pepper, wall ginger, prick madam, gold chain and bird's bread. In 'The Borough', the poet George Crabbe (1754–1832) writes of the stonecrop's favoured habitat:

> At the wall base the fiery nettle springs,
> With fruit globes and fierce with poison'd stings;
> Above (the growth of many a tear) is spread
> The yellow level of the stone-crop's bed . . .

Old herbalists used the plant to deal with internal and external bleeding. Boiled in beer, it was recommended for fevers, expelling poisons, and as the simple *par excellence* for ague. Fresh bruised stonecrop was applied directly to piles.

In the language of the flowers the stonecrop means tranquillity, and astrologically it comes under the sign of the moon.

Blackberry   see **Bramble**

Blackcurrant
Ribes nigrum

The generic name is derived from the Arabic word for a certain shrub with acid juices; *nigrum* means black. Blackcurrants do not seem to have been mentioned by earlier writers, although John Gerard, speaking of gooseberries, does make a passing reference to what must have been the redcurrant, *Ribes rubrum*: 'We have also in our London gardens another sought altogether without prickles, whose fruit is very small, lesser by muche than the common kind, but of a perfect red colour'.

The fruit is delicious in pies, puddings, jams and jellies, and as a cordial; it is rich in vitamin C. The young leaves steeped in spirit have the flavour of brandy.

Blackcurrant is the birthday flower for 22 August, meaning, 'You please all'. In the language of the flowers currant blossom signifies, 'Your frown will kill me'.

Black knapweed
Centaurea nigra

In classical legend the centaur Chiron healed wounds with this plant, hence the generic name; *nigra* means black. Other knapweeds are the brown, greater and Jersey knapweed. (*C. jacea, C. scabiosa* and *C. paniculata*.) The plant has many country names including knopweed, knobweed, horse-knot, horse-nobs, bottle-weed, bull-weed, hardheads, Harry head, iron knobs, shaving brush and topknot. All knapweeds, whether growing or dried, are avoided by cattle, and botanical books refer to it as 'a bad weed among grass'. Nevertheless it was used as a love oracle, as the rural poet John Clare (1793–1864) describes in *The Shepherd's Calendar* of 1827:

> They pull the little blossom threads
> From out the knapweed button heads
> And put the husk wi many a smile
> In their white bosom for awhile
> Who if they guess aright the swain
> That loves sweet fancy trys to gain
> Tis said that ere its lain an hour
> Twill blossom wi a second flower.

The root was used by early herbalists to stop bleeding from the mouth and nose, and to treat sore throats, ruptures and bruises. Modern herbalists boil the root in water to produce a catarrh remedy. Astrologically knapweed is under the dominion of Saturn.

Blackthorn
Prunus spinosa

The generic name is Latin for plum, while the common name probably comes from the colour of the bark, which is much darker than that of the hawthorn. The shrub is also known as sloe. It is symbolic of austerity, difficulty and ill luck, and in Christian legend the crown of thorns was said to have been made from its branches. For this reason monks considered it unlucky to bring a spray of blackthorn blossom into the house and even to this day it is regarded as an omen of death. However formerly it was used as a New Year decoration when there is no blossom – branches were fashioned into a wreath, scorched over a fire, and decorated with mistletoe. As a fertility offering, branches were baked in the oven, taken out to the fields and burnt, and the ashes scattered over the earliest sown wheat.

Witches were believed to carry a blackthorn rod with which they caused miscarriages, and were as a result burnt with them as their chief instrument of torture. Many superstitions are associated also with blackthorn fruit. 'Many sloans, many groans' is self-explanatory, but a deeper significance was that a hard winter was to come, causing poverty and possible death. Another saying was 'Many sloes, many cold toes'. A cold spell with sharp winds often occurs during the flowering period of the shrub, and in some parts of the country this is known as a blackthorn winter.

Sloes can be made into a strongly flavoured wine and the whole fruit added to gin, producing sloe gin. Sloes are also bottled, buried deep in the earth and brought out at Christmas to be eaten as a preserve. During the nineteenth century the sloe acquired a doubtful reputation as the juice was used in making *ersatz* port wine while the dried leaves were mixed with a small quantity of tea leaves (then an expensive commodity) and passed off as real tea.

The bark was used medicinally, and for tanning leather: it produces a reddish brown shade, while the fruit gives a rosy colour. Blackthorn wood is used in marquetry, having fine, dark markings on a light matrix.

Bluebell
Endymion non-scriptus

Endymion was a beautiful youth who fell in love with Juno and was condemned to perpetual sleep by Jupiter. Older writers often referred to this plant as the **harebell** (in fact a different plant altogether), English jacinth or wild hyacinth. There are numerous local names including blue bonnets, blue bottle, cross flower and crow bells. The effect of the hazy mass of rich colour like a carpet laid under the trees in spring is described by Patric Dickinson (1914–):

> Like smoke held down by the frost
> The bluebell wreathe in the wood.

It is reputed to bloom on St George's Day, 23 April. In former times blue was worn on that day:

> On St George's Day, when blue is worn,
> The blue Harebells in field adorn.

Although the rhyme refers to 'harebells' it is the bluebell that is in flower at this time. The two plants have often been confused, and in Scotland the harebell is still called the bluebell.

A mysterious aura surrounds the plant. In legend bluebells are fairy flowers, and it was believed that if a child picked them, alone in a wood, it would never be seen again. If an adult did so he or she would be led around by a pixie until found by someone who would lead the person to safety. 'In and out of the dusky bluebells' is a children's singing ring game which in reality is a fairy or magical song with sinister overtones:

In and out of the dusky Bluebells
In and out of the dusky Bluebells
In and out of the dusky Bluebells
  I am your master
Tipper-ipper-apper-on your shoulder
Tipper-ipper-apper-on your shoulder
Tipper-ipper-apper-on your shoulder
  I am your master.

In the Middle Ages the sticky sap was used to fasten feathers to the shaft of arrows, while the Elizabethans used it for stiffening muslin and as a paste for sticking paper. It is the birthday flower for 30 September and symbolizes solitude and regret.

Bog asphodel
Narthecium ossifragum

Older writers claim that *Narthecium* comes from Greek *narthex*, a rod. *Asphodelus* is a Greek name for the true asphodel, to which this British species bears some resemblance. In ancient Greece the flower was dedicated to the memory of departed souls and used at funeral ceremonies and planted on graves to provide nourishment for the departed.

Within I enclose the dead,
But without I have mallow and asphodel.

In Greek mythology asphodel was one of the flowers that formed the couch of Zeus and Hera. Nevertheless it was a flower of death that grew in Hades. Later asphodel was dedicated to the Virgin Mary. The plant has a long history in England: *Hastula regia* – king's spear, as the plant was known – is mentioned in the Anglo-Saxon translation of the *Herbarium* of the second-century B.C. Roman writer Apuleius.

Bog asphodel was sometimes used as a substitute for saffron, and during the seventeenth century the plant was gathered from the moors and used as a yellow hair dye. In the Middle Ages the root was used as food and referred to as 'food for a king'.

Asphodel is the birthday flower for 13 July, bearing the sentiment memorial sorrow; it is a symbol of death and eternity. In the language of the flowers it means, 'My regrets follow you to the end of the world'.

Borage
Borago officinalis

The name probably comes from Latin *burra*, a hairy garment, alluding to the hairy leaves which give a distinctive flavour to drinks. Older writers suggested that the name was a corruption of *corago*, from *cor*, heart, and *ago*, I bring, because the plant was used to prepare stimulating drinks. Other common names are herb of gladness and bee bread. The plant named *Euphrosynon* by the Greeks was most probably borage; they put it in their wine to give a feeling of wellbeing. The juice of the plant has the smell and flavour of cucumber.

Writings dating back to the thirteenth century refer to borage as a salad herb. In 1502 it is recorded as a valuable asset to the still room. The brilliant blue flowers were formerly candied as a decorative sweetmeat. Today borage is used to flavour bean and pea soup and stews. A sprig of borage cooked with cabbage improves its flavour. The plant can be boiled as a vegetable or added to spinach, in equal proportions. It is a classic garnish for punches.

Medicinally, borage cordials were prescribed for prolonged illness such as consumption, swooning and palpitations of the heart, and for increasing milk production in nursing mothers. In Robert Burton's *Anatomy of Melancholy* of 1621 we find:

> Borage and Hellebore fill two scenes,
> Sovereign plants to purge the veins
> Of melancholy, and cheer the heart
> Of those black fumes which make it smart

However a warning reminded the patient that an overdose produced a less cheerful symptom – death. The leaves, mixed with those of **fumitory**, provided a remedy for cleansing the blood and soothing the irritation caused by ringworm, scabs and sores.

Astrologically borage is under the dominion of Jupiter and the sign of Leo. In the language of the flowers it symbolizes bluntness and talent.

Box
Buxus sempervirens

The generic name is the Latin name of the tree and is derived from *sempes*, always, and *vivo*, alive, alluding to the tenacity of this plant. The word *buxus* also denotes a flute, and the ancients prized the wood for making musical instruments. Box has a long history, and is mentioned by Isaiah in the Bible. In ancient Rome box was sacred to the wind deity, Mercury, messenger of the gods. However the ancient Greeks regarded it as a funeral and shrine tree. This association with death was perpetuated in the north of England as late as the nineteenth century, when it was customary to place a bowl full of box sprigs by the door of a deceased person's house. After viewing the body before the funeral the mourners each took a piece of the shrub and later, as the coffin was lowered into the grave, they walked past and threw in the twigs. The poet Wordsworth (1770–1850) recalls the burial of a child:

> The basin of Box-wood, just six months before,
> Had stood on the table at Timothy's door;
> A coffin through Timothy's thresh-hold has passed
> One child did it bear, and that child was his last.

There is reason to believe that the Romans cultivated box on English hillsides for civic and religious festivals. Box Hill in Surrey is named after the plant. Turner, a distinguished writer on plants, wrote in 1551: 'It groweth on the mountains in Germany plentifully, wild, without any setting; but in England it groweth not by itself, in any place that I know, though there is much in England.'

Topiary was popular in England during the sixteenth and seventeenth centuries; box and juniper were the favourite shrubs. The Elizabethans also surrounded small beds of flowers and herbs with it to form a low hedge. Box wood was often used as an inlay in other woods.

Boughs of box used to be gathered at Whitsuntide to decorate fireplaces, and it was formerly used in place of willow on Palm Sunday. The *Domesday Book* records that a tenant rendered a bundle of box twigs as part of his payment, on Palm Sunday.

Box is the birthday flower for 17 September, and is a symbol of grace, prosperity and stoicism; it bears the sentiment 'tattling' ('given to idle talk').

Bracken see **Common bracken**

Bramble

Rubus fruticosus

Rubus, meaning red, is the Latin name of the plant. A quaint legend concerning the origin of the plant relates that the cormorant was once a wool merchant who went into partnership with the bat and the bramble. They loaded up with wool a large ship which was wrecked, and the company became brankrupt. Since that time the cormorant is forever diving into the sea to find the vessel, the bat skulks about till midnight to avoid his creditors, and the bramble grasps at passing sheep to make up his loss by taking their wool.

In the Christian tradition it is an emblem of Christ and the Virgin Mary; it is also a Hebrew symbol of divine love and the voice of God. The burning bush from which the angel of the Lord appeared to Moses was said to be the bramble. Superstition held that it was unlucky to eat blackberries after 11 October, Old Michaelmas Day. After that date the fruit was cursed and spat upon by the devil, because, when he was cast out of heaven, he fell into a blackberry bush.

An arch of bramble was alleged to be an effective cure for man and horse. If a shrew ran over a horse it 'enfeebled its hind quarters and made him unable to go'. The horse could be cured by being drawn backwards through an arch of bramble. Strangely enough, this treatment would also cure blackheads and heal boils in humans. In some countries, it is claimed, whooping cough was cured by passing the patient through an arch seven times, saying:

> In bramble, out cough,
> Here I leave the whooping cough.

An interesting combination of Christian and pagan practices is to be found in a charm for burns: nine blackberry leaves were dipped in holy water and applied to the affected area, whilst repeating three times to each leaf:

> There came three angels out of the east,
> One brought fire and two brought frost,
> Out fire, in frost,
> In the name of the Father, the Son and the Holy Ghost.

In the ancient world people thought the fruit and flowers were effective against snakebite. A Roman physician considered bramble roots boiled in wine a valuable medicine for mouth and throat complaints. Old English herbalists, who used many of the recipes of Roman writers, thought every part of the bramble useful medicinally. Even young shoots eaten as a salad 'would fasten teeth which were loose'. Piles, too, benefited from the internal or external use of the fruit.

The cutting down of hedges in recent years has drastically reduced what was once a common fruit, although garden varieties are still popular; both make excellent jam. The berries, which can be bottled or frozen, also make an excellent wine and a cordial to relieve sore throats. The juice from the fruit yields a dye that is grey on wool and slate blue on silk, while the green shoots produce a black dye.

Bramble is the birthday flower for 19 July, and a symbol of death, envy, lowliness, pain, grief, wickedness, remorse, weariness, riches that destroy the soul, that which holds the rose and beauty of soul. Astrologically it is under the dominion of Venus in the sign of Aries.

Broom
Cytisus scoparius

Scoparius means broomlike, and the common name is from Old English *brom*. Country names include golden chain, green wood, basom and cat's peas. In heraldry broom is the insignia of knighthood. It was the emblem of the Plantagenet family, whose coat of arms depicts a genet passing through two sprigs of broom. In a legendary story Geoffrey, Duke of Anjou, father of Henry II, saw a broom shrub clinging firmly to a crumbling, rocky surface. Breaking off a yellow-flowering sprig, he placed it in his cap, saying, 'Thus shall that golden plant ever be my cognizance, rooted firmly amid rocks, and yet upholding that which is ready to fall. I will bear it in my crest, amid battlefield, if need be, at tournaments and when dispensing justic.' Broom was worn by all his descendants down to Richard III. In Christian legend the noisy popping sound of the seed pods earned this member of the pea family a rebuke from the Virgin Mary when she was in hiding from Herod's soldiers, intent on the murder of all baby boys, as she feared it would draw attention to her hiding place.

Superstitions surrounding broom vary. To some people it was a magical plant of phallic significance provided it was not gathered in May, the Roman month of death, otherwise ill luck would befall the transgressor. In many countries it was believed that:

> If you sweep the house with blossom'd broom in May,
> You are sure to sweep the head of the house away.

Nevertheless, because of its profusion of flowers a bundle of broom tied with ribbons was carried at country weddings as a symbol of good luck and plenty. Another delightful and practical wedding custom was to strew herbs, flowers and rushes along the bridal path:

> The wheaten ear was scatter'd near the porch,
> The green broom blossom'd strew'd the way to church.

Heavy blossom on broom was seen as a sign of a fruitful harvest. At Whitsun it was used as a church decoration, and later in the year it was said to coincide with the cuckoo leaving the country:

> Nor does she cease
> Her changeless note, until the Broom, full blown,
> Gives warning that her time for flight has come.

The juice of the young boughs was prescribed for dropsy, ague and generally 'helping pains', and was used in tanning leather. A bright yellow dye can be obtained from the plant. In the language of the flowers broom symbolizes humility, neatness and servility, and astrologically it is under the dominion of Mars.

Buckthorn
Rhamnus catharticus

The generic name is from Greek *rhamnos*, branch, and the specific means purging. It is the Christian symbol of martyrdom and some sources claim that the crown of thorns was of buckthorn (see **blackthorn**). In ancient Greece it was chewed in the belief that it had the power to ward off evil spirits and ghosts. The reputation of the plant as protection against witchcraft was well-known during the Middle Ages in England:

> These rhamnus' branches are
> Which, stuck in entries, or about the bar
> That holds the door, kill all enchantments,
>   and charms that do harms
> To men or cattle.

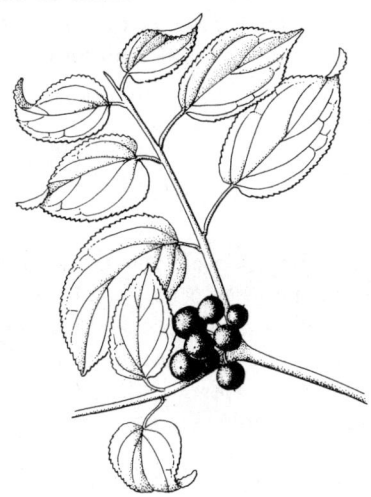

Buckthorn is a powerful cathartic, and was seldom used alone on account of the severity of its action. The berries were used medicinally in the form of a syrup with various spices 'but their use produced an intolerable thirst' and were eventually considered unsafe.

The unripe berries yield a yellow dye, the ripe ones, combined with other ingredients, sap green. The bark also produces a yellow dye. In the language of the flowers buckthorn symbolizes trial, cares, tribulation, exile and sin.

Bugle
Ajuga reptans

The generic name comes from Greek, *a*, not, and *zeugon*, yoke – as with many common herbs, considerable medicinal power was attributed to it. *Reptans* is Latin for creeping, referring to the plant's habit. The common name is based on the generic name, though in his *Popular Names of British Plants*, published in 1863, Prior claims that the true derivation is from medieval Latin *bugulus*, a small glass pipe used in female headdress in the Middle Ages, to which the bluish corolla of this plant bears some resemblance. Other common names include baby's rattle, thunder and lightning, wild mint, sickle-wort, herb carpenter and middle comfrey.

Mildly narcotic, the plant was said to relieve stomach upsets, quinsy and coughing, heal wounds, reduce the pulse rate, control the spitting up of blood in tuberculosis, and generally to assist the digestive system. An old writer tells us: 'It is so singular good for all sorts of hurts in the body, that none that know its usefulness will ever be without it.'

Astrologically bugle is under the dominion of Saturn.

Bulrush
Typha latifolia

The generic name comes from Greek *typhos*, marsh, the natural habitat of the plant. The specific name means broad-leaved. In the Christian tradition it is a symbol of the multitude and the faithful. Various artists have represented Jesus holding a bulrush in his hand, when, in mockery, a reed was given Him as a sceptre.

In his *Shepherd's Calendar* John Clare describes bulrush-cutting:

> The gipsy down the meadow brook
> Wi long pole and reaping hook
> Tyd at its end amid the streams
> That glitters withe hot sunbeams
> Reaches and cuts the Bulrush down
> And hawks them round each neighbouring town.

The downy tufts were used for stuffing mattresses and pillows, and the long leaves were made use of in thatching and in making baskets and mats. Coopers sometimes used to put the leaves between the staves of the casks to prevent leakage. Nowadays we use bulrushes for their decorative rather than their functional qualities – picked as they near perfection, they make excellent material for the flower arranger.

In the language of the flowers bulrush symbolizes independence, and it is the birthday flower for 20 July.

Burdock   see **Greater burdock**

Butcher's broom
Ruscus aculeatus

The generic name, *Ruscus*, is thought to have originally been *Bruscus*, from Celtic *bruskelen*, box holly. *Aculeatus* means prickly. Old common names for the plant are ruscus, bruscus, knee-holme, kneeholly, kneehulver, Jew's myrtle and pettigree. The name butcher's broom came from the simple fact that the boughs of the plant were used to sweep out butchers' shops. However, another source suggests that it was used to preserve meat from mice and rats, and again, in W.A. Bromfield's *Flora Vectensis*, published in 1856, he declared that butchers decorated their Christmas sirloins with sprigs of the plant.

Because the greenish white flowers are so small they are often overlooked. Bishop Mant (1776–1848) wrote of the plant:

> Mid barren heaths the Butcher's Broom,
> On thorn-tipt leaves its lovely bloom
> Infixes, when the central eye
> Shoots to a purple nectary;
> Bright mid the greenish petals shows,
> And dark greenleaf where on it blows.

The scarlet berries, which have a sweet flavour, contain orange seeds which herbalists crushed with the leaves to make a poultice for broken bones. A mixture made from the roots and taken in wine was said to be an excellent treatment for bowel and kidney complaints, jaundice, headaches and menstrual problems.

Astrologically butcher's broom is a plant of Mars.

Butterbur
Petasites hybridus

The generic name is derived from Greek *petatos*, a covering for the head, referring to the plant's huge, broad leaves. Butterbur was used as a love oracle. A young unmarried woman had to sow the seeds half an hour before sunrise in an isolated place, saying:

> I sow, I sow,
> Then come my own dear,
> Come here, come here,
> And mow and mow.

Having spoken, she would then see her future husband. However, if she was afraid of what she saw the phrase 'Have mercy upon me' caused the figure to disappear instantly. This method was considered rather desperate and was only used as a last resort.

The root of the plant is white with a thick black skin, strong-smelling and bitter-tasting. It was formerly used to reduce fevers and was believed to be so effective against the plague that it was known as pestilence-wort. Powdered and taken in wine, it was also used to induce sweating for bladder complaints, as a heart stimulant, to treating menstrual problems and as a cure for flat and broad worms.

Buttercup see **Meadow buttercup**

Cabbage
Brassica oleracea

The generic name is the Latin word for cabbage, while *oleracea* means of the garden. In former times it was customary when a cabbage was cut to mark the remaining piece of stalk in the form of a cross: this was meant to ensure the growth of new green shoots and to protect the plant against the devil. When it was used as a means of telling one's fortune the whole plant had to be pulled up in the dark with one's left hand; the amount of earth left clinging to the root indicated one's future financial prospects – the more earth, the richer one would be.

Culpepper believed that, despite the fact that the plant was 'extremely windy' it was helpful for those suffering from gout or poor eyesight. In the language of the flowers the cabbage symbolizes gain and profit, and is an emblem of the self-willed. Astrologically it is under the dominion of the moon, and it is the birthday flower for 19 September.

Camellia
Camellia japonica

The camellia is a native of Japan and China and derives its name from Jacob Kamel, a Jesuit missionary who broght this beautiful shrub to Europe in 1739.

The romantic image of the flower was established in a nineteenth-century novel by Alexandre Dumas *fils, La Dame aux Camélias,* which was later made into an opera, *La Traviata,* by Verdi. The novel was based on the real-life story of Alphonsine Plessis, with whom both the composer Franz Liszt and Dumas were in love. Tragically, she died of tuberculosis at the age of twenty-three. As camellias were her favourite flower they filled her coffin with them and placed them on her grave.

In the language of the flowers the camellia signifies excellence, fragility and loveliness. A red camellia means innate worth, and a white one perfect loveliness.

Campion

And we'll pause and gather a glorious wreath
From the flowers that are shelter'd the corn beneath.
There are velvet campions, both white and red,
And poppies, like morning-glories spread.
AGNES STRICKLAND (1796–1874), 'FLOWERS OF THE CORNFIELD'

Red campion
Silene dioica

The generic name now applied to campions is a Greek word for another plant. *Silene* is from the Greek *sialon*, saliva, which the gummy exudations on the stems resemble, and *dioica* is the Greek for opening in two parts. The common name may come from the Latin *campus*, an open field or plain, where the plant grows, although it is also found in hedgerows. However it was sometimes called champion, and may have been so named because the flower was used to make garlands or chaplets for the victors in public games or tournaments.

In folklore red campion is dedicated to Robin Goodfellow, and was sometimes called Robin Hood or Robin's flower. It was also known as bachelors' buttons, as were other flowers, from the days when men wore flowers in their buttonholes. 'To wear bachelors' buttons' denoted that a young man was unmarried.

The plant used to be applied to sores and ulcers, and was taken in red or white wine to treat internal bleeding and bladder and kidney complaints. In the language of the flowers red campion symbolizes gentleness; it is the birthday flower for 20 October. Astrologically it is in the dominion of Saturn.

White campion
Silene alba

Alternative names for the plant are grandmother's nightcap, milkmaids, summer saucers and white Robin Hood. A more sinister name was mother-dee, because picking the flower allegedly brought death to one's mother. Other country names for white campion are vesper flower and evening flower.

The Elizabethans used white campion with other scented flowers in pot-pourri. Herbalists recommended a decoction of the plant to stop internal bleeding, and it was also applied externally for a similar purpose. A mixture produced from the plant was taken for bladder and stomach complaints, snakebites and the plague, and was used for cleansing ulcers and sores. Astrologically, white campion is assigned to Saturn.

Candytuft
Iberis umbellata

The generic name comes from Iberia, an old name for Spain, where the plant is native. *Umbellata* is from the Latin *umbella*, sunshade, and describes the structure of the flower cluster. Candytuft refers to its place of origin, Candia, the old name for Crete. Country names for the plant include Billy come home soon, sciatic cress and Spanish tufts.

Dioscorides, the Greek writer and contemporary of Pliny, wrote a book called *De Materia Medica* on the use and identificatin of medical herbs; this, with the works of Galen (A.D.131–201) and the better-known Hippocrates (469B.C.–399B.C.), formed the basis of herbal treatment for well over a thousand years. Dioscorides says that in his time candytuft seed was used as a mustard, and served with meat. In Elizabeth I's day Gerard was well pleased with 'the comely flowers that bringeth forth for decking up of gardens and houses', and grew them from seed.

In the language of the flowers, candytuft symbolizes indifference.

Canterbury bell
Campanula medium

The generic name is a diminutive of Latin *campana*, bell, from the shape of the corolla. During the sixteenth and seventeenth centuries it was known as Coventry bell, while another plant, *Campanula trachelium*, was known as Canterbury bell, probably because its flowers resembled the horse bells of the Canterbury pilgrims. The name Coventry bell may have been applied because the plant grew in that area – there is no specific evidence for this, but some plants certainly were named after their locality.

The plant is dedicated to St Augustine, and is thought to have been grown in English gardens for over three hundred years following its introduction from southern Europe. In the language of the flowers the Canterbury bell carries the sentiment gratitude and is a symbol of constancy in adversity. It is the birthday flower for 21 July.

Caraway
Carum carvi

The name comes from a place called Caria in Asia Minor. The seeds, an acquired taste, have been used in English and European cooking for centuries, particularly in bread and cakes. Caraway comfits used to be eaten each morning and after meals as an aid to digestion. The Elizabethans used the seeds to flavour apples, and the custom of serving roast apples with a little saucerful of caraway was maintained at Trinity College, Cambridge, until the end of the nineteenth century.

Medicinally, the powdered seed was used as a poultice to draw out bruising. Distilled water from the seed acts as a gripe water, and was given to children for the relief of colic. Caraway roots are said to strengthen the stomach of elderly people. Culpepper wrote: 'Carraway seed hath a moderate sharp quality, wherbey it breaketh wind and provoketh urine, which also the herb doth. The root is better food than parsnips; it is pleasant and comfortable to the stomach, and helpeth digestion.' The plant yields an aromatic oil.

Astrologically, caraway is under the dominion of Mercury.

Carnation
Dianthus caryophyllus

The name *Dianthus* signifies Jupiter's flower, or divine flower, and was given to the genus by the Greek philosopher and botanist Theophrastus in the fourth century B.C. *Caryophyllus* means having clovelike leaves, referring in this instance to the plant's scent; the name was first given to the Indian clove tree, and was later transferred to the carnation because of this distinctive smell. Carnation is derived from the Latin *caro*, flesh, because the flower was thought to be so coloured. Pliny, writing in the first century A.D., says that the clove carnation was discovered in Spain in the days of his approximate contemporary the Emperor Augustus. The Greeks and Romans used it in their garlands.

In Christian legend the pink carnation is a symbol of mother love. The flowers are said to have first appeared on earth when Mary's tears fell to the ground on her agonizing walk to Calvary. It was probably introduced into England at the time of the Norman Conquest. Chaucer refers to the carnation as the clove gilofre, and Shakespeare calls it the gillyvor.

The flower was used to give a spicy flavour to drinks, and one of its names was sops-in-wine. During the seventeenth and eighteenth centuries the carnation was used in soups and sauces and for vinegars. The flowers were candied and preserved. Herbalists used the plant to treat heart and brain diseases, to expel poisons and soothe fevers.

Astrologically the carnation is under the dominion of Jupiter. It is the birthday flower for 19 December, symbol of divine love, fascination and woman's love. The yellow carnation means disdain and the striped carnation, refusal.

Carrot   see **Wild carrot**

Catmint
Nepeta cataria

A number of herbaceous plants were known by the Romans as *Nepeta*, including catmint or catnep. Gerard referred to the plant as *Herba cattaria* because cats like to roll in it and nibble the leaves. Abraham Cowley wrote of this habit:

> Lavender, Cornrose, Pennyroyale, sate,
> And that which cats esteem so delicate.

An old saying suggests a solution to the problem:

> If you set it, the cats will eat it,
> If you sow it, the cats wont know it.

Chewing the root of the plant was said to give one courage, and public hangmen were alleged to use it when carrying out their duties. The tops and leaves of catmint make a herbal tea which was used in the treatment of nervous headaches, irritability, wind, colic and hysterics. More recent herbalists rcommended the tea for feverish colds because it induces perspiration and soothes the nervous system, sending the person to sleep. In Peachey's *Compleat Herbal* of 1694 catmint was recommended for 'Obstructions of the Womb, for Barrenness, and to hasten delivery, and to help Expectoration'.

Astrologically it is a plant of Venus.

Cedar of Lebanon
Cedrus libani

The generic name is of Arabic origin, via Greek, from *kedron* or *kedros*, power. The ancient Egyptians used cedar resin as an embalming agent to preserve the bodies of their dead:

> . . . the agelong, spicy strength
> Of the Lebanon cedars, shimmering with needles, and stout
> With their perching cones. And Solomon passed to his rest.

In the Christian tradition the cedar is an emblem of Christ, and in the Jewish one it is a symbol of fragrance, empire and nobility. The cedar cone has always been regarded as a life charm. Shakespeare refers to the tree in *Henry IV*:

> Thus yields the cedar to the axe's edge,
> Whose arms gave shelter to the princely eagle,
> Under whose shade the ramping lion slept,
> Whose top-branch overpeer'd Jove's spreading tree,
> And kept low shrubs from winter's powerful wind.

English herbalists used the cedar fruit for urinary complaints and for bringing on menstruation. In the language of the flowers the tree means 'I live only for you', and symbolizes pride, mercy, majesty, strength and beauty. A cedar leaf in the language of the flowers means 'Think of me'.

Celandine

The greater and lesser celandines are not related, the former being a member of the poppy family and the latter belonging to the buttercup family, and bear no resemblance except in the yellow colour of their flowers. They are grouped here for convenience.

Greater celandine
Chelidonium majus

The generic name is from Greek *chelidon*, swallow, from the belief that the flower appeared with the swallows and died when they departed. Country names for the plant include swallow-wort, tetterwort, witch's

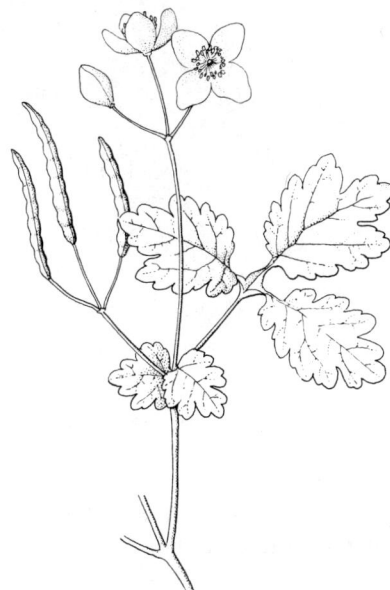

flower, wart plant and yellow spit. Pliny, who recorded the virtues of this plant, said that swallows anointed the eyes of their young with the juice of the greater celandine.

Certainly the juice was applied to the eyes and head of human beings and used to treat tetters (skin diseases), ringworm and warts. A decoction of the herb was said to ease toothache, while the powdered root laid on a loose or hollow tooth would cause it to fall out. During the twentieth century it has been used as a purge, for spleen and liver complaints, and in the form of a poultice for ulcers and skin diseases.

The greater celandine is a plant of the sun and the sign of Leo. It is the birthday flower for 9 October and signifies, in the language of the flowers, withered hope.

Lesser celandine
Ranunculus ficaria

The generic name is derived from Latin *rana*, frog, the habitat of the animal and of plants of the buttercup family being similar; the specific name is from *ficus*, fig, an allusion to the fig-shaped root tubers. A popular name for the plant was pilewort, from Latin *pilum*, ball, alluding to the small knobs on the roots, at the same time indicating its remedial use for haemorrhoids.

The beauty of this, one of the earliest European spring flowers, has

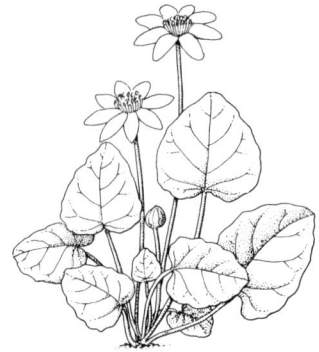

made it popular amongst poets. Wordworth had it carved on his white marble tomb, and wrote of it:

> There's a flower that shall be mine
> 'Tis the little celandine.

Superstitious people carried the plant, with a mole's heart, as a talisman against enemies and lawsuits. The bitter and often poisonous qualities of the buttercup family did not prevent it being used as a cure for jaundice and warts. Children rubbed their teeth with the leaves to whiten them.

In the language of the flowers lesser celandine carries the sentiment 'Joy to come', and it is the birthday flower for 22 July. Astrologically it is under the dominion of Mars.

Centaury   see **Common centaury**

Chamomile   see **Common chamomile**

Charlock
Sinapis arvensis

The generic name is derived from Greek *sinapi*, mustard. *Arvensis* comes from the Latin, pertaining to fields or cultivated land. Charlock is from Old English *cerlic*. An alternative common name for charlock is wild mustard, and it was used as a substitute for **mustard**. Older books refer to it as chadlock, cadlock, cherlock or carlock, the last of which is used by John Clare in his *Shepherd's Calendar*:

> And carlock yellow as the sun
> That o'er the may fields thickly run.

Other country names include bread and marmalade, runch balls, yellow top and yellow weed.

The young tops of charlock used to be boiled and eaten as a vegetable in June, when the plant was abundant in the cornfields.

Cherry   see **Dwarf cherry**

Chervil   see **Garden chervil**

Chestnut

The horse chestnut and sweet chestnut belong to different botanical families but are grouped here for convenience.

Horse chestnut
Aesculus hippocastanum

The generic name is from Greek *esca*, nourishment. A flour was formerly ground from the kernels of the sweet chestnut. The nineteenth-century poet Tennyson refers to the formation of the leaf and the fruit in one of his many poems:

> The drooping chestnut buds appear
> To spread into the perfect fan
> Above the teeming ground.

and

> Calm in the morn without a sound,
> Calm as to suit a calmer grief,
> And only thro' the faded leaf
> The chestnut pottering to the ground.

The fruit of the horse chestnut is commonly known as a conker, and the game of conkers has long been a favourite pastime of children. To play the game one bores a hole through the centre (a meat skewer is the ideal tool) through which a string is then threaded and knotted at one end. One child holds a string dangling a conker, and the other tries to crack it with his own conker. The players alternate positions, each in turn trying to hit the other's nut, until one is broken. The winning conker becomes a 'oner' and so on, according to the number of victories scored. In Worcestershire there is an old rhyme about being the starter of the game:

> Hobley, hobley, ack,
> My first crack.

Herbalists used the horse chestnut in the relief of piles and other rectal complaints. Begged or stolen, it was believed to be a charm against rheumatism. Planted near a house, the tree is thought to keep away gnats.

Horse chestnut is the birthday flower for 1 October and symbolizes luxury; the spiky burr surrounding the nut typifies darting, radiating, piercing fire.

Sweet chestnut
Castanea sativa

Named after Castanum in Thessaly (Greece) where it grew in abundance, the tree was introduced to Britain by the Romans. Early writers called it the Sardian nut, Jupiter's nut and husked nut.

Chestnut wood was used for hop and vine poles and in the later stages of winemaking:

> With close-grained chestnut-wood of sovereign use,
> For casking up the grape's most powerful juice.

The bark was used by tanners, and the leaves, although tending to crackle, were a popular form of mattress stuffing.

Boiled or roasted chestnuts have long been a favourite Christmas dish. Milton describes his own fireside, which must have been typical:

> While hisses on my hearth and pulpy pear,
> And blackening chestnuts start and crackle there.

Although chestnuts were a popular traditional food, and street sellers were once part of the English scene, they were more popular with the French and Italians who used them in pies, stews and fritters. In England, too many chestnuts were thought to 'make the blood thick, and caused headaches' (Culpepper). The modern luxury confection *marrons glâcés* consists of the nuts, boiled and crystallized.

Dried chestnuts beaten to a powder and mixed with honey was a remedy for lung complaints. The bark, leaves and fruit are still used by modern herbalists for respiratory conditions and fevers.

In the Christian tradition the sweet chestnut signifies chastity, and the triumph of virtue over temptations of the flesh. In the language of the flowers, it means 'Render me justice', and symbolizes luxury. To dream of cooking chestnuts signifies that the dreamer will be exploited, and to dream of eating them suggests a difficult business situation.

Chickweed   see **Common chickweed**

Chicory
Cichorium intybus

The generic name is a Latin adaptation of the Arabic word for one member of the family. *Cichorium* comes from the Greek *kichore* meaning salad or root vegetable. The plant is also known as succory. A species of chicory is believed by some old writers to have been among the 'bitter herbs' which God (*Numbers* 9:11) commanded the Israelites to eat with lamb, when the Passover was instituted.

In legend Succory was a beautiful young woman whom the sun wished to marry. Since she refused his advances he changed her into a plant destined to have its face lifted towards him from morning until night. Because of the response of the flower to the sun's rays, it was believed that, by sympathetic magic, the water distilled from the flowers would improve fading eyesight. Chicory was formerly grown as an aphrodisiac, although on no account could the plant be simply pulled out of the ground: it had to be removed with a piece of gold or a stag's horn, a version of the disc-shaped gold sickle which was used in ritual to represent sunlight, warmth and fertility. (The Druids used a golden sickle – the crescent moon – to cut the sacred Mistletoe for ceremonial purposes.) The most auspicious days for picking the plant were St Peter's Day (27 June) and St James's Day (25 July). If the cutter spoke during this time he would die. Superstition also held that those who carried the plant were rendered invisible, and that the leaf would open locked doors if held against a lock.

Herbalists used the plant to treat dropsy and jaundice. The roots of the plant can be ground and blended with coffee to make it go further, a practice still common in France, while the young green leaves, finely chopped, and blanched tops, makes an excellent salad.

Astrologically chicory comes under the dominion of Jupiter. In the language of the flowers it symbolizes frugality.

Chives
Allium schoenoprasum

The generic name is the Latin name of the plant and is the same for all members of the onion family. *Schoenoprasum* is the Greek name for a leek. The origin of this onion-flavoured herb goes back to the ancient Chinese, and the use of chives throughout Asia and the Mediterranean regions was well documented before the Christian era. The Romans are said to have introduced the plant to Britain, where it used to be known as chibbole or chibbal (similar to modern Italian *cipolla*, onion).

Eaten raw, they were believed to send vapours to the brain, causing troublesome sleep and affecting the eyesight, although herbalists maintained that if correctly prepared they made an 'excellent remedy for the stoppage of urine' (Culpepper). The superstitious regarded chives as a protective plant against the evil eye and misfortune generally.

This excellent garden herb can be used in egg, cheese, fish and meat dishes, sauces and salads, as in this poem by Reginald Arkell (1882–1959):

> A salad fit for a king
> I sing;
> With chives and marjoram, lemon thyme –
> A crime
> To leave out parsley and sprigs of mint –
> A hint
> Of sage and bay will crown the head
> (in soup or stew)
> Of the newly-wed!

Astrologically chives are under the dominion of Mars.

Christmas rose
Helleborus niger

The generic name is derived from two Greek words, *hellion*, to kill, and *bora*, food; *niger* means black. Gerard suggests that the Christmas rose was so called because it 'bloweth about the birth of Our Lord Jesus Christ'.

> The Christmas Rose, the last flower of the year
> Comes when the holly-berries glow and cheer,
> When the pale snowdrop rises from the earth,
> So white and spirit like 'mid Christmas mirth.

In the Christian tradition, a medieval nativity play tells of the origin of the flower. It is said that a young country girl who accompanied the shepherds when they visited Jesus in the stable wept because she had no gift to offer the baby. An angel, seeing her sorrow, led her from the stable, and on touching the cold earth a Christmas rose appeared. With joy, the girl was able to offer that flower as her token, and it has become an emblem of the Nativity. The flower is also dedicated to St Agnes, patron saint of young virgins, and in some parts of the country is known as St Agnes flower.

Among its other alternative common names are Christ's herb, Christmas herb and black hellebore, bcause, according to Farrer, its heart [root] is black, while 'its face shines with a blazing white innocence'.

Formerly hellebore was called melampode, after Melampus, a Greek physician active around 1400 B.C., who, according to Pliny, treated nervous disorders. Apparently he first observed its effects when he was working as a shepherd, and is alleged to have cured the daughters of

Proetus, King of Argus. John Clare, in his *Shepherd's Calendar* refers to its use in the treatment of sheep:

> My silly sheep like well below,
> They need not melampode;
> For they bene hale enough, I trow,
> And liken their abode.

Both 'melampode' and a herb called terebinth (a shrub yielding a balsamic resin called Chian turpentine) were used to treat diseased goats, and humans were said to benefit from drinking the milk of the animals as well as eating the herb on its own. The roots were dried and collected in the autumn, and used to treat dropsy, hysteria and nervous disorders generally. Treatment was followed by a cold bath. Nevertheless the root is so poisonous that, when powedered, it was mixed with meal to kill mice!

The superstitious would cure sick or bewitched cattle by inserting a piece of hellebore root in the ear of the beast for twenty-four hours. They also blessed their cattle with hellebore as a protection against witchcraft in the first place. Houses were purified with it, because the smell of the plant was thought to drive away evil spirits. Later Christmas roses were planted near cottage doors to protect the occupants from evil spirits who might try to cross the threshold, which was alleged, together with the chimney, to be a vulnerable place when dealing with the supernatural.

Lengthy religious rites used to accompany the gathering of the roots for medicinal purposes. A circle was drawn around the plant with a sword, and prayers were offered to Apollo and to Aesculapius, the god of medicine. It was essential that an eagle did not hover nearby, otherwise death would overtake the gatherer within the year, and it was advisable to eat garlic to mask any odour from the plant. The Christmas rose has been associated with witchcraft for a very long time and inevitably variations and contradictions in its use have arisen. The Gauls are said to have tipped their arrows with a variety of hellebore before hunting, but in the belief that it tenderized the meat rather than for any superstitious reason.

Christmas rose is the birthday flower for 25 December, Christmas Day, and is an emblem of the Nativity of Christ.

Chrysanthemum
Chrysanthemum sinensis × indicum

In the generic name *chyros* means golden in Greek, and *anthos*, flower. Although cultivated for hundreds of years in the Far East, the flower has a comparatively short history in England. It was first imported towards the end of the eighteenth century, although a few varieties were introduced to Holland a littler earlier. By the 1860s the National Chrysanthemum Society was holding exhibitions of both Japanese and Chinese species. The early Chinese flowers were mostly incurved although later interest moved towards the Japanese loose or recurved varieties.

The flower typifies the Orient as the rose typifies the western world, and the Chinese cultivate certain varieties of chrysanthemum for their edible petals, a colourful addition to any salad. An emblem of the solar wheel, which was based on a belief that some flowers open and close daily at determinate hours, and the flower of Sagittarius, the chrysanthemum is the birthday flower for 24 December and symbolizes abundance, regal beauty, wealth, and cheerfulness in adversity. The red chrysanthemum carries the sentiment 'I love you', while the white one signifies truth and the yellow one dejection and slighted love.

Clary
Salvia sclarea

The generic name is from Latin *salveo*, I heal, from the supposed properties of the genus; clary comes from *clarus*, clear. Apothecaries made eye salves from the plant, which account for two of its popular names, clear eye and Christ's eye (*Oculus Christi*). In those days of primitive medicine a whole seed was sometimes placed under the eyelid and left until it dropped out. Several administrations were thought 'to take off a film which covereth the sight; a handsome and safer remedy, it is a great deal easier than to tear it off with a needle' (Culpepper). Neither remedy sounds particularly pleasant. The virtues of the plant were held in such esteem that it was alternatively named *Officinalis Christi*, which some writers thought quite blasphemous.

The whole plant has an aromatic odour similar to garden **sage**, which explains yet another of its common names, wild sage. Clary seeds, beaten to a powder and taken in wine, were recommended as an aphrodisiac. The leaves were used in pot-pourri and as a flavouring for omelettes. Astrologically the plant is assigned to the moon.

Cleavers   see **Common cleavers**

Clover
Trifolium

The generic name means three-leafed in Latin. The common name is the clavers of the Middle Ages. The Anglo-Saxons called it cloeferwort, probably from Latin *clava*, a club or cudgel, the club of our playing cards. It was also known as trefoil. Red clover (*T. pratense*) is the most extensively cultivated of the many species of *trifolium*.

Hope was depicted by the ancients as a little child, standing on tiptoe holding a clover in its hand. The Druids held the plant in great regard as a charm against evil spirits. During the period when witches and fairies seemed to be part of everyday life the clover was considered by both peasant and knight a potent charm against their influences. The falchion or sword arm was the correct place to display it. The following is quoted in Hilderic Friend's *Flowers and Flower Lore*:

> Woe! Woe! to the wight who meets the green knight,
> Except on his falchion arm
> Spell-proof he bears, like the brave St Clair,
> The holy Trefoil's charm

A four-leaf clover hidden in the cowshed protected the cows from magic and ensured plenty of butter. Wearing a four-leaf clover was thought to cure various diseases, including lunacy, to averting the evil eye, and to assist the wearer to escape military service. According to folk rhyme:

> One leaf for fame,
> And one for wealth,
> One for a faithful lover,
> And one to bring you glorious health
> Are in a four-leaf clover.

A four-leaf clover was thought to give second sight, and to dream of it suggested a happy marriage. A five-leaf clover was considered as unlucky as a four-leafed one was lucky.

Two rhymes couple the clover with the **ash**, one a form of love divination:

> If you find an ash leaf or a four-leafed clover
> You'll see your true love ere the day be over.

The other is a couplet indicating good fortune and luck:

> With a four-leaved Clover, a double-leaved Ash, and green
> topped Seave,
> You may go before the queen's daughter without asking leave.

A form of love oracle was suggested in the old saying:

> A clover, a clover of two,
> Put it in your right shoe,
> The first young man [or woman] you meet,
> In field, lane or street,
> You shall have him, or one of his name.

The clover leaf is an emblem of spring, season of renewal, the trefoil being a trinity symbol. Red clover symbolizes industry; purple clover means, 'Not only gay but good'; crimson clover (*T. incarnatum*) means prudent and watchful; and white clover (*T. repens*) in the language of the flowers signifies, 'Think of me'. A four-leafed clover symbolizes good fortune, and in the language of the flowers means, 'Be mine'. A good wine can be made from the red and white clover.

Coltsfoot
Tussilago farfara

The generic name is from Latin *tussis*, cough, and the plant was used medicinally in treating that complaint; the specific is from Pliny's word for the white poplar – both plants have downy leaves. The common name is derived from the shape of the leaf. Many other country names of similar origin, include foalswort, ass's-foot, horsehoof, hallfoot and bullsfoot. A popular name of ancient origin was *Filius-ante-patrem*, son-before-the-father, because the flowers appear before the leaves.

In summer the seed head is crowned with a hairy pappus which country people used as a weather omen. If the down flies off when there is no wind it is a certain sign of rain. The soft seed heads were used for stuffing pillows and the leaves as tinder.

For centuries herbalists have used coltsfoot for chest complaints. As a remedy for a cough Pliny suggested that the dried leaves and roots of the plant should be burnt, preferably over **cypress** charcoal, and the smoke drawn up into the mouth through a reed and swallowed. A little wine could be sipped between inhalations. Later the plant was mixed with **yarrow** and **rose** leaves to make a tobacco which was a herbal remedy for asthma. Coltsfoot lozenges were sold during the Victorian era, and the plant was still being used during this century in treating whooping cough.

Astrologically coltsfoot is under the dominion of Venus. In the language of the flowers it means 'Justice shall be done', and symbolizes maternal care.

Columbine
Aquilegia vulgaris

The generic name is from Latin *aquila*, eagle, because the nectaries are said to resemble the claws of that bird. Columbine is from Latin *columba*, dove – the flower was thought to look like a nest of doves.

> O columbine, open your folded wrapper,
> Where two twin turtle-doves dwell!

A native plant, columbine has been cultivated in gardens for hundreds of years, and is also known as doves in the ark, granny-bonnets, culver-wort, skull caps and fool's cap.

The flower was one of the badges of the House of Lancaster. In the

Christian tradition it is dedicated to Christ and the Holy Ghost, and is depicted with seven petals instead of the usual five, to typify the gifts of the Holy Spirit; counsel, fear, knowledge, piety, strength, understanding and wisdom.

Herbalists prescribed columbine seeds for measles, smallpox and jaundice, although Linnaeus alleged that children died through taking it. The seeds, taken in wine, were said to bring on childbirth. A lotion concocted from the leaves was used to treat ulcerated mouths and sore throats.

Columbine is the birthday flower for 1 April and symbolizes desertion, inconstancy and folly. In former days it was the insignia of a deserted lover. A couplet in the 'Britannia's Pastorals' of William Browne (1592–?1643) refers to this symbolism:

> The Columbine by lonely wand'rer taken,
> Is there ascribed to such as are forsaken.

Comfrey see **Common comfrey**

Common alder
Alnus glutinosa

The generic name is the classical Latin word for the tree. Alder and variants of it go back beyond Old English. Some etymologists derive the name for this lover of damp habitats from an ancient word for water, *al*. A very durable wood, especially underwater, it was used in building early boats, piles and water pipes.

In Celtic mythology it is the tree of the resurrection, marking the emergence of the solar year. Alder typifies fire, from the red of its trunk; water, from the green flowers; and earth, from the brown of its bark.

Its medicinal properties were well known to herbalists, who used the bark as a gargle for sore throats and a compound of the leaf to treat burns and inflammations. The leaf could also be applied directly to parts so affected. Placed beneath the feet, they were said to bring relief to the weary traveller. The surface of the leaf, which is clammy, was recommended by Culpepper 'to be gathered while the morning dew is upon them, and brought into a chamber troubled with fleas, will gather them there unto, which being suddenly cast out, will rid the chamber of those troublesome bedfellows'.

Alder is under the dominion of Venus and the astrological sign of Pisces.

Common bracken
Pteridium aquilinum

The generic name is from Greek *pteron*, wing, from the appearance of the fronds; *aquilinum* means eagle-like. The names brake and bracken are very old and suggest the plant's habitat, as brake is derived from a word meaning uncultivated land. Rustic wisdom can be quite baffling to the modern reader, as in this charming but not readily comprehensible rhyme which was once in common usage:

> When the fern is as high as a spoon,
> You may sleep an hour at noon;
> When the fern is as high as a ladle,
> You may sleep as long as you're able;
> When the fern begins to look red
> Then milk is good with brown bread.

Many people considered bracken to be a holy plant because the marks on the root when the plant is cut are said to resemble the Greek letter Χ, meaning Christ. Others thought the dark markings in the cellular mass showed the figure of an **oak** tree, said to have first appeared after Charles II had sheltered in one after the Battle of Worcester in 1651.

The superstitious believed that some plants had the power to impart their particular qualities to the wearer. The seeds of certain plants were invisible to the naked eye, and presumed therefore to confer invisibility on those who carried the plant. In Shakespeare's *Henry IV*, Gadshill remarks: 'We have receipt of fern-seed . . . we walk invisible.' The reply, however, expresses a more practical view: 'Now, by my faith, I think you are more beholden to the night than to fern-seed for your walking invisible.' It was accepted in many parts of the country that fern seed was visible only on St John's Eve at the precise moment the saint was born, which was obviously the most propitious time to gather it.

> But on St John's mysterious night,
> Scared to many a wizard spell,
> The hour when first to human sight
> Confest, the mystic fern-seed fell.

As late as 1870, in Lancashire, it was firmly believed that to swallow seed gathered on the family Bible gave invisibility. Ideally the seeds were collected in silence and allowed to fall on a pewter dish. The bracken had to be bent over with a **hazel** twig and the seeds allowed to drop untouched by human hand.

Another ritual associated with the plant at midsummer required the roots of the male plant to be dug up, carved into the shape of a human hand, and baked in an oven. The shrivelled result, known as dead man's hand or St John's hand, was carried as a charm against witches and evil spirits, protecting one's person, home and land.

One variety of fern was an important ingredient in love philtres, as a Gaelic song reveals:

> Twas the maiden's matchless beauty
> That drew my heart anigh,
> Not the fern-root potions,
> But the glance of her blue eye.

Bracken was grown on the roofs of houses as protection against thunder and lightning, and burning it was thought to have some influence on local rainfall.

There was a widespread belief in the healing properties of fern, particularly if picked during the waning of the moon, for sprains and inflammations. The stems and fronds were used in dietetic drinks and medicines, and the juice for eye inflammations. As a guarantee against toothache for a whole year superstitious people swore by the biting of a fern seed in spring.

Bracken is the birthday flower for 24 March. It symbolizes confidence, fascination, sincerity and humility.

Common centaury
Centaurium erythraea

For the origin of the generic and common names see **black knapweed**; the specific name means red, referring to the pink flowers. An old name for the plant was birthwort. Because of its bitter taste herbalists referred to it as *fel terrae*, earth gall. A healing and tonic effect was attributed to it; Culpepper wrote: 'Tis very wholesome, but not very toothsome.' Centaury was the main ingredient of the Duke of Portland's Powder, so named because it is said to have cured him of gout. Albertus Magnus, the thirteenth-century German scholar, claimed a more unusual use for the plant: 'Magicians assure us that this herb has a singular virtue for if it is mixed with the flood of a female hoopoe [a bird] and put in a lamp with the oil, all those present will see themselves upside down with their feet in the air.'

Centaury is an obvious weather oracle, closing in damp weather or when the sky is overcast. It symbolizes felicity and delicacy, and astrologically it is under the sign of the sun.

Common chamomile
Anthemis nobilis

The generic name comes from Greek *anthos*, flower, and the specific meaning, noble, is a testimony to the excellence and superior value of the plant. The common name is also Greek in origin and is derived from *chamos*, on the ground, and *melos*, apple. Chamomile was one of the sacred herbs of Saxon times, the others being **mugwort, plantain, watercress, nettle, crab apple, chervil** and **fennel**, and fragrant, fresh chamomile would be strewn over the bare stone or wooden floors of their homes. Chamomile was believed to have the power to revive other plants growing nearby.

Because it is a fast-growing aromatic plant lawns were sown with it. In Shakespeare's *Henry IV* Falstaff remarks: 'Though the camomile the more it is trodden on the faster it grows, yet youth the more it is wasted the sooner it wears.' Though chamomile lawns were fashionable in Tudor times, grass has almost completely taken over; however, a well-established lawn can still be found in the grounds of Buckingham Palace today.

The medicinal qualities of the plant were said to be at their most potent when the flowers were fully expanded. Muslin bags full of flowers were steeped in water and used as fomentations to treat facial swellings caused by abscesses. They also made a very pleasant scented bath. Chamomile tea was a very popular beverage consisting of two heaped teaspoonsful of chamomile flowers to a large cup of boiling water, left to brew for ten minutes; the effect was said to be rather like a sedative. Beatrix Potter's Peter Rabbit was given chamomile tea to soothe him after his adventure in Mr McGregor's garden. This preparation was also used as a facial skin tonic and a hair rinse, especially to lighten fair hair. A preparation of chamomile is a twentieth-century tonic for dyspepsia and stomach complaints and menstruation problems. William Browne, writing in 'Britannia's Pastroals', said that it was good for fish:

> Another from her banks in sheer good will,
> Brings nutriment for fish, the camomile.

The flower heads yield a yellow dye.

Astrologically chamomile is under the dominion of the sun. It is the birthday flower for 17 December and symbolizes energy in adversity, and love in austerity.

Common chickweed
Stellaria media

The generic name is from Latin *stella*, star, which the expanded flowers resemble in shape. Other common names are chick wittles, chickweed, skirt and buttons, chickenwort, tongue grass and white bird's eye. The plant is rich in copper and used to form a valuable addition to people's diets. It was eaten as a salad plant and as a cooked vegetable, similar to spinach.

Herbalists recommended poultices of chickweed to treat carbuncles and abscesses, and an infusion of the plant as an eye lotion. A slimming potion of ancient repute consisted of a distillation of chickweed, with lemon or orange peel added; this 'tea' was also said to soothe upset stomachs. Michael Drayton wrote:

> His chickweed cures the heat that in the face doth rise;
> For physic, some again he inwardly applies.

Chickweed was prescribed for cramp, one recipe consisting of a handful of the plant and a handful of red **rose** leaves boiled in a quart of muscadine (grape juice) reduced by a quarter; sheep's foot oil was then added. The resulting compound was applied to the affected area which would then 'with God's blessing, cure the malady three times the dressing'.

In the language of the flowers chickweed means 'Will you meet me'. The plant symbolizes a rendezvous. It is the birthday flower for 2 May, and astrologically is a herb of the moon.

Common cleavers
Galium aparine

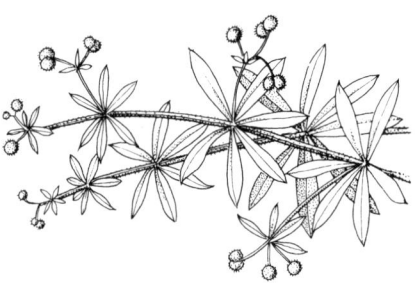

The generic name is from Greek *gala*, milk; some of the species were used to curdle milk. The common name refers to the plant's habit of clinging to the coats of passing animals and the clothes of humans, providing an excellent method of seed dispersal. Children enjoy secretly throwing the plant on to the backs of unsuspecting friends, where they will cling until detected. Country names include burweed, stickleback, sweethearts, catch grass and love man, and like **silverweed** it is known as goosegrass, from its reputation as a food for geese.

Herbalists used the distilled water of the plant to treat jaundice, the juice of the leaves to stop bleeding and, finely chopped in spring, 'to cleanse the blood'. In the present century it was recommended for kidney and bladder complaints, fevers and acute diseases. Cleavers seeds were used as a substitute for coffee. Astrologically the herb is under the dominion of the moon.

Common comfrey
Symphytum officinale

The generic name is from Greek *sympho*, unite, from its supposed healing properties, and the common name is a corruption of *confirma* – both are an allusion to the knitting of broken bones, which the herb was said to bring about. The plant was named by Dioscorides some two thousand years ago. It has several common names, many referring to its healing properties – knitbone, consolida, nipbone, bruisewort and boneset; others include church bells, suckers and Abraham Isaac and Jacob, the last from the variation in colour of the flowers.

Herbalists applied comfrey leaves externally to sprains, swellings and bruises, and as a poultice on severe cuts, boils and abscesses. By reducing the swelling around fractures it was believed to unite bones. The root was first pounded to a mucilaginous mass. The juice was used to wash the limb and the pulp drained through a linen cloth and packed around the bone as it lay in a wooden trough splint. Michael Drayton recommended it also for lung complaints:

> Campana here he crops, approved and wonderous good;
> As comfrey until him that's spitting blood.

The root was still in use during the twentieth century as a remedy for bleeding from the lungs, coughs and dysentery, and for treating ulcers, bruises, fresh wounds and sore breasts. However, recent reports suggest that comfrey tea, which has enjoyed some popularity, may be dangerous.

Astrologically comfrey is under the dominion of Saturn and the sign of Capricorn, which suggests that it is cold in quality.

Common dodder
Cuscuta epithymum

The generic name is thought to be derived from Arabic *kechout*. Popular names for the plant include lady's laces and bride's laces because of the stringlike stems; less flattering names include devil's guts, hellweed and strangle-tare, from its characteristic of winding itself around other plants and ultimately strangling them to death.

Dodder was used to treat 'melancholy diseases of the head, brain and spleen', as well as swooning and fainting, and heart complaints. As a parasite herb it symbolizes meanness. Astrologically it is under the dominion of Saturn.

Common duckweed
Lemna minor

The generic name is Greek for some unspecified waterweed. English country names include dig meat, duck pond weed and Jenny green teeth. The last of these refers to a sinister, magical creature said to hide beneath the floating plants – a useful 'bogey-man' legend quoted by parents to frighten their children away from dangerous waters.

Herbalists used the plant with barley meal as a poultice to treat gout. Distilled duckweed water was used for fevers and internal inflammation, swelling in the scrotum and of the breasts 'before they have grown too much', and redness of the eyes. Fresh leaves were applied to the head to relieve headaches. The plant is under the dominion of the moon and the sign of Cancer.

Common fumitory
Fumaria officinalis

The generic name is medieval Latin, meaning smoke from the earth. Pliny wrote that as smoke causes the eye to water so does fumitory when applied to them, hence its name. The so-called 'smoke' of the plant was believed by ancient exorcists to have the power to drive out evil spirits. Dioscorides claimed that it prevented new eyelashes growing. Country names for the plant are beggary and mother of thousands.

Herbalists used fumitory juice with **dock** and vinegar for cleansing scabs, sores and pimples. A distillation of the herb, with honey and water, was recommended as a gargle and as a preventative against plague. John Clare refers to the cosmetic use of the plant:

> And fumitory, too, a name
> That superstition holds to fame
> Whose red and purple mottled flowers
> Are cropt by maids in weeding hours
> To boil in water milk and way [whey]
> For washes on a holiday
> To make their beauty fair and sleek
> And scour the tan from summer's cheek.

Fumitory is the birthday flower for 1 September, and symbolizes the spleen. In the language of the flowers it means 'ill at ease'. Astrologically it is under the sign of Saturn.

Common lime
Tilia × vulgaris

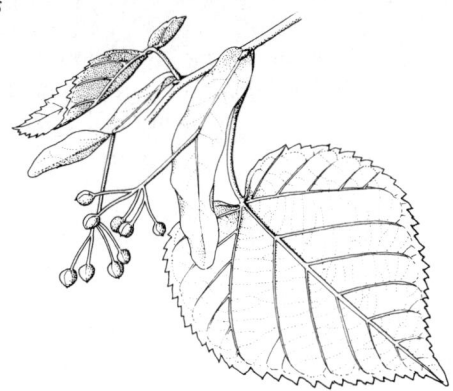

The generic name is the word the Romans used. The word lime is derived from Anglo-Saxon *lind* (hence its alternative name, linden), shield, as the wood, which is easy to work, was used for making shields; *lind* became *lynde*, then *line*.

The lime is a symbol of wedded love, an attribute it acquired probably through the legend of a good shepherd named Philemon and his wife, Baucis, who lived in a Phrygian village and entertained the gods Zeus and Hermes when, disguised as humans, they were unable to find shelter for the night. As a reward for their kindness Zeus granted them the wish that one day they would die together. In due course Philemon became an oak, symbol of hospitality, and Baucis a lime, the emblem of conjugal affection.

To the superstitious the lime was a life index tree for the family to whom it belonged. A fallen branch foretold a death in that family.

Herbalists steeped the bark of the tree in water until a thick mucilaginous substance formed which was applied to burns and scalds. The leaves, boiled in water, provided a lotion used as a mouthwash for children and to treat sores, ulcers, freckles, wrinkles and other skin complaints. A concoction of lime was applied to stimulate hair growth. Lime flowers were used in a cure for epilepsy. In fact just sitting under the tree was thought to be beneficial – it was probably connected with their fragrance, to which the nineteenth-century poet Matthew Arnold refers in *The Scholar Gypsey*:

> And air swept lindens yield
> Their scent, and rustle down their perfum'd showers
> Of bloom on the bent grass where I am laid,
> And bower me from the August sun with shade.

Lime wood is close-grained and ideal for carving. Much of the exquisite work of the master craftsman Grinling Gibbons (1648–1720) was carried out in lime.

Astrologically the lime is under the dominion of Venus. It is the birthday flower for 7 February and symbolizes gentleness, hospitality, modesty, pliancy, sweetness and, as mentioned above, conjugal love.

Common milkwort
Polygala vulgaris

The generic name is derived from two Greek words meaning much and milk, from the ancient belief that the plant increased milk production in animals. Country names for the plant include hedge hyssop, procession flower, cross flower and rogation flower. Many of them are associated with the old religious observance of Rogation Days, the three days leading up to Ascension Day when the litany used to be sung in public procession. Rogation Days were also known as Gang Days from the custom of 'ganging' round the parish to beat the bounds. On Ascension Day children, accompanied by clergy and other parish officials, walked their parish from end to end; the boys were lashed with **willow** wands on the boundary lines to teach them the confines of the parish. A pole decorated with milkwort and other flowrs was carried by charity children, and garlands were also made of the flower. The procession is mentioned as early as A.D.550. Gerard speaks of the practice in Tudor times: 'It [milkwort] serveth well to decking up of houses and banquetting-rooms, for places of pleasure, and for beautifying of streets in the Crosse or Gang Week, and such like.'

In the language of the flowers milkwort means a hermitage.

Common reed
Phragmites communis

The generic name is from Greek *phragma*, materials for an enclosure. The long stems of the reed were widely used from early times in thatching house roofs and barns.

In Greek mythology Prometheus brought fire to mankind in a hollow reed. Syrinx, the daughter of the river god Ladon, pursued by Pan, prayed to the gods to be transformed into a reed. Pan's pipes were fashioned from the reed for this reason, as the seventeenth-century poet Andrew Marvell recounts:

And Pan did after Syrinx speed,
Not as a nymph, but for a reed.

Astrologically the plant is assigned to Venus. A single reed is the birthday flower for 17 October and symbolizes blessedness, complacence and writing. A split reed is the plant for 6 October and symbolizes folly and indiscretion. The reed also signifies authority, frailty, marsh, instability, literature and music. It is the Christian symbol of humility and justice.

Common rock-rose
Helianthemum nummularium

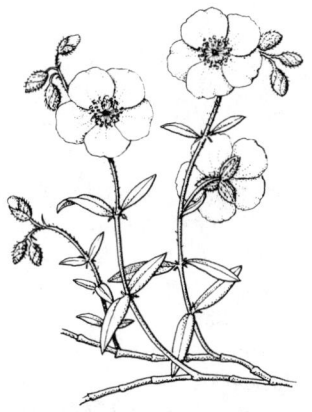

The generic name is from Greek *helios*, sun, and *anthos*, flower, because the flowers expand in sunshine. The bright yellow flower well deserves its country names of beauties of the sun and sun roses.

Herbalists used a variety of the plant as a pessary to soften the womb in childbirth. Alternatively they would burn rock-rose on hot coals – the smoke was believed to penetrate the womb and bring down the afterbirth. A special recipe, which also included myrrh, was used to prevent hair falling out.

Astrologically the rock-rose is governed by the sign of Jupiter. It is the birthday flower for 16 December and symbolizes security.

Common Solomon's seal
Polygonatum multiflorum

The generic name literally means many-knee-jointed, referring to the distinctive markings on the stem or root. Dioscorides wrote that the plant was so named because that's what the shape of the rhizome resembled. Ambiguity surrounds the common name, however; some sources say that the white pendant blossoms suggest a hanging bunch of seals, others that the flat, round scars on the rootstock resemble what is referred to as a Solomon's seal – a name given by Arabs to a six-pointed star. A third source points out that as the flower stems decay the main stalk becomes scarred; the marks resemble seals, and the roots were thought to have medicinal properties for sealing wounds. Old country names for Solomon's seal include ladder to heaven, David's harp and Solomon's heal.

The root of the plant, mixed with cream, was a well-used remedy for bruises, in particular for those 'gotten by falls of woman's wilfulness, in stumbling upon their hasty husband's fists', a reflection of the times. The root provided remedies to stop bleeding, knit broken bones, cure baldness and vomiting, and seal open wounds. A distillation of the whole plant removed freckles, spots and marks, leaving the skin 'fresh, fair and lovely'. During the present century the plant was used to treat chronic dysentery, piles and inflammation of the stomach. An inhalation from the delicate flowers was said to inspire painters and poets.

Astrologically Solomon's seal is under the dominion of Saturn.

Common sorrel
Rumex acetosa

The generic name was the Latin word for the plant. Country names are numerous and include sour dock, sour suds, sour grass, green sauce and green sorrel.

During the Tudor period the plant was a popular salad herb and green vegetable; it was later replaced by French sorrel. Chopped finely with vinegar and sugar, it was known as green sauce. Sorrel was also used as a tenderizer – meat was wrapped in sorrel leaves, whose acidity was said to have a beneficial action on tough meat. A pleasant wine can be produced from the flowers.

Early herbalists suggested that the plant refreshed the spirit 'overspent with the violence of furious or fiery fits of ague to quench thirst and procure an appetite in fainting and decayed stomachs' (Culpepper). Sorrel juice, blended with vinegar, was recommended for ringworm, and a syrup of **fumitory** and sorrel was used to treat irritating skin infections. The entire herb was used to treat scorpion stings and a cooling drink dispensed for fevers and to prevent scurvy.

Sorrel is under the astrological sign of Venus and is the birthday flower for 17 March; it symbolizes paternal affection, and resignation in sorrow.

Common toadflax
Linaria vulgaris

The generic name is from Latin *linum*, flax, which the leaves of some species resemble. According to one old writer the name toadflax was given it because the flower has 'a mouth like unto a frog's mouth'. It is also known as butter and eggs, the pale yellow part of the flower suggesting butter and the orange part an egg yolk; other names include flax-weed, patten-and-clogs, wild snapdragon and gallwort. To quote Culpepper: 'In Sussex we call it Gallwort, and lay it on our chickens water to cure them of the gall; it relieves them when they are dropping.'

The flowers yield a yellow dye. Medicinally they were used for skin infections. Toadflax juice or a distillation of the plant was used as an eye remedy, while a decoction of the leaves and flowers was supposed to expel stillborn babies. The plant was favoured for the treatment of liver complaints.

Astrologically it is under the dominion of Mars.

Common valerian
Valeriana officinalis

The generic name is from Latin *valere*, to be healthy, on account of its medicinal virtues. Some older writers, however, attribute the name to a physician, Valerius, who is said to have been the first person to have used the plant medicinally. Other names for the plant are drunken sailor, bouncing Bess, pretty Betty and all-heal, a name also given to **mistletoe**. The possible intoxicating effect of the plant could explain some of the common names, because it has a strong odour, particularly when bruised. Another old and expressive name for the plant was phu: cats are said to be very attracted to the herb and delight in rolling about in it. Rats are similarly affected, and the plant was once used as rat bait – it is said that this was the secret of the Pied Piper of Hamelin's success in defeating the plague of rats.

The Romans cannot have found valerian too unpleasant as it was popular as an incense plant. In the Middle Ages the roots were used to perfume linen and clothing. Valerian was also used as an aphrodisiac and it was said if a girl wore valerian she would never lack lovers.

Medieval herbalists recommended it as a specific for cramp:

> Valerian then he crops, and purposely doth stamp,
> To apply into the place that's haled with cramp.

A gipsy recipe for the treatment of epilepsy consisted of one ounce of valerian root, boiled in one and a half pints of water until it reduced to a pint; the dosage was one wineglass four or five times a day. Valerian tea, brewed from the dried roots, is alleged to be one of the strongest herbal sedatives. During the twentieth century valerian has been used to treat epilepsy, nervous headaches and, as a medical placebo, hypochondria.

Astrologically the plant is under the dominion of Mercury. It is the birthday flower for 16 March and symbolizes a good disposition.

Coriander
Coriandrum sativum

The generic name is possibly derived from a Greek word meaning bug, referring to the odour of the seeds. It was frequently known also as coliander. The plant, particularly the seed, was familiar to the ancients as a condiment and a medicine. It is mentioned in the Bible, in the Book of Numbers, as one of the bitter herbs of the Passover.

Roasted and taken in wine, coriander seeds were recommended by herbalists as a cure for worms; taken after meals they were thought to be an aid to digestion and to prevent sickness by closing up the entrance to the stomach. The green plant, boiled and mixed with white bread-crumbs, made a poultice for swellings and inflammations. The seeds were also used to disguise the taste of less pleasant medicines.

Today the seeds are used to flavour curries, confectionery and any dish containing apples. Coriander is the birthday flower for 12 December and in the language of the flowers symbolizes concealed merit and hidden wealth. Astrologically it is under the dominion of Saturn.

Corn cockle
Agrostemma githago

Older writers claim that *Agrostemma* is of Greek origin, meaning crown of the field. The name cockle or cokyl was used in reference to weeds generally. In the Christian tradition it suggests wickedness (weed) invading the goodness (garden) of the church. In the Bible, when Job protests his integrity, suggesting that if he be false, 'Let thistles grow instead of wheat, and cockle instead of barley', there is no doubt that he meant weeds. Nevertheless, the true corn cockle is one of the plants of Palestine. In Agnes Strickland's 'Flowers of the Cornfield' the reference is quite clear too:

> And poppies, like morning-glories spread,
> That flash and glance with their scarlet shoes,
> The bending ears of the wheat between;
> And mark, when it bows to the breezes sway,
> How it shows the cockle in rich array.

Cockle seed mixed with corn was believed to cause giddiness. The small black seeds were said to be poisonous, and when ground with the flour later appeared as black specks in the bread.

Corn cockle is the birthday flower for 11 December, and signifies absence. Astrologically it is assigned to the dominion of Saturn.

Cornflower
Centaurea cyanus

For the derivation of the generic name see **black knapweed**; *cyanus* refers to the beautiful blue colour of the cornflower. In Greek mythology Cyanus was a fair young devotee of the goddess Flora, who passed his days weaving garlands of flowers in the cornfields for the various floral festivals. On his death, as a reward for his devotion, Flora transformed his body into a cornflower, the flower he believed to be the most beautiful of all, and which lay scattered around him when he died. The cornflower has several country names such as bachelors' buttons, corn blue-bottle, blue-cap, blue-bonnet (a Scottish name) and hurt-sickle: the last arose from the plant's reputation for blunting the sickles formerly used to cut corn.

> A treach'rous guest, destruction though dost bring
> To th' inhospitable field where thou dost spring,
> Thou blunt'st the very reaper's sickle, and so
> In life and death becom'st the farmer's foe.

Formerly the flower was used as a form of love divination. If it was carried in a young man's pocket and survived, he would marry his current sweetheart, but if the flower died, she would find someone else.

> If my lover loves me, and loves me well
> So may the fall of the morning dew
> Keep the sun from fading they tender blue.

Children made wreaths of cornflower heads by stringing the outer florets with a needle and thread; the ends were secured and the circlet pressed between the pages of a book. Flowers treated this way retain their colour for a long time, and because the dried petals of the cornflower do last well they are still popular for pot-pourri. Artists, particularly miniaturists, would pound the fresh central florets in a mortar and use the residue as a pigment.

Medicinally, the fresh leaves taken in wine were considered a remedy for plague and other infectious diseases. The juice of the plant, placed on fresh wounds, promoted rapid healing; mouth ulcers and eye complaints were also treated with the cornflower. The powdered leaves were used for bruises and internal bleeding, and with the addition of **plantain** and **marestail** as an antidote for snake and scorpion bites.

The cornflower is under the astrological sign of Libra and the dominion of Saturn. The flower signifies delicacy, and a dweller in heavenly places.

Cottage pink
Dianthus plumaris

The generic name signifies Jupiter's flower or divine flower from the Greek *dios*, divine, and *anthos*, flower. Gerard claims to have given the plant its specific name, *plumaris*, because of its cut or feathered petals. The name pink is said to be a combination of a Dutch word and an English word meaning a small winking eye, referring no doubt to the eye at the centre of the flower. The word pink (as in pinking shears) also describes a scalloped edge, another feature of the petals. Pink, as the name of a colour, was unknown when the plant was introduced.

In medieval art the pink symbolizes divine love and signified that a lady was engaged to be married. In heraldry it typifies admiration. The pink is the birthday flower for 31 May and symbolizes amiability, morning light, timidity, welcomeness and divine love.

Cowslip
Primula veris

The generic name is a form of Latin *primus*, first; *veris* refers to spring. Cowslip comes from Old English *cuslippe*. Old herbals call the plant herb Peter and St Peter's wort, as the cluster of blossoms resembles a bunch of keys, the emblem of the apostle. Petty mullein was also used, because the plant was originally thought to be a small species of mullein. Another old

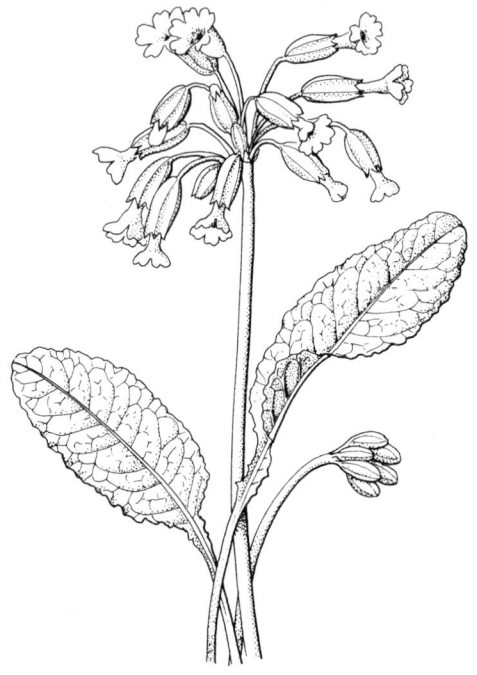

country name, paigle, gave rise to the saying 'As blake as a paigle', blake meaning yellow.

Cowslips were said to remove blemishes and wrinkles, the magic being in the spots on the petals. Shakespeare wrote in *A Midsummer Night's Dream*:

> In their gold coats spots you see;
> Those be rubies, fairy favours,
> In those freckles live their savours.

An old country custom associated with the plant was to string up sixty or so of the umbels, pressing them carefully together and tying them with string to form a ball. In *The Shepherd's Calendar* John Clare refers to this rural practice:

> And cowslip cucking balls to toss
> Above the garlands swinging light
> Hang in the soft eves sober light
> These maid and child did yearly pull
> By many a folded apron full.

Welsh girls used the balls as a love oracle, throwing them from one to another and singing:

> Titsy tosty, tell me true
> Who shall I be married to.

The names of local bachelors would be called out, and the one mentioned before the ball was dropped would be the future husband of the girl who had previously been designated by her friends. Cowslips were scattered around the maypole on May Day, a survival of pagan sacrificial rites. It was generally believed if the cowslip was planted upside down the flowers would come up red or as a **primrose**. Another attribute that it shares with the primrose is that of supposedly being able to open caves where treasure was hidden.

The leaves were used as a salad herb and for dressing wounds. A decoction of the flowers was thought to cure trembling and generally strengthen the brain and nervous system. Cowslip flowers, dried in the sun, were made into a conserve with sugar. The fresh blossoms, added to tea, were believed to make it wholesome and refreshing. Cowslip wine, which has a pleasant flavour, had an excellent reputation as a sedative, as those who have drunk the wine in any quantity will have discovered. A treatment said to be soothing and beneficial to the skin was a cowslip bath, which required three handfuls of fresh or dried flower heads to be steeped in hot water for fifteen minutes in a muslin bag; the scented water was then added to the bath where it could be massaged into the body.

Astrologically the cowslip is under the sign of Venus. It is the birthday flower for 22 September and symbolizes pensiveness, winning grace, rusticity and comeliness. In the language of the flowers it means, 'You are my divinity'.

Crab apple
Malus sylvestris

The generic name is Latin for apple; the specific refers to woodland. Crab apples were once used as love oracles. It was the custom at Michaelmas (29 September) for girls to gather the fruit and arrange them in a loft to form the initials of their various boyfriends. Whichever initial was found to be still perfect on Old Michaelmas Day (11 October) represented the strongest attachment and obviously the best choice as a husband.

The juice of the crab apple is very sour, and in the days when vinegar

was commonly used for making whey, syllabubs and other confectionery the fruit was gathered and used as a substitute. The 'vinegar' was also applied to burns and scalds and used as a medicine for colds. A brew consisting of ale, nutmeg, ginger, sugar and toasted crab apples was formerly drunk at Lammastide (1 August). The drink was also popular at christenings, and Shakespeare refers to it in *A Midsummer Night's Dream* ('gossip' here is an old word for a godparent):

> And sometime lurk I in a gossip's bowl
> In very likenesss of a roasted crab;
> And when she drinks, against her lips I bob,
> And on her wither'd dew-lap pour the ale.

In the language of the flowers, crab apples signify irritability.

Cranesbill   see **Meadow cranesbill**

Creeping cinquefoil
Potentilla reptans

The generic name is from Latin *potens*, powerful, referring to the properties supposedly held by some of the species. Cinquefoil, as well as some of the country names – five-leaved-grass, five fingers, sinkfield, synkefoyle and cynkfoly – allude to the plant's five-fingered leaf, which was believed to symbolize the five senses. John Clare refers to the significance of the five leaflets in *The Eternity of Nature*:

> Her ways are mysterys all yet endless youth
> Lives in them all unchangeable as truth
> With the odd number five strange natures laws
> Play many freaks nor once mistake the cause

Another alternative common name was St Anthony's turnip.

The plant was credited with the power to keep witches and evil spirits at bay, although it was also a herb of witches, who made a special ointment consisting of the juice of cinquefoil, wolfsbane and smallage, wheatmeal, and the fat of children taken from their graves. The herb was also used as a love oracle: placed under the pillow it would ensure that one would get one's lover 'as sure as the dead man lies in his grave'. Cinquefoil is known as an emblem of the dead.

The Potentillas were known to Dioscorides and named by Theophrastus for their potent value in curing fevers. Today herbalists use the plant for its astringent properties, in mouthwashes and gargles, and for nosebleeds. Fishermen used to bait their hooks with corn boiled with cinquefoil, **marjoram**, **nettle**, **thyme** and **houseleek.**

A herb of Jupiter, cinquefoil is the birthday flower for 13 April and in the language of the flowers symbolizes maternal affection. In heraldry the plant typifies hope and joy.

Crocus
Crocus vernus

The generic name is from Greek *krokos*, saffron; *vernus* refers to the spring. In Greek mythology Crocus was a youth who loved the nymph Smilax. Since his great love was not returned, he pined away and died. The gods took pity on him and changed him into a crocus, while Smilax became a **yew** tree.

In ancient times the flower was used to decorate marriage beds. According to Homer, the Greek poet, it was one of the flowers that formed the couch of Zeus and Hera. The Romans used the crocus as a strewing flower in their banqueting halls, and floated them on the water of ornamental streams and fountains in their gardens.

The crocus is dedicated to St Valentine, since it is supposed to flower on 14 February. Anne Pratt wrote:

The crocus blows before the shrine,
At vernal dawn of St Valentine.

It is the birthday flower for 16 April and symbolizes youthful gladness.

Crown imperial
Fritillaria imperialis

The generic name is from Latin *fritillus*, dice box, referring to the chequerboard markings on the flowers of some of the species. The plant is a native of Persia, introduced to Europe during the sixteenth century. The name crown imperial is said to have been given by Alphonsus Pancius, physician to the Duke of Florence, because it was first grown in the Imperial Gardens of Vienna. Originally it was known as the Persian lily. A Persian legend tells of a queen whose fidelity was questioned by her husband; an angel, full of pity for the sad queen, changed her into the flower. Until she is reunited with her husband the tears (nectaries at the base of the petals) will remain.

  Christian legend relates how, with the exception of the crown imperial which was formerly white, all the flowers in the Garden of Gethsemane bowed their heads during the Agony of Our Lord. Since that time it blushingly hangs its head in shame – with tears of repentance in the flower's eyes.

Since the flower's introduction it has been dedicated to St Edward, the tenth-century king and martyr who was murdered by his stepmother while drinking a stirrup cup. Superstition alleges that the plant flowers on the day he died, 18 March. In a raw state the roots are said to be poisonous, but once cooked they become harmless and were frequently used in soups and stews.

Crown imperial is the birthday flower for 13 January and signifies majesty and power.

Cuckoo flower
Cardamine pratensis

The generic name is derived from two Greek words meaning heart and fortify and the plant is supposed to have strengthening properties; *pratensis* is a Latin word signifying meadow-growing. The name cuckoo flower, or *Flos-cuculi*, means 'when the cuckoo is in full song' and refers to the flowering period. The name was given to several plants, particularly **ragged robin**. Country names include lady's smock and milk maids, from the fancied resemblance to linen spread out on the grass to bleach in the sun. The pale mauve flowers do often appear white in the sunlight.

Traditionally cuckoo flower was a plant of the fairies and it was unlucky to bring it into the home. If the flower was accidentally woven into a May Day garland it had to be taken to pieces and remade. In Christian legend it is dedicated to the Virgin Mary.

Although the plant was thought inferior to **watercress**, herbalists recommended it for digestive complaints, hysteria, epilepsy and scurvy. The leaves, which are very pungent, can be used as a salad plant.

Astrologically cuckoo flower is under the dominion of the moon, and it is the birthday flower for 21 August. In the language of the flowers it signifies ardour.

Cyclamen   see **Sowbread**

Cypress   see **Italian cypress**

Daffodil

Narcissus pseudo-narcissus

In Greek mythology Narcissus was a young man who spurned the love of the nymph, Echo, who died of a broken heart in a cave; her bones turned to stone and all that was left was the echo of her voice. The gods punished Narcissus by causing him to fall in love with his own image which he saw reflected in the water. He died of languor, being unable to avert his gaze. Then the gods, pitying him, changed him into the flower which bears his name. The daffodil was formerly known as affodil, affodilly and daff-a-down-dilly. On seeing their first daffodil of the spring children would recite:

> Daff-a-down-dilly has now come to town
> In a yellow pettycoat and a green gown.

The daffodil is the flower of Lent and was known as Lent lily or lents; it was sold at this time by poor children for pins, as it was thought unlucky to take money. Another name, lide-lily was used in some counties – lide signifying the month of March.

Daffodil and **yew** together are an emblem of the Resurrection, making them a suitable decoration for churches at Easter. In Roman mythology, Proserpina (a Latin corruption of the Greek Persephone), wore a wreath of daffodils when she was abducted and taken to the Underworld. Shakespeare wrote:

> O Proserpina,
> For the flowers now, that frightened thou let'st fall
> From Dis's waggon! daffodils
> That come before the swallow dares and takes
> The winds of March with beauty.

The word 'take' is used here in the Elizabethan sense, meaning to charm or bewitch.

Many flowers that hang their heads were considered unlucky and in some parts of England it was thought unlucky to bring it into the house. To point at a daffodil was supposed to prevent it blooming. In Wales, to be the person who finds the first flower means that you will have more gold than silver in the coming year. It was widely believed that a plant could indicate one's fortune. The poet Robert Herrick (1591–1674) refers to this allusion:

> When a daffodil I see
> Hanging down her head t'wards me,
> Guess I may what I must be
> First, I shall decline my head;
> Secondly, I shall be dead.
> Lastly, safely buried.

Daffodils today are almost certainly the best-known and best-loved flowers of spring, and eveyone knows Wordsworth's wonderful evocation of them:

> And then my heart with pleasure fills
> And dances with the daffodils.

Medicinally daffodil juice mixed with honey, frankincense and myrrh was used to treat discharging ears. A plaster consisting of roots and **barley** meal was applied to dissolve hard swellings. Boiled roots were employed as an emetic.

Daffodil is the birthday flower for 23 August and symbolizes unrequited love. It is a flower of narcotic properties, hence deceitful hope. In heraldry the daffodil stands for chivalry, and it is the floral emblem of Wales.

Dahlia
Dahlia pinnata

The dahlia is named after Dahl, the Swedish pupil of the great eighteenth-century botanist Linnaeus, and is a native of Mexico. It was introduced to Europe in 1789 and to England, at Kew, in 1798. The petals, like those of the **chrysanthemum** and **marigold** can be eaten in salads.

It is the birthday flower for 24 August, and is symbolic of dignity, elegance, pomp and instability. In the language of the flowers it means, 'Forever yours'.

Daisy

Daisy
Bellis perennis

The generic name is from Latin *bellus*, pretty or charming, though an alternative source claims that it is from *bellum*, because 'it is fitted to heal wounds in war'. Early physicians and apothecaries named it *Consilida minor*, because it was supposed to heal or consolidate wounds. The common name is a corruption of day's eye, from the Old English *daeges eage*. Chaucer comments:

> Well by reason men it call maie
> The Daisie, or els the Eye of the Daie.

Country names for the plant include day's eye, bairnwort, brinswort, little star, white frills, miss modesty and twelve disciples.

In the Christian tradition, it is an emblem of Christ and the Virgin Mary. It is also the flower of St Margaret, whose feast day falls on 20 July, and the flower was dedicated to her by the monks in olden times. An earlier name for the plant was in fact herb Margaret.

An old country name for the plant, measure of love, indicates its use as a love oracle. Girls still pick off individual petals, saying alternately 'He loves me' and 'He loves me not', the last petal giving the answer. Another form of love divination required a young girl to pick a bunch of daisies with her eyes closed – the number of flowers would indicate the number of years before she married. In Shakespeare's *Hamlet*, Ophelia gives Queen Gertrude a daisy to signify 'that her light and fickle love ought not to expect constancy in her husband'. Pleasant dreams of loved ones could be realized by placing a daisy root under the pillow.

The root worn or carried about one's person was a remedy against accidents or illness, though this also applied to other roots. Daisy roots were believed to stunt the growth of humans, a superstition which may have come from the notion, mentioned earlier, that everything had the power to inflict its own personality on others.

The flowering of the daisy is significant and various superstitions and sayings exist, such as 'Spring has come when you can place your foot on three daisies'. In some parts of the country the number of flowers is seven or nine. If you fail to tread on the first daisy you see in the spring, it is said that daisies will grow over you or your loved one before the year is out.

As the plant is under the dominion of Venus, it was considered an excellent remedy for wounds of the breasts. Oils, ointments, plasters and syrups were made from it. Bruised leaves were applied to the testicles to reduce swelling, and a distillation of the flower was recommended as a liver tonic. During the fifteenth century the plant was listed as a salad herb.

The daisy is the floral representative for July, the birthday flower for 17 April, and symbolizes adoration, innocence and virginity. In the language of the flowers it means, 'I share your sentiments'.

Michaelmas daisy
Aster novi-belgii

The generic name is a Greek word meaning star. The michaelmas daisy was formerly known as starwort and aster. The first aster to be known as michaelmas daisy was originally called *Aster tradescantii* and was brought to England from America in 1633 by John Tradescant, son of Charles I's Dutch gardener. This late-flowering plant produces tiny white flowers with yellow centres, unlike the garden hybrids of today, produced from American species, the biggest group being *Aster novi-belgii*.

The flower is dedicated to St Michael, whose feast day now falls on 29 September. The name michaelmas daisy came into use after 1752 when Pope Gregory's revised calendar was adopted, causing Michaelmas Day to fall earlier and to coincide with the flowering of this plant. A quotation from an early *Calendar of English Flowers* establishes the time of flowering:

> The Michaelmas Daisies, among dede weeds,
> Bloom for St Michael's valourous deeds;
> And seems the last of floures that stode
> Till the feast of St Simon and St Jude.

The feast day of the last two saints falls on 28 October.

Impatient sweethearts used the flower as a love oracle, removing the petals one by one, and saying 'He loves me' and 'He loves me not' until one remained, giving the answer. A similar custom applies to the **daisy**.

In the language of the flowers the michaelmas daisy means afterthought, because it begins to bloom when other flowers are scarce.

Ox-eye daisy
Leucanthemum vulgare

The generic name is derived from the Greek word for white and *anthos*, flower. The ox-eye daisy is also known as marguerite, dog daisy, moon daisy, maudlin daisy, whiteweed golding and goul or gool. The old gool-ridings of Scotland were established to exterminate this so-called weed from the cornfields: the penalty of a castrated ram was paid by the farmer with the largest crop of gools.

It is dedicated to St John, and consequently was an emblem in the floral displays of Midsummer Day, his feast day. Children used to string the flower heads together in a pretty imitation of the feathers worn by soldiers on their hats. However, they were warned not to rub their eyes after handling the flowers, as they were supposedly harmful. The flower was thought to be a remedy against fleas and was mixed with straw and grasses in the bedding of domestic animals.

Ox-eye daisy is the birthday flower for 29 October and symbolizes an obstacle, and disappointment. In the language of the flowers it means, 'Be patient'. The flower is a good luck talisman and a sun emblem.

Dame's violet
Hesperis matronalis

The generic name comes from a Greek word corresponding to vesper or evening. These are the flowers

> . . . That keep
> Their odour to themselves all day
> But when the sunlight dies away,
> Let the delicious secret out
> To every breeze that roams about.

In spite of its common name it is unrelated to the true violets. Other names for the plant are night rocket, night-odorous stock, summer lilac, sweet rocket, eveweed and rogue's or queen's gillofers.

Although seldom seen in gardens today, the plant was a favourite of the Elizabethans who considered its perfume superior to all others. Ladies used to place the flowers in their bedchambers and apartments. In the language of the flowers dame's violet means coquetry.

Dandelion
Taraxacum

The generic name is a corruption of a Persian word meaning bitter pot-herb. Dandelion comes via Middle English *dent de lyoun* from French *dent de lion*, lion's tooth – an allusion to the jagged, toothlike edges of the leaves. Country names for the plant include clock flower, devil's milk plant (from the white sap), tell time and what o'clock.

Until recent times it was widely believed that to smell the flower would cause bedwetting. Earlier popular names, such as pee-a-bed, wet-a-bed, pis-a-bed and pismire, support this superstition. The plant certainly does contain stimulating elements that would affect the kidney and the bladder. A tea made from the leaves or roots was thought to combat anaemia, rheumatism and skin complaints. As late as the present century the plant was used to treat dyspepsia, diseases of the liver and spleen, and stomach and bowel conditions. The juice of the stem is a well-known country cure for warts.

A form of coffee can be made from the dried root. The roots and leaves are used for making a beer and the flowers for winemaking. Dandelion leaves can be eaten raw in salads or boiled as a vegetable.

William Howitt (1792–1879) refers to a favourite pastime of children who blow off the downy dandelion heads, each puff counting for one hour, until every seed has scattered in the wind.

> Dandelion, with globe of down
> The schoolboys clock in every town
> Which the truants puffs amain,
> To conjure lost hours back again.

The seed head was also used to interpret the depths of a lover's feelings. If all the seeds flew away in one puff the blower was loved passionately; a few seeds remaining indicated some unfaithfulness; and many seeds indifference.

The dandelion is a sun emblem governing the sign of Leo and assigned to the planet Venus. It is the birthday flower for 27 September, symbolic of grief, bitterness and coquetry. As a bitter herb it is a symbol of Christ's Passion.

Daphne
Daphne mezereum

For the derivation of the name, see **bay**. The pink, crimson or white flowers precede the leaves of this fragrant flowering shrub. In her poem, 'To the Mezereon in December' Mrs Tighe writes:

> Odours of spring, my sense ye charm
> With fragrance premature,
> And mid these days of dark alarm,
> Almost to hope allure.

Daphne symbolizes fame and glory, and in the language of the flowers means 'Sweets to the sweet'.

Herbalists used the bark and root, although the effects, both internally and externally, could be quite violent. The bark, soaked in vinegar and

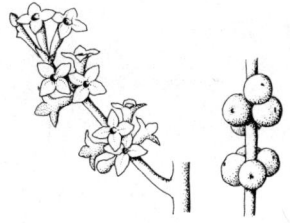

applied to the skin, caused blistering, a variation on the old practice of leeching, which was said to draw out 'humours'. The bright scarlet berries are poisonous.

Darnel
Lolium temulentum

Darnel is thought to be the *infelix lolium* mentioned by Virgil. Country names for the plant include sturdy and ryle, although a much older one is dwake, which was applied to corn cockle and weeds generally:

> Darnel, and all the idle weeds that grow
> In our sustaining Corn.

wrote Shakespeare, who viewed it with disfavour when it adulterated bread:

> Good morrow, Gallants! want ye Corn for bread?
> I think the Duke of Burgundy will fast,
> Before he'll buy again at such a rate;
> 'Twas full of Darnel; do you like the taste?

Ancient and nineteenth century botanists attributed poisonous properties to the plant. The symptoms resulting from eating the seeds were tremors, vomiting, staggering and impaired vision. Medicinally, darnel meal mixed with salt and **radish** roots was used in the treatment of gangrene, leprosy sores and ringworm. Darnel meal applied as a poultice was said to draw out splinters and broken bones from the flesh. The plant, boiled in red wine, provided an interesting medicine for kidney and gynaecological complaints.

Astrologically darnel is under the influence of the planet Saturn. It symbolizes vice.

Devilsbit scabious
Succisa pratensis

The generic name is derived from the Latin *succido*, to cut off from below, and *pratensis*, found growing in meadows. Scabious is derived from Latin *scabies*, itch, for which skin irritations some of the species were supposed to be a remedy. The root has a peculiar bitten-off appearance, alleged to have been caused by the devil creeping underground and biting it off to prevent man using it as a cure. Superstitious people believed that picking the plant caused the devil to appear at your bedside during the night. Other country names for the plant are forebitten more and pincushions, the latter descriptive of the shape of the blue-purple flower head.

In ancient times herbalists applied the bruised plant to the body to draw out pieces of broken bone, arrow heads and foreign bodies embedded in the flesh. Later, the roots boiled in wine were used as a preventative medicine for plague, and a cure for poisoning by potion or snakebites, bruises, blows and falls. An ointment was made from the powdered root to soothe skin diseases. Applied to a bruise, the whole plant or root was alleged to remove any discolouration, while a lotion disinfected ulcers and cuts. A cosmetic preparation for the removal of pimples and freckles consisted of the green parts of the plant boiled in water and mixed with borax.

Devilsbit scabious is the birthday flower for 8 August; it symbolizes unfortunate love.

The beautiful blue **garden scabious** (*scabiosa atropurpurea*) is also known as sweet scabious, mournful widow and pincushion flower. It is the last of these names that Victoria (Vita) Sackville-West, the writer and creator of the beautiful garden at Sissinghurst Castle in Kent, recalls in *The Garden*:

> . . . or scabious tall
> That country children call
> Pincushions, with their gift
> Of accurate observance and their swift
> Naming more vivid than the botanist.

Garden scabious is the birthday flower for 26 June, and symbolizes widowhood. It was considered an appropriate flower for a widow to include in her bouquet when in mourning for a husband.

Dill
Anethum graveolens

The generic name is from Greek *ano*, upwards, and *theo*, I run, in reference to the plant's rapid growth. The common name is derived from an Old English word. Dill is an aromatic herb with a sweetish flavour, used medicinally by the ancient Egyptians. The Romans brought the plant to England and their poets sang its praises.

Dill seeds have a mildly soporific effect, and dill water was and is still used to calm fretful babies, particularly those suffering from colic. For hundreds of years dill has been used to settle stomach complaints, and in the sixteenth century Michael Drayton mentions it in a different medical context:

> The wonder working dill he gets not from these,
> Which curious women use in many a nice disease.

Because the plant is under the dominion of Mercury it was thought to strengthen the brain. In the Middle Ages the plant was thought to have protective virtues:

> Trefoil, Johnswort, Vervaine, Dill
> Hinder witches of their will.

During the seventeenth and eighteen centuries dill seeds, known also as meeting house seeds, were eaten during church services. Whether this was to ease the congregation through lengthy sermons or to provide a source of nourishment must remain open to speculation.

Dill is a culinary herb which can be used in salads, sauces, soups and egg, cheese, meat, fish and poultry dishes. The seeds are used in distilling gin.

Dock
Rumex

The generic name is the Latin word for the plant which is perhaps the best-known member of the dock family, widely recognized as a remedy for **nettle** stings. In Chaucer's time rubbing the affected area with a dock leaf was thought to be effective only if the following charm was pronounced simultaneously:

> Nettle out, Dock in,
> Dock remove the nettle sting.

Country names for dock include land robber, celery seed, donkey's oats and batter dock.

Herbalists used dock seeds to treat tuberculosis and stomach complaints. The roots were boiled in vinegar for bathing skin infections, and the distilled water of plant and root was thought to clear the skin of discolourations and freckles. In his *Banquet of Senses* the Latin poet Ovid (43B.C.–A.D.18) suggests a different remedy; he speaks of 'soveraine Rumex that doth rancour kill'. Docks cooked with meat were thought to make the water boil sooner. Before paper was in common use the broad, cool leaves were used to wrap up butter and cheese for market.

Astrologically the plant is under the sign of Jupiter. Dock is the birthday flower for 26 September and symbolizes, in the language of the flowers, patience and shrewdness.

Dodder   see **Common dodder**

Dogwood
Cornus sanguinea

The generic name is the Latin word for the shrub. The specific name was given it because the bark on the older branches is red and eye-catching in winter, about which Victoria Sackville-West wrote:

> See the red dogwood, lacquered by the rain,
> That's touch, that's savage, that will stand the strong
> Usage of Winter till Spring again
> Clothe with less lovely leaf its Indian vein.

One of its alternative names, for this reason, was bloody twig; others are wild cornel, dog-berry, hound's-tree and gaten-tree.

Dogwood berries are bitter, astringent and rich in oil, which in some parts of Europe used to be extracted and used as a fuel for lamps. The hard wood was once used for making pikes and javelins, although it is more likely to have been the cornelian cherry (*Cornus mas*) to which the first-century B.C. Roman poet Virgil refers in his pastoral poem, the *Georgics*:

> The war from stubborn myrtle shafts receives,
> From Cornel's jav'lins, and the tougher yew
> Receives the bending figure of a bow.

Smaller pieces of wood were fashioned into skewers, lace bobbins, toothpicks and arrows. A tonic medicine prepared from the bark, was considered inferior in quality to that produced from the dogwood in North and South America. The flowering time of the dogwood was used as a weather oracle:

> When the dogwood flowers appear
> Frost will not again be here.

In the language of the flowers dogwood means 'Love undiminished by adversity'. It symbolizes beauty, durability, faithfulness, firmness and stability.

Duckweed   see **Common duckweed**

Dwarf cherry
Prunus cerasus

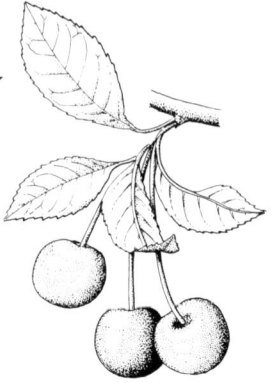

For the derivation of the generic name see **blackthorn**. Cerasus was a city of ancient Pontus, in Asia Minor, which later became Kerasoun. The cherry tree was brought to Europe by a Roman general, Lucullus, in 67 B.C. at the end of the Mithridatic Wars, which were fought in this part of the ancient world. When tribute was paid to him, he placed the cherry tree in the most conspicuous place among the spoils of gold, silver and other treasure, as a sign that it was of more value than anything else. It is almost certain that the cherry was introduced to England by the Romans.

The morello, may duke and Kentish cherries are considered to be derived from the wild or dwarf cherry. Other native wild cherries are the (*P. avium*), which is the most widely distributed, and the bird cherry (*P. padus*). The first recorded orchard was called the New Garden, to which Michael Drayton refers in his *Polyoblion*:

> WhenThames-ward to the shore which shoots
>   upon the rise,
> Rich Tenham undertakes thy close'ts to suffice
> With cherries which we say the summer in doth
>   bring
> Wherewith Pomona crowns the young and lustful
>   Spring.
> Whose golden gardens seem the Hesperides to
>   mock,
> Nor here the damson wants, nor dainty Apricock.

The cherry is associated with the cuckoo. On hearing the first cuckoo it was customary to turn over one's money, saying:

> Cuckoo, cherry tree
> Catch a penny and give it to me.

Children would shake a cherry tree in flower, saying:

> Cuckoo, cherry tree
> Good bird tell me
> How many years before I die.

The number of 'cuckoos' in the bird's call supplied the answer. This association with the cuckoo seems to stem from the tradition that the bird must eat three good meals of cherries before he is allowed to stop singing. Another legend tells of Jesus giving St Peter a cherry, chiding him, gently, not to scorn small things.

Herbalists used the gum of the cherry tree, dissolved in wine, for coughs and sore throats. The mixture was also said to sharpen the eyesight and increase the appetite. The fruit can be used to flavour liqueurs, wine brandy and vinegar, and is delicious for tarts, puddings, cakes and jams. A chocolate-coloured dye can be produced from the bark.

Cherry blossom signifies spiritual beauty, and in the language of the flowers means 'Do me justice'. The cherry tree means Great Divine Spirit, education, truth. A white cherry tree signifies deception. The fruit symbolizes merrymaking, virginity and, in the Christian tradition, the delight of the blessed and the fruit of paradise. The bird cherry symbolizes hope.

Elder
Sambucus nigra

The generic name is probably connected with Latin *sambuca*, harp, for which the wood was anciently used; *nigra* means black. Elder may be derived from Saxon *eller*, to kindle, from the custom of blowing through the stems to revive dying embers, or it may be named after Hulda, Norse goddess of love, marriage and fecundity, to whom it was sacred.

The tree has always had evil associations in folklore and legend, and is connected with death and witchcraft. In some parts of England it was considered unlucky to have elder in the home as it was said to bring in the Devil; to burn the wood on the hearth would bring death to a member of the family. If an elder tree was chopped down the Elder Mother who lived in it would cause the wood to creak or warp if it was used for furniture. However, chopping down the tree could be made safer by reciting this rhyme to the tree spirit:

> Owd girl, give me thy wood,
> And I will give thee some of mine,
> When I grow into a tree.

The wood was never used in shipbuilding or for meat skewers. In Ireland elder sticks were supposed to be used by witches as magic horses. The Rollright Stones in Oxfordshire, an impressive circle of about seventy standing stones, are alleged to be a king and his army turned to stone by a witch who had changed herself into a nearby elder tree; on Midsummer Eve the local people would hold a feast and bleed the 'witch'. According to medieval legend Judas Iscariot hanged himself from an elder tree; the mushroom-like excrescences which grow on the branches are known as Judas (or Jew's) ears, and are said to have grown there since that time.

Nevertheless, in some parts of England the tree had the reputation of giving protection, and was grown close to the house to guard the occupants against witchcraft. Planted near the larder window it was supposed to keep away flies. Elder was also planted near graves to give protection to the body after death. An elder twig carried in the pocket when riding a horse was supposed to prevent saddle sores.

The elder has been called the medicine chest of the country, as its medicinal properties have been valued since the time of the Ancient Britons. The more superstitious herbalists believed that the value of the plant was enhanced if it grew in the decayed stump of a hollow tree where birds had dropped the seed. There is an old remedy for a cough:

> For a cough take Judas Eare
> With the paring of a Peare;
> And drinke this without feare;
> If you will have remedie.

The plant was also used to cure the bites of adders and mad dogs, and to alleviate toothache and melancholy. The berries, fresh or dry, were used to treat dropsy, and the juice of the green leaves sniffed up the nostrils 'purgeth the brow'. Elder shoots boiled like asparagus, or the young leaves and stalks, were recommended for expelling phlegm and the juice of the root was said to be an emetic. Elderflower tea was prescribed to stimulate the glandular system, and a salve was made from the blossoms.

The young branches are full of pith, which schoolboys carefully removed to leave a hollow pipe, the first steps in making music or, more likely, a peashooter. A sprig of white elderberry flowers placed beneath the pastry gives a delicious flavour to gooseberry pie. Unfolded flower buds, pickled, were one of the best substitutes for capers, and the berries make an excellent wine which, served hot and spiced, was traditionally given to visitors on Christmas Eve. Elderflower champagne is a popular product made from the flowers. Elderflower water was formerly a favourite cosmetic preparation and eye lotion, and the leaves and berries were also used for the complexion. Various dyes can be produced from the elder, the leaves giving a green one, the berries, a blue-lilac and the bark, black.

Astrologically elder is under the dominion of Venus. It is the birthday flower for 29 March and symbolizes compassion and zealousness.

Elecampane
Inula helenium

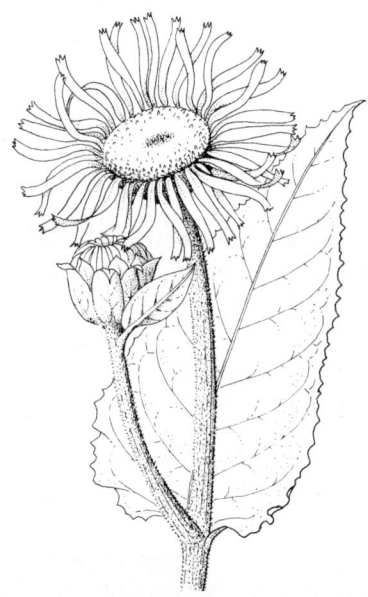

The botanical name literally means Helen's Helen. In legend the celebrated Helen, daughter of Zeus and Leda, is said to have had her hands full of flowers when she eloped with Paris and brought about the Trojan War. Elecampane is derived from *Inula campana*, meaning Helen's bell, which was corrupted by 'the Doctor' in the old mummers' plays to hell-and-come-pain. Helen dropped the elecampane she was carrying and it was claimed for the fairies. Elfwort and elfdock are old country names for the plant, which was said to have formed part of the Fairy Garland.

The Romans and Greeks prized elecampane particularly for the roots, used both as a vegetable and for medicinal purposes. It is evident from old manuscripts that monks, too, believed in the healing qualities of the plant: '*Enula campana* will restore health to the heart,' says one of them. In the Middle Ages it was the digestive system which was said to benefit and the plant was used as a medicinal sweetmeat. Elecampane lozenges were sold by Victorian druggists, and as late as this century the root was still being used to treat skin diseases and chronic infections of the lung. It was also prescribed for a variety of sheep ailments.

Bruised elecampane leaves, steeped in wine and mixed with **bilberries** produce a rich blue dye. The plant is under the dominion of the planet Mercury.

Elm
Ulmus

The generic name is the Latin word for the tree, which has given it its Anglo-Saxon name, *ulm* or *elm*. Several species grow in Britain, and when mature it is a magnificent tree, but Dutch elm disease has wreaked havoc on the elm population and only a few areas are disease-free.

The ancients twined their vines around elm trunks, and the wedding of the elm to the vine was often alluded to by Roman poets. However, it is in the work of the seventeenth-century poet John Milton that we find:

> They led the Vine
> To wed the Elm; she, spoused, about his twines
> Her marriageable arms, and with her brings
> Her dower, the adopted clusters to adorn
> His barren leaves.

The elm is the Christian symbol of strength. According to Norse mythology, the whole human race sprang from the **ash**, from which the man, Ask, was made, and the elm, from which the woman, Embla, was shaped. In parts of England the maypole was an elm trunk which was brought home on 30 April to be painted and decorated in preparation for May Day. Formerly elm branches were carried during the beating of the bounds ceremony (see **common milkwort**). When the burning of a Yule log was a traditional event, a heavily cross-grained block of elm was popular among the servants because, as long as the wood burnt, they could drink the best and strongest cider.

The size of elm leaves was a guide to the sowing of various crops:

> When Elm leaves are as big as a shilling,
> Plant Kidney Beans, if to plant 'em your willing.
> When Elm leaves are as big as a penny,
> You must plant Kidney beans, if you mean to have any.

Elm leaves falling out of season was a bad omen, signifying that the cattle would become diseased.

Medically the bark was used as a remedy for skin diseases and burns. The water in which elm root had been boiled was added to what must have been an endless selection of remedies for 'falling off of the hair' (Culpepper). Bruised elm leaves were placed on open wounds as healing agents, while the bark, ground with brine and made into a poultice, was said to ease the pain of gout.

Astrologically the elm is under the dominion of Saturn. In the language of the flowers it signifies beauty, charm, dignity, graciousness, courtesy, stateliness and shade.

Enchanter's nightshade
Circaea lutetiana

The generic name is from the classical goddess Circe, notorious for her evil spells and enchantments. She married the King of Sarmatia, whom she poisoned, and built herself a magnificent palace on the island of Aeaea. By means of a magic potion all who landed were changed into animals. Nevertheless Ulysses resisted this metamorphosis by eating a mythical herb, given to him by the god Mercury:

> Black was the root, but milky white the flower,
> Moly the name, to mortals hard to find.

The plant itself has no active properties and was not used in enchantments. It is thought that the name was transferred in error from the mandrake (*Mandragora*). The mandrake used to be called nightshade, having been originally classified, along with the other nightshades, with the family Solanaceae.

The specific name of the plant is said to be from Lutetia, the ancient name for Paris. The delicate pink flowers symbolize witchcraft.

Evening primrose
Oenothera biennis

The generic name is a Greek word supposed to be derived from *oinos*, wine, and *thera*, booty. A very old name for the plant was *onagra*, ass food – botanists changed the name of the plant because the roots were used before a meal as an incentive to wine drinking, as one would eat olives or peanuts today. Evening primrose is not mentined by the earliest writers, although Parkinson names it in his *Garden of Pleasant Flowers*, published in 1629, as the tree primrose of Virginia. It is known that the plant was first sent from Virginia to Padua in 1619, and introduced into England about the same period. The poet John Keats (1795–1821) wrote of the plant:

> A tuft of evening primroses,
> O'er which the mind may hover till it dozes;
> O'er which it well might take a pleasant sleep,
> But that 'tis ever startled by the leap
> Of buds unto ripe flowers.

The sweet-scented evening primrose is also known as evening star.

Today there is a theory that the oil extracted from the seeds is helpful in generating a body chemical which relieves pre-menstrual tension.

In the language of the flowers evening primrose means constancy.

Eyebright
Euphrasia officinalis

The generic name is said to be derived from Greek *euphrosyne*, gladness, because of the valuable properties attributed to the plant. The common name signifies its use in the treatment of eye complaints. Milton represents the Archangel Michael as clearing Adam's vision with eyebright:

> Michael from Adam's eyes the Filme remov'd
> Which that false Fruit that promised clearer sight
> Had bred; then purg'd with Euphrasie and Rue
> The visual Nerve, for he had much to see.

The juice or distilled water of eyebright was dropped into the eye as a solution or taken in wine or broth as a medicine; one particular recipe required the addition of dried **sage**, mace, **fennel** and sugar. The Scots used an infusion of the plant in milk. A modern eye lotion consists of thirty drops of tincture of eyebright in a wineglass of rosewater.

Astrologically it is under the dominion of the sun and the sign of Virgo. In the language of the flowers eyebright means, 'Cheer up'.

False acacia
Robinia pseudacacia

Linnaeus named the genus in honour of Jean Robin, a French botanist. *Acacia* is derived from Greek *akis*, a sharp point. False acacia was thought to be identical with the African acacia, and was introduced from America in 1620. It is also known as the locust tree, silver chain and white laburnum, the last two names describing the flowers.

Acacia is the birthday flower for 14 September, and signifies platonic love and friendship. In the language of the flowers it means 'You have elegance and grace'. The tree is a symbol of fecundity, immortality of the soul and menstruous blood, symbolized by its gum. As a tree with thorns it is emblematic of divine power to repel evil.

Fat hen
Chenopodium album

The generic name means goose and little foot. Provincial names for the plant include goosefoot, good King Henry, all good, dirty Dick, muck hill weed, midden myles, dung weed, bacon weed and lamb's quarters; fat hen was the *melde* of the Anglo-Saxons.

The plant formed part of the diet of Neolithic, Bronze Age and Early Iron Age people, and later the Romans. The seeds were harvested and ground into flour for gruel and bread, which was quite nutritious and not unpleasant to taste. Fat hen was formerly regarded as a vegetable because of its nutrition value. In Europe the fatty seeds of the plant were among the early food grains, and were found amongst the other grains and seeds in the stomach of Tolund Man, of the first century B.C., before he was sacrificed in his Danish bog. He was discovered in 1950. A red dye can be obtained from the plant.

Fennel
Foeniculum vulgare

The generic name is derived from Latin *foenum*, hay, to which the smell of fennel has been compared. The common name has come down from Old English. In the south it is sometimes known as devil-in-a-bush, because the strong smelling flower is surrounded by the leaves.

Fennel is one of the oldest cultivated herbs, originating from the Mediterranean countries. Ancient Egyptian records reveal that the plant was in use long before the Christian era. The old Greek name for the herb was *marathron*, derived from *maraino*, to grow thin, which no doubt accounts for its reputation as a slimming aid. Athletes are said to have eaten it when competing in the Olympic Games because it strengthened them without making them fat. Wreaths of fennel were worn by the victors. It was also believed to improve poor eyesight. The poet Henry Wadsworth Longfellow (1807–1882) describes the virtues and uses of the plant in *The Goblet of Life*:

> The fennel with its yellow flowers,
> That, in an earlier age than ours,
> Was gifted with the wonderous powers
> Lost vision to restore.
> It gave new strength and fearless mood,
> And gladiators fierce and rude
> Mingled it in their daily food
> And he who battled and subdued,
> The wreath of Fennel bore.

Compresses steeped in fennel tea were placed on the eyes, or an infusion was used to bathe them. Wrinkles were treated with a face pack of fennel, tea and honey. Old herbalists boiled the herb in wine as an antidote for mushroom poisoning and snake and scopion bites: snakes were said to eat the plant before shedding their skin. Oil of fennel was used to perfume soaps, and the dried leaves for pot-pourris or powdered for sachets.

Fennel was supposed to be an aphrodisiac: to eat conger and fennel, 'two-hot things', indicated sexual licence. Bunches of the herb were hung up in the home to protect the occupants against evil spirits, and over the doors at midsummer to keep witches at bay. Ghosts could be kept out by stuffing keyholes with the seeds. Incantations were often part of the ritual of administering herbs, and the Holy Herbs Charm, one that included **thyme** and fennel, runs:

> Thyme and Fennel, two exceeding mighty ones,
> These herbs the wise Lord made
> Holy in the Heaven, He let them down,
> Placed them, and sent them into the seven worlds
> As a cure for all, the poor and the rich.

Fresh or dried fennel can be used in soups, stews, meat, salads, poultry and fish dishes. It was said particularly to help the digestion of fish, and was used during Lent. Cucumbers and fruits used to be pickled with it, and the seeds used in fruit pies and also bread 'to give it better relish'. One should find fennel rather than cultivate it, warns an old proverb: 'Sow fennel, sow sorrow.'

Astrologically fennel is governed by Mercury under Virgo. It is the birthday flower for 5 December, and symbolizes strength. In the language of the flowers it means 'worthy of praise'. The plant is an attribute of the Virgin Mary.

Feverfew
Tanacetum parthenium

According to Plutarch (A.D.46–120), the Greek biographer, the herb was named *parthenium* because it was used to save the life of a man who fell from the Parthenon, when it was being built. *Tanacetum* is thought to come from the Greek *athanatos*, immortal, an allusion to the long-lasting flowers of this plant. The name feverfew is a corruption of *febrifuge*, referring to the medicinal properties of the plant in the treatment of fevers and agues. It is also known as featherfew from the feathery appearance of the leaves. Other country names include bachelors' buttons, stink daisies, flintweed, devil daisy and flirtwort.

For medicinal use the herb was boiled in white wine, nutmeg and mace and taken to cleanse the womb, expel afterbirth, encourage menstruation and treat female complaints generally. A special remedy concocted from the plant was an antidote for 'too liberal use of opium'. As a cosmetic preparation, the distilled water was recommended to remove freckles, spots and skin blemishes. Modern herbalists recommend feverfew tea for migraine.

The plant has a powerful but not particularly unpleasant odour, although it is said to be unattractive to bees. Dried feverfew leaves used to be packed in muslin bags and employed as a moth deterrent, and could be bought in the streets of London. Astrologically feverfew is a plant of Venus.

Field forget-me-not
Myosotis arvenis

The generic name is from a Greek word meaning a mouse's ear, referring to the shape of the leaves. An improbable romantic legend tells how the flower received its common name. A knight and his lady were walking by a fast-flowing river; the knight, wishing to please his love, attempted to pick the bright blue flower growing on the bank close to the water's edge. Unfortunately he slipped and fell into the water. Throwing the flowers to his beloved, he called 'Forget me not' before being swept away and drowned. Country names include mouse-ear and scorpion grass. All the forget-me-not species are known coloquially as scorpion grass, which is an old name given them because of the way the flower stem curls round towards the extremity.

Historically, the flower is connected with the House of Plantagenet. Henry of Lancaster, who later became Henry IV, chose the forget-me-not as his badge when in exile.

Traditionally the flower was exchanged by friends on 29 February, and was also given to people starting a journey on that particular day. In fable, like the **primrose** and the **cowslip**, it was believed to have the power to open caves containing treasure. Steel tempered with forget-me-not juice was said to be hard enough to cut stone. Herbalists used the plant to cure the bite of mad dogs and snakes.

The forget-me-not symbolizes constancy, remembrance and true love. In the language of the flowers it means exactly what its name says.

Field madder
Sherardia arvensis

The generic name was given to the plant in honour of the English botanist W. Sherard (1659–1728). Although the plant produces a rose-coloured dye it was Dyer's madder (*Rubia tinctoria*) which was grown extensively for this purpose and during the Middle Ages yielded one of the most commonly used red dyes. Before the introduction of aniline dyes in the nineteenth century the madder was cultivated in large quantities throughout Europe. Today the revival of interest in crafts has resulted in these old vegetable dyes once again being used by spinners and weavers to produce more subtle shades than the chemical industry can offer.

Superstitious people used to believe that if they held madder in their hand it could change the colour of their urine to that of blood. Herbalists applied the beaten root and leaves of the plant to the skin to remove freckles and scurf. The root, boiled in wine or water, was a remedy for jaundice, although if honey was added it could be used for sciatica, palsy and bruising: for the last it could be taken internally or applied externally.

Madder is the birthday flower for 8 September and is a symbol of backbiting, calumny and talkativeness. Astrologically it is assigned to Mars.

Field maple
Acer campestre

The generic name is the Latin word for the tree, meaning sharp; maple wood was used to make sharply pointed weapons such as spears, pikes and lances. Centuries ago, bowls and trenchers too were commonly made of maple. Milton wrote in *Comus*:

> For who would rob a hermit of his weeds
> His few books, or his beads, or maple dish,
> Or do his grey hairs any violence?

Some of these bowls were elaborately carved with legends in English or Latin and scenes of animals, flowers and fruit. The Elizabethan poet Edmund Spenser (?1552–99) describes such a vessel:

> A mazer ywrought of the maple warre,
> Wherein is enchased many a fayre sight
> Of bears and tygers, that maken fiers warre,
> And ever them spread a goodly wilde vine,
> Entrailed with a wanton yvy twine,
> Thereby is a lambe in the wolve's jawes;
> But see how fast runneth the shepherd swain,
> To save the innocent from the beaste's pawes.

St Christopher was a popular subject; he was usually found carved in the bottom, in theory to comfort the drinker as he drained his bowl.

The bright autumn colours of the maple typify past happiness, because the leaves fade early and suggest transitoriness. Legend has it that children passed through the branches of the tree would have a long life. Medicinally the leaves and bark were used for liver complaints.

Astrologically maple is under the dominion of Jupiter and is the birthday flower for 12 March; it is symbolic of conjugal love, earthly happiness, retirement and reserve.

Figwort
Scrophularia

The generic name derives from the disease called scrofula, more often known as the King's Evil because the monarch's hands were supposed to have miraculous powers to cure it, for which the plant was formerly thought to be a specific. It is known in parts of Britain as crowdy-kit, a corruption of the Welsh *crwth*, fiddle – two of the stalks rubbed together sound rather like a violin. Other country names are fiddlers and fiddlesticks, throatwort, poor man's salve, stinking Roger and cut finger.

In the belief that it congealed the blood, herbalists used the plant to control external and internal bleeding. Piles, leprosy, spots and freckles were also treated with it. A remedy for scrofula consisted of figwort and houndstongue leaves mixed with the flowers of **foxglove** and white dead **nettle**.

Astrologically figwort is under the domination of Venus. It is the birthday flower for 15 August and symbolizes neglected beauty.

Flax
Linum

The generic name is Latin for flax. It is one of the oldest cultivated plants, and seeds and pieces of linen have been found in prehistoric dwellings. References to it are found in both the Old and the New Testament.

In Norse mythology the plant is protected by Hulda, goddess of love, marriage and fecundity, who gave flax to mortals and taught them how to spin and weave. For many centuries wool and linen were the only materials available to the ordinary people. The sight of a farmer sowing flax gave rise to the remark: 'There goes a man who is sowing his shirt.' To encourage a good harvest the farmer would sit on his seed bag three times, facing east, before he started sowing. (A few stolen seeds in the bag also helped.) Later, on Midsummer Night, the farm workers would jump over fires to ensure a good yield. Further encouragement was given by ringing the church bell on Ascension Day.

People knew that the growing of flax impoverished the soil, which accounted for the unpopularity of the plant. In Tusser's time English farmers were compelled by law to sow one rood of flax in every 60 acres. As well as being cultivated for the fibres, the plant has seeds which yield linseed oil.

Herbalists recommended flax seed tea for coughs and bronchial diseases, as well as inflammation of the urinary organs, lungs and bowels. An infusion of the plant was sometimes used for piles and dysentery, probably injected by means of an enema. A reference by Shakespeare in *King Lear* suggests a further use of the plant, to heal wounds:

> Go then; I'll fetch some Flax and white of eggs
> To apply to his bleeding face.

The flowers were believed to give good protection against sorcery.

Flax, which is under the dominion of Venus, is the birthday plant for 28 August. It symbolizes domesticity, industry, fate, gratitude and simplicity. In the language of the flowers it means 'I feel your kindness'.

Forget-me-not   see **Field forget-me-not**

Foxglove
Digitalis purpurea

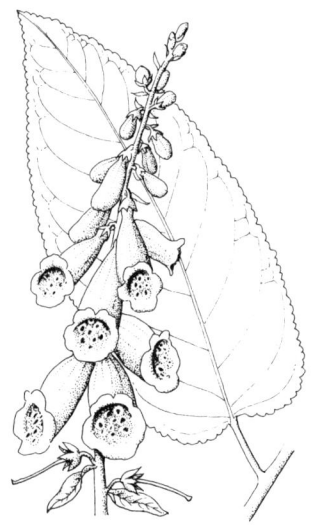

The generic name is from Latin *digitus*, finger, and is said to have been given it by Leonard Fuchs, in his *Herbal*, published in 1542. The idea of the 'foxglove' is fancifully expressed by Abraham Cowley:

> The Foxglove on fair Flora's hand is worn,
> Lest while she gathers flowers she meet a thorn.

The plant has strong asociations with folklore generally and fairies in particular; many of the country names, such as fairy caps, fairybells and fairy thimbles, allude to this belief. Other names include folks glove, dog's lugs, dead men's bells, King Edward, butcher's fingers and throatwort. The earliest known version of the name foxglove, is found in a plant list compiled in the reign of Edward III in the fourteenth century – Foxes glofa. However, the plant does resemble a favourite instrument of earlier times, a ring of bells on an arched support called a tintinnabulum.

A Shropshire witch is reputed to have discovered digitalis, which in modern times is still used as a heart stimulant, albeit in a synthetic form. An early botanical writer advised:

> The Foxglove leaves, with caution given,
> Another proof of favouring Heaven
> Will happily display;
> The rabid pulse it can abate,
> The hectic flush can moderate,
> And bleast by Him whose will is fate,
> May give a lengthened day.

In previous centuries the plant had to be picked with the left hand, from the north side of a hedge (modern experiments, however, have proved that this kind of thing is not just an ignorant superstition – some plants are more potent when picked at certain times). Digitalis is a dangerous drug in unskilled hands, and no one should attempt to try it out for themselves.

Fritillary
Fritillaria meleagris

For the derivation of the generic name see **crown imperial**. *Meleagris* is from a Latin word meaning guinea fowl; like the generic name, it alludes to the markings on the flower, which also explains one of the country names for the plant – chequered daffodil. This and ginny hen flower were the names by which Gerard referred to it. Less attractive ones include snake's-head and snake-flower (the drooping head being compared with that of a reptile), widow veil, madam ugly, turkey eggs, drooping lily, toad's head, leopard's lily, leper's lily and lazar's bell; it must have looked like the bell that lepers rang, warning of their approach.

The discovery that the fritillary was a rare native plant was made in the

mid-eighteenth century. Earlier botanists supposed it had been brought to England by the Huguenots in the sixteenth century. In the language of the flowers the fritillary symbolizes persecution.

Fumitory   see **Common fumitory**

Garden chervil
Anthriscus cerefolium

The botanical name appears to be derived from Greek, and means rejoicing in its leaves. An alternative common name is Honiton lace. The hern is thought to have been introduced by the Romans, and the Anglo-Saxons continued to use it after them.

In spring, chervil is one of the first herbs available in large quantities, and its blood-cleansing qualities have been known for a long time. The juice of the plant was formerly used as a cleansing lotion, and for jaundice, gout and chronic skin complaints.

The herb is used fresh in various salads, omelettes, cream cheese, soups and stews; fish, poultry and game dishes; and it can be sprinkled on certain vegetables. The French include it in *fines herbes*, which consists of equal quantities of chopped **tarragon, chives, parsley** and chervil. A revival of interest in the use of herbs has been seen in the past few years. Nurseries selling herb plants are now quite commonplace, although a small number of dedicated growers have always existed. Astrologically the herb is under the sign of Jupiter and signifies sincerity.

Garden scabious see **Devilsbit scabious**

Garlic see **Ramsons**

Gentian
Gentiana

The plant is said to have been named after Gentius, King of Illyricum (roughly, modern Yugoslavia), whom it is claimed discovered the medicinal virtues of the plant about two thousand years ago. The yellow-flowered G. *lutea*, the great yellow gentian, is said to be the first foreign gentian cultivated in England. Many other species of gentian grow wild in Britain, some of them bearing the more familiar deep blue flowers. The plant was also known as felwort and bitterwort.

Herbalists used powdered gentian root in wine for snakebite, liver complaints, stomach pains and bruises; also for pains in joints due 'to cold or bad lodgings', and as a tonic for weary travellers. Injuries to the udders of cattle were treated with a lotion made from the gentian, which was alleged to heal the wounds instantly. Today gentian is still used as a tonic and an antiseptic. Formerly the plant was imported in quantity for medicinal purposes, causing the botanist J.R. Thornton, in his *A Family Herbal* published in 1814, to write, 'Our English gentians have most probably the same virtues as the foreign . . . yet we often seek at a distance what lies at the very threshold of our doors.'

In the language of the flowers a closed gentian means, 'May your dreams be sweet'. Fringed gentian, *Gentianella ciliata*, signifies 'I look to heaven' and symbolizes October. In his poem 'Bavarian Gentians' D.H. Lawrence (1885–1930) wrote:

> Not every man has gentians in his house
> In soft September, at slow sad Michaelmas.

Gentian is the birthday flower for 27 November and the flower of the zodiac sign of Scopio. It symbolizes autumn loveliness.

Geranium
Pelargonium

The common name comes from Greek *geranos*, crane, a bird to whose beak the fruit of the plants bears a fancied resemblance. The Geraniaceae family is divided into three groups, the true geraniums or cranesbills (see **meadow cranesbill**), the pelargoniums or storksbills, and the erodiums or heronsbills. Pelargoniums (from *pelarges*, stork) are the plants which are commonly but incorrectly referred to as geraniums, and which are discussed here. These popular bedding plants were developed during the early eighteenth century by crossing *P. zonale* with *P. inquinans.* They have roundish lobed leaves with a horseshoe marking, and the flowers range from white, through pink and orange to red. Other varieties were grown for their sweet smell and variegated foliage. The Turks believe that *P. zonale* was originally the **common mallow**. The prophet Mohammed is said to have hung his shirt on the plant to dry; when he removed it, the geranium was revealed. All members of the Geraniaceae have tonic properties.

In the language of the flowers the geranium typifies gentility. A dark red geranium symbolizes melancholy and is the birthday flower of 24 November. The ivy-leaved geranium is a bridal favour, and in the language of the flowers means, 'I engage you for the next dance'. The lemon geranium (*P. citriodorum*) symbolizes an unexpected meeting. The nutmeg geranium (*P. fragrans*) symbolizes an expected meeting, and is the birthday flower for 1 January. The rose geranium (*P. capitatum*) is the birthday flower for 4 March, symbolizing preference. A scarlet geranium symbolizes comfort and gaiety and is the birthday flower for 1 December. A silver-leafed geranium symbolizes recall and is the birthday flower for 26 November.

Germander speedwell
Veronica chamaedrys

The generic name *Veronica* comes from Latin *vera*, and Greek *icon*, meaning true image. Legend has it that the handkerchief of St Veronica was imprinted with the impression of Christ's face when He used it to wipe away sweat during the journey to Calvary. From the fancied resemblance on the flower to Christ's face it was named after its sainted owner. The plant is also known as birds-eye, blue speedwell, blue eyes, eyebright (not to be confused with the true **eyebright** *Euphrasia officinalis*) and cat's-eye:

Ah! the blue Germander Speedwell,
On the grassy bank that groweth;
Ah! the little twinkling Cat's-eye
Twixt the April showers bloweth.

The name speedwell is said to have been given to the plant because the flowers fall quickly after it is picked. Birds-eye comes from the bright blue colour of the flowers, similar to the eye colour of some species of birds. In the language of the flowers, germander speedwell symbolizes womanly fidelity, and it is a herb of Mercury.

Gladiolus
Gladiolus

The name is derived from Latin *gladius*, sword, referring to the shape of the leaves. One of the earliest references to the plant occurs in Lyte's *Niewe Herball* of 1518. In 1597 two European species were being grown, but many new species have been introduced over the centuries. The autumn varieties are the hardiest and it is to these that Norman Gale refers in his poem 'Michaelmas Daisies':

When June is kissing England at the flowertide of the year;
The gladiolus in his bulb considers plans for beauty
To flame along the border when his miracle is clear.

In herbal medicine poultices were made from the roots for drawing out thorns and splinters. Ground to a powder, the seedpods and seeds were taken in goat's or ass's milk as a remedy for colic. In the language of the flowers gladiolus signifies, 'You pierce my heart', and it means ready and armed.

Globe flower
Trollius europaeus

The generic name is believed to derive from Latin *trulleus*, basin, although modern writers suggest a German word for the plant, *troll-blume*, literally troll flower. In folklore it is said to have originated from the trolls of Scandinavia who claimed it for their own, unlocking the flower at night and dropping venom into the cup to poison dairymaids and herdsmen. Many old books refer to it by the Scottish name lucken

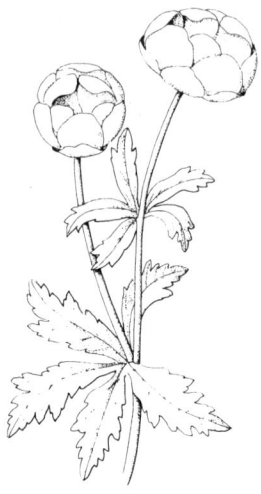

gowan: 'lucken' means closed or shut up, while 'gowan' comes from Gaelic *galan*, bud or flower, or *gollande*, an old form of golden. It is the lucken gowan that is mentioned in 'The Gentle Shepherd' by the Scottish poet Allan Ramsay (1686–1758):

> We'll put the daisies on the green,
> The lucken gowan frae the bog;
> Between hands now and then we'll lean,
> And sport upon the Velvet fog.

Fog in this context is a dialect word for moss.

The globe flower was formerly used in wreaths and garlands, for well dressing, for funeral and wedding chaplets, and for the decoration of houses and churches.

Goatsbeard
Tragopogon pratenis

The generic name is derived from two Greek words – *tragos*, goat, and *pogon*, beard. When the flower reaches maturity it grows into a 'downy blow ball' similar to the dandelion. Ben Jonson mentions this dainty head:

> Her treading would not blend a blade of grass
> Or shake the downey blow ball from his stalk.

As the flower closes at noon and expands with the sun it is also known as noon flower and go-to-bed-at-noon:

> The goats beard, which each morn abroad goes peep,
> But shuts its flower at noon, and goes to sleep.

wrote Abraham Cowley. Another country name is star of Jerusalem.

Goatsbeard is the flower of St Joseph, probably because Mary's husband is invariably depicted as an older man with a beard. The plant formerly served a culinary purpose: the roots would be eaten as we today eat parsnips, and the young stalks cut into lengths and cooked like asparagus.

Golden rod
Solidago virgaurea

The generic name is from Latin *solido*, I make whole, on account of the plant's supposed qualities in healing wounds. *Virgaurea* means rod-like. Golden rod is also popularly known as yellow rod, cast-the-spear, woundwort (in common with other plants sharing this ability) and farewell summer. It is in the context of the last of these names that the nineteenth-century poet John Greenleaf Whittier refers to the flower in 'The Last Walk in Autumn':

> Along the rivers summer walk,
> The withered tufts of asters nod;
> And trembles on its arid stalk
> The hoar plume of the golden-rod.

Herbalists considered the plant inferior to none as a healer of both internal and external injuries. A lotion extracted from golden rod had an excellent reputation in the treatment of ulcers, especially in the mouth and throat and around the sexual organs. This remedy was also said to make loose teeth secure. The plant was used as a remedy for various kidney complaints and, more recently, for tuberculosis, hay fever and persistent colds. The plant and flower heads yield a yellow dye.

Golden rod is the birthday flower for 30 November, and is symbolic of encouragement and precaution. Astrologically the herb is assigned to the planet Saturn and the sign of Virgo. Believers in the occult thought that the plant could point the way to hidden springs of water and treasures of gold and silver.

Gooseberry
Ribes grossularia

For the derivation of the generic name see **blackcurrant**. The common name is said to be derived from gorse and berry, because both plants are prickly. An alternative source suggests that it was used to make a sauce for goose. Gerard certainly mentions the fruit being used as an accompaniment for meat and giving a pleasant flavour to broth.

The shrub would seem to have been introduced to England before 1276, as gooseberry plants are recorded at that time in Edward I's garden at Westminster. In his *Shepherd's Calendar* John Clare describes some of the nineteenth-century gooseberries:

> When grandams . . .
> Come wi' their baskets heaped with fruit to sell
> That thither all the season did pursue
> Wi' mellow gooseberrys of every hue
> Green ruffs and raspberry reds and drops of gold
> That makes mouths water often to behold.

Gooseberry pie and baked custard were traditional Whitsuntide food. An old superstition held that eating the fruit at this time prevented people making fools of themselves for the rest of the year. (Gooseberry fool, however, a pudding made of scalded gooseberries mixed with cream, derives its name from French *fouler*, to press or crush.) Gooseberries are also used to make jellies, jams, wine and champagne.

Several old sayings are associated with the plant, such as 'He played old gooseberry with me', meaning that liberties were taken with one's person, possessions and property. 'To play gooseberry' is to be an unwanted third in the company of lovers. The 'big gooseberry season' was a mid-Victorian phrase similar to the modern 'silly season', applied to the time of the year when the Law Courts and Parliament were in recess and fashionable people had left town. Newspaper editors, with nothing more exciting to fill their pages, resorted to stories of giant gooseberries, sweet peas and marrows.

Herbalists prescribed the fruit, scalded or baked, to improve the appetite and to 'stay the longings of pregnant women'. The riper berries were recommended for stomach disorders and the young leaves for expelling stones in the bladder or kidneys.

The birthday plant for 28 September, the gooseberry is astrologically under the sign of Venus. In the language of the flowers it is symbolic of anticipation and regret. It is emblematic of a pearl of great price – in other words a designation of wisdom.

Gorse
Ulex europaeus

The generic name is the ancient Latin name for these spiny evergreen shrubs. Gorse is from Old English *gorst*, a waste, in reference to the shrub's natural habitat of moorland and common.

In the Druidic calendar it typifies the young sun at the spring equinox when fires of gorse, moor whin or furze, as it is also known, were lit on the hills. At midsummer, blazing branches were carried around the herds of cattle to ensure their good health during the coming year. Because gorse is said to be visited by the first bees of the year, it was believed to be enchanted and consequently used as a charm against witches. However in some areas it is considered unlucky to bring it into the house, which contradicts its former use in other parts of Britain in bridal bouquets.

A common country saying warns:

> When furze is out of bloom
> Kissing is out of season.

Fortunately, a few blossoms can be found at almost any time of year. An old Scottish saying can be treated almost as lightly:

> When the whin gangs out of bloom
> Will mean the end of Edinburgh town.

Reference to the shrub in December appears in Allan Johnson's *A Suffolk Calendar*, where it is associated with a custom commemorating St Stephen's Day, 26 December, also known as Wrenning Day, when a wren was stoned to death in memory of the saint's martyrdom.

> The wren, the wren, the king of all birds,
> Was caught St Stephen's Day in the furze
> Then pray kind gentleman, give him (or us) a treat.

The bird was carried round on a bush by boys begging for money.

Herbalists used the flowers for kidney complaints and in the treatment of jaundice – the colours of flowers often dictated their use for various complaints, and yellow ones generally provided an endless source of remedies, particularly (for obvious reasons) for jaundice. The bark, flowers and young shoots produce a yellow dye which was used to colour Highland tartans.

In the language of the flowers gorse is symbolic of anger, enduring affection and love for all seasons. Astrologically a plant of Mars, it is the birthday flower for 28 November.

Grape
Vitis vinefera

The generic name is the Latin name for a vine. The grape is the oldest of all cultivated fruits, and some of the world's most ancient writings describe man cultivating the vine and harvesting the fruit for food and drink. The vine has been widely grown in England for hundreds of years since the Romans first introduced it. After a long period of decline, English winemaking is now on the increase again.

In the Christian tradition it is an antidote to the fatal apple. It typifies the blood of Christ, the Eucharist and good works. A bunch of grapes symbolizes the blood of Christ, the wine of God's kingdom. Grape with wheat ears symbolizes the bread and wine of the Eucharist. By drinking wine, the fruit of the grape, and eating bread, produced from grain, Christians preserve the early relics of plant worship. The grape is an attribute of Christ, as well as Caleb, Dionysus, Joshua, Mithras, Bacchus and other gods of wine and fertility.

Herbalists recommended a lotion of boiled grape leaves for sore mouths, and grape leaves and **barley** meal as poultices. Country people called the droppings of the vine, when it was cut in the spring, tears; they were used in syrups to 'stay woman's longings and for urinary complaints'. A toothpaste which was claimed to make black teeth as white as snow was mixed from the ashes of the vine.

In the language of the flowers the grape signifies fruitfulness, good cheer, good fellowship, pleasure, lust and youth. The wild grape is the birthday flower for 18 April and signifies charity and rural felicity.

Grass   see **Scented vernal-grass**

Greater burdock
Arctium lappa

The generic name is derived from Greek *arctos*, bear, alluding to the rough, furry texture of the bracts around the flowers; *lappa* is from Celtic *llap*, hand, because the sharply hooked bracts attach themselves to any passing animal, which then acts as a form of seed dispersal. Country names for the plant include gipsy's rhubarb, touch-me-not, sweethearts, happy major, clot bur, great bur and hur bur. In *Hamlet* Shakespeare places it in humble company:

> Crown'd with rank fumiter and furrow weeds,
> With bur-docks, hemlock, nettles, cuckoo flowers,
> Darnel, and all the weeds that grow
> In our sustaining corn.

During the Middle Ages burdock, then known as bardona, was regarded as an important ingredient in the cure of gall and kidney stones. The roots, preserved in sugar, were used for lung complaints, although Sir Robert Walpole (1676–1745), the first English Prime Minister, praised a mixture of the roots as a remedy for gout. Burdock was perhaps best known as a cure of rheumatism – the large leaves were applied to affected areas. medical botanists thought it more effective than sarsaparilla, at one time considered the *ne plus ultra* in rheumatic complaints. The leaves were also laid on open wounds, acting as a healing agent, and the seeds used for bladder and kidney disorders. This versatile plant also had a reputation for purifying the blood and treating skin complaints. Gerard recommended eating the stalks raw or boiled in broth as an aphrodisiac. Aphrodisiac or not, they can certainly be cooked and eaten as a substitute for asparagus.

Astrologically burdock is assigned to Venus. In the language of the flowers it means 'Touch me not', and carries the sentiment importunity.

Greater stitchwort
Stellaria holostea

For the derivation of the generic name see **common chickweed**. In the Middle Ages the word was used to denote a number of plants with a star-shaped leaf or flower.

> I am the 'flower of sorrow'
> So they say
> No glory can I borrow
> From the May
> Yet, starlike, mid the green
> My fragile flowers are seen,
> So faith her steadfast eye
> Lifts to the sky.

Holostea is composed of two Greek words and means all bone, the most probable explanation being that the stems are swollen at the leaf junction and snap very easily, giving the plant the popular name of all bones. However, some early botanists saw a resemblance between the stem of the plant and the bones of the human hand. Other country names are devil's corn, devil's eye snappers and white Sunday, a day on which it was reputed to be gathered.

Superstitious people believed that stitchwort formed part of the Fairy Garland, and for this reason it was considered unlucky – if one picked the flower one would be 'pixy-led'. At a time when all plants were reputed to have some medicinal value, stitchwort was regarded as an antidote for the discomfort one feels after over-exertion, which we call stitch. The leaves were formerly ground and used as a cure for boils.

Ground elder
Aegopodium podagraria

The generic name is derived from two Greek words – *aix*, goat, and *podion*, little foot, from a supposed similarity to them in the leaves. The plant, which is unrelated to elder, is also known as goutweed, goat's foot, bishop's elder, bishop's weed, ashweed, herb Gerard, Jack-jump-about and dog elder; these names are explained below.

Ground elder is particularly associated with monasteries, castles, abbeys and the ruins and sites of old settlements. It was introduced during the Middle Ages both as a pot-herb and for medicinal use. In the treatment of gout it was so successful that it was assumed to be a gift from Gerard, to whom afflicted persons used to pray for relief from this complaint. Monasteries were the centres of early medical treatment, and their herb gardens were well stocked in readiness for travelling patients. Passing bishops are said to have taken advantage of the cure, hence the alternative names bishop's weed and bishop's elder, mentioned above. Ground elder spreads very quickly, its flat seed vessels being thrown about at the slightest movement – hence the name Jack-jump-about.

Modern herbalists prescribe the plant in the treatment of arthritic and rheumatic pains, generally as an infusion. The boiled leaves and roots are applied as a poultice to alleviate these conditions.

Ground ivy
Glechoma hederacea

Older writers claim the generic name originates from one given by Dioscorides, from Greek *glenchon*, mint; the specific name means ivylike. Popular names for ground ivy (no relation to ordinary ivy) include cat's foot, blue runner, ale-hoof, hen and chickens, tunhoof, hedgemaids and gill-creep-by-the-ground. Many of the popular names originate from the fact that the plant was used in brewing before the introduction of **hops**. Gill is from the French *guiller*, to ferment ale. Hops were used in continental Europe much earlier than in England, where the plant was thought injurious to health. Because ground ivy was used to clarify ale it could be found in most cottage gardens, and with other herbs was sold in the streets of London:

> Here's fine Rosemary, Sage and Thyme.
> Come, buy my Ground Ivy.

Ground ivy leaves were dried and taken as snuff. A special beverage known as gill tea was thought to purify the blood and was also used for kidney complaints, coughs and indigestion. As late as the twentieth century the leaves were popular in the treatment of jaundice, asthma and diseases of the kidneys and lungs. The juice dropped in the ears stopped 'singing tones', and was also used as a gargle to relieve sore throats. Farriers recommended the juice of the plant to treat eye complaints in horses. Astrologically ground ivy is assigned to the planet Venus.

Groundsel
Senecio vulgaris

The generic name is derived from Latin *senex*, old man. According to an old herbal, 'The flower of this herb hath white hair, and when the wind blowth it away, then it appeareth like a bald headed man.' Groundsel comes via the medieval word *grundeswyle*, from Old English *gundaeswelgae*, earth glutton, the fast-growing habit of the plant was always apparent. In the North of England a popular name for the plant was grundy-swallow. Its profuse growth made it a cheap and readily available food for pigs, rabbits, goats and poultry.

Herbalists recommended a decoction of groundsel tea for scurvy and bilious attacks. The plant was also used to treat jaundice, kidney and liver complaints and vomiting. A soothing hand lotion was produced from an infusion of the plant. An old remedy to cure toothache involved first digging up the plant with an iron tool; the afflicted tooth was then touched with the groundsel five times, after each of which the patient had to spit three times. If the herb was replanted in its original place the pain was supposed to cease.

In the Scottish Highlands women wore an amulet of groundsel root as protection against the evil eye. Astrologically, groundsel is under the dominion of Venus.

Guelder rose
Viburnum opulus

The generic name is the Latin word for the tree. Guelder is from Guelders in the Netherlands, the native country of the plant. In spite of its common name it is not a member of the rose family. In his poem 'The Winter Walk at Noon' the eighteenth-century poet William Cowper describes both 'roses':

> The scentless and the scented rose, this red
> And of an humbler growth, the other tall,
> And throwing up into the darkest gloom
> Of neighbouring cypress, or more sable yew,
> Her silver globes, light as the foamy surf
> That the wind severs from the broken wave.

It is also known as rose elder, water elder, titsy totsy, wild pincushion tree, mugget rose and snowball tree, from its balls of white flowers.

It is the birthday flower for 29 September. In the language of the flowers the guelder rose signifies age, though still young in heart and spirit.

Harebell
Campanula rotundifolia

The generic name is Latin for little bell – an obvious allusion to the shape of the dainty pale mauvish-blue flowers. Some writers suggest that the common name was given because it grows particularly well on dry pastures frequented by hares. A more probable explanation comes from the fact that it was sometimes spelt hairbell because of the light, delicate stems from which the bell-like flowers hang. Country names include sheep bell, old man's bell and ding dongs, and in Scotland it is known as the bluebell, as in the following lines by the poet James Grahame (1705–1811):

> . . . Nature gives a parting smile
> As yet the blue-bell lingers on the sod
> That copes the sheepfold ring; and in the woods
> A second blow of many flowers appears,
> Flowers faintly tinged, and yielding no perfume.

The presence of the harebell indicates barren soil, as noted in these lines by the poet and critic George Meredith (1828–1909):

> On the windy hills
> Lo, the little harebell leans
> On the spire grass that it queens
> With bonnet blue!

In the Christian tradition the harebell is a flower of the Virgin Mary, and for this reason is known also as lady's thimble. In Roman Catholic countries it is dedicated to St Dominic (1170–1221). In the language of the flowers, it symbolizes childhood, grief, humility and submission.

Hawkweed
Hieracium

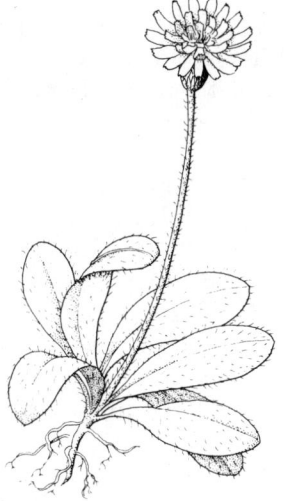

Older writers claim that *hieracium* is derived from Greek *hierax*, hawk, because birds of prey were believed to strengthen their eyesight on this genus of plants, of which several species grow wild in Britain. Children blew on the multi-plumed seed heads to discover if they lived in the north, south, east or west, each puff indicating a point of the compass, until the seed head was bare. Sweethearts used the flower as a love oracle. W.B. Scott (1745–1836) asks:

> Will he come? I pluck the flower leaves off,
> And at each, cry yes, no, yes;
> I blow the down, of the dry hawkweed
> Once, twice, hah! it flies amiss!

Hawkweed formerly had a good reputation as a medicinal herb. The juice taken in wine, night and morning, was believed to help in the treatment of jaundice. The green plant, bruised and mixed with salt, was applied to wounds. Mixed with breast milk, it was used as an eye remedy. Hawkweed is alleged to soothe the stomach and help the digestive system.

Astrologically hawkweed is under the dominion of Saturn. It is the birthday flower for 21 November and is symbolic of quick-sightedness.

Hawthorn
Crataegus monogyna

The generic name is from Greek *kratos*, strength, alluding to the hardness of the wood. Hawthorn is said to be a corruption of Old English *hagathorn* or *haegthorn*. It is also popularly known as white thorn, bread and cheese tree, maybush and maytree. The name bread and cheese tree is derived from the pleasant flavour of the berries and leaves. May is the most popular name of the tree, from the time of flowering, here recalled by the poet and essayist Leigh Hunt (1774–1859):

> O thou merry month complete,
> May, thy very name is sweet!
> May was maid in olden times,
> And is still in Scottish rhymes;
> May's the blooming hawthorn bough,
> May's the month that's laughing now.

The hawthorn is best known for its association with May Day. Bourne, in his *Antiquities*, tells us that 'all ranks of people went a maying'. Young people went out to the woods to gather branches of may, a merry occasion with music and horn-blowing. At sunrise they returned to decorate their homes with the blossom. Innocent as this custom was in design, it became, particularly round the larger towns, more like the ancient Floralia from which it derived, and the virtuous gradually withdrew as the celebrations became more decadent; church reformers, keen to abolish May Day festivities generally, gradually succeeded in doing so. Floralia was a festival celebrated by games, mimes and much licence in honour of Flora, the Roman goddess of flowers and spring, from 28 April to 1 May. Flora was said to give sweetness to honey, fragrance to blossom, aroma to wine and charm to youth and she is portrayed as a young woman garlanded with flowers. Hawthorn was often the wreath of the Green Man or Jack-in-the-green, who, concealed in a wicker frame decorated with may branches, took part in the chimney sweeps' revels on May Day. In Devon water was thrown over those not wearing a sprig of hawthorn on May Day.

The dew from the hawthorn was believed to make plain girls beautiful, especially on May Day or to endow 'fair' girls with lasting beauty:

> The fair maid who the first of May,
> Goes to the field at the break of day,
> And washes in dew from the Hawthorn tree
> Will ever after handsome be.

Hawthorn was also used as a love oracle on May Eve, when a girl would hang a branch of hawthorn on a signpost. Whichever way it was pointing in the morning, her future husband would come from that direction. But should it have fallen to the ground . . . no marriage at all! The first branch of blossom which she saw in the spring she had to break partly through and leave hanging. That night she would dream of her future husband, returning in the morning to pick the branch.

The many superstitions surrounding the hawthorn vary from county to county, although it was generally accepted that chopping down hawthorn trees brought great harm to family, home and cattle. To this day many people will not have hawthorn blossom in the house because it is associated with misfortune, and it was considered dangerous to sit under a hawthorn tree in May because the fairies would gain power over you. However, in some parts of Britain a bunch of hawthorn gathered on Palm Sunday or Ascension Day was placed in the rafters by someone unconnected with the house in the belief that it would give protection from witches, spirits and storms. The protective virtues of the hawthorn against injury in a storm are set against those of other trees:

Beware of an oak,
It draws the stroke,
Avoid an ash,
It courts a flash,
Creep under the thorn,
It will save you from harm.

In Cambridgeshire a sprig of hawthorn was placed on the last wagonload of corn of the harvest. At Helston in Cornwall a sprig of hawthorn and a clod of earth were placed at each boundary stone. In Herefordshire a hawthorn globe hung in farm kitchens throughout the year; on New Year's Day it was taken down in the early morning and burnt in the field which was to be sown first that season. This ceremony, called Burning the Bush, was carried out by the men; the women, meanwhile, fashioned a new globe to ensure good crops the following season. In some counties **mistletoe** was used in a similar way.

Historically the hawthorn was used as a crest by the Tudors. The device was chosen because at the Battle of Bosworth, which ended the Wars of the Roses and brought the House of Tudor to the English throne, the crown of the defeated Richard III was found in a hawthorn bush. An old proverb refers to the incident: 'Cleave to the crown, though it hang in a bush.'

In Greek mythology, hawthorn lighted the altar temples of Hymen, the god of marriage, and the flowers were used in bridal wreaths. In the Christian tradition it is a holy tree associated with the Virgin Mary. In fact no tree would appear to be more subject to speculation in Christian legend than the hawthorn, for it is alleged to be the Glastonbury Thorn.

The story goes that Joseph of Arimathea, who received Christ's blood on the cross in the Holy Grail, came to England to preach the Gospel. Having arrived on the high ground of the Isle of Avalon, he thrust his staff into the ground and slept. On awakening, he found that it had changed into a tree bursting with snowy white blossom. Taking this as a sign, he built a chapel which later became a magnificent abbey. The tree was alleged to produce flower buds on Chrismas Eve, which bloomed on Christmas Day and withered away the following night. Details concerning this remarkable tree became widely known from stories told by the travelling monks. Many people collected its blossoms and pieces of thorn were exported. By the reign of Queen Elizabeth I the tree had two trunks, one of which was cut down by a zealous Puritan. According to a writer of the time, this desecration did not go unpunished – 'some of the prickles flew into his eye, and made him monocular'. The remaining trunk was cut down during the reign of Charles I. During the nineteenth-century two old trees still flowered in late January, allegedly offshoots from the original tree. It is impossible to account for the winter flowering of this hawthorn, except to say that it must have been from natural causes. Christmas flowerings by other hawthorn trees have been recorded.

Old herbalists recommended the fruit, known as haws, bruised and boiled in wine, to be taken as a remedy for severe pains. Distilled water of the flowers and the haws was said to draw out splinters. As a remedy for dropsy, seeds inside the haws were beaten to a powder and taken in wine. Modern herbalists use the leaves and berries as a tonic for cardiac and asthmatic patients. A good liqueur is made from hawthorn berries infused in brandy and the berries make an interesting wine. The dried leaves can be added to tea.

Astrologically hawthorn is assigned to Mars and bears the sentiment of contentment. It is symbolic of fertility, marriage, hope, self-denial and spring.

Hazel
Corylus avellana

The generic name is the Greek word for hazel. Hazel is derived from Old English *haeal* or *haesel*. Hazel is the tree of poetic art which produces flowers (beauty) and fruit (wisdom) simultaneously.

Branches of the tree were carried by the Romans in the form of a burning torch at wedding eve ceremonies to ensure a peaceful and happy union. In Norse mythology it is the tree of Thor, son of Woden, god of war. The Celts associated the tree with fire and fertility, and small twigs were thought to protect the house against lightning. In Ireland cattle were driven through blazing fires on Midsummer Night and their backs singed with hazel rods, which were then put aside for cattle droving during the coming year. In medieval times the hazel rod served in court, rather like a water-divining rod, to discover murderers and thieves.

A Y-shaped hazel twig is commonly used for divining water and other substances. The diverging arms are held firmly in the hands with the unforked part pointing outwards:

> And as within the hazel's bough
> A gift of mystic virtue dwells,
> That points to golden ores below
> And in dry desert places tells
> Where flow unseen the cool, sweet wells. . .

Superstition held that, to be effective, a divining rod should be cut facing east, so that the rod caught the first rays of the morning sun.

Hazel wands appear to have had religious associations, as a token of certain pilgrimmages. In several places the remains of staves have been found in the graves of ecclesiastics. Many superstitions surround the tree. For instance, it was said to confer invisibility on the wearer. Hazel twigs were worn by sea captains in their hats as a protection against bad weather. A breastband of hazel was placed on horses to protect them from evil spirits. In the past, when people believed in the existence of elves and fairies, churches were decorated with evergreens to make them feel welcome. Shakespeare refers to the equipage of a fairy:

> Her chariot is an empty hazel-nut,
> Made by the joiner squirrel, or old grub,
> Time out of mind the fairies' coach-builder.

In the Midlands a good crop of nuts was a sinister omen. An old saying ran:

> 'Many nuts, many pits.'

A pit meant a grave. Nevertheless, in other parts of Britain many nuts indicated a large number of babies being born during the year. Hazelnuts were especially associated with Halloween, which in parts of England was also known as Nutcrack Night. They were used as a form of love divination, and the following lines from *A Suffolk Calendar* describe the ritual:

> Two hazel nuts I threw into the flame,
> And to each nut I gave a sweetheart's name:
> This with the loudest bounce me sore amaz'd
> That in a flame of bright colour blaz'd,
> As blaz'd the nut, so may thy passion grow
> For 'twas thy Nut that did so brightly glow!

A briefer alternative was that a nut would be named after each girl present and then thrown into the fire. As a suitor was named, the relationship would be indicated by the nut:

> If you love me, pop and fly,
> If not, lie and die.

Among many herbal remedies and old wives' tales, a double hazelnut carried in the pocket was said to protect one against toothache. The dried husks and nut shells were taken in red wine for menstrual problems. A mixture was produced for coughs and lung complaints from the nut kernels which, roasted and sprinkled with pepper, were also recommended to be eaten before going to bed as a treatment for colds. Adder bites were alleged to be cured by placing a cross-shaped piece of hazel wood on the affected area. Hazel leaves were thought to increase a cow's milk yield.

The tree is assigned to Mercury and symbolizes justice, reconciliation and truth. In the language of the flowers 'Be wise and desist'. It was given by a girl to a boy as a sign of discouragement since the time of Agricola.

Heather
Calluna vulgaris

The generic name is from Greek *kalluno*, cleanse or adorn. Heather, the familiar rosy purple covering of late summer heath and moorland, was formerly used in winemaking, apparently enjoying royal favour:

> Though unobtrusive all thy beauties shine
> Yet boast thou rival of the purple vine!
> For once thy mantling juice was seen to laugh
> In pearly cups, which monarchs loved to quaff.

The burning of heather was said to bring rain. The tips of the plants, picked just prior to flowering, are used to produce an olive yellow plant dye (see *The Use of Vegetable Dyes* by Violetta Thurston).

In the language of the flowers, red heather is a plant of passion, while white heather protects against acts of passion. It is sacred to the Sicilian love goddess Erycina, an alternative name for Venus.

Hedge bindweed
Calystegia sepium

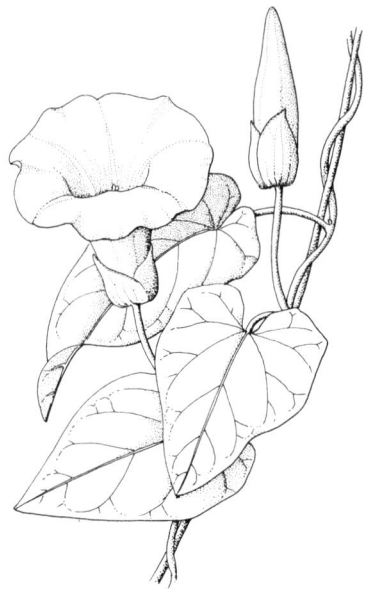

The generic name is from Greek *kalyx*, calyx, and *stegon*, cover, referring to the large bracts which conceal the calyx. In the Middle Ages it was regarded as the Devil's plant and became known as devil's guts. The twining nature of the plant is reflected in its common name:

> . . . Up tall
> Turrets of sorrel the bindweed climbs
> Like a spiral staircase.

wrote Norman Nicholson (1914–). However it was not to the climbing habits of the plant that Walter de la Mare (1873–1956) was referring when he wrote:

> The bindweed roots pierce down
> Deeper than men do lie
> Laid in their dark-shut graves
> Their slumbering kinsmen by.

Bindweed is the birthday flower for 12 April and in the language of the flowers it carries the sentiment obstinacy. Hedge bindweed signifies humility, and great bindweed (*C. silvatica*) insinuation.

Heliotrope
Heliotropium europaeum

The generic name is derived from two Greek words: *helios*, sun and *trope*, turning, as the flower is supposed to turn towards the sun, following its course. Another name for the plant is turnsole, for the same reason, and it is known as cherry pie, from a similarity in the fragrance. Heliotrope was introduced to England, via France, from Peru before 1757.

In Greek mythology the origin of the plant is ascribed to the death of Clytie, daughter of Oceanus, who pined away in hopeless love for the sun god, Helios, and was transformed into a heliotrope.

> A symbol of unhappy love
> Sacred to the slighted Clytie.

Nowadays heliotrope is not a popular plant, although one older writer declared: 'The heliotrope bears to the flower garden the same relation that the soul does to beauty, or love to youth.'

During the Middle Ages, when flower dials were popular, particularly in monastery gardens, heliotrope marked one of the hours, each of which had a floral symbol:

First hour	Budding roses
Second hour	Heliotrope
Third hour	White roses
Fourth hour	Hyacinths
Fifth hour	Lemons
Sixth hour	Lotus blossom
Seventh hour	Lupins
Eighth hour	Oranges
Ninth hour	Olive leaves
Tenth hour	Poplar leaves
Eleventh hour	Marigolds
Twelfth hour	Pansies and violets

In 'The Garden' Andrew Marvell describes a floral dial which was said to mark the hours according to the time at which the flowers opened and closed:

> How well the skilful gardener drew
> Of flowers and herbs this dial new!
> There from above, the milder sun

Does through a fragrant zodiac run,
And, as it works, the industrious bee
Computes the time as well as we.
How could such sweet and wholesome hours
Be reckoned but with herbs and flowers.

Medicinally the leaves were applied to areas pained with gout. The seed and juice, mixed with fat, were put on warts and cysts, particularly on the face and eyelids. Boiled with the spice cumin, the plant was used to treat urinary complaints and to encourage speedy delivery in childbirth. An astringent tincture manufactured from heliotrope was said to be of 'great service in clergyman's sore throat'.

Astrologically heliotrope is assigned to the sun, typifying that which follows the sun, and is symbolic of devotion, faithfulness and eagerness. In the language of the flowers it means, 'I remain true'.

Hemlock
Conium maculatum

The generic name is the Greek word for hemlock; older writers claim that it is derived from Greek *konos*, spinning top, because the poison in the plant first causes vertigo, then death. *Maculatum* refers to the distinctive mottling on the stem. Hemlock may come from Old English *hem*, border or shore, and *leac*, leek or plant. Country names include bad man's oatmeal, devil's blossom, gipsy flower and scabby hands. Country people call many species of the carrot family, to which this plant belongs, kecksies; hemlock itself they call kex.

In ancient Greece and Rome executions were carried out by making the victim drink a cup of hemlock. Socrates, the great Greek philosopher, condemned to death for the corruption of youth by introducing new gods (thus being guilty of impiety) is alleged, while surrounded by his followers in prison, to have taken hemlock and died. Hemlock was swallowed, willingly, by ancient philosophers who had grown weary of life; these occasions lacked neither ceremony nor style, as the candidates crowned themselves with garlands and made their farewells to assembled guests before taking their fatal potion. The effects of drinking hemlock are described by Keats in 'Ode to a Nightingale':

My heartaches, and a drowsy numbness pains
My sense, as though of hemlock I had drunk.

This highly poisonous plant has long been associated with the Devil and witchcraft:

> . . . By the witches' tower,
> Where hellebore and Hemlock seem to weave
> Round its dark vaults a melancholy bower
> For spirits of the dead at night's enchanted hour.

wrote Thomas Campbell (1777–1844). Medicinally the bruised leaves were said in earlier times to relieve swollen, red eyelids if they were placed on the brow. The root, roasted in embers and wrapped in wet paper, was applied to areas affected by gout. In twentieth-century medicine, the leaves and seeds were used to treat neuralgia, syphilis, asthma and chronic rheumatism. Hemlock is said to be poisonous to cows but not to horses, sheep and goats.

Astrologically hemlock is a plant of Saturn, and it is the birthday flower for 15 February. A herb of evil omen, it is symbolic of death by poisoning. In the language of the flowers it means 'You will cause my death'.

Hemp
Cannabis sativa

Cannabis comes from the Greek *cannabis*, hemp. One of the oldest plants in cultivation, it was grown primarily for its strong waterproof fibres, formerly used in ropes and sailcloth. The plant is now better known for a resin exuded by the female flower, *charas* or *hashish*. The drug marijuana is composed of the whole of the flowering head, but contains less resin and alkaloids than *hashish*.

The plant has a long history. By 500B.C. it had spread from South Siberia to India, Aisa Minor and North Africa; much later it arrived in the Americas. Cannabis appears in Arabic literature; for instance in the *Thousand and One Nights* reference is made to a large dose of the drug in the following words: 'Had an elephant smelt it he would have slept from night to night.'

The name *hashish* is a derivation of Al-Hasan ibn-al-Sabbah, a fanatical devotee of Islam, who terrorized the Persian Empire with his followers, *Hashishins* or Assassins. Their fury was increased by taking the drug, and the strange visions they experienced were explained away by Al-Hasan as a foretaste of the Moslem paradise.

In medieval Europe hemp was prescribed for gout, cystitis, urinary pains through infection, and childbirth. The fresh root, mixed with oil and butter, was used for gunpowder burns, and an infusion of the plant for coughs, bleeding from the mouth, jaundice and obstructions of the liver and spleen. Latterly cannabis has been used for easing pain and calming people with nervous disorders, and as a sedative. While it would seem no more harmful than tobacco or alcohol, the medical possibilities have yet to be fully explored.

The harvesting and dressing of the hemp crop was a lengthy process: the male plants were pulled out first, and later, when the female plant was ready, the seed heads were removed before the bundles were placed in water.

> Good flax and good hemp, to have of her own,
> In May a good housewife will see it be sown;
> And afterwards trim it, to serve at a need,
> The fimble to spin, and the karl for her seed.

It is the birthday flower for 24 June, and was used as a love charm:

> Hemp seed I sow, hemp seed I sow,
> The young man that I love
> Come after me, and mow

I sow; I sow;
Then my own dear
Come here, come here
and mow; and mow.

Henbane
Hyoscyamus niger

The name *Hyoscyamus* was given to the plant by Dioscorides, and is derived from Greek *hyos* and *cyamos*, meaning hog's bean, as that animal was said to eat the fruit. Hogbean, henbell and devil's eye are all country names for the plant. It has a very unpleasant smell which is particularly apparent when the leaves are bruised, and is referred to by John Clare in his *Shepherd's Calendar*:

And hunting from the stackyard sod
The stinking henbane's belted pod
By youths vain fancy sweetly fed
Christening them his loaves of bread.

For centuries the plant has been associated with witchcraft; its effect in potions was to produce convulsions and, it is said, temporary madness. When henbane was burned on a fire, the fumes were believed to conjure up the spirits of the dead and give one the power of clairvoyance. However, bathing the feet in henbane before going to bed was considered an excellent cure against insomnia! In *Barnaby Rudge* Charles Dickens refers to this property of the plant: 'The prospect of finding anybody out in anything would have kept Miss Miggs awake under the influence of Henbane.'

In earlier times herbalists used the leaves boiled in wine as a fomentation to reduce swellings in the scrotum and in women's breasts, and to alleviate gout and aching joints. Applied with vinegar to the forehead and temples, it was said to relieve headaches and bring sleep to feverish patients. For centuries henbane was prescribed for toothache. Because of its narcotic properties, it was used in medicine to treat rheumatism, gout, bronchitis, asthma, whooping cough and consumption, often as a substitute for opium. The plant yields hyoscine, the poison used by Dr Crippen to murder his wife in 1910.

Astrologically henbane is under the sign of Saturn, and in the language of the flowers it suggests imperfection.

Herb Bennet
Geum urbanum

The generic name is from Greek *geue*, taste well or give relish, while *urbanum* means city dweller in Latin. Country names for the plant include wood avens, colewort, way Bennet, yellow herb, blessed herb and holy herb. Many of the plant's European names are a corruption of herb Bennet. Benedict was one of the first saints to have a flower named after him.

The plant was believed to be a protective one and it was said of it: 'Where the root is in the house the devil can do nothing, and flies from it; wherefore it is blessed above all herbs.' Herb Bennet was considered sacred, and is frequently found in decorative work in church architecture and painting. In medieval times the upper leaves, with three leaflets and five gold petals, symbolized the Holy Trinity and the five wounds of Christ on the cross.

Herbalists used the roots of the plant, green or dry, boiled in wine, for all 'inward wounds' and chest complaints. If herb Bennet could have cured half the complaints with which it was credited it would have been truly a blessed herb!

The root, which is slightly astringent, was used to prevent ale turning sour, giving a distinctive clove-like flavour to the drink, and as a substitute for cloves in apple tarts. A hot cordial can be made from the leaves. Astrologically herb Bennet is governed by Jupiter.

Herb Paris
Paris quadrifolia

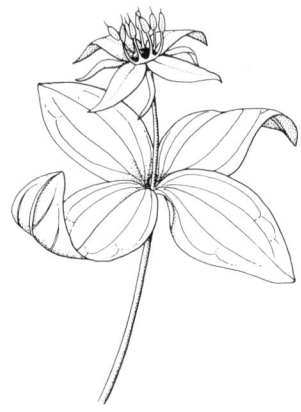

The generic name comes from Latin *par*, equal, on account of the unvarying number of leaves. A singular plant with a long stem, it has four large, pointed leaves and a solitary green flower, hence one of its country names, four-leaved grass. In parts of Scotland herb Paris is also known as devil-in-a-bush because the foul-smelling flower is surrounded by the four leaves; for similar reason southerners refer to **fennel** by the same name. It is also known as true-love-knot, and was used in a rather complicated love divination ceremony. Two girls would sit in a room from midnight until one o'clock without speaking. During this time they removed from their heads a hair for every year of their life, and placed them on a linen cloth with the plant. After the clock struck one, each hair had to be burnt separately and this charm pronounced:

> I offer this my sacrifice,
> To him most precious in my eyes,
> I charge thee now come forth to me
> That I this minute may thee see.

The future husband would appear and walk about the room and then vanish, neither girl being able to see the other's lover.

Medicinally the plant was an antidote for poison, in particular aconite. The root, powdered and taken in wine, was used to treat colic, while the juice of the leaves, applied to the fingernails and toenails, was alleged to heal sores very quickly. Astrologically it is a plant of Venus.

Herb Robert
Geranium Robertianum

For the derivation of the generic name see **geranium**. It has been suggested that the plant was named after Robert, Duke of Normandy, for whom the *Ortus Sanitatis*, for some hundreds of years a standard herbal, was written by J. Von Cube in 1490. Another source suggests that the herb was used in Germany to cure a disease known as Robert's plague. Yet a third claims that St Robert, a Benedictine Abbot whose feast day was celebrated on 29 April, when the flower is in bloom, cured diseases with the plant and gave his name to it. The plant has rather a disagreeable smell, which led to the country name of stinking Bob. It is also known as death-come-quickly, from an old superstition that death will follow if it is picked and brought into the house. Among its other names are herb robin, ragged robin, red robin, fox geranium and kiss-me-quick.

Having certain styptic properties, this species has been used to staunch blood both internally and externally. It has also been employed to treat ulcers, piles and nephritis. Astrologically the plant is under the dominion of Venus.

Hogweed
Heracleum sphondylium

The generic name is derived from Hercules, the mythical character from classical literature, who is said to have brought this or some allied plant into medicinal use; a French author suggests that he was not only a great hero but also a doctor and botanist. The plant is popularly known as cow parsnip, cow parsley and keck.

The seed and root of the plant were recommended by old herbalists to be boiled in oil and rubbed on the heads of those 'labouring under a phrenzy'. The root was used as a medicine for coughs, epilepsy and jaundice, and as a remedy to remove the hard skin covering abscesses by scraping it on to the affected part. Hogweed mixed with **rue** was said to revive people suffering from drowsiness. An attempt was once made to manufacture sugar from the thick dried stalks of the plant.

Holly
Ilex aquifolium

Holly or holm is from Old English *holen* or *holegn*, a word derived from Latin *ulex*, which in the Middle Ages was confused with *ilex*, the holm oak of the ancients. *Aquifolium* signifies needle-leaved in Latin. The holly was also formerly known as holme, hulver or hulfere. Chaucer wrote:

> This herbere was full of flowers gende,
> Into the which as I beholde 'gan,
> Betwixt an Hulfere and a woodbende,
> As I was ware, I saw where lay a man.

In ancient Rome the holly was an emblem of goodwill and was sent as a gift during the festival of Saturn, celebrated on 17, 18 and 19 December. The Christmas custom of decorating houses and later churches is very old, and probably has its origins in this Roman custom. The early Christians incorporated many so-called pagan practices into their faith, and gradually their origins were conveniently forgotten. The holly and **ivy** are typical, as they were used in fertility rites during the Fire Festival (Christmas), the prickly holly suggesting the male principle and the entwining ivy the female principle.

At a time when people believed in elves and fairies, holly, like a number of other trees, was hung in churches as a sign of welcome. However it is now used as a decoration symbolic of eternal life. Being an evergreen and having red berries it is associated with good luck almost everywhere. A tree growing near the house was believed to protect the occupants against thunder and lightning. the dark green leaves and red berries, inside or outside of the house, provided an additional safeguard from demons, witches and the Evil Eye.

Holly is still the most popular of all evergreens used to decorate homes at Christmas, although in the past a variety of branches were used:

> Spread out the laurel and the bay,
> For chimney-piece and window gay,
> Scour the brass gear – a shining row
> And Holly place with Mistletoe.

Nevertheless the holly must be hung before the **mistletoe**, otherwise ill luck will come down the chimney on Christmas Eve. After the Christmas festivities, holly must be taken down no later than Epiphany Eve (5 January) although an older tradition says Candlemas (2 February). However a sprig of holly should be retained to protect the house against lightning, particularly if there is no tree growing outside. Holly branches should never be burnt green, otherwise death will visit the family. To stamp on a holly berry or bring holly into the house in flower is also unlucky. Many berries foretell a hard winter.

Superstitious people believe that the male or prickly holly is lucky to men, and the smooth, variegated type, she-holly, to women. The variegated variety was used as a form of love divination. Nine holly leaves had to be gathered at midnight on a Friday and placed in a three-cornered handkerchief, which was then tied with nine knots and concealed under the pillow before going to bed. Absolute silence was essential from the time of the gathering of the leaves until dawn. A somewhat drastic country remedy for chilblains was to thrash them with a holly branch 'to let the chilled blood out'.

Holly is the birthday flower for 5 March, symbolic of domestic happiness, foresight, friendship and good wishes. In the language of flowers it means, 'Am I forgotten?' In the Christian tradition, the thorns typify the Passion of Christ, the red berries drops of blood. An old rhyme suggests that:

The holly bears a berry red,
The ivy bears a black 'un,
To show that Christ His blood did shed,
To save our souls from Satan.

Hollyhock
Althaea rosea

The generic name is from Greek *althaia*, cure, referring to the healing properties of some of the species. Some sources suggest that the hollyhock was introduced by the Huguenots in the late sixteenth century, although in a herbal published in 1551 Turner speaks of the common holyhoke. *Hoc* is the Old English word for mallow. The wild plant still grows profusely in Palestine, which supports another suggestion, that the 'holy hoc' was first introduced by the Crusaders. The word hollyhock means holy great one.

> Here beside the modest stock
> Flaunts the flaring hollyhock;
> Here without a pang, one sees
> Ranks, conditions, and degrees.
>
> AUSTIN DOBSON, 'A GARDEN SONG'

Herbalists used the root of the plant, dried and powdered, in wine to kill worms in children, disperse blood clots, help ruptures and prevent miscarriages. Culpepper advised that 'the root is very binding, and may be used to advantage both inwardly and outwardly, for incontinence of urine, immoderate menses, bleeding wounds, spitting of blood, the bloody flux, and other fluxes of the belly.'

Hollyhock is the birthday flower for 25 June, and symbolizes ambition, fecundity and fruitfulness. The white hollyhock symbolizes female ambition.

Honesty
Lunaria biennis

The generic name is derived from the Latin *luna*, moon, referring to the form of the seed vessels. Confusion surrounds the early history of honesty because old writers referred to another plant as lunaria, believing it to have magical powers:

> . . . Whose virtues such
> It in the pasture only with a touch,
> Unshoes the new-shod steed.

This unusual explanation almost certainly covers up the work of an inferior blacksmith. Honesty has many delightful country names, most of which refer to the distinctive silver, disc-like seed pods whose transparency is said to have given rise to the common name. The plant is also known as satin flower, money flower, silver plate, silver pennies, money-in-both-pockets, pennies-in-a-purse, pennieflower, silver bloom, prick-song-wort and lunarie.

Since the eighteenth century honesty has been popular in dried winter floral arrangements. The plant should be cut with long stems on a sunny day when the seed pods are dry, tied into bunches, and hung upside down in a light, airy room. When past their best the seed pods can be sprayed silver or gold as a Christmas decoration. The roots of the plant were formerly eaten in salads. Like all members of the cabbage family or Cruciferae (the name comes from the characteristic cross shape made by the petals) they were considered beneficial to the health. This gave rise to the saying '*In cruce salus*' – health is in the cross. In the language of the flowers honesty means fascination and, not surprisingly, honesty.

Honeysuckle
Lonicera periclymenum

The genus was named in honour of Adam Lonicer, a German botanist. The name honeysuckle was given in the mistaken belief that bees extracted honey from the flower. Popular names include woodbine, woodbind, caprifoly and goat's-leaf – alluding to the fact that goats fed on the leaves. In Greek antiquity the honeysuckle was an object of religious worship, paralleling the lotus bud. The poet William Cowper describes the growth of this fragrant climber:

> As Woodbine weds the plant within her reach,
> Rough elm or smooth-grain'd ash, or glossy beech,
> In spiral rings ascends the trunk, and lays
> Her golden tassels on the leafy sprays;
> But does a mischief while she lends a grace,
> Slackening its growth by such a strict embrace.

The sweet scent of the honeysuckle has over the years endeared the plant to many poets. Chaucer wrote of the charming custom of girls wearing wreaths of flowers:

> . . . Wore chapelets on hir hede
> Of fresh wodebind, be such never were
> To love untrue, in word, he thought, he ded.

Medicinally the juice of the plant was taken as an antidote for snakebite. The infected area was bathed with the water in which the plant had been boiled, and the plant itself then laid on the wound. The seeds and flowers, boiled and mixed with oil, provided a poultice for swellings. A preparation of honeysuckle was also used as a contraceptive. Modern herbalists recommend the flowers as a cure for asthma, and a syrup, also concocted from the flowers, for lung complaints and digestive disorders and as a gargle.

Honeysuckle is the birthday flower for 25 November and symbolizes bonds of love, constancy and domestic happiness. In the language of the flowers it means, 'I will not answer hastily'. Astrologically the plant is under the dominion of Mercury.

Hop
Humulus lupulus

Humus (of which *Humulus* is a derivative) is Latin for soil, in which the plant thrives. *Lupulus* is probably from *lupus*, wolf, because like the animal this climbing plant lightly embraces the host plant before strangling and subsequently destroying it. Some writers, however, think that the word came from *lupinus*, as it is well known that the Egyptians used **lupin** seeds to give a bitter flavour to their beer. Hop is from Old English *hoppian*, to climb. The plant is best known for its use in brewing – the fruit has a number of glandular hairs which exude a chemical known as 'bitters'. The cultivated hop is said to have been introduced in the early sixteenth-century, in the reign of Henry VIII:

> Hops, reformation, bays and beer
> Came into England all in one year.

For a long time hops were thought to spoil the flavour of the beer, and actually endanger the lives of beer drinkers. However by 1572 it was listed as a necessary item in the garden. In Tusser's *Five Good Pointes of Husbandrie*, published in 1551, he gives advice on the cultivation of hops:

> Choose soil for the hop of the rottenest mould
> Well doonged and wroght, as a garden plot should;
> Not far from the water (but not overfloune),
> This lesson well-noted, is mete to be knowne.
> The sun in the south or else southlie and west,
> Is joy to the Hop, as welcomed ghest
> But wind in the north, or else northerly east,
> To Hop is as ill as a fray in a feast.

It used to be the custom for anyone visiting a hopfield to contribute 'foot money' to prevent luck leaving the fields. Traditionally a Queen of the Hops was crowned at the end of the season. A branch that had grown contorted and twisted was saved by the hop picker as a good luck charm.

Early herbalists recommended the seeds as a means of killing worms in the body. The flowers and fruit were used for expelling poison and as a syrup for stomach and liver complaints. Later hops were used to treat insomnia: a pillow stuffed with the fruiting heads was very popular – George III is reputed to have used one regularly and they are still sold today, thanks to the revival of interest in herbal remedies. Hops were also prescribed for poultices to relieve pain. A yellow powder, obtained by threshing the hops, was a powerful twentieth-century antaphrodisiac for soothing the genital organs and painful erection due to gonorrhoea and allied diseases.

In the kitchen, the young tops of the wild hop can be tied in bundles, boiled and eaten as a vegetable. It is the birthday flower for 7 April and symbolizes injustice, passion and pride.

Horsetail   see **Marestail**

Houseleek
Sempervivum tectorum

The specific name is derived from Latin *semper*, always and *vivo*, I live; *tectorum* means of the roof. In rural districts it was planted on cottage roofs in the hope that 'the dread rattling thunder which rifts Jove's stout oak with his own bolts may pass harmlessly over the lowly weed'. John Leyden (1775–1811) recalls a thatched cottage where the weary traveller could rest with simple people:

> The clay built wall with woodbine twisted o'er,
> The House-leek clustering green above the door;
> While through the sheltering elms that round them grew
> The winding smoke arose in columns blue.

The association of houseleek with lightning explains some of the plant's country names such as Jupiter's beard, Thor's beard and Jove's beard

(Jupiter or Jove, and Thor, being the gods associated with thunder and lightning in classical and Norse mythology respectively). It is also known as healing blade, hen and chickens, syngreen, St George's beard and, most extraordinarily, as welcome-home-husband-however-drunk-you-be.

The superstitious not only believed in the protective powers of the plant against lightning, but thought that it warded off evil spirits and illness and prevented fire. This association with fire made it a natural choice to relieve burns and scalds. The plant was widely used for a variety of ailments. Older writers indicate that it was bound about the forehead 'to ease the headache, and distempered heat of the brain in frenzies or through want of sleep'. Medieval herbalists boiled the juice of the plant in milk to quench thirst in fever, and blended it with honey as a soothing syrup for sore throats. The juice was also mixed with cream to treat erysipelas, a skin complaint which at one time reached epidemic proportions. Warts and corns were treated with the juice, as were bee and nettle stings and eye and ear complaints. Modern herbalists use the juice, or the plant itself, for bruises, cuts and swellings, and to treat ringworm and shingles.

Houseleek is under the dominion of Jupiter. In the language of the flowers it symbolizes domestic economy and industry.

Hyacinth
Hyacinthus orientalis

The generic name comes from a Greek deity of spring vegetation, Hyakinthos, who was loved and accidentally killed by Apollo; the flower of the hyacinth is supposed to have sprung up from the blood of the dead youth. The petals were said to be marked with the Greek letters, αι, αι (alas, alas), although there are no indications of this in the modern plant

> The hyacinth betrays the doleful 'AI',
> And culls the tribute of Apollo's sigh,
> Still on its bloom the mournful flower retains
> The lovely blue that dyed the stripling's veins.
>
> CAMEONS LUSIAD IX

In the Christian tradition the flower typifies desire for heaven, peace of mind and prudence. It is dedicated to the Virgin Mary. In classical mythology the hyacinth was one of the sweet-scented flowers that formed the couch of Hera and Zeus. In ancient Greece wreaths of hyacinth and **parsley** were worn on the heads of bridesmaids.

Hyacinth is the birthday flower for 7 March, and symbolizes faith, prudence, wisdom, woe and resurrection. The hyacinth is symbolic of things sorrowful and sad.

Hydrangea
Hydrangea macrophylla

The name is derived from two Greek words: *hydros*, water, and *aggos*, jar, in reference to the cup form of the capsule. The popularly supposed connection with water is a fallacy. The plant was introduced to England in about 1736. The dried flower heads provide beautiful material for winter flower arrangements, which can be sprayed silver or gold for Christmas. Hydrangea is the birthday flower for 5 January. It is symbolic of remembrance, boastfulness, heartiness and cold beauty, because it is a beautiful flower without scent.

Hyssop
Hyssopus officinalis

The generic name is the Latin word for this sweet herb. This species, however, is not the one mentioned in the Bible. Hyssop is one of our oldest garden herbs. It is listed by Michael Drayton in his *Chaplet of Herbs* in the poem 'Herbularis':

> With Hyssop as an herb most prime
> Herein my wreath bestowing.

It was certainly grown during the fifteenth century, and probably even in the thirteenth, by Cistercian monks, and it was a popular strewing herb.

In the Christian tradition it typifies baptism, innocence regained and purgation. In folklore it relates to the **cedar** as **mistletoe** does to the **oak**. Mythologically the union of hyssop and cedar typifies the whole course of the sun, from its birth at the winter solstice to its prime at the summer solstice, and its decline back to the winter solstice. Thomas Macaulay, the nineteenth-century poet and historian, wrote:

> He is indeed a kind of semi-Solomon
> He half knows everything from the cedar to the hyssop.

Hyssop seeds, pounded into a salve, were used medicinally to cleanse 'old and filthy sores' (Culpepper). Fresh bruised leaves mixed with sugar were said to heal wounds quickly, a remedy mentioned by the poet Spenser: 'Sharp isop, good for green wounds' remedies.' Boiled in wine, the plant soothed inflammations and removed bruise marks. However, boiled with figs it made an excellent remedy for quinsy, and boiled with vinegar and gargled it provided relief for toothache. A twentieth-century remedy for the treatment of chronic bronchitis consisted of hyssop, **sage**, alum and honey.

Hyssop is the birthday flower for 14 January and symbolizes humility, purification, holiness and cleanliness. Astrologically it is a herb of Jupiter under the sign of Cancer.

Iris   see **Yellow flag**

Italian cypress
Cupresses sempervirens

The generic name is derived from Greek *kuo*, I produce, and *parises*, equal, in reference to the symmetrical growth of many of the species. The cypress was introduced into the Mediterranean regions by the Phoenicians, who came from Asia Minor and colonized the island of Cyprus, which derived its name from the tree.

In Greek mythology Cyparissus, a special friend of Apollo, accidentally killed the god's sacred stag. Suffering deep remorse, he begged the gods to allow his grief to last forever. They changed him into a cypress tree, which became the symbol of the immortal soul and eternal death. In ancient Greece the tree was an attribute of Aphrodite, goddess of love and beauty; in the annual procession to commemorate the death of Adonis she carried cypress. In Roman mythology cypress was dedicated to Dis, Pluto and Silvanus.

Marlowe wrote of:

> Sylvanus weeping for the lovely boy
> That is now turn'd into a cypress tree,
> Under whose shades the wood-gods love to be.

In both Greek and Roman mythology cypress was the emblem of the gods of the Underworld, the Fates and the Furies. Formerly it was the custom to place cypress branches at the door of a house containing a dead body; it was also carried by mourners in a funeral procession, as a sign of irrevocable death – once cut, it will never grow again.

The tree which furnished the wood of Christ's cross was a constant source of conjecture among early writers. Four types of wood were suggested by Bede (673–735), the scholar and historian: cypress, **cedar**, **pine** and **box**, and this was generally accepted by contemporary monks. However a translation of some Latin lines on the subject reveals:

> Nailed were His feet to Cedar, to Palm His hands,
> Cypress His body bore, title on Olive stands.

The four types of wood were supposed to represent the four quarters of the globe.

Herbalists used cypress leaves, boiled in sweet wine or mead, for healing wounds and to staunch the flow of blood, and mixed with **barley** meal as a poultice for carbuncles and ulcers. The fruit was used for complaints associated with the circulation. An infusion of leaves and fruit in vinegar was used to dye the hair black.

Cypress is the birthday flower for 11 February, signifying a just man. It is symbolic of death, despair, eternal sorrow, immortality, mourning and rebirth. Astrologically it is assigned to Saturn.

Ivy
Hedera helix

The generic name is the Latin word for the plant. The dark evergreen ivy is a well-known climbing plant; Charles Dickens wrote of it:

> The stateliest building man can raise,
> Is the ivy's food at last.
> Creeping on where time has been,
> A rare old plant is the ivy green.

Country names for the plant are love stone and bindwood.

Ivy is a burial flower because it symbolizes immortality, and an evil omen because it kills whatever it embraces. Its spiral growth is dedicated to the Resurrection, and the plant itself is a Christian symbol of attachment, death and undying affection. It was the tree of the eleventh Druidic month – 1–20 October in the modern calendar. In Greek antiquity the ivy wreath is the emblem of Thalici, muse of comedy and idyllic poetry. It is dedicated to Bacchus and was thought to prevent

drunkenness: his priestesses carried staves or javelins entwined with the plant during their sacrificial rites.

A bunch of ivy on a pole was one of the first inn signs. This custom gave rise to the saying: 'A good wine needs no bush', suggesting that the reputation should be good enough without further advertisement.

Superstitious people used ivy as a means of divination. One ceremony took place on New Year's Eve, when an ivy leaf was placed in a bowl of water and left, untouched, until Twelfth Night. If the leaf remained fresh it foretold a happy year to follow; however black spots appearing near the apex of the leaf warned of leg and foot complaints; spots in the centre only suggested that the stomach would be affected, while markings towards the stalk indicated head and neck problems. General decay of the leaf meant an early death. Less drastic was the use of ivy as a love oracle. A girl would place a leaf in her pocket and go for a walk: the first man she met, married or otherwise, would eventually become her husband. Ivy growing on the wall of a house protected the occupant against witches – however if the plant withered, disaster was inevitable. In Wales the withering of the ivy meant that the house would pass into other hands, either through financial problems or lack of heirs.

Pliny observed that the yellow berries were a good remedy against jaundice and prevented drunkenness. The mythological background of the ivy perpetuated the plant's association with alcoholic drinks. Ivy leaves boiled in wine were recommended, on the 'hair of the dog' principle, for a hangover. Water and wine mixed in a bowl carved from ivy wood were said to separate automatically, which led people to believe that the leaves and berries were beneficial after a period of excessive drinking. Ivy wood cups were used as drinking vessels for children suffering from whooping cough, suggesting a stronger belief in the container than in the contents. A wreath of ivy was a decorative remedy against falling hair. The juice of the berries or leaves sniffed up the nose was said to clear the brain and eyes, and to cure nasal complaints. Fresh leaves boiled in vinegar were applied to the side to relieve 'stitch' and general aches and pains, and corns were allegedly cured by binding them with ivy leaves soaked in vinegar. A vinegar produced from ivy berries was a well-known remedy during the Great Plague of London of 1665.

Ivy is the birthday flower for 13 March, symbolizing a need for support, ambition, fidelity, immortality, tenacity, wedded love and obscurity. In the language of the flowers it means, 'I die where I cling'. A sprig of ivy is the birthday flower for 24 September, symbolic of longing. In the language of the flowers it signifies, 'I desire to please'. Astrologically, ivy is a plant of Saturn.

Jasmine

The generic name *Jasminum* is the Latin version of the Persian name for these sweet-scented shrubs and climbers.

White jasmine
Jasminum officinale

This jasmine is the fragant late summer flowering climber:

> Your sweetness by the truant wind is driven,
> As summer weary with its fragrance sighs.

wrote Isidore Ascher.

In the language of the flowers white jasmine symbolizes amiability. It is used in the distillation of scent and reacts exceptionally well to one of the oldest methods of perfume extraction, *enfleurage*: spread fresh flowers over lightly oiled sheets of glass. After a day or so replace the old flowers with new ones and carry on the process in this way until the oil has absorbed sufficient of the jasmine's fragrance and is bottled for use. Anyone who grows white jasmine can succeed with this method.

Winter jasmine
Jasminum nudiflorum

The winter or yellow jasmine was introduced by Robert Fortune, the plant collector, from China in 1844. It is usually trained as a climbing shrub, as described by the Poet Laureate, Sir John Betjeman (1906–84):

> But winter jasmine used to cling
> With golden stars ashine
> Where rain and wind would wash and swing
> The crudely painted sign.

Winter jasmine is the birthday flower for 22 April, symbolizing elegance, grace, modesty, divine hope and heavenly felicity. It is a flower of the Epiphany, celebrated on 6 January, and an attribute of the Virgin Mary.

Jonquil
Narcissus jonquilla

For the derivation of the generic name see **daffodil**. The jonquil is a fragrant scented narcissus that takes its name from Spanish *junquillo*, rush, on account of the shape of the leaves. The principal species were cultivated during the sixteenth-century and were introduced from the Iberian Peninsula. Gerard grew the plant and the seventeenth-century botanist, John Parkinson, mentions a double variety. Double jonquils were planted out in the gardens of Blenheim Palace, which was Queen Anne's reward to John Churchill, 1st Duke of Marlborough, for his defeat of Louis XIV in 1704. It seems logical that it was at this time that they acquired the name Queen Anne's jonquil. In 'To a Snowdrop' Wordsworth refers to the sweet scent of the flower:

> . . . Blue eyed May
> Shall soon behold this border thickly set
> With bright jonquils, their odours lavishing
> On the soft west wind and his frolic peers.

Jonquil is the birthday flower for 12 September and symbolizes desire, evening fragrance and longing. In the language of the flowers it means, 'I desire your affection'.

Juniper
Juniperus communis

The generic name is the Latin word for the tree. In Christian legend the Virgin Mary took refuge with the child Jesus behind a juniper bush when fleeing from Herod into Egypt.

The ancients thought that the pungent smoke produced by the green branches was incense to the infernal gods. In medieval times this odour was believed to smoke out witches and keep evil spirits at bay. Bishop Hall (1764–1831) mentions an allusion to this belief in his *Satires*:

> And with glasse stills and sticks of Juniper,
> Raise the black spright that burns not with the fire.

The berries were burnt at funerals to frighten away evil spirits. In Wales chopping down a juniper tree was regarded as a misfortune, resulting, it was feared, in a death in the family, most probably one's own. To dream of the actual tree was also unlucky although a dream about the berries only was not. Juniper used to be hung in Scottish cowsheds as a protective plant against the evil eye.

The fruit of the juniper, which resemble small berries, rather than cones, yield an oil used in medicine and gin; the word gin is derived from the French for juniper, *genièvre*. Oil of juniper is still being used this century for urinary complaints, dropsy, piles and worms, and the ash from burnt juniper wood as a remedy for gum complaints. Physicians thought that ten or twelve of the dark purple berries, taken while fasting, were beneficial in treating lung diseases. An infusion from the tree was said to restore lost youth.

Because the wood is aromatic, spits, for roasting meat, and spoons were made from it, in the belief that they imparted a pleasant flavour to the food. The scent of the tree made the leaves popular for strewing. For the same reason it was also burnt, and Queen Elizabeth I used it to fumigate her bedchamber.

Juniper is the birthday flower for 3 October, symbolic of fecundity, asylum, longevity, remembrance, succour and protection.

Knapweed   see **Black knapweed**

Knotgrass
Polygonum aviculare

The generic name is derived from two Greek words: *polys*, many, *gonu*, a knee joint. The plant was used by witches to stunt the growth of children thus enabling them to be used as dwarves in travelling circuses and fairs. This practice was familiar to Shakespeare, who says in *A Midsummer Night's Dream*:

> Get you gone, you dwarf,
> You minimus of hindering Knotgrass made;
> You bead! You acorn!

Early herbalists used knotgrass juice in red wine to stop bleeding from the mouth, to relieve stomach pains and diarrhoea, and as a treatment for worms. The juice, applied to the temples or squirted up the nostrils, was thought to relieve nose bleeding. When applied to fresh wounds, the healing properties of the plant were thought to be beneficial. Modern herbalists make an ointment from the plant to treat cuts and sores. Astrologically, knotgrass is assigned to the planet Saturn.

Laburnum
Laburnum anagyroides

The hardy deciduous tree of our gardens and parks was introduced in about 1596, and is a member of the pea and bean family, the *Leguminosae*. It is also known as golden chain because of the beauty of the bright yellow flower racemes, and bean-trefoil and pea-tree, referring to the leaves and seed pods respectively. Laburnum flowers in late spring and early summer:

> Like a fountain, o'er the meadow,
> Gold the green laburnum showers;
> Spouting up a glossy column,
> Dripping down in amber showers.

The seeds are a violent emetic and are very dangerous to children. Ironically, in the well-known poem by Thomas Hood (1798–1845), 'I Remember, I Remember', when the poet recalls his happy childhood years he mentions this very tree on a family occasion:

> And where my brother set
> The laburnum on his birthday –
> The tree is living yet.

All parts of the tree are poisonous although rabbits are reputed to be particularly fond of laburnum bark.

Laburnum is the birthday flower for 8 January, symbolizing pensive beauty.

Lady's bedstraw
Galium verum

For the derivation of the generic name see **common cleavers**; some of the species were used to colour and curdle milk. In the North of England it was used as a substitute for rennet and in Gloucestershire mixed with **nettle** juice in making the famous Double Gloucester cheese. Cheese-renet is an old name for the plant.

Lady's bedstraw or Our Lady's bedstraw was called bedstre in former times. In legend it is said to have formed part of the bedding in the stable where Jesus Christ was born, and in a painting of the Nativity by the French artist Nicolas Poussin (1593–1665) the 'straw' in the manger is said to be lady's bedstraw. At various times the Virgin Mary was assigned flowers relating to her person, such as lady's slipper, lady's mantle, lady's smock, lady's fingers and lady's tresses. Other popular country names for this plant are maid hair and wild rosemary.

Herbalists recommended bruised leaves or flowers placed in the nostrils as a remedy for nosebleeds. A soothing ointment for burns and scalds was also made from the plant. The flowers, sprinkled in water, were said to soothe the feet of the weary traveller. The root of lady's bedstraw yields a rust-coloured dye, and the stems and flowers, boiled in alum, a yellow one.

Lady's mantle
Alchemilla vulgaris

The generic name is a Latin word indicating the plant's use in alchemy, from Arabic *alkemelych*. A country name for the plant is lion's foot, from a supposed resemblance of the outspread leaves to the pug mark of a lion. The common name has a slightly more romantic derivation, as the leaves were thought to have a similar shape to the mantles worn by ladies.

The crystal drops which form on the leaves were collected and sold as a cosmetic preparation for restoring female beauty, however faded! In the Middle Ages, this so-called dew was carefully gathered and used in a preparation called philosopher's stone, a hypothetical substance which alchemists alleged converted all baser metals into gold.

The plant has strong astringent and styptic properties and was used for healing wounds and staunching the flow of blood. Culpepper, without feeling the need to elaborate, said, 'It is one of the most singular wound herbe there is.' Although originally used for wounds it was later more popular for female ailments, and acquired the title of 'a woman's best friend'. If a woman took the distilled water of the plant for twenty days it was believed to aid conception, while a decoction of the herb placed in the bathwater prevented miscarriages. Modern herbalists thought it helpful, before and after a confinement, in retaining one's figure. A pillow filled with flower heads was said to induce sleep. Arab and gipsy herdsmen also placed great faith in the plant, but used it as the main ingredient in a tonic for horses, goats and sheep.

In the language of the flowers lady's mantle symbolizes fashion. Astrologically it is a herb of Venus. Many centuries ago the plant was known as 'the magic herb'.

Lady's slipper
Cypripedium calceolus

The generic name is from Greek *Kupris*, Venus, and *pedilon*, slipper. the common name for this lovely orchid is suggested by the maroon flower sepals and large inflated yellow lip. It was a rare plant even a hundred years ago, when these lines were written: 'The indiscreet zeal of simplers to possess this beautiful rarity, and the ravages of certain gardeners impelled by filthy lucre, have nearly exhausted several of its favourite haunts.'

The fibrous roots were used medicinally during this century in the treatment of epilepsy, nervous headaches, hysteria and neuralgia. An old gipsy recipe for the treatment of headaches and neuralgia consists of one ounce of the root boiled in a pint of water for ten minutes, strained and bottled; a wineglassful should be taken during the attacks. This remedy was also taken as a sedative.

Lady's slipper is the birthday flower for 23 April and symbolizes capricious beauty and fickleness. In the language of the flowers it means, 'Win and wear me'.

Larkspur
Delphinium consolida

The generic name is derived from Greek *delphin*, dolphin, which animal
the upper sepals are thought to resemble. *Consolida* is from the Latin verb
to heal, or fill in; a number of plants were described in medieval herbals
as 'filling in' wounds. Alternative names such as lark's-claw, lark's-toe
and lark's-heel arise from comparisons with the various parts of that
bird. Shakespeare, and John Fletcher (1579–1625) in particular use the old
name, lark-heel. In 'The Bird of Song' we find:

> With Hairbells dim;
> Oxlips in their cradles growing,
> Marigolds on death-beds blowing
> Lark-heels trim.

Larkspur seeds were well known during the Tudor period as being good
for 'the stinging of scorpions' and could, if thrown in the path of a
'venomous beast' immobilize it until 'the herbe be taken away'. Seeds
were also used to destroy body and hair lice.
   In the language of the flowers pink larkspur symbolizes fickleness, and
purple larkspur naughtiness.

Lavender
Lavandula spica

The generic name is said to be derived from Latin *lavo*, I wash: for many
centuries lavender has been used to scent soaps and bath water. The
Greeks gave it the name *nardos*, from Naarda in Syria, after which it
became known as nard. The plant is said to have been introduced to
England in about the mid-thirteenth century, although as it was a
favourite of the Romans it could have been earlier.
   Lavender bags have been used to perfume linen for hundreds of years.
The lavender faggot was also popular,

> '. . . made of the spikes before the flower is fully blown; From
> about twelve to twenty heads of lavender should be placed evenly
> together, and one end of the narrow ribbon tied tightly round the
> whole, close under the heads to form a bow, leaving the remainder
> of the ribbon, about a yard long. The stalks are then bent
> backwards over the heads of lavender and the ribbon wound
> spirally round the faggot, passing it alternately over two stalks and

under the next two until the heads are covered. The winding ribbon and the stalks are fastened firmly by a bow and about three inches of stalk left below the last bow.'

Lavender inspired one of the best-known cries of London:

> Lavender, sweet blooming Lavender
> Six bunches a penny today.
> Lavender, sweet blooming Lavender,
> Ladies, buy it while you may.

Charles VI of France had the cushions in his palace stuffed with the flower heads to create a pleasant odour and deter insects, particularly moths.

Lavender was given by lovers as a sign of affection. In his 'Pastorals' of 1619 Michael Drayton wrote:

> He from his lasse him lavender hath sent,
> Showing her love and doth requit all crave.

However, if lavender thrives in a garden it was said that the daughter of the house would never marry, from which came the saying: 'Lavender will only grow in old maid's gardens.'

Herbalists recommended two teaspoonsful of the distilled water of the flowers to restore a lost voice, and to calm the tremblings and passions of the heart. A mixture of lavender, horehound, **fennel, asparagus** root and a little cinnamon was used to treat epilepsy and giddiness of the brain, and as a gargle for toothache.

In the language of the flowers the plant signifies distrust, acknowledgement and assiduity. It is the birthday flower for 9 January, and astrologically it is a herb of Mercury.

Leek
Allium porrum

The generic name is the Latin name for garlic, while *porrum* means leek. The leek is the national emblem of Wales, and many reasons have been put forward for this. One source suggests that when the Saxons invaded Britain in 640 the Britons, to distinguish friend from foe, wore leeks taken from a garden near the battlefield. The Britons' subsequent victory is believed to have established the custom of wearing the leek on St David's Day. In *Henry V* Shakespeare says it is 'an ancient tradition begun upon an honourable respect and worn as a memorable trophy of pre-deceased valour'. There is a possibility that it originated from the custom of farmers contributing leeks to the common repast which commemorated mutual assistance in ploughing.

   The leek was used as a love oracle: if a girl walked backwards into a garden at Halloween and placed a knife among the leeks, she would see a vision of her future husband. Medicinally the leek was boiled and applied to relieve the discomfort of piles. Baked, it was a popular antidote against eating too many mushrooms! It is the birthday flower for 9 February and symbolizes liveliness.

Lemon
Citrus limonia

> Know'st thou the land where the lemon-trees bloom,
> Where the gold orange glows in the deep thickets gloom,
> Where a wind ever soft from the blue heaven
> And the groves are of laurel and myrtle and rose.

wrote the eighteenth-century German poet and dramatist Johann Wolfgang von Goethe of the longing for the warm and sunny south which the lemon tree epitomises. The generic name is the Latin word for some other plant, but it was applied by Linnaeus to this genus which also includes oranges, limes and grapefruit. The lemon is a variety of citron which was first known to the Europeans as the Median apple, having been brought originally from Media (an ancient region south west of the Caspian Sea):

> Nor be the citron, Media's boast unsung
> Though harsh the juice and lingering on the tongue.

In Christian art the lemon is an attribute of the Virgin Mary. It is sometimes depicted as the fruit of the Tree of Knowledge and Evil.

Oil of lemon, obtained from the fresh rind of the fruit, is used in perfumery and to give an agreeable taste to medicine. **Angelica** root, gold and lemon juice was given as an antidote against the plague, and distilled water drawn from the inner pulp of the fruit was used to clear spots and freckles and to prevent scurvy on long voyages. A general remedy for scabs and itches was to sprinkle powder of brimstone on half a lemon, roast it and rub it into the affected part. Apparently it was very good for crab lice, too.

The fruit is very popular today for flavouring and garnishing a variety of drinks, puddings, vegetables, meat and fish dishes. The juice is used in curing colds and is a useful item in a slimmer's diet.

The lemon is the birthday plant for 11 January, symbolizing discretion, pleasant thoughts and zest. Lemon blossom is the birthday flower for 12 January, symbolizing love's fidelity.

Leopardsbane
Doronicum pardalianches

The generic name *doronium* derives from the Arabic *doronigi* or *doronakti*. The species is alleged to take its name from Greek *pardalio*, leopard, and *agcho*, strangle, because the plant was formerly used to destroy wild animals. Conrad Gesner, the sixteenth-century Swiss naturalist, is said to have shortened his own life by conducting experiments with various plants on his own body. In the *Historia Plantarus* it is recorded that he took some leopardsbane in the morning, fasted, and two hours later wrote to a friend commenting on his excellent state of health. Approximately one hour later he was taken ill and died. Nevertheless, Gerard, the Elizabethan gardener, grew the plant in his garden, was quite sceptical about the claims made against the *Dornicum*, as it was known at the time, and wrote of instances when it had been eaten with great relish and lasting enjoyment!

Writing in *A New Herball* William Turner (1508–68), 'the father of British botany', observed 'the Arabian commendeth this herbe very much agaynst diseases of the herte, and holdes that is goode agaynst poyson and venome'. Traditionally, however, it is an ingredient for a witch's brew:

> I've been plucking (plants among) . . .
> Hemlock, hanbane, adders tongue,
> Nightshade, moonwort, leopards bane.

Lettuce
Lactuca sativa

The generic name is derived from Latin *lac*, milk, which the juice of the plant resembles in colour:

> Lettuce of lac derivyed is perchaunce;
> For milk it hath or yeveth abundaunce.

There are several flowering varieties. The lettuce probably came to England via the Romans, and was cultivated by the Anglo-Saxons who named it sleepwort from its supposed narcotic properties.

It is the Hebrew symbol of the coming of spring, suggesting the perpetual renewal of life and ever-sustaining hope of human redemption. Some superstitious people believed that too much lettuce growing in the garden would adversely affect the fertility of a wife, a surprising observation since the plant was thought by others to be an aphrodisiac. In classical mythology Venus laid the body of her lover on a bed of lettuce, and Juno, wife of Jupiter, is said to have conceived Hebe, who became a cup-bearer to the gods, after eating lettuce.

Early English herbalists mixed lettuce juice with oil of **roses** and applied it to the temples to ease headaches. The medicinal properties of the garden plant are contained in the milk. Twentieth-century herbalists used it to allay coughs and irritability when opium disagreed with a patient. Boiled lettuce was said to help the digestive system and to relieve stomach pains. Applied to the veins, heart and liver, the juice was thought to strengthen them, although people who had respiratory complaints were strictly forbidden to use it.

Lettuce is astrologically under the dominion of the moon. The plant is the birthday flower for 20 March and is symbolic of cold-heartedness and temperance.

Lilac
Syringa

The generic name is derived from Greek *syrinx*, pipe or tube. This fragrant, spring-flowering shrub is believed to have been introduced to England during the sixteenth century from Persia:

For though the bridal cherries bring
Delight with neighbour pears,
The top of magic comes when Spring,
Made vocal by her fragant wares,
Cries, 'Lilac! Lilac! Lilac!'

wrote Norman Gale, while William Cowper (1731–1800) refers to the different shades:

The lilac various in array, now white,
Now sanguine, and her beauteous head now set
With purple spike pyramidal; as if
Studious of ornament, yet unresolved
Which hue she most approved, she chose them all.

Like many sweet-smelling white flowers lilac is associated with death, and some people even today will not have it in the house. In some parts of England it is known as may (**hawthorn**), which may have contributed to this unfortunate association. A five-petalled flower is also a bad omen.

Purple lilac is the birthday flower for 25 July and symbolizes fastidiousness and first love. In the language of the flowers it means, 'Do you still love me'. White lilac is the birthday flower for 24 July, and is a symbol of purity and youthful innocence. **Mock orange** blossom is often incorrectly known as syringa.

Lily

The two lilies described here are not related – the belladonna lily is in fact a member of the daffodil family – but have been grouped here for convenience.

Belladonna lily
Amaryllis belladonna

The generic name refers to a rustic sweetheart – a shepherdess who appears in the pastoral poems of Virgil and Theocritus, and who was later referred to by Milton:

> To sport with Amaryllis in the shade,
> Or with the tangles of Naera's hair . . .

Belladonna means beautiful lady. The flower was introduced from South Africa and the large rosy-pink flowers have a fruity scent.

The belladonna lily is the birthday flower for 22 February. It carries the sentiments beauty, pride, timidity and vanity.

Madonna lily
Lilium candidum

The generic name is a Latin word akin to Greek *leirion*, meaning the madonna lily. It was formerly known as the white lily, and the present name dates only from the nineteenth century. The lily was probably introduced by the Romans, and the earliest English references to the flower are in the writings of the Venerable Bede, who died in 735. He made the lily the flower of the Resurrection of the Virgin, the white petals signifying her body and the yellow anthers her soul. The lily is said to bloom first on the Feast of the Visitation, 2 July:

> From Visitation to S. Swithin's showers
> The lilie White reigns Queen of the flowers.

The lily and the **rose** have long been rival candidates for the title of Queen of Flowers. William Cowper suggested a solution in a poem:

> Within the garden's peaceful scene
> Appeared two lovely foes,
> Aspiring to the rank of Queen,
> The Lily and the Rose. . . .
>
> Your's is she said, the noblest hue,
> And yours the statelier mien,
> And till a third surpasses you
> Let each be deemed a Queen.

In Christian art it takes precedence over all other flowers and is depicted in many of the great religious paintings. It is an attribute of Jesus Christ and the Virgin Mary. In Christian legend the lily is alleged to have sprung from the repentant tears of Eve as she left the Garden of Eden. In Greek mythology it is the flower of Hera, goddess of light, sky, marriage and motherhood. A Roman legend reveals that Jupiter caused Somnus, god of sleep, to prepare a sleeping draught for Juno, goddess of light, sky, marriage and motherhood, who soon fell into a profound sleep. Jove then placed a baby to her breast in order that it might drink of the divine milk that would ensure its immortality. The little Hercules, over-eager, drew the milk too quickly and some drops fell on to the earth. The white lily, emblematic of purity, sprang up.

Although the lily has a predominately religious background a few superstitions were associated with it. In the Midlands, for instance, it was thought to keep ghosts away from the garden. For a man to step on a lily meant loss of purity for the ladies of the household. A profusion of flowers meant that bread would be cheaper, although smelling a lily caused freckles. However, to dream of a lily meant good luck.

The Elizabethans used the bulb to treat boils. Another recipe for the same complaint required forty madonna lily petals to be steeped in brandy and laid rough side up on the infected area. Cakes consisting of juice of the bulb mixed with **barley** meal were used to treat dropsy. The root was used to relieve burns, scalds, erysipelas and quinsy.

The lily signifies bashfulness, celestial beauty, beatitude, chastity, divine nuptials, eternal love, grace, heavenly bliss, queenliness, showiness and sinlessness. It typifies the Annunciation, good works, innocence and the joyful mysteries of the rosary. It is the flower of Easter and the flower of the age of the spirit to come, when men will live in plenitude and love. Astrologically it is under the dominion of the moon.

Lily of the valley
Convallaria majalis

The generic name is derived from Latin *convallis*, valley, and *majalis*, May-flowering. Popular names for the plant today are May lily, Our Lady's tears, ladder-to-heaven and lily-constancy. Older names were glovewort, because it was recommended for sore hands, and mugget, from the French *muguet*.

As lily of the valley blooms in May it was customary to decorate churches with them at Whitsuntide, to which they are dedicated. During the time when Lady chapels were built to honour the Virgin Mary, they and other types of **lily** were a popular decoration. In pagan times the flower was dedicated to Ostara, the Norse goddess of the dawn. The profusion of flowers reputed to bloom in St Leonard's Forest, Sussex, is said to have been caused by the blood of a local patron saint who was wounded while slaying a dragon which had terrorized the local inhabitants. In the West of England, to plant a bed of lily of the valley was a bad omen, an invitation to an early death.

Water distilled from the flowers was thought by some people so precious that it was stored in gold or silver vessels. Both distilled water and wine in which flowers had been soaked were used to restore lost speech, strengthen the brain and heart, and treat gout and apoplexy. An eye lotion was also prepared from these distillations. In recent times valvular diseases of the heart were treated with a preparation of lily of the valley. An essence distilled from the flowers has been used for many years in perfume. Although no details of content or potency are available, the plant was used as a love potion.

Lily of the valley is the birthday flower for 7 September, signifying return of happiness, purity and sweetness as George Croly (1780–1860) wrote:

> White bud! thou'rt emblem of a lovelier thing –
> The broken spirit that its anguish bears
> To silent shades, and there sits offering
> To heaven the holy fragrance of its tears.

Astrologically it is under the dominion of Mercury.

Lime   see **Common lime**

Lobelia
Lobelia

The plant is named after Mathias de l'Obel (1538–1616), who was botanist to James I. *Lobelia cardinalis* was an early introduction (1637) from what can only be described as a very large and varied genus. Queen Henrietta Maria, the wife of Charles I, is alleged to have remarked on the likeness of the flower's colouring to the scarlet stockings of a cardinal, hence cardinal flower.

A blue, American, lobelia (*syphilitica*), known as blue cardinal, was introduced before 1665. Linnaeus gave the plant the unusual specific name because his pupil Pehr Kalm, who had visited America, discovered that it was used by the Red Indians in the treatment of venereal disease. Although the recipe for the supposed cure was later obtained, for the interest of European doctors, very little is known of the result.

The familiar small, blue, trailing or bedding lobelias all came from the Cape of Good Hope, and it is probably to these that Constance Goodwin refers to in 'The Flight of The Rose':

> Roses – red roses – and jessamine white,
> Sunflowers yellow, lobelia blue
> Blossomed and twined in sweet flowerful delight
> Glowing with colours when darkness took flight.

In the language of the flowers lobelia symbolizes malevolence.

London pride
Saxifraga × *urbium*

The generic name is from Latin *saxum*, rock, and *frango*, I break. Many of the species grow in the crevices of stone walls. Country names for the plant include Queen Anne's needlework, because of the delicate red spots traced on the white petals, resembling some design or type of stitchery which are part of the mystery of embroidery. As the plant was said to grow freely in Ireland, particularly near Killarney, it was known as St Patrick's cabbage. None-so-pretty is another alternative common name. In legend it is supposed to have sprung up to comfort a monk named Bresal, who had spent some time in Spain and longed to see its familiar vegetation again.

It is difficult to determine when it was first established in England, because of confusion with a speckled variety of **sweet William**, known in the seventeenth century as the pride of London. A Dr Molyneuxe, writing in 1697, refers to a flower 'vulgarly call'd by the gardeners London Pride; I suppose because of its pretty elegant flower,' which may have been what we call London pride today. Bishop Mant aptly describes the delicate bloom:

> Its disk of white on upland wolds
> The pretty Saxifrage unfolds
> With lucid spots of crimson pied,
> Hence brought, and hail'd the City's Pride.

London pride is the birthday flower for 27 July, and symbolizes frivolity.

Loosestrife

Though sharing a common name, purple loosestrife is quite unrelated to yellow loosestrife and the other two species which grow in Northern Europe.

Purple loosestrife
Lythrum salicaria

The generic name is from Greek *lythron*, blood, alluding to the colour of the flowers, and Latin *salicaria*, from *salix*, willow, alluding to the willow-like leaves. Older botanists did in fact class the plant among the willowherbs. The plant is commonly found on riverbanks and moist ground, as Matthew Arnold describes in 'Thrysis':

> Where is the girl, who, by the boatman's door
> Above the locks, above the boating throng,
> Unmoor'd our skiff, when, through the Wytham flats,
> Red loosestrife and blonde meadow-sweet among,
> And darting swallows, and light water-gnats,
> We tracked the shy Thames shore.

Country names include grass polly, soliders and foxtail. Herbalists past and present use a distillation of the plant to strengthen and preserve the eyesight, and to remove dust and particles of foreign matter. A distillation of the plant was mixed with unsalted butter, sugar and wax and boiled to make an ointment for open wounds; the fresh green leaves were applied to ulcers.

Astrologically, purple loosestrife is under the dominion of the moon and the sign of Cancer.

Yellow loosestrife
Lysimachia vulgaris

According to Pliny, Lysimachus was a king of Sicily who first used this plant to his advantage and later introduced it to his people. A more probable explanation is that the name in Greek has the same meaning as the English. It is also known as yellow willowherb and yellow saugh.

Placed beneath the yoke of oxen while ploughing, the plant kept them quiet; restive horses could be subdued in the same way. By the sixteenth century the plant had an established reputation as a fly repellent, which John Fletcher mentions in 'The Faithful Shepherdess':

> Yellow lysimachus, to give sweet rest
> To the faint shepherd, killing, where it comes
> All busy gnats, and every fly that hums.

In marsh and fenland areas the plant was burnt at night for this purpose. Culpepper wrote, 'the smoke hereof being burned driveth away flies and gnats which in the night time molest people in marshes and fenny countries'.

Herbalists recommended the plant for stopping bleeding from the mouth, nose and open wounds. It was also often used as a gargle for sore mouths, and as an antiseptic wash for the sexual organs.

Lords and ladies
Arum maculatum

The generic name is the Greek word for the plant. According to Dr R.C.A. Prior, writing in the nineteenth century, the common name derived 'from children so calling the flower spikes as they find them to be purple or white, a name of recent introduction to replace certain older and generally very indecent ones'. Other names include cuckoo pint, angels and devils, bloody fingers, bullocks, devil's man and woman, Jack in the green, bobbin and Joan, priest's hood, parson in the pulpit, wake robin, wild arum, calfsfoot, cows and calves, and Gethsemane. The last of these names was acquired because it is said to have been growing at the foot of the cross; drops of blood fell on its leaves, and from this time it has been so marked.

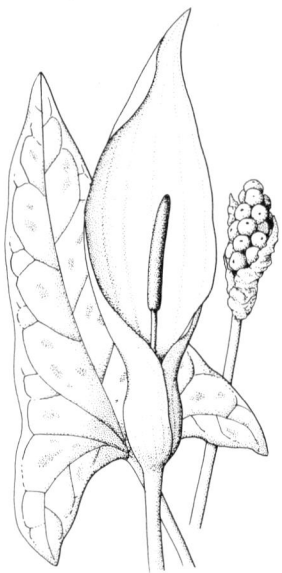

Those deep unwrought marks
The villager will tell you
Are the flowers portion from the atoning blood
On Calvary shed beneath the cross it grew.

Similar tradition surrounds the **redshank**. Lords and ladies flowers in
April and May, after which the familiar cluster of scarlet berries appears:

The Arum there,
Now leafless, lifts its ruby screptre-red
As coral rocks that stud the sea Nymph's bed.

A story attributed to the time of Aristotle, three or four hundred years
before Christ, relates that bears, half starved after hibernation, were
completely restored by eating lords and ladies, suggesting a belief in the
power of the plant to restore life. The plant was also used by young men
as a love charm. To ensure the choice of the prettiest partner at a dance,
they would place a piece of lords and ladies in their shoe, saying:

I place you in my shoe
Let all the young girls be drawn to you.

During Elizabethan times a starch for stiffening linen was produced from the plant. The root was also used as a soap.

Herbalists placed the dark green, glossy, arrow-shaped leaves on the body to treat skin complaints and draw poison from wounds and ulcers. A tiny quantity of fresh or dried root was supposed to be an excellent remedy for poison or the plague. A mixture of powdered root and sugar was prescribed for coughs, and the berries crushed in brandy were given for loss of appetite. The juice of the leaves was used for treating 'stinking sores in the nose, called polypus' (Culpepper). Formerly the root was used commercially and sold as Portland Sago. In the language of the flowers lords and ladies symbolizes zeal.

Lovage
Levisticum officinale

The generic name is said to be a corruption of the Latin *Legusticum*, now Liguria, the Italian province where the plant abounds. An old alternative common name was sea parsley. In the legends and folkore of many countries the herb is reputed to be of help in matters of the heart, suggesting a reputation as an ingredient for love philtres. A tall garden herb, lovage is native to Southern Europe and was introduced to Britain via the monastery gardens of the Benedictine monks. When crushed, the leaves smell of celery. The stalks and leaves, dried or fresh, can be eaten as a vegetable. The unusual yeast flavour of the plant, which gives strength to soups, broths, and casserole dishes, also enhances fish, game, poultry and salads. A fragrant herbal tea can be brewed from the dried leaves, and a pepper made from the powdered seeds and roots. A cordial known as lovage, whose other ingredients were **yarrow** and **tansy**, used to be sold in inns all over Britain.

Herbalists recommended a distillation of the plant for throat infections and quinsy. The leaves, bruised and fried in hog's lard, were applied, hot, to boils, the powdered root was given in wine to help the digestive system; the Greeks and Romans chewed lovage for the same reason. The Scottish Highlanders used to eat lovage in the morning to preserve them from infection during the day. Anne Pratt, the Victorian botanist, wrote: 'The Shetland islanders who eat it as salad, as well as boil it, call it "sirenas".'

Love-in-a-mist
Nigelia damascena

The generic name is from Latin *niger*, black, from the colour of the seeds, which are aromatic and slightly narcotic. The specific name was given because the plant was said to have been brought to Europe from Damascus in about 1570. Love-in-a-mist is also known as love-in-a-puzzle, fennel flower, Jack-in-prison, prick-my-nose, devil-in-a-bush (because the horned capsules peer from a bush of finely divided fringe) and St Catherine's flower (it is dedicated to that saint) from a resemblance between the shape of its flowers and the wheel on which St Catherine was executed.

Love-in-a-mist is the birthday flower for 13 September, symbolizing embarrassment and perplexity.

Love-lies-bleeding
Amaranthus caudatus

> Love-lies-bleeding in the bed wherever
> Roses lean with smiling mouths or pleading:
> Earth lies laughing where the sun's darts clove her:
> Love lies bleeding.
>
> A.C. SWINBURNE (1837–1909)

The generic name is from Greek *amarantos*, unfading – the flowers hold their colour for a long time. Wordsworth wrote about the plant:

> You call it, 'love-lies-bleeding' – so you may,
> Though the red flower, not prostrate only droops,
> As we have seen it here from day to day,
> From month to month, life passing not away.

Although known to Gerard and Parkinson as the great purple flower gentle, the first reference to love-lies-bleeding would appear to be in John Rea's *Flora, Ceres and Pomona* of 1665.

It is the birthday flower for 31 March and symbolizes desertion. In the language of the flowers it means, 'Hopeless but not heartless'.

Lungwort
Pulmonaria officinalis

The generic name comes from Latin *pulmo*, lung, whose shape the spotted leaves are said to resemble. An old Somerset name was bloody butcher, referring in a macabre way to the bloodstained traditional blue apron worn by butchers; the probable explanation is that the flowers change from a rose colour to mauve and blue. As with several other plants that have white-spotted leaves, folklore suggests that they were formed by drops of milk from the Virgin Mary's breasts falling on to the leaves, accounting for the name Our Lady's sile. Other country names include soldiers and sailors, Adam and Eve, Joseph and Mary, hundreds and thousands, Mary's tears, spotted dog, beggar's basket and Jerusalem cowslip – there is a similarity in the form of the flower to the cowslip, but they are not related.

Because of the shape of the leaves herbalists used the plant to treat pulmonary complaints, in the mistaken belief that like heals like. It was also reputed to 'drive away sorrows, pensiveness and to comfort and strengthen the heart'. A lotion distilled from the plant was used to 'wash ulcers in the privy parts of man or woman'. Belief in the plant's medicinal value was accepted without question, for many centuries. Culpepper's remedies also extended to animals: lungwort boiled in beer was considered to be an excellent remedy for 'broken-winded horses'.

Lungwort comes under the dominion of Jupiter in astrology.

Lupin
Lupinus

> Old Time, has made a nosegay. He is welcome to his plucking
> Of tiger-lilies, lad's love, and the tall cathedral spires
> Of lupins.

NORMAN GALE

The botanical name is said to be derived from *lupinus*, wolf, because these plants were supposed to destroy fertile soil. *Lupinus albus* is said to be the first cultivated variety grown in England, and was mentioned by Turner in 1568. The Romans grew the lupin as a food for man and beast. Protogenus, a painter who lived in Rhodes during the third century B.C. is alleged to have existed on lupin seeds (to stimulate the imagination) and water while painting a hunting scene. The ancient Egyptians used lupins in brewing.

Herbalists recommended lupin seeds taken with honey for obstruction of the liver, to encourage the passing of urine, and believed that with myrrh it 'expelleth a dead child'. A meal ground from lupin seeds and boiled with vinegar was applied to ulcers, sores, smallpox marks, bruises and pimples. A lupin ointment, still in use during the eighteenth century as a beauty preparation for ladies, was recommended by Rev. William Hanbury to 'smooth the face and soften the features and make the few charms they possess a little powerful'.

Lupin is the birthday flower for 8 November, symbolizing voraciousness. In the language of the flowers the white lupin means 'always happy', and the rose lupin fancifulness. Astrologically it is under the influence of Mars.

Maidenhair fern
Adiantum capillus-veneris

The generic name comes from Greek *adiantos*, dry, denoting the peculiar tendency of the fronds to throw off water. Pliny observed that if the plant was plunged into water it always remains dry. *Capillus-veneris* means Venus' hair. The plant is also known as Maria's fern or virgin's hair.

The fern was universally regarded as a cure for lung complaints, including coughs, catarrh and breathing difficulties. It was also recommended for jaundice and swollen joints. A recipe for preventing baldness and helping the hair to grow thick and well-coloured consisted of maidenhair, wild celery, oil and wine.

Astrologically the plant is under the dominion of Mercury. Maidenhair is the birthday flower for 22 March and symbolizes discretion, secrecy and the secret bond of love. It is dedicated to the Virgin Mary, Venus and Aphrodite.

Mallow

Common mallow
Malva sylvestris

The generic name is the Latin word for mallow, derived from Greek *malakos*, softening, referring to the emollient properties of the mucilage which it contains. The most frequent country name is cheeses, because of the plant's rounded, flattened seed case which closely resembles a Dutch cheese. John Clare recalls the name, when children in autumn would be

> . . . sitting down, when school was o'er,
> Upon the threshold of the door,
> Picking from mallows sport to please,
> The crumpled seed we call'd a cheese.

Superstitious people used to regard the seeds as a food of the fairies and the plant is still sometimes known as fairy cheese. Mallow leaves have large pointed lobes with an almost toothlike edge, which may explain another name, rags and tatters. A charming Islamic legend of how the common mallow was transformed into the pelargonium is recounted under **geranium**.

The ancient Greeks planted mallow and asphodels (see **bog asphodel**) round their tombs in the belief that the seeds gave nourishment to the dead. An inscription on a tomb bears testimony to this:

> Without, I am nourished by mallow and asphodels,
> Within, I am filled with the bones of the dead.

Herbalists recommended that washing the head with mallow leaves and flowers over a long period prevented baldness. Michael Drayton, in his 'Polyolbion', gives a long list of plants prized for their medicinal virtues, including mallow:

> The med'cinable mallow here,
> Assuaging sudden tumours.

The leaves, boiled in wine and water, were 'very convenient for agues'; placed over the eyes, they were said to relieve irritation and pain from wasp stings. A mixture of the seed in milk was used for chest complaints. Poultices made from boiled mallow leaves and **barley** meal were used to soothe inflamed testicles. The juice of the plant was used to induce childbirth or, more specifically, a speedy delivery. Mallow flowers boiled in oil or water were recommended as a gargle to relieve sore throats. Superstitious people took a concoction of boiled mallow roots and raisins early in the morning as a temporary protection against evil – the effect lasting for one day only.

Astrologically, the mallow is assigned to Venus. In the language of the flowers it symbolizes mildness and beneficence.

Marsh mallow
Althaea officinalis

The generic name is derived from Greek *althaia*, cure. The healing powers of both the seeds and flowers of the plant were well known to the ancients. An old name for the marsh mallow was mortification plant, as the roots were used to check mortification of the flesh in the form of an infusion 'injected into the body through the orifices'. During this century the powdered root, as well as the leaves and flowers, were made into poultices, and the root alone was used in the treatment of lung, bowel, bladder and stomach complaints.

The marsh mallow played an unusual role in less sophisticated times. When people were accused of a crime they used to have to undergo a trial by ordeal to prove their innocence. However, if one was of poor health or of delicate appearance one was excused the rigours of combat for what must have been considered the less fearful experience of grasping a red-hot iron. If no burns appeared on the hand it was seen as proof of innocence. The so-called trial was held in a church during mass. An inspection of the prisoner was made by the clergy only, which enabled the accused, shielded by friends, to coat his hands with a substance consisting of marsh mallow, fleabane and white of egg, which was said to protect the skin from burning.

Until fairly recent times the root of the plant was used in the production of the confection called marsh mallow – it is now made synthetically. Marsh mallow is the birthday flower for 5 February, symbolizing bachelorhood, beneficence and consent, and is assigned to Venus.

Maple   see **Field maple**

Marestail
Hippuris vulgaris

The generic name is Greek and signifies a mare's tail – the plant has an erect, jointed stem which is branched at the base only and tapers to a point. It is sometimes confused with the horsetail (*Equisetum*), which does not bear any flowers. Horsetail juice was used by herbalists to stop internal and external bleeding and to treat ulcers. A quantity of the distilled water taken two or three times eased 'disagreeable sensation of the bowels'. Warm juice applied to the genital organs or anus was said to cure any inflammation.

Marigold

> Nor shall the marigold unmentioned die,
> Which Acis once founded out in Sicily;
> She Phoebus loves, and from him draws his hue,
> And ever keeps his golden beams in view.

Marigold
Calendula officinalis

The generic name is from Latin *calendae*, the first day of the month, because marigolds can be found flowering somewhere in every month of the year. Older writers claim that the marigold is so called in honour of the Virgin Mary. John Gay (1685–1732), poet and author of *The Beggar's Opera*, in his 'Pastoral' asks:

> What flower is that which bears the Virgin's name,
> The richest metal added to the name?

A native of India, the marigold was already familiar in the thirteenth century, as evidenced by numerous references in medical manuscripts. Thomas Hyall, writing in 1577, refers to marigolds as husband's dyall, 'in that the same shewth to them both the morning and evening tide'. William Shakespeare said 'the Marigold goes to bed with the sun and with him rises weeping'. A reference to the sun was also made by Charles I, in a couplet written when he was imprisoned in Carisbrooke Castle:

> The Marigold observes the Sun
> More than my subjects me have done . . .

Other country names for the flower are gold ruddes, jackanapes-on-horseback and summer's bride.

A love salve consisting of **marjoram**, **thyme**, **wormwood**, marigold, honey and white vinegar was prepared for St Luke's Day, 18 October (St Luke was regarded as a lucky saint for lovers). Anyone wishing to dream of their future spouse had to anoint their breasts, hips and stomach with the ointment. While lying down in bed the following rhyme had to be repeated three times:

> St Luke, St Luke, be kind to me,
> In dreams let me my true love see!

Herbalists recommended the juice of the leaves mixed with vinegar to soothe swellings, and the flowers, fresh or dried, in possets and broths. Marigold was also used as a cleansing herb for smallpox, and a tisane made from the flowers was thought to be helpful to people suffering from catarrh. According to Culpepper a poultice made of 'dry flowers in powder, hog's grease, turpentine and resin, applied to the breast, strengthens and succours the heart infinitely in fevers, whether pestilential or not'. Our ancestors believed the plant could 'drive evil humour out of the head'. Modern herbalists recommend an infusion of marigold for indigestion, gall bladder disorders and the complexion. The flower petals give both colour and flavour to salads and omelettes, and a yellow dye can be produced from them.

Marigold is the birthday flower for 15 January, symbolic of cruelty in love, grief and pain. Astrologically it is assigned to the sun, and the zodiac sign of Leo. As a flower of the sun, it was considered very lucky in the home. Almost all yellow flowers were considered to be protective, as they reflected the sunlight. The flower is now dedicated to Lady Day, 25 March, although it was formerly used as a decorative flower for the festivals of ancient gods. A bouquet of marigold and **poppies** expresses sympathy and lightened cares. When the flower is mixed with others it marks the thread of life made up of joys and sorrows.

French marigold
Tagetes patula

The generic name is derived from Tages, who in Etruscan mythology was the grandson of Jupiter; he was a boy of great widsom who is said to have instructed the Etruscans in the art of augury. The plant originated in Mexico, and it is thought that the Huguenots brought it from Europe to England. According to some sources it is said to have first bloomed in this country on 24 August the year after the Massacre of St Bartholomew's Eve in 1572, when 30,000 Huguenots were murdered in France.

In spite of its unpleasant odour, the plant eventually became a popular garden flower, although often admired at a respectable distance. Early records mention the distrust it aroused, mainly on the grounds that anything that smelt so disagreeable must be poisonous.

The French marigold is the birthday flower for 29 May, symbolizing jealousy.

Marjoram
Origanum

The generic name is derived from two Greek words: *oros*, mountain, and *ganos*, joy; this is said to be from a romantic idea that the 'plants are as a crown of rejoicing to the heights on which they grow'. The plant is also known as oregano, and joy of the mountain. Several species exist. The winter or pot marjoram (*O. onites*) is relatively hardy; its date of introduction is not known. The sweet marjoram (*O. majorana*), an annual, was a favourite of the ancient Greeks and has been cultivated in England since the fourteenth century. Our native wild marjoram (*O. vulgare*), as fragrant and as useful as the garden varieties, grows on English hillsides.

The ancient Greeks crowned newly married couples with wreaths of marjoram because it was thought to have been raised by Venus and to have derived its pleasant fragrance from her touch. They also planted it on graves in the belief that if it flourished it was a good omen for the future life of the occupant. In England, every spring or prime, as Spenser describes it, witches were said to purify themselves in a bath containing herbs:

> Till on a day (that day is every prime),
> When witches wont do penance for their crime
> I chaunst to see her in her proper hew,
> Bathing herself in origane and thyme.

The Tudors liked it as a strewing herb. Later, marjoram juice was used to clean furniture. In thundery weather, a bunch of the herb was placed by milk containers to prevent the contents turning sour. The flower heads yield a dye that is purple on wool and brown on linen.

All the marjoram species were used medicinally for a variety of complaints. Powdered marjoram sniffed up the nose 'provoked sneezing' and thus 'purgeth the brain'. Mixed with honey, it was used to remove bruises and marks on the skin. A strong aromatic oil was extracted from the herb and applied to stiff joints and muscles. The juice was said to relieve toothache and earache, and to act as a hair restorer. Dried marjoram leaves were used for poultices. Wild marjoram was said to be an antidote for **hemlock**, **henbane** or opium (see **opium poppy**). It is an excellent culinary herb in soups and salads, in meat, egg, cheese and fish dishes, and is used particularly in certain Italian recipes.

Astrologically marjoram is under the dominion of Mercury. It is the birthday flower for 1 June, symbolizing blushes.

Marsh marigold
Caltha palustris

The generic name is from Greek *calthus*, cup, which the flower resembles; *palustris* means marsh-growing, in reference to the plant's habitat. Country names include kingcup, mollyblobs, water caltrops, May blobs, horse blobs, water dragon, water blabs, meadow rout and Mary-bud. It is unrelated to the real marigolds, although they derive their common name from the same source: all these flowers were used in church festivals during the Middle Ages as an emblem of the Virgin Mary. Shakespeare refers to them by one of the alternative names:

> Winking Marybuds begin
> To ope their golden eyes . . .

and John Clare, in 'Sport in the Meadow' by yet another:

> And water blabs and all their golden kin
> Crowd round the shallows by the striding brig.

Superstitious people used to believe it was unlucky to take the flower into the house before 1 May, although in some counties it was used as a decoration on May Day. The flowers were arranged in bunches and hung upside down in the house or woven into garlands and wreaths to festoon the doors and entrances to homes.

For culinary purposes the leaves can be cooked and eaten as spinach. Pickled in vinegar, the flower buds taste like capers. The flowers, mixed with alum, produce a strong yellow dye.

Marsh marigold is the birthday flower for 10 March, symbolizing brilliancy. In the language of the flowers it means, 'I wish I were rich'.

Meadow buttercup
Ranunculus acris

Buttercups and daisies,
Oh, the pretty flowers;
Come ere the Springtime,
To tell of sunny hours.

MARY HOWITT (1799–1888)

The generic name is derived from Latin *rana*, frog, because the numerous members of this genus like a similar habitat. *Acris* is a Greek derivative, meaning bitter. All the Ranunculaceae, the buttercup family, have acrid poisonous properties and tend to be avoided by cattle. Country names for the plant include crowfoot, bachelors buttons, (shared, as mentioned before, with several other plants) and crazy, as many people believed the plant caused madness. Shakespeare's 'cuckoo-buds of yellow' are thought to be buttercups.

The name buttercup does suggest obvious associations. Irish farmers rubbed their cows' udders with the flower on May Day in the belief that it increased the milk yield. Today, children still hold the flower under each other's chins to discover who likes butter – a yellow reflection is supposed to reveal the ones who do! Making buttercup and daisy chains is a quiet country pastime that has been played on sunny days, amusing children and adults, for hundreds of years.

Buttercup is the birthday flower for 18 September. It symbolizes childishness, ingratitude, mockery, riches and spite.

Meadow cranesbill
Geranium pratense

For the derivation of the generic name see **geranium**. Old common names include king's hood, Odin's flower, Odin's grace and blue basins, although the Elizabethans preferred crowfoot cranes-bill.

All the cranesbill family had a good reputation as herbs for healing wounds. Taken in wine, meadow cranesbill was said to deal with internal bleeding and bruising, and a fomentation of the plant was applied to fresh wounds and ulcers. Powdered and taken over a long period, the herb was recommended in the treatment of ruptures, gout and painful joints in young and old. Twentieth-century herbalists recommend the plant as an excellent gargle for sore throats and ulcerated mouths.

In the language of the flowers, meadow cranesbill symbolizes envy. Astrologically the plant is assigned to Mars.

Meadow saffron
Colchicum autumnale

The generic name is derived from Colchis, a place in classical mythology famous for medicinal herbs, where it was reputed to grow in abundance. It is similar in appearance to autumn crocus (*C. nudiflorus*), but though sometimes confused, and sharing the same properties, they are not the same species. In classical legend meadow saffron is said to have sprung up from spilt drops of the liquid given by Medea to restore Jeson to youth. The plant is known by several other names, including naked ladies, naked boys, naked nannies and upstart. Victoria Sackville-West recalls two of them:

Or those pure chalices that Kentish men
Called Naked Boys, but by a lovelier name
Others call Naked Ladies, slender, bare
Dressed only in their amethystine flame,
The Meadow Saffron magically sprung
By dawn in morning orchards in the grass.

The corm of the plant was used medicinally when it had reached about the size of a chestnut, and was thought to be at its most potent after one year. The root is the source of the drug Colchicine, still considered a valuable remedy for gout and rheumatism. An infusion, with the addition of sugar, formed a syrup for pulmonary complaints. The plant was familiar to the Egyptians since 1800 B.C. In ancient Greece Theophrastus, philosopher and friend of Plato and Aristotle, said that it was eaten by slaves to make themselves ill when they had been 'provoked or offended'. The Elizabethan antidote for those who had eaten too much meadow saffron was alleged to be cow's milk, otherwise 'death presently ensueth'.

Meadow saffron is the birthday flower for 3 April. In the language of the flowers it means, 'My best days are past'.

Meadow saxifrage
Saxifraga granulata

For the derivation of the generic name see **London pride**; many of the species grow from the crevices of rocks. Older writers maintain that the name came not from the habitat but from the plant's power to dissolve stones in the body. The pebble-like tubers attached to the roots would, according to the *Doctrine of Signatures*, indicate its use for 'gravel'. Michael Drayton also recommends the plant:

> So saxifrage is good, and harts tongue for the stone
> With agrimoney and that herb we call St John.

A mixture of the root or powdered seed taken in white wine cleansed the stomach and lungs.

The dainty white flower is also known as bulbous saxifraga, breakstone and dry cuckoo. A native plant, its double form has been cultivated and named pretty maids, the flower of the nursery rhyme:

> Mary Mary quite contrary
> How does your garden grow?
> With silver bells and cockleshells
> And Pretty Maids, all in a row.

Meadowsweet
Filipendula ulmaria

> The almond-scented Meadow-sweet, whose plumes
> Of powerful odour incense all the air.

The generic name is from Latin *filium*, thread and *pendulus*, hanging. *Ulmaria* is from *ulmus*, elm – the plant's leaflets resemble those of the elm tree. The cream-flowered plant is also known as queen of the meadows and bridewort, from a fancied resemblance to the feathers formerly worn by brides, or from the very old custom of strewing flowers along the path of a bride walking to church. Two older names, medewort and meadowswete, may have associations with the plant's use in flavouring mead. Steeped in ordinary wine, the flowers were said to give it the aroma of malmsey. Culpepper said that a leaf in a cup of claret would give it 'a fine relish'. Chaucer mentions a drink made from meadwort, called save.

The lapsed office of King's Herb-strewer was revived for the coronation of George IV, who ascended the throne in 1820. A woman held the office and wore for the occasion a white gown, a gold-trimmed red mantle, and on her head a wreath of **laurel** and **oak**. Her attendants, six girls wearing white gowns adorned with flowers and leaves, scattered

various sweet-smelling herbs in the path of the king. William Allingham (1824–1889) wrote:

> There, once upon a time, the heavy King,
> Trod out its perfume from the Meadowsweet,
> Strown like a woman's love beneath his feet,
> In stately dance or jovial banqueting.

Although meadowsweet was widely used, superstitious people regarded it, along with many other sweet-smelling white flowers, as an omen of death and refused to have it in the house. Others believed that its scent would induce a deep sleep from which there was no awakening.

Herbalists recommended meadowsweet tea, an infusion of the flowers sweetened with honey, as a remedy for diarrhoea, dysentery, fevers and blood disorders, to stop vomiting and 'take away fits of ague' (Culpepper). Distilled water of the leaves was used for eye complaints, while an infusion obtained from the dried plant provided both the ingredients for a cold cure and a flavouring for soups. The roots, beaten or ground with meal, were used as a substitute for flour. Apart from these medicinal and culinary uses, the plant has a root which yields a black dye which was very popular in the Highlands of Scotland. July was recommended as the most suitable time of year for digging up the root.

Astrologically it is assigned to Venus and is the birthday flower for 17 May, symbolizing uselessness.

Medlar
Mespilus germanica

The generic name is from Greek *mesos*, half, and *pilos*, ball, in referene to the shape of the fruit, not unlike a giant brown rosehip. The tree, native to Europe, produces a fruit much prized in the past. Shakespeare said that it was only fit to be eaten when rotten. The fruit should, in fact, be picked when it is over-ripe, and can be baked whole, made into a jelly, or skinned and eaten with cream. Chaucer wrote appreciatively of the tree:

> And as I stood and cast aside mine eie,
> I was ware of the fairest medle-tree,
> That ever yet in al my life I sie.
> As ful of blossomes as it might be;
> Therein a goldfinch leaping pretile
> Fro' bough to bough, and as him list, he eet
> Here and there of buddes and floweres sweet.

Various medicinal virtues were attributed to the fruit, particularly as an aid to improving the memory. Powdered dried leaves were sprinkled on open wounds to staunch the flow of blood and heal torn flesh. The stones, powdered into wine in which **parsley** roots had been infused, formed a popular remedy for dissolving kidney stones. The fruit was eaten during pregnancy to prevent 'longings after unusual meat' and, according to Culpepper, a plaster of the ripened fruit could also be applied to the back, as a preventative measure against miscarriage.

Astrologically, the medlar is under the dominion of Saturn.

Michaelmas daisy   see **Daisy**

Mignonette
Reseda odorata

The generic name is derived from Latin *resedo*, I calm, from the supposed soothing effect of some plants of this genus. The poet William Cowper called this sweet-smelling flower the Frenchman's darling!

> The sashes fronted with a range
> Of the fragrant weed,
> The Frenchman's Darling.

Since the time of Pliny, herbalists have used the plant to reduce swellings and soothe inflammation. The superstitious favoured a ritual to ensure success, including the charm: 'Reseda, cause these maladies to cease. Knowest thou, knowest thou, who has driven these pullets here? Let the roots have neither head nor foot.' The rhyme was repeated three times, spitting on the ground each time.

It is the birthday flower for 30 January, symbolic of health. In the language of the flowers mignonette means, 'You are better than handsome', and 'Your qualities surpass your charms'.

Milkwort see **Common milkwort**

Mimosa
Acacia decurrens dealbata var.

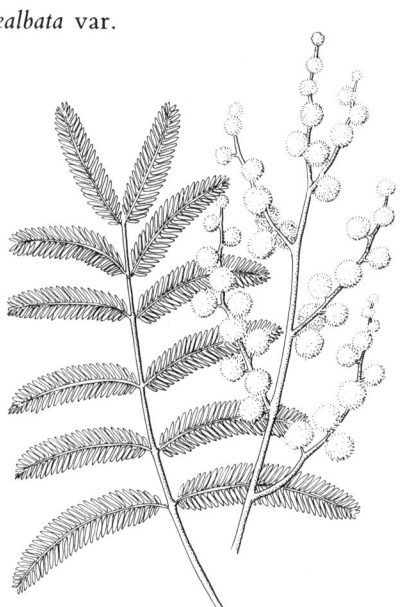

For the derivation of the generic name see **false acacia**; *dealbata* means whitened. Although it is popularly known as mimosa, the correct name of this Australian plant with fluffy yellow flower balls is silver wattle. Mimosa was introduced to Western gardens in 1820. The shrub is said to droop its branches whenever anyone approaches, and the common name reflects the idea, as the plant was thought to mimic the motions of animals.

Although beautiful and fragrant, mimosa is considered by some unlucky to bring into the house. It is the birthday flower for 5 November, symbolic of exquisiteness, fastidiousness and sensitivity.

Mistletoe
Viscum album

The generic name is the Latin word for the plant, derived from Celtic *gwid*. The name mistletoe is from Old English *mistiltan*, from *mistil*, different, and *tan*, twig – because this parasite is so unlike the tree on which it grows. One old tradition maintains that the Cross was made of mistletoe, which had up to that time been a large tree; thereafter it was condemned to the life of a parasite. The plant grows on various trees, particularly **apple** and **oak**. Mistletoe is also known as mislin-bush, kiss and go, and churchman's greetings.

The Ancient British druids venerated mistletoe. Traditionally the plant was cut with a golden sickle and used during rites accompanying the sacrifice of a white bull:

> The fearless British priests, under the aged oak,
> Taking a milk-white bull, unstained with the yoke,
> And with an axe of gold, from that Jove-sacred tree
> The Mistletoe cut down.

After the ceremony the branches were distributed among the worshippers to be suspended from the ceiling in their homes to ward off evil spirits. The druids believed that the berries were the fertilizing dew of the supreme deity. The association of the plant with the pagan druids and their custom of human sacrifice probably explains why mistletoe is never used in church decoration.

In mythology there is a link of sexual significance with the twin berries of the mistletoe. In the classical tradition Uranus was castrated by his son Cronus with a golden sickle. His testicles fell into the sea, changing into blood and foam, from which rose Aphrodite (Venus), the goddess of love. The twin leaves and berries are also symbolic of the celestial twins. In Scandinavian legend Balder, god of light and son of Odin and Frigga, is said to have been slain with an arrow of mistletoe. The plant was dedicated to Frigga, goddess of love, and many customs would seem to have originated from this. The practice of kissing under the mistletoe suggests a belief in its phallic power. It was customary for the man to remove a berry at the end of each kiss; after the last berry was removed the kissing stopped. This pleasant Christmas practice dates back to the seventeenth century, and is flourishing today, even if occasionally aided by plastic mistletoe.

In feudal times mistletoe boughs were gathered on Christmas Eve to decorate the homes. However it was unlucky to cut the plant before Christmas Eve – to hang it in the house before Christmas could only mean death for a member of the household.

> On Christmas Eve the bells were rung;
> On Christmas Eve the mass was sung . . .
> The hall was dress'd with Holly green;
> Forth to the woods did merry-men go
> To gather in the Mistletoe;
> Then open'd wide the baron's hall
> To vassal, tenant, serf and all.

However in some counties it was unlucky to have mistletoe in the house before New Year's Eve, on which night the old mistletoe, which had hung there for the past year, was taken down and burnt and replaced by new sprigs.

One exception to cutting mistletoe at Christmastime was Halloween. Small sprigs were worn round the neck as a witch repellent, but they had to be cut with a new dagger, the gatherer having first walked round the oak tree three times. A sprig laid in a child's cradle was supposed to protect it from fairies. The first cow that calved after New Year was fed mistletoe to ensure a healthy herd.

The Elizabethans used a preparation of mistletoe both internally and externally. One herbalist maintained that mistletoe which grew on oak trees was valued more highly only because it was more difficult to come by but as late as the reign of George I it was praised as a remedy against epilepsy. In earlier times a branch of mistletoe was hung round the neck of the sufferer, but later a preparation was made from the slightly astringent, non-poisonous berries. One cure for epilepsy consisted of enough powdered mistletoe to cover a medium-sized coin, taken in black **cherry** water or beer, for some days near a full moon. The juice of bruised mistletoe was used as ear drops. Country people ate the berries when they had the stitch after over-exerting themselves.

Astrologically mistletoe is under the dominion of the sun. It is the birthday flower for 6 February, symbolic of difficulties. In the language of the flowers it means, 'You are a parasite', and 'I surmount all obstacles'.

Mock orange
Philadelphus coronarius

The generic name is derived from Ptolemy Philadelphus, a king of Egypt who had an intense affection for his brother (which is what the word means in Greek). For this reason, mock orange is dedicated to his memory and is a florigraphical sign of fraternal love. The shrub is also known (incorrectly) as syringa, which is **lilac**. This sweet-smelling, white-flowered shrub was introduced to England during the sixteenth century.

Syringa tea was drunk by Captain Cook's crew on their voyage to Australia. Although the leaves have an unpalatable taste, a tonic produced from them was considered a good remedy against scurvy.

Mock orange is the birthday flower for 16 May and symbolizes brotherly love as mentioned above, and memory. In the language of the flowers it means, 'You shall be happy yet' and 'Remember me'.

Monkshood
Aconitum napellus

The generic name of this poisonous plant is derived from Greek *akon*, dart. In former times it was referred to as blue aconite, and later as Odin's helm, Thor's hat or Tyr's helm, the shape of the flower suggesting the headgear of the fighting gods of Northern Europe. When the Benedictine monks came to these countries their cowl replaced the helm of Tyr in people's imaginations, and the plant became monkshood. The Anglo-Saxons named it *thung*, a word applied to highly poisonous plants. Other popular names were friar's cap and blue rocket.

In legend the poisonous qualities of the plant are ascribed to the foam that dropped from the mouth of the three-headed dog Cerebus when Hercules, performing his twelfth labour, dragged the monster from the nether regions. Aconites sprang up wherever a drop of spittle fell. In classical mythology, monkshood was mixed in the drink Medea offered to Theseus which he threw to the ground, where it fermented until the marble cracked.

In the ancient world the plant belonged to Hecate, the moon goddess of the witches. The 'flying ointment' which was thought to assist witches in their flight contained monkshood and **deadly nightshade**. The combined effect of such drugs could produce a sensation of flying. Under the Roman Emperor Trajan (c. 53–117) growing monkshood was an offence punishable by death, because the dangerous qualities of the plant were well known.

Among other uses the plant was employed as a deadly bait against wolves, and no doubt received one of its other popular names, wolfsbane, for this reason. The juice was widely used in ancient times for poisoning wells and springs, usually as a defensive action against invading armies. The plant had the reputation of being most suitable for poisoning one's wife or husband, but only among the common people; those of rank preferred **hemlock**.

Not all the uses to which the plant has been put have been negative ones. Herbalists, who generally used the leaves and roots separately, applied the roots in particular as a remedy against the bites of venomous creatures, and the shoots against vegetable poisons. During the present century monkshood has been used in the treatment of neuralgia, epilepsy, paralysis, gout and fevers.

Monkshood is under the astrological influence of Saturn and is the birthday flower for 9 September. It signifies deadliness, illicit love, remorse, vendetta and misanthropy. In the language of the flowers it means, 'Your disdain will kill me'. Winter aconite (*eranthus hyemalis*) means lustre in the language of the flowers.

Morning glory
Ipomoea

> Thy silence answers life was mine!
> And I, who pass without regret or grief
> Have cared the more to make my moment fine,
> Because it was so brief.
>
> FLORENCE COATES, 'THE MORNING GLORY'

Ipomors is from the Greek *ips*, bindweed, and *homoios*, like, referring to its twining habits. The seeds of the plant arrived from South America via Italy, and were first grown and described by John Goodyer in 1621: '. . . like a little ball, like those of the bindweed, but of a delicate azure or as if it were a color blew and redd mixed together, with five strokes or lines on the inside, like redd dark crimson velvet'. The flowers, which last for only one day, are at their best in the morning.

In the 1960s it was thought that morning glory seeds had a hallucinatory effect. This was eventually disproved.

It is the birthday flower for 4 August and symbolizes affection. In the language of the flowers it means, 'She loved you'.

Moschatel
Adoxa moschatellina

The generic name, which is from Greek, signifies inconspicuousness, relating to the plant's humble growth – it can be found in shady lanes and banks. Bishop Mant describes the habitat of this greenish-yellow flower:

> There, in the hollow lane, whose sides
> The nature rock o'er reaching hides,
> While from its moss-green fissures well
> The trickling drops, the Moschatel,
> Peep'd meekly from her rocky bed.

Moschatel has several names, such as musk crowfoot, derived from the distinctive musky odour that the whole plant diffuses. The name Good Friday flower seems to have originated from it always being in flower at that time. Five-faced bishop, Town hall clock, glory less, bulbous whiskers and hollow root are all country names of the plant.

The plant is a symbol of Christian watchfulness, because the four petals of the flower face north, south, east and west. In the language of the flowers moschatel symbolizes weakness.

Motherwort
Leonurus cardiaca

The generic name is from Greek *leon*, lion, and *ouros*, tail, from a supposed resemblance to the plant, which is said to be a native of Tartary (Central Asia). Lion's tail is a country name for it.

Known as the herb of life, it gave rise to an amusing saying: 'Drink Motherwort and live to be a source of continuous astonishment and grief to waiting heirs.' Herbalists advised that it 'cured melancholy, strengthened the heart and made the soul merry': a syrup or conserve named *cardiaca* was made from the plant. In a powdered form, motherwort was prescribed for gynaecological complaints and 'to make women joyful mothers of children, and settle their wombe'. Chest complaints, urinary disorders, cramp and convulsions were all said to be relieved by the use of motherwort. More recently the tops and leaves of the plant were still widely used for nervous complaints, many chronic disorders, and menstrual problems.

Motherwort is under the dominion of Venus and the sign of Leo. It is the birthday flower for 25 January, symbolizing concealed love.

Mugwort
Artemisia vulgaris

The generic name comes from Artemis, the Greek form of Diana, goddess of the moon. All the plants in the genus *Artemisia* are dedicated to her. Apuleius wrote, 'Of those worts that we name Artemisia, it is said that Diana did find them and delivered their powers and leechdom to Chiron the Centaur, who first set forth a leechdom, and he named these worts from the name Diana, Artemis, that is, Artemisias.' Nevertheless some sources think the name is from Artemisia II, the Carian queen, who built the famous Mausoleum for Mausolus, which was adorned with the works of Greek sculptors of the age. Country names for mugwort include apple pie, dog ears, mugwood and sailor's tobacco – the leaves were often used as tobacco.

Mugwort was believed to protect against witchcraft, and was credited with many other powers. The plant was highly regarded, as the following lines indicate:

> Eldest of worts
> Thou hast might for three
> And against thirty
> For venom availest
> For flying vile things
> That through the land rove.

Carried in the hand, it prevented the traveller becoming tired. Pilgrims placed the herb in their shoes in the belief that they would have the strength to walk long distances. *The Art of Simpling*, published in 1652, said: 'If a footman take mugwort and put it in his shoes in the morning he may go forty miles before noon and not be weary.' Alternatively one could place the herb in one's bath to relieve fatigue. Mugwort was also carried as a charm against the plague, ague, carbuncles and lightning. Superstitious people vowed that coal could be found under the plant on Midsummer Eve, and even some respectable authors of the period endorsed this belief. Nevertheless Paul Barbette, writing in 1675, says: 'These authors are deceived, for they are not coales, but old acid rootes, consisting of much volatile salt, and are almost always to be found under Mugwort; so that it is only a certain superstition that old dead rootes ought to be pulled up on the Eve of St John the Baptist about twelve.'

Medicinally, the plant has been associated with childbirth for centuries. Mixed with myrrh, it was used as a pessary to speed up birth and the expulsion of the placenta. In his *Polyolbion* of 1622 Michael Drayton prescribes: 'The belly hurt by birth, by mugwort to make sound.' The leaves, dried and powdered and taken in wine, were said to relieve sciatica, while a lotion consisting of mugwort, **chamomile** and **agrimony** was applied to areas affected by cramp. Before **hops** were used generally in brewing, in some parts of the country people continued to use mugwort as it was thought it made beer more intoxicating.

Mugwort is the birthday flower for 3 November, symbolizing happiness. Astrologically it is a herb of Venus.

Mulberry
Morus nigra

The generic name is the Latin word for the tree, although older writers claim that it is a Greek word for fool. However it is also reputed to be the wisest of all plants, as it never buds until the cold weather is past. *Morus nigra* (meaning black) is the common species, though white and red ones also exist.

According to classical legend, the fruit of all mulberry trees was originally white, but was darkened by the blood of Thisbe and Pyramus, whose deaths arose out of a tragic misunderstanding. Thisbe had arranged to meet her love Pyramus near a white mulberry tree. Arriving before him she was startled by a lion and fled, dropping her veil, which the animal smeared with blood before wandering away. Pyramus, on finding the veil, thought Thisbe was dead and killed himself. Later Thisbe returned; finding his body, she stabbed herself in her grief. The blood of the lovers was said to have changed the colour of the berries.

In ancient China the bark of the mulberry was used to make paper hundreds of years before Europeans had any knowledge of the art of papermaking. The bark was mashed up, so that the woody fibres were broken up and pulled apart. The tiny fibres were then allowed to sink through water on a grating where they formed a tangled felt which could be compressed together into a thin sheet.

Mulberry must have been a common tree in Anglo-Saxon times, as a favourite drink, called morat, consisted of honey flavoured with mulberries. The mulberry has connections with Shakespeare, who planted a tree which was later cut down. In 1769, when the famous David Garrick received the Freedom of Stratford-upon-Avon, the key was presented in a carved box made from the wood of that tree. A cup was also made, which Garrick held on the occasion of Shakespeare's Jubilee (Shakespeare would have been 200 in 1704) while he sang one of his own compositions:

> All shall kneel to the Mulberry tree;
> Bend to the blest Mulberry;
> Matchless was he who planted thee;
> And thou like him immortal shall be.

In the West of England the mulberry was a weather oracle – the appearance of the leaves signifies that the frosts are over.

'Here we go round the mulberry bush' is an old ring game in which children join hands and dance round in a circle singing a song in which these words are the title and the refrain.

Herablists applied mulberry leaves, beaten in vinegar, to burns. Untreated leaves were said to stop bleeding from the mouth, nose or haemorrhoids. The juice of the leaves was prescribed as an antidote for snakebite and **aconite** poisoning.

Mulberry is the birthday flower for 19 June, symbolizing kindness, offset by sharpness and wisdom. Mercury is said to rule the tree.

Mullein
Verbascum

Older writers claim that the generic name is from Latin *barba*, beard, from the shaggy leaves of some of the species. Mullein is said to be derived from Old English, *moleine*, from Latin *malandrium*, meaning the malanders or leprosy. The name of the complaint in its medical form, *malandre*, became applicable to cattle diseases (lung troubles among others), so that the plant remedy became mullein or bullock's lungwort. It was also used to treat a disease contracted by peasants who tended the cattle, and was known as clown's lungwort.

Mullein has many other country names, such as candelaria, a Roman name, from the custom of stripping off the leaves and flowers and dipping the thick resinous stalk in tallow to make candles. From this source also comes torch weed. The plant is covered with whitish hairs which, when dried, provided valuable tinder for kindling, explaining such names as fluffweed, hare's beard, old man's flannel, velvet dock and feltwoot. The leaves were also used to make wicks for candles, hence candel-wick plant. In old books the name hag-taper, hig-taper or agg-leaf is used, probably a further reference to tapers, or candles. *Haege* or *haga* was the Old English word for hedge. However, another source ascribes these names to the belief that the plant was repellent to witches (hags).

> The hag is astride
> This night for to ride,
> The devil and she together.

It is also known as hedge taper, high taper and Our Lady's candle and torches. Other names include Jupiter's staff and Aaron's rod, suggesting that it might have been regarded as warding off lightning.

Herbalists used to steep fresh mullein flowers in olive oil and expose them to sunlight to produce drops for earache. A distillation of the flowers, taken morning and evening for several days, was thought to relieve gout. The juice of both leaves and flowers acted as a wart remover, and the powdered dried flowers were taken to relieve colic. Twentieth-century remedies include the leaves, dipped in hot vinegar and water, applied as a fomentation for mumps and tonsillitis, or used as an inhalation. Boiled in sweetened milk, the leaves were used for bowel complaints, and an infusion of leaves and flowers was drunk freely by sufferers from coughs, colds and bronchitis.

Astrologically mullein is under the dominion of Saturn. It is the birthday flower for 22 January, symbolic of nature. In the language of the flowers it means, 'Take courage'.

Mustard   see **White mustard**

Myrtle
Myrtus communis

The generic name is the Greek word for the plant, which was sacred to Aphrodite or Venus. 'Sacred to Venus is the myrtle shade,' wrote John Dryden (1631–1700). According to one myth the plant received its name from Myrsine, a favourite of the Roman goddess of wisdom, Minerva. The reason why the shrub was dedicated to Venus is not known for certain. It may be because it grows near the natural element of the goddess, the sea, or that the fragrance of the flowers and permanent nature of the foliage make it a suitable tribute to the goddess of beauty. Venus is said to have hidden behind a myrtle tree on Cytherea when satyrs disturbed her while bathing, and she is said to have worn a wreath of myrtle when she was crowned after springing from the foam of the sea. Her head was decked with the plant when Paris awarded her the golden apple, the prize for her supreme beauty. The Graces who attended her also wore chaplets of this aromatic shrub. Like the **rose**, myrtle was considered symbolic of love, and the ancient Greeks planted groves of myrtle around the temples dedicated to Venus.

The myrtle leaf is punctured with tiny holes, a reminder of the legend of Phaedra, wife of Theseus, who fell in love with her stepson, Hippolytus. While he exercised his horses in the arena, Phaedra sat under a myrtle tree to await his return; she passed the time away by piercing holes in the leaves with a hairpin. In the Moslem tradition, when Adam was driven out of the Garden of Eden he took three things – wheat, as the chief of all kinds of food; dates, as the chief of fruits; and myrtle, as the chief of all sweet-scented flowers in the world. When Greek immigrants sailed to find a new colony, which they hoped would be favoured by Aphrodite, ruler of the sea, they carried boughs of myrtle to indicate the end of an old cycle and the beginning of a new one.

There can be no doubt that the plant's association with love and beauty led to some delightful English customs. Country brides carried a sprig of myrtle, an emblem of fertility, in their bouquets, which also included orange blossom and **rosemary**. After the ceremony a bridesmaid planted a sprig in the bride's garden, no doubt accounting for the number of myrtle bushes found in old cottage gardens. On St John's Eve in the North of England a girl would lay a sprig of myrtle on her prayer book with the words: 'Wilt thou take me [speaking her name] to be thy wedded wife?' The closed book was then placed under her pillow and if the next morning the sprig had disappeared she would marry her present sweetheart. The leaves were also used as a love oracle. If they crackled in the hand, one's beloved was faithful. In Wales, a myrtle bush was planted either side of the door to keep peace and love in the house: to dig them up was seen as tempting providence. The people of Somerset believed it to be the luckiest plant to have in a window box – however, it had to be planted by a good woman! In the language of the flowers myrtle symbolizes amiability, maidenhood, pleasure, love in absence and victory. It is the Christian symbol of the conversion of the purity of Virgin Mary and of her influence over the unruly impulses of the human soul.

Narcissus
Narcissus

> Narcissi, the fairest among them all,
> Who gaze on their eyes in the streams recess
> Till they die of their own dear loveliness.
>> PERCY BYSSHE SHELLEY (1792–1822)

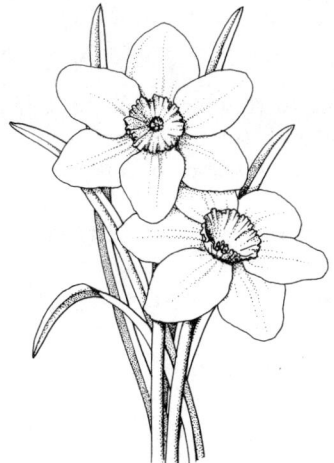

For the classical legend concerning the derivation of the name see **daffodil**. In Greek mythology the plant is dedicated to Hades, the underworld, or to Pluto, god of the underworld, and hence means death of a beautiful youth, or the decay that precedes new life. The Three Fates wore wreaths of the flowers, the scent of which was said to be so painfully sweet that it caused madness, a stark reminder that narcissism, the symbol of egotism and conceit, will be punished in the end. The tazetta or bunch-flowered narcissus are the oldest variety associated with man, and were used as a funeral flower by the ancient Egyptians.

In the language of the flowers narcissus means, 'You love yourself too well'. It is the birthday flower for 28 January, symbolic of coldness, self-love, stupidity and one who constantly gazes at his own image. The narcissus is a Christian symbol of divine love over sin, eternal life over death, and sacrifice over selfishness.

Nasturtium
Troplaeolum majus

The generic name is derived from Greek *tropaion*, trophy, the pillar set in a battlefield on which captured armour was hung – the round leaf was thought to suggest a shield, and the flower a spear-pierced, bloodstained golden helmet. Nasturtium is derived from Latin *nasus tortus*, distorted nose, on account of the plant's pungent smell; the flower shape itself is similar to that of a nose. Because of its pungent taste it was originally named in error, because of its similarity to **watercress**, *Nasturtium officinale*. The nasturtium was introduced from its native Peru, via Spain, in 1597, although this was not the same variety that Victoria Sackville-West refers to in *The Garden*; that one arrived at a later date, 1684.

> And gay nasturtium writhing up a fence
> Splotching with mock sunlight sunless days
> When latening summer brings the usual mist.

The fresh flowers and leaves can be eaten in salads, and the seeds pickled or dried and powdered and used as a mustard. Herbalists believed that the plant would 'purge the brain and quicken the spirit'.

Nasturtium is the birthday flower for 1 November. In the language of the flower it symbolizes patriotism; a scarlet flower signifies splendour.

Nettle
Urtica dioica

The generic name is from Latin *uredo*, burning itch, from the stinging properties of the plant. Nettle is from Old English *netel*, derived from a word meaning needle. Country names include naughty man's plaything, devil's leaf and hokey pokey.

Nettle, **sowbread** and hellebore (see **Christmas rose**) were the ingredients of a popular love potion. Many charms were associated with the plant: one such cure for a fever involved grasping a nettle and pulling it up by the roots, at the same time speaking the patient's name and that of his or her parents. Nettles growing in the shade were considered to be the most effective. Nevertheless approaching a nettle required a little dash and boldness:

> Tender-handed touch a nettle,
> And it stings you for your pains,
> Grasp it like a man of mettle,
> And it soft as silk remains.

A charm for curing poor eyesight was to blow through a hole in a nettle leaf into a child's eye; however this could only be practised by 'a woman who had never seen her father' and before 'she puts her hand to anything for the day'. In Yorkshire, nettles were used in ceremonies to exorcise the Devil. A bunch of nettles was hung near beehives to drive away frogs and likewise in the larder to deter flies.

In Northern Europe and Scotland nettle was used as a thread, but eventually replaced by **flax** and **hemp**. The poet Campbell recalls: 'In Scotland I have eaten nettles, slept in nettle sheets, and dined off a nettle tablecloth. My mother thought nettle cloth more durable than any other species.' Other domesitc uses ranged from a nettle oil to a decoction of the plant in place of rennet for curdling milk. The leaves yield a green dye, and the roots boiled with alum a yellow one. Formerly stone fruit such as plums were wrapped in the leaves, because it was thought that the bloom would be retained for a longer period. The young shoots were boiled and eaten as a vegetable. Porridge, soup, tea, wine and beer can all be produced from this otherwise unfriendly plant.

Nettle tea was said to relieve gout, asthma, bronchitis and rheumatic complaints, and was used as a gargle for throat infections. It was perhaps best known, however, as a tonic to enrich the blood, and was hawked in the streets of London with the cry: 'Nettles with tender shoots to cleanse the blood.' An old rhyme advised all young ladies to take a spring tonic:

> If they would drink nettles in March
> And eat mugwort in May,
> So many fine maidens
> Wouldn't go to clay.

Further medicinal uses included the treatment of stings, dog bites, rashes and gangrenous wounds and sores. The seeds or leaves, bruised and pushed up the nostrils, were said to stop nose bleeds and remove polypi; a leaf pressed to the roof of the mouth was an alternative method. During the Roman occupation of Britain, when the invaders must often have despaired of our weather, the soldiers are said to have suffered from rheumatism, relieving the pain by whipping each other with a variety of nettle. Another source suggests that they used them as a 'warming up exercise' in cold climates.

Astrologically under the dominion of Mars, nettle is the birthday flower for 31 October and bears the sentiment cruelty; it is symbolic of courage and envy. In the language of the flowers it means, 'You are spiteful.'

Nightshade

Black nightshade
Solanum nigrum

> Harebell shall haunt the banks,
> And thro' the hedgerows peer
> With wind and snapdragon
> And Nightshade's flower of fear
>
> ROBERT BRIDGES (1844–1930)

The generic name is from Latin *solamen*, solace or consolation; *nigrum* means black, referring to the colour of the berries. Black nightshade is also known as hound's berry, garden nightshade and common nightshade. The berries are at their most poisonous when green and immature.

Herbalists used the juice of the plant externally for gout, earache and ringworm; and mixed with vinegar as a mouthwash. A cloth soaked in the juice was applied to the testicles to reduce swelling. The juice of the herb and berries, mixed with oil of **roses** and a little vinegar and beaten in a mortar, made an ointment for inflamed eyes.

Astrologically under the sign of Saturn, black nightshade is the birthday flower for 23 January, and in the language of the flowers means 'Your thoughts are dark'. The plant is symbolic of scepticism, sorcery, witchcraft, obscurity and death.

Deadly nightshade
Atropa belladonna

In Greek mythology Atropa was the eldest of the Three Fates: the generic name indicates inflexibility and inability to be redirected. Atropa held the shears which cut the Thread of Life of mortal beings without regard to age, sex or quality – an allusion to the poisonous nature of the plant. *Belladonna* is the old name for the plant, derived from Latin and meaning beautiful lady: ladies formerly used a preparation of the plant as an eye lotion to dialate their pupils. A country name, fair lady, refers to the enchantress Hecate, the Greek goddess who presided over the lower world and knew the names of all the plants, teaching their special qualities to her daughters. Consequently all plants of a poisonous nature were sacred to her. Because of its large black berries it was also known as black cherry, devil's berry and devil's herb. Another name, dwale, is derived from a French word meaning mourning. In Chaucer's time the plant was used in sleeping draughts, hence his remark: 'There needeth him no dwale.'

The 'insane root which takes the reason prisoner', mentioned by Shakespeare, is thought to be deadly nightshade.

The poisonous qualities of the plant were well known centuries ago. Plutarch relates that it was the poison (probably put in drinking-water wells) that killed Marcus Antonius' soldiers during the Parthian Wars. Similarly, George Buchanan (1506–82) recorded that the Scots, under a truce agreement with Sweno the Dane, mixed the juice of the plant with the Danish army's supplies, which so intoxicated the enemy that the Scots were able to destroy most of their force.

Gathering deadly nightshade created problems for superstitious people, as the Devil was said to watch over the plant by day and night. First, a black hen had to be released as a diversion – the Devil would be unable to resist chasing it, leaving the collector free to pick the plant. A collar of deadly nightshade was believed to prevent cattle from becoming enchanted, while a horse that had been ridden by a witch could be cured by placing a wreath of the herb around its neck. Human beings did the same thing to combat spells. The stem, cut into small pieces and threaded to form a necklace, was believed to prevent teething fits in babies.

Medicinally the plant was used as a remedy for neuralgia, whooping cough, gout, rheumatism, paralysis, and diseases associated with the nervous system. It is the birthday flower for 15 July, bearing the sentiment a fatal gift, and symbolizes loneliness and silence.

Woody nightshade
Solanum dulcamara

For the derivation of the generic name see **deadly nightshade**, above. *Dulcamara* means bittersweet, another name for the plant, when first tasted the stems are bitter, followed by a sensation of sweetness. In some old herbals it is called amaradulcis. It was also known as felonwort, originating from the plant's effectiveness in the cure of abscesses, which at that time were commonly known as felons. Country names include poison flower, shady night, snake flower and witch flower.

The bright red berries are reputed to be wart removers. During the present century scaly skin, and skin conditions resulting from syphilis, were treated with woody nightshade.

It is the birthday flower for 19 July and in the language of the flowers bears the sentiment truth. Astrologically the plant is under the sign of Mercury.

Oak
Quercus

The generic name is the Latin word for the tree. The oak is the largest and longest-lived of Britain's native trees.

Our ancestors worshipped the oak as the first tree created and as one of the oldest means of divination by interpreting the voice of the supreme diety in the rustling of its branches. The tree was sacred to the sky and thunder gods, particularly Jupiter, the supreme deity of Roman mythology, and for this reason it was known as Jove's tree. Because it was his special tree it was believed that it could not be struck by lightning in a storm:

> Strike Elm, strike Rowan
> Not the Oak

The Greeks dedicated the tree to Zeus, because his oracle was located in a grove of oaks.

An old New Year's Eve custom was as follows:

> From the wood some oak leaves bring
> That were green in early spring;
> Scatter them about the bier
> Of the now departing year.

Oak trees were frequently used to mark the boundaries of English parishes. It was customary when villagers walked in procession round the boundary, as they did every year (see **milkwort**), to recite passages from the Gospels. Robert Herrick wrote:

> Dearest, bury me
> Under the holy oak, or gospel tree
> Where though thou see'st not thou may'st think upon
> Me, when thou goest Procession.

Many acorns indicate a long, hard winter. In the spring the sign to look for is the oak bursting into leaf, which can be used as a weather oracle:

> If the Oak is out before the Ash,
> 'Twill be a summer of wet and splash;
> But if the Ash is before the Oak
> 'Twill be a summer of fire and smoke.

or

> Oak before Ash, only a splash;
> Ash before Oak, in for a soak.

The druids venerated the oak, on which the sacred **mistletoe** grew; this may explain why people in earlier times feared that felling an oak tree brought about death. For centuries the wood has been used in building, ship building, furniture making and carving. Oak galls, produced on oak leaves by the poisonous secretion of an insect, were formerly used to make ink. The acorn was the staple of the Nordic peoples until replaced by cereals.

The oak is a symbol of England and formed the badge of the Stuarts. Formerly oak leaves and oak apples (galls) were worn in buttonholes and caps on 29 May to commemorate the birthday of Charles II, who is said to have concealed himself in an oak tree after the Battle of Worcester in 1651. A childhood rhyme still chanted in fairly recent times by school-children recalls the occasion:

> Royal Oak Day
> The 29th of May
> If you don't give us a holiday
> We will all run away.

Herbalists used the inner bark of the tree and the skin of the acorn as a cure for lung complaints. A charm for curing gout consisted of taking nail clippings and hairs from the sufferer's leg, placing them in a hole bored into an oak tree, and closing it with cow dung. After three months the complaint was supposed to disappear.

In the language of the flowers an oak leaf is the birthday flower for 24 January, symbolic of bravery, flames, humanity and welcome. The oak tree is a symbol of courage, independence, faith, longevity, fire, royalty, stability, honour and reward.

Oat
Avena sativa

The generic name is the Latin word for the plant. Superstition used to surround the sowing of the seed, which varied in different parts of the country:

> Upon St David's Day
> Put oats and barley in the clay.

and

> Who Janivere sows oats,
> Gets gold and groats;
> Who sows in May,
> Gets little that way.

If spring is so late that farmers cannot sow the seeds until the cuckoo is heard, or the summer so wet that the hay cannot be gathered until the woodcock appears, farmers will experience great losses. This is the explanation for the saying:

> Cuckoo Oats and Woodcock Hay
> Make a farmer run away

An indication of a good crop is a drop of rain or dew hanging from a head of oat on Midsummer Day.

Medicinally, poultices of oatmeal and oil of **bay** were used to treat leprosy and abscesses. Oatmeal taken with sugar was recommended for coughs and colds. A cosmetic preparation for the treatment of freckles and spots consisted of oatmeal boiled in vinegar, and oatmeal still provides a basis for cosmetics and soap today.

In the language of the flowers the oat means, 'I love your music', alluding to the shepherd's pipe which can be made from the straw. The stem is cut to a required length and stopped at one end by a knot, near which an incision is cut to form a reed. Shakespeare refers to the custom:

> When shepherds pipe on oaten straws,
> And merry larks are ploughman's clocks.

In *The Shepherd's Calendar* John Clare refers to another old custom:

> The young girls whisper things of love
> And from the old damsels hearing move
> Oft making 'love knotts' in the shade
> Of blue green oat or wheaten blade.

Onion
Allium cepa

The generic name is Latin for garlic. Onion comes from the French *oignon*, bulb; the Old English name was *ine*. The onion is of great value in the vegetable garden, and to ensure a good crop the ideal day for sowing the seed was supposed to be St Gregory's Day (12 March). It was used as a weather oracle:

> Onion's skin very thin,
> Mild winter coming in,
> Onion's skin thick and tough
> Coming winter cold and rough.

As a love charm, the onion was favoured on St Thomas' Eve (21 December). A girl would peel a large red onion into which she would stick nine pins (nine has always been a mystical number), one in the centre and the others radially, saying:

> Good St Thomas, do me right,
> Send me my true love tonight,
> In his clothes and his array,
> Which he weareth every day,
> That I may see him in the face,
> And in my arms may him embrace.

To be completely successful, the onion had to be placed under the pillow. Alternatively, one could scratch the initials of possible suitors on various onions and place them in the chimney corner – the first one to sprout indicated the future husband.

The use of onions to promote tears artificially is very old: it is mentioned by Pliny and there are frequent references to it by old English writers. Tears, however, do flow naturally when one is near the peeled vegetable. Shakespeare refers to this in *All's Well that Ends Well*:

> Mine eyes smell Onions, I shall weep anon:
> Good Tom Drum, lend me a handkercher.

The ancients used the onion for divining purposes. It was also used as an anti-witch charm, but it would only work, apparently, if cut or peeled. The outer skins of the onion produces a golden brown dye.

For hundreds of years it has been associated with herbal remedies. In *The Englishman's Doctor* of 1608 we find:

> If your hound by hap should bite his master,
> With honey, rew and onyons make a plaister.

A remedy for plague, sores and ulcers involved making a hole in the centre of an onion, filling it with treacle, and roasting it in the embers of a fire. The outer skin was thrown away and the remainder beaten to a pulp and applied to the infected area. A roasted onion held to the ear was thought to relieve earache. Chilblains were rubbed with salt and onions. Bruised onion, mixed with salt and honey, was meant to be a wart remover. Hair growth was encouraged by rubbing a bald patch with honey and onion. The juice of the vegetable was applied to burns and scalds and, perhaps strangest of all, it was alleged that toothache could be cured by placing an onion skin over the patient's big toe! In some areas the juice was mixed with sugar as a remedy for children with coughs and colds, and roasted onion applied as a poultice to draw suppurating boils and tumours. It also reduces swelling and is very effective against wasp and bee stings and it used to be given to people suffering from diphtheria to prevent them suffocating as their throat swelled up.

The onion symbolizes unity, primal cause, oneness, eternity and immortality, and the universe is suggested by its many veils of skin. To dream of an onion means good luck. Astrologically it is under the dominion of Mars.

Orchid

Bee orchid
Ophrys apifera

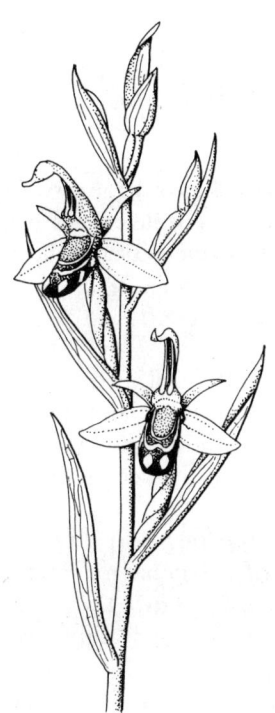

The generic name is the Greek word for the plant; however, older writers claim that it is the Greek for eyebrow, and Pliny, a great authority on natural history, says that the plant was used to darken ladies' eyebrows. *Apifera* in Latin means bee-bearing – honey bee flower is a country name for the plant – because of its appearance. Nature contains many curious examples of mimicry, and looking at the bee orchid one can be in no doubt as to why the flower was so named. John Langhorné (1735–1779) describes the flower and its deceptive appearance as he approached:

> See on that flowret's velvet breast
> How close the busy vagrant lies!
> His thin-wrought plume, his dewy breast,
> The ambrosial gold that swells his thighs.

However, as the poet came nearer:

> I sought the living Bee to find,
> And found the picture of a Bee.

In the language of the flowers bee orchid means error and industry.

Early purple orchid
Orchis mascula

The generic name is a Greek word for testicle, given to a plant with a double tuberous root. Early purple orchid is one of the commonest of our fifty native orchids: its name indicates the colour and flowering time. However, there are many of similar shade and all are rare. Alfred Noyes (1880–1958) refers to their habitat:

> For still as the bell in the sunset toiled,
> The meadow sweet and the marygold
> And the purple orchis kissed their ankles
> And lured them over the listening wold.

This particular flower is the long purple of Shakespeare's *Hamlet*. In the scene where the body of the unhappy, mad Ophelia floats down the river, decked in a garland of meadow flowers, the following lines describe the floral tributes of her deathly passage:

> There with fantastic garlands did she come
> Of crow-flowers, nettles, daisies and long purples
> That liberal shepherds give a grosser name,
> But our cold maids do dead men's fingers call them.

Early purple orchid was also known as dead man's hand and dead man's thumb. The handlike shape of the palmate tubers gave credence to these names and much cruder ones too. Sometimes the plant was referred to as Adam and Eve. In order to establish which was Adam and which was Eve tubers were dropped in water: the one that sank was Adam, and the one that floated Eve.

Orpine
Sedum telephium

For the derivation of the generic name see **biting stonecrop**. The plant's tenacity for life, even when picked, gained it the name livelong, and from the custom of being gathered on Midsummer Eve it was also called midsummer men.

Orpine was once used as a love oracle. A betrothed girl would gather two orpine plants on Midsummer Eve and set them on a wooden plate, from which she could estimate her lover's fidelity: the bending of the leaves to the right or left indicated whether a lover was true or false. An alternative method of divination involved fixing a leaf in an upright position: if on the following morning it was found to incline to the right, the lover would come from that direction and be true; however if it inclined to the left the lover would be unfaithful. Reference is made to the custom in *The Cottage Girl*, published in about 1786:

> Oft on the shrub she cast her eye,
> That spoke her true-loves secret sigh;
> Or else, alas! too plainly told
> Her true-love's faithless heart was cold.

Orpine taken into the house on Midsummer Eve was also said to give protection against illness and lightning.

It is the leaves and juice only that are of use to herbalists. The juice, beaten with oil, soothed burns and scalds, while the freshly picked leaves were laid on wounds, bound to the throat in the treatment of quinsy, and applied to ruptures. Astrologically the plant is assigned to the moon.

Osier
Salix viminalis

The generic name is the Latin word for willow; *viminalis* means long and tender – like osier shoots.

Osier beds or holts were very common in England even in comparatively recent times. Being flexible, the shoots were widely used for basket making and for various kitchen utensils:

> For first an osier colender provide
> Of twigs thick wrought: such toiling peasants twine,
> When through streight passages they strein their wine.

A legend claims that when the devils were banished from the earth, a few were caught up in **birch** branches, which made them suitable material for a witch's steed. The traditional witch's broom consists of birch twigs, attached to an **ash** handle to prevent drowning, and bound with osier, which is dedicated to Hecate, goddess of witchcraft.

Osier is the birthday flower for 31 July. It symbolizes frankness.

Ox-eye daisy   see **Daisy**

Pansy   see **Wild pansy**

Parsley
Petroselinum crispum

The generic name derives from Greek *petros*, rock, and *selinun*, parsley, and was given to the plant by Dioscorides. In the Middle Ages it became *Petrocilium*, which was then anglicized as petersylunge, persele, perseley and finally parsley. With the possible exception of mint (see **spearmint**), parsley is one of our most widely known herbs, used fresh or dried in a variety of ways including salads, soups, stews and sauces, and as a garnish. It was a side dish at ancient banquets, especially the Jewish Passover feast.

The Greeks crowned their victors at the Isthmian Games with chaplets of parsley. Their gardens were generally bordered with parsley and **rue**, from which came the saying, when a garden was only in the planning stage: 'We are only in the parsley and rue.' The plant was originally dedicated to Persephone, daughter of Demeter and Zeus, and was used during Greek funeral rites. Apart from being spread over the dead it decorated the graves:

> Garlands that o'er thy door I hung
> Hang withered now, and crumble fast,
> Whilst parsley, on thy fair form flung,
> Now tells my heart that all is past.

In early Christian times it was dedicated to St Peter.

Both sowing and picking parsley are shrouded in superstition. The ideal day to sow parsley is Good Friday, when the plant is free from the evil influence of the Devil, although in some parts of England it was thought that the seeds had to go down to the Devil seven times before any growth appeared above the soil at all. The fact that it is a slow-growing plant lent credence to this belief. In East Anglia, if any lady other than the mistress of the house planted the seeds, she would become pregnant. The remedy for this lay in the cause, because parsley eaten three times daily was supposed to induce an abortion! Parsley should never be given away by the owner, otherwise you give away your luck, although to help oneself to another person's plant was protection enough. To speak a person's name while picking parsley was meant to cause their death within seven days. Never cut parsley when you are in love, people used to say, because your lover will die. Disaster was supposed to come to a family who transplanted the herb. Two old sayings associated with the plant are: 'Only the wicked can grow parsley' and 'Parsley flourishes where the Missus is master', neither of which could be regarded as encouraging reasons for having a plentiful supply of the herb.

Parsley chewed after drinking is said to disguise the smell of alcohol. Apart from this socially useful attribute it had a number of uses in herbal medicines. The seeds, sprinkled on the head three times a year, were thought helpful in restoring hair in cases of baldness. Parsley infused in water collected during a thunderstorm was used as an eye-strengthening lotion. The leaves, mixed with bread or meal, were applied to inflamed eyes; this mixture could also be fried and applied to a woman's breast to disperse any hard lumps during breast feeding, and to remove the discoloration from bruises. The juice, mixed with a little wine and dropped into the ear, dealt with any problems in that part of the anatomy. Livestock could benefit also, as parsley was used to treat sheep diseases.

Parsley is a plant of Mercury and is the birthday flower for 30 October. In the language of the flowers it is a symbol of victory, death, feasting and fickleness. Parsley round a **carrot** signifies fecundity.

Pasque flower
Pulsatilla vulgaris

The generic name is derived from Latin *pulso*, I beat. The common name arises from the Paschal or Passover ceremonies at Eastertime, when the flower is in bloom. Victoria Sackville-West wrote of it:

> The Pasque-flow'r which ignores
> A date the moon ordained, but takes its rule
> From sun and rain, as both by chance occur;
> Yet some years by a nice coincidence
> Opens upon our very Easter-day
> (When the sun dances or is said to dance)
> Lavender petals sheathed in silver floss
> Soft as the ruffle of a kitten's fur;
> That pulsatilla, 'shaken by the wind',
> That fragile native of the chalky Downs.

The petals yield a bright green dye, and the whole plant a richer shade of green. The pasque flower was used, as were other wild flowers, to stain eggs, which were later beautifully decorated and presented as Easter gifts.

It is a poisonous plant, whose properties can seriously affect the heart rate. The leaves and flowers, distilled in water, were given as an unpleasant-tasting emetic, although the root itself has a sweet flavour. However any remedy in which the pasque flower was used was said to be more effective when taken by a blonde-haired lady with blue eyes.

In the language of the flowers pasque flower means, 'I have no claims', and it is the birthday flower for 22 June. In folklore it was said to bloom only where Saxon or in some cases Danish blood had fallen. This legend is also said to apply to **monkshood**.

Passion flower
Passiflora

The generic name is from Latin *passio*, passion, and *flos*, flower. The conformation of the flower contains symbols of the Crucifixion:

> The leaf symbolizing the spear.
> The five anthers the five wounds.
> The tendrils, the cords or whips.
> The column of the ovary, the pillar of the cross.
> The stamens, the hammers.
> The three styles, the three nails.
> The fleshy threads within the flowers, the crown of thorns.
> The calyx, the glory of nimbus.
> The white tint, purity.
> The blue tint, heaven.

The flower remains open for three days, symbolizing the three years of the ministry.

The passion flower, a native of southern Brazil, arrived in England in about 1690. It is the birthday flower for 23 June, and symbolizes holy love, religious fervour and susceptibility.

Pea

The peas are all members of the very large pea family, the Leguminosae, which includes vetches, gorses, brooms and clovers.

Broad-leaved everlasting pea
Lathyrus latifolius

The generic name was given by Theophrastus to certain leguminous plants, although the exact species cannot be traced. Linnaeus took it over to name this genus. The common name is a translation of the French *pois éternel*. J. Hulme refers to this annual plant in *Favourite Flowers* as one of the commonest yet most beautiful adornments of old fashioned gardens:

> And where I often, when a child, for hours
> Tried through the pales to get the tempting flowers,
> As lady's laces, everylasting peas,
> True-Lovers-Lie-Bleeding, with the hearts-at-ease,
> And golden rods, and tansy running high,
> That o'er the pale tops smiled on passers-by.

In the language of the flowers it signifies, 'Appoint a meeting', symbolizing lasting pleasure.

Garden pea
Pisum sativum

The generic name is Latin for pea. Some sources suggest that it came from Pisa, the Italian town, where the plant grew wild. In old English manuscripts pea is written as pease.

Various rhymes are associated with sowing peas and ensuring a good crop. In Scotland, peas were never sown until the first swallow appeared, while in England, Tusser advised:

Sow peas and beans in the wane of the moon
Who soweth them sooner he soweth too soon.

or

Sow beans and peas on David and Chad [1 and 2 March]
Be the weather good or bad.

A sign earlier in the year would have indicated whether a good or bad crop was to be expected:

On Candlemas Day if the thorns hang a drop,
Then you are sure of a good pea crop.

In Browne's 'Brittania Pastorals', reference is made to the use of peas as a love charm:

The peascod greens, oft with no little toyle,
He'd ask for in the fattest fertil'st soyle,
And rend it from the stalke to bring it to her,
And in her bosom for acceptance wooe her.

Peascod wooing was a popular country custom. A pod containing nine peas was considered lucky – if placed by a girl on the lintel of the kitchen door, the first man to pass through became her lover. In some parts of the country it was customary for the girl to write on a piece of paper:

Come in, my dear
And do not fear.

The paper was then placed in a pod under the door, and the first man to enter would become her husband. There are several regional variations of these charms.

The pea was formerly used as one of the many cures for warts. Each wart was touched with a pea, which was then wrapped in paper and buried. As the vegetable decayed, the wart was supposed to disappear.

The Greeks and Romans served boiled peas as a light refreshment during the interval in their theatres. Today it is perhaps one of the most widely eaten vegetables in the world.

In the language of the flowers, the pea is symbolic of respect. It is the birthday flower for 17 February.

Sweet pea
Lathyrus odoratus

> Here are sweet peas on tip toe for a flight
> With wings of gently flush o'er delicate white
> And taper fingers catching at all things,
> To bind them all about with tiny rings
>
> JOHN KEATS (1795–1821)

For the derivation of the generic name see **broad-leaved everlasting pea**, above. The sweet pea is a Sicilian wild flower, and the first written records of the plant were made by Father Cupani in *Hortus Catholicus*, published in 1697. It was introduced to England at the beginning of the eighteenth century, the original flowers were rather straggly and limited in colour. The plant improved when Silas Cole, gardener to Earl Spencer of Althorp Park in Northamptonshire, produced the first of the waved sweet peas.

The sweet pea if the birthday flower for 1 February, and symbolizes delicacy and departure. In the language of the flowers, it means, 'Remember me'.

Peach
Prunus persica

The generic name is Latin for cherry and plum; *persica* means Persian. In *Emblems*, published in 1612, Henry Peacham (1576–1642), describes an English fruit garden, confirming that the peach has been established in England for hundreds of years.

> The Persian peach and fruitful quince,
> And there the forward almond greive,
> With cherries knowne no long time since,
> The winder warden, orchards pride,
> The philibert that loves the wall,
> And red green apple, so envide
> Of school boys passing by the pole.

Early herbalists produced a conserve from the leaves and flowers for the treatment of jaundice, while powdered leaves and flowers were sprinkled over wounds to staunch the flow of blood and act as a healing agent. Considerable attention has been given over the centuries to finding a cure for baldness – the bruised kernel of a peach stone, boiled in vinegar and applied to the head, was one of the many remedies dreamed up. The flowers, steeped overnight in warm wine, strained and taken in the morning, produced a pleasant laxative; herbalists use a preparation of the leaves for inflammation of the stomach and bowels, and to treat whooping cough. A tonic was mixed from a quarter ounce of bruised kernels and a quart of honey.

The 'penalty of the peach' was a method of capital punishment in ancient Egypt. The kernels of the fruit are poisonous and were ground up to be eaten.

Peach blossom is the birthday flower for 25 April and symbolizes a bride and the season of spring. In the language of the flowers it signifies, 'I am your captive'. Astrologically the peach is assigned to Venus.

Pear
Pyrus communis

> Who could forget the beauty of the blossom
> And after April, when May follows
> And the white-throat builds and all the swallows
> Hark, where my blossom'd pear-tree in the hedge
> Leans to the field and scatters on the clover
> Blossoms and dewdrops . . .
> ROBERT BROWNING (1812–89), 'HOME THOUGHTS FROM ABROAD'

The generic name is Latin for a pear. Considering the harsh taste of the wild pear, few would suspect it to be the origin of today's delicious cultivated fruit. The tree grows slowly, which is said to have given rise to the saying:

> Plant your pears,
> For your heirs.

The cultivated pear was probably first introduced to Britain by the Romans, although other varieties from the continent came in later. Shakespeare does not seem to have had a very high opinion of foreign pears, as this quotation from *All's Well that Ends Well* confirms: 'Your virginity, your old virginity, is like one of our French withered Pears, it looks ill, it eats drily; marry, 'tis a withered Pear, it was formerly better; marry, yet 'tis a withered Pear.'

Formerly Warden pears, grown at Old Warden Abbey, were used in a traditional local delicacy which was sold on the feast of St Simon and St Jude (28 October) accompanied by the cry:

> Who knows what I have got?
> In a pot hot?
> Baked wardens . . . all hot,
> Who knows what I have got?

The Catherine pear was probably named after St Catherine, the martyr, just as the Martin-pear is the variety that ripened round about Martinmas. The poet John Suckling (1609–42) compares a bride's cheeks to the former fruit in his 'Ballad upon Weddings':

> For streaks of red were mingled there
> Such as are on a Catherine pear
> (The side thats next the sun).
>
> Her lips were red, and one was thin
> Compared to that was next her chin,
> (Some bee had stung it newly).

From the Choke-pear, which has a rough astringent taste, developed the custom of referring to anything that stopped speech, such as an unanswerable argument or a biting remark, as a choke pear. John Lyly (?1554–1606) reveals in *Euphues*: 'He gave him a choake-peare to stoppe his breath.' Prior, on the other hand, thinks that this could be an allusion to the death of Emperor Claudius' son, Druscus, who choked on a pear. Tradition has it that King John was poisoned by an unknown ingredient which was added to a dish of pears given to him by the monks of Swinstead.

According to *A Suffolk Calendar* the first appearance of the fruit indicated the quality of the crop:

> If St Margaret [20 July] brings the first pear,
> Pears will abound for the rest of the year.

A well sunk close to a wild pear tree is said to produce water which will cure gout. Culpepper is alleged to have written: 'All the sweet and luscious sorts, whether manured or wild, do help to move the belly downwards, more or less.' Modern herbalists use them for diabetics, in preference to other fruit which have a higher sugar content. Cooked with mushrooms, a pear is believed to act as an antidote if a poisonous mushroom is accidentally included in the dish. The fruit make an excellent drink called perry, while the leaves produce a dull yellow dye.

The pear is under the dominion of Venus. The tree is the birthday flower for 12 June, symbolizing satire. In the language of the flowers it means 'Do not foget'. The pear symbolizes the heart. Pear blossom is the birthday flower for 17 August, symbolizing affection, and in the language of the flowers means 'not altogether lovely'. The pear was once thought to be a more powerful charm against evil than the **rowan**.

Pellitory of the wall
Parietaria judaica

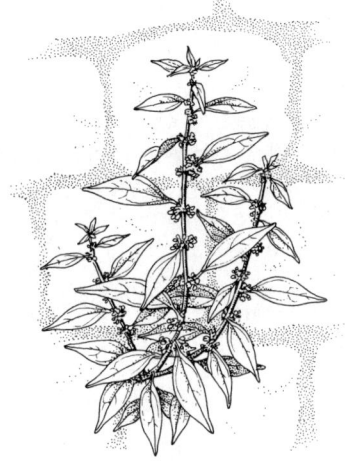

The generic name is derived from Latin *paries*, wall, from the habitat of the plant, which is common on church stonework, old walls and ruins generally:

> Where the abbey's height appears,
> Hoary 'neath a weight of years,
> Where the mouldering walls are seen
> Hung with Pellitory green.

Chaucer refers to the plant by an old English name, paritorie, which was a favourite rural medicine at that time:

> His forehead dropped as a stillatorie,
> Were full of plantaine, or of Paritorie.

Herbalists used a decoction of the herb to ease labour pains and to bring on menstruation. With a little sweetening added, it was used as a gargle. The juice of the plant, held in the mouth, was a remedy for toothache; if oil of **roses** was added to the juice it was said to 'cleanse rotten ulcers and running sores in childrens heads preventing the hair from coming off'. A teaspoonful of the juice, boiled into a syrup with honey and drunk every morning, was recommended to treat dropsy. Pellitory of the wall was also used in the treatment of haemorrhoids, and, mized with goat's tallow, for gout. Farmers placed the plant among heaps of corn infected by weevils, to clear their crop of the insects.

Astrologically the pellitory comes under the dominion of Mercury.

Pennyroyal
Mentha pulegium

The generic name is the Latin word for mint, while *pulegium* is a corruption of Latin *pulex*, flea. Many writers believed pennyroyal to be the Dictamne of the ancients. Virgil wrote of deer wounded by the huntsman's arrows being cured by eating the plant. The legend has often been alluded to by poets, one example being Virgil:

> And whilst I wander, like the wounded deer,
> That seeks for Dictamne to recure his scarre.

Pennyroyal is also known as pudding grass, from its use as a flavouring for haggis pudding or hackt meat; 'pudding' in this context was actually a stuffing for meat.

The plant was grown medicinally, and used for this purpose until quite recently to procure abortions, and to expel stillborn babies and the placenta. It was a natural choice for a witch's garland in the not too distant past: however, having pennyroyal growing in the garden was said to give protection against the evil eye. The plant was applied as a plaster to carbuncles and blotches on the face, and boiled in wine with honey and salt as a remedy for toothache. Taken in wine, the plant was considered to be of 'singular service' to those stung by 'venomous beasts'. Applied to the nostrils with vinegar, it was guaranteed to revive a swoon. Dried pennyroyal was used by sailors on long voyages to freshen their drinking water and destroy fleas in their cramped and generally unsatisfactory accommodation. Nevertheless, the plant's use in the late twentieth century is confined to the relief of colic.

Pennyroyal is a plant of Venus, symbolizing fleeing. In the language of the flowers it means, 'You had better go'.

Peony
Paeonia

The generic name is derived from the Greek physician Paeon, who first used the plant for medicinal purposes. The ancient Greeks believed it to be of divine origin – an emanation of the moon with the power to shine at night. According to Homer, it was with the peony that Pluto, after being wounded by Hercules, was cured. *P. officinallis* is the old May-flowering, cottage garden flower of which there are many varieties. It was formerly referred to as piny or piony. Browne, in his 'Pastorals', mentions the flower in a floral custom long discontinued:

> So did the maidens with their various flowers
> Deck up their windows, and make neat their bowers
> Using such cunning, as they did dispose
> The ruddy piny with the lighter rose.

In Victorian times, necklaces made from the plant, known as piney beads, were worn by children to help teething and prevent convulsions. Children in Elizabethan times also wore them around their necks, but for a different reason: Gerard wrote, 'The seeds of the Peony gathered in the wane and hanged about the necks of children is good against the hauntings of fairies and witches.' This so-called magical plant had to be gathered and administered with care. Like the mystical mandrake, it had to be pulled out of the ground by a rope attached to a dog. The intended patient was not allowed to taste the root if a woodpecker was in sight, as this would cause blindness. The ideal time for the plant to be administered was at night when the moon was at a given phase. Peony was reputed to drive away evil spirits, avert tempests and, by growing near a house, protect the occupants from injury.

In order of importance, herbalists prized first the roots, then the seeds, flowers and leaves. The root was used to cleanse the womb after childbirth, and the black seeds were recommended to be taken night and morning as a remedy for nightmares. Lunacy and epilepsy were also treated with the plant.

Peony is the birthday flower for 21 July, symbolizing anger, indignation and shame. Astrologically it is a herb of the sun and comes under the sign of Leo.

Periwinkle
Vinca

The generic name is derived from a Latin word meaning bind, because of the twisting nature of the plant, which was used for funeral wreaths. Other country names for the plant are blue buttons, devil's eye and sorcerer's violet, the last from the use claimed to be made of the plant by witches and wizards in their charms. Chaucer knew the plant as the parvenke:

> Parvenke is an erb grene of colour
> In tyme of May he beryth blo flour.

In Wales, it was thought very unlucky to uproot the periwinkle from a grave, otherwise one might be haunted by the occupant. In medieval times this association with death was extended to criminals, who wore garlands of periwinkle on their way to the gallows. The plant was used in love philtres and as a counter charm against evil spirits. In his *Herbal* Culpepper advises that the leaves eaten together 'by man and wife cause love between them'. One unsavoury recipe with the same intention consisted of powdered periwinkle, **houseleek** and earthworms, to be taken with meals by a man and his wife.

Herbalists recommended binding periwinkle leaves round the legs to prevent cramp. The plant was also used for boils, toothache and nosebleeds, and more recently in the treatment of diabetes, leukaemia, skin diseases and ulcerated throats.

Astrologically periwinkle is under the sign of Venus. It is the birthday flower of 31 January, symbolizing tender recollections. The blue periwinkle is the birthday flower for 18 August and symbolizes early friendship. However white periwinkle is symbolic of the pleasures of memory.

Pheasant's eye
Adonis annua

The name pheasant's eye is descriptive, and like the gamebird the plant has, in botanical terms, a bright red corolla with a dark centre. In Phoenician mythology Adonis was born of a tree, into which his mother had transformed herself. As a youth he was killed by a wild boar or bear while hunting, and his blood is said to have stained the flower petals red. Revered by the Greeks as the god of plants, he was believed to disappear into the earth in the autumn and reappear for the spring rites. The festival which commemorated his death was celebrated after the harvest. In the spring, quick-germinating seeds of **fennel**, **barley**, **wheat** and **lettuce** were sown in earthenware pots. These little artificial gardens were displayed with images of the god and afterwards thrown into the sea or fountains: their brief existence typified the life of Adonis. A quotation from Shakespeare alludes to this:

> Thy promises are like Adonis gardens
> that one day bloom'd and fruitful were the next.

The plant is also known as Adonis flower and Jack in the green. Some popular old names were rose a rubie and red maythes.
    Pheasant's eye is the birthday flower for 16 September. It symbolizes memories.

Phlox
Phlox

The name is the Greek word for flame, and was used by Theophrastus in reference to some flower of that colour, never since identified. Phlox was introduced to England from America in 1725. It is mentioned in F. Shove's poem 'The Watermill':

> . . . the Phloxes in the garden beds
> Turn red, turn grey
> With the time of day,
> And smell sweet in the dusk,
> Then die away . . .

    In the language of the flowers phlox means 'trying to please you'. It is the birthday flower for 26 May.

Pink   see **Cottage pink**

Plane
Platanus

The generic name is the Latin word for the tree. The London plane, *P. hybrida*, the species most commonly seen in Britain, is a comparatively recent introduction which appeared in about 1670 at Oxford. The tree has taken very well to town life, particularly in London, and is a welcome sight when in leaf or decked with snow.

> The chestnut's proud, and the lilac's pretty,
> The poplar's gentle and tall,
> But the plane tree's kind to the poor dull city –
> I love him best of all.

wrote Edith Nesbit (1858–1924), the poet and author of children's books.

The Greeks and the Romans admired plane trees and planted many of them. Nevertheless in England, from Turner's evidence published in 1578, plane trees were generally very scarce in the sixteenth century. He wrote: 'I never saw any Plaine tree in Englande, saving once in Northumberlande besyde Morpeth, and an other at Barnwell Abbey besyde Cambryge'. However, Shakespeare referred to the tree:

> I have sent him where a Cedar,
> Higher than all the rest, spreads like a Plane
> Fast by a brook.

The tree is the Christian symbol of charity and moral superiority. In Greek mythology the plane is dedicated to Zeus, the greatest of Greek gods, primarily worshipped as god of the sky. The Romans dedicated the tree to the same god in their mythology, Jupiter, pouring libations of wine over its roots.

Herbalists prescribed the leaves of the dwarf plane, boiled in wine, for eye complaints; the bark, boiled in vinegar, was given for toothache.

Plane is the birthday flower for 24 October. It symbolizes genius, magnificence, ornamentation and shelter.

Plantain
Plantago

The generic name may be derived from Latin *planta,* the sole of the foot.
The plant is also known as white man's foot and Englishman's foot,
because it is believed to grow wherever an Englishman settles. Henry
Wadsworth Longfellow (1807–82) uses one such name in 'Hiawatha':

> Wheresoe'er they tread, beneath them
> Springs a flower unknown among us,
> Springs the 'white man's foot' in blossom.

Another name is waybroad, which is of Saxon origin, and a corruption
of wabron or wabret, a name used by Leyden: 'The Wabret-leaf that by
the pathway grew . . .'. In legend the waybroad was a maiden searching
for her absent lover. Eventually she was changed into the flower which is
a very common wayside plant. Since that time, every seventh year, it
becomes a cuckoo or the cuckoo's servant, the dimmick. It is under the
name waybroad that it is mentioned in an eleventh-century book of
recipes by Aelfric (?955–1010):

> And thou, Waybroad
> Mother of Worts
> Open from the Eastward
> Mighty within,
> Over thee carts creaked,
> Over thee queens rode,
> Over thee brides bridalled
> Over thee bulls breathed.

There are several species of plantain; buckshorn plantain (*P. coronopus*)
was used as an oracle to forecast the harvest:

> If dry be the buck's horn
> On Holy Rood morn,
> 'Tis worth a chest of gold
> But if wet it be seen
> Ere Holy Rood e'en
> Bad harvest is foretold.

Ribwort plantain (*P. lanceolata*) was used as a love oracle. To discover
whether a lover would remain true and become one's husband, three
stalks stripped of their flowers were laid in a left shoe and placed under

one's pillow. If the lover was to become the husband the stalks would be in full bloom by morning. If, on the contrary, he was to prove untrue, the stalks would remain blossomless.

The Saxons bound plaintain leaves to their heads with red wool to cure headaches, while the Elizabethans, according to Michael Drayton, used 'wholesome plantain, that the paine of eyes and ears appease'. However, it was as a wound-healing herb that it was held in universal esteem. In Shakespeare's *Romeo and Juliet* Romeo, referring to a grazed shin, remarks: 'Your Plantain-leaf is excellent for that.' W. Shenstone (1714–1763) also mentions a variety of plantain: 'And Plantain ribb'd, that heals the reaper's wounds.' Quite possibly binding a wound with a large, cool leaf did act to some extent as a healing agent. The juice was used for several illnesses. A mixture of the roots and tops was prescribed for syphilis, and the bruised leaves applied to insect bites, ulcers, erysipelas and wounds. Reputable writers recorded that 'When the toad was about to encounter the spider it ate of the Plantain-leaf, and that if wounded, it sought again the same remedy.' Likewise they wrote that it was considered such a healer that, put into a pot where pieces of meat were boiling, it could make them into one whole piece!

In the language of the flowers, the plantain is a Christian symbol of the multitude seeking salvation. Astrologically it is under the sign of Venus.

Plum   see **Wild plum**

Pomegranate
Pumica granatum

The botanical name comes from Old French *pume grenate*, pomegranate apple. The pomegranate was introduced to England in 1548.

In Greek antiquity, it is said to have sprung from the blood of Dionysus, the god of wine. The fruit is an attribute of Persephone, daughter of Demeter and Zeus, as goddess of the underworld.

Historically, the fruit was adopted by Henry IV from the Moorish kings of Grenada as his device, with the motto: 'Sour, yet sweet' – implying that, in a good king, severity should be tempered with mildness. The calyx does resemble a crown. Later, it became the emblem of Catherine of Aragon, the first wife of Henry VIII. It is recorded that in a court masque in her honour, a bank of **roses** and pomegranates typified the union of England and Spain. Her daughter, as Queen Mary, took the pomeranate and white and red roses as her device.

Medicinally, the seed within the fruit and the rind were used in complaints associated with the blood, such as menstruation and spitting blood. The fruit was also used to treat ulcers in the ears and nose, and dropsy; loose teeth were supposed to be fixed after taking pomegranate. A solution extracted from the flowers was claimed to produce similar results. Pomegranate rind was an ingredient in the blackest and most durable writing ink.

Pomegranate blossom is the birthday flower for 10 June, signifying foolishness and mature elegance. The pomegranate itself means concord, the female principle, hope, immortality, love, union and virginity. It is thought by some to be the Tree of Knowledge. Astrologically the plant is under the dominion of the sun.

Poplar

The blinding sky's unkind,
The day has dust and glare,
The poplar keeps the wind
In her cage of light and air;
Makes of her leaves a snare
To keep the wind confined.

KATHERINE TYNAN, 'POPLAR'

Black poplar
Populus nigra

For the derivation of the generic name see **aspen**. In Greek mythology
the poplar was dedicated to Hercules, god of superhuman strength and
vigour, who destroyed Cacus in a cavern on the poplar-covered Mount
Aventine. The victorious Hercules bound a branch of the tree around his
head. When he descended into the infernal regions the excessive heat
caused profuse perspiration on his forehead, which blanched the under
surface of the leaves, while the smoke of the eternal flames blackened the
upper surface, resulting in the dark and light shades of the leaf. Later,
when any sacrifice was made to Hercules, the worshippers wreathed
their heads with poplar leaves. Triumph in battle was celebrated with
garlands of poplar, to commemorate their great predecessor's victory.

The crushed buds yield a fragant substance which was used by
herbalists to treat various diseases. The juice of the leaves, warmed and
dropped in the ears, was recommended for earache, and the seeds in
vinegar for epilepsy. An ointment compounded from the poplar was
used to dry up the milk in women's breasts.

Black poplar is the birthday flower for 11 June, symbolizing courage.
Astrologically it is under the dominion of Saturn. It is the Christian
symbol of the Holy Rood, and in heraldry signifies aspiration.

White poplar
Populus alba

O cool and beautiful
Her leaves of silver-grey
Hang in the wind so cool
In the blind and breathless day

In Roman mythology the white poplar was formerly the nymph Leuce, beloved of Pluto, ruler of the infernal regions. When she died he changed her into the tree. According to Greek mythology when Phaeton, son of Phoebus (the sun), died, his sisters, the Heliades, who wept for him, were metamorphosed into white poplars by Zeus and their tears, which continued to ooze throgh the bark, changed into amber. The ancients believed that amber was formed from the clammy substance which dropped from poplar trees into rivers. The tree was also dedicated to Time, because its leaves appear to be constantly in motion, dark on one side and light on the other, indicating the alternation of night and day.

Herbalists used the young buds, bruised and taken with a little honey, to improve the eyesight. The powdered bark was mixed into a drink as a remedy for sciatica, and the juice of the leaves, as with black poplar, for earache. Modern herbalists use the bark as a tonic to relieve flatulence and indigestion.

In the language of the flowers the white poplar symbolizes resurrection, courage, time and the female principle. Astrologically assigned to Saturn, it is the emblem of shieldmakers.

Poppy

Opium poppy
Papver somniferum

The generic name is the Latin word for poppy; *somniferum* means sleep-producing; Latin *opium*, from Greek *opion*, means opium or poppy juice. Because of the narcotic content of some of the varieties it is associated with sleep and drug taking.

The plant was certainly being used in England for its opium content as early as the sixteenth century, and probably since Roman times, as they were certainly aware of its properties. By the nineteenth century it was being grown on quite a large commercial scale: it is estimated that about 50,000 lb were being consumed annually. A Miss Kent writes in 1823 about the poppy, concerning 'the solution of opium in spirits of wine . . . now called laudanum, or loddy, so much used instead of tea by the poorer class of females in Manchester and other manufacturing towns'. William Wilberforce, leader of the anti-slavery campaign, is alleged to have taken laudanum daily for the last forty-five years of his life. Robert Clive, the military genius who secured India for the British was a self-confessed addict who was later to die of an overdose. Wordsworth would seem to have been the only poet of his day who did not indulge in its use. Patent preparations containing the drug were sold throughout the country under innocuous-sounding names. However the invention of the hypodermic syringe in 1851, whereby liquids could be directly injected into the bloodstream, did regulate what had hitherto been a rather haphazard means of dosage. The commercial interest involved was such that two wars were fought between England and China. However in England's defence it must be said that the full horror of the effects of the drug was unknown to most people at that time.

Opium is produced from the sap extracted from the green seed heads. The seeds within the capsule do not contain opium, but are rich in oil which was used for making bread and for fuel in lamps.

In Roman mythology the poppy is associated with Somnus, god of sleep, who is usually depicted as a youth of pleasing appearance carrying a poppy and a horn from which he dispenses sleep. He is said to have created the plant for Ceres, goddess of the harvest, to help her sleep restfully, because the crops were being neglected due to her tiredness. Ceres is usually depicted wearing a garland of corn and poppies. Cybele, the mother of the gods, wore a crown of poppies, the numerous seeds being an emblem of fertility.

In Greek mythology the flower is associated with Hypnus, god of sleep, who was loved as a benefactor of mankind and as a bringer of rest and freedom from pain. He is usually depicted with his eyes closed, carrying a poppy. His son Morpheus (the word from which morphine is said to be derived) is connected with dreams and is invariably portrayed as a young man with wings, carrying a bunch of poppies, scattering their sleep-producing leaves to the winds. In Christian architecture a poppy flower of formal design often appears at the termination of a bench pew: it signifies heavenly sleep.

In folklore poppy leaves are known as tell-tale leaves, for when they are crushed in the hand they make a crackling sound from which a lover can discern whether he is loved or not. Theocritus wrote:

> By a prophetic poppy leaf I found
> Your changed affection, for it gave no sound
> Though in my hand struck hollow as it lay,
> But quickly withered like your love away.

It was thought unlucky to bring wild poppies (common poppy, *P. rhoeas*) into the house. In fact, it was considered wiser not to pick them at all, as headaches, blindness and earache were said to result from too close contact with the plant.

The red poppy is the birthday flower for 10 May, symbolizing consolation. The scarlet poppy means fantastic extravagance; the variegated poppy, flirtation. The white poppy is the birthday flower for 8 May and symbolizes forgetfulness and sleep. Astrologically the poppy is a flower of the moon.

Yellow horned-poppy
Glaucium flavus

> A poppy grows upon the shore,
> Burst her twin cups in summer late:
> Her leaves are glaucus-green and hoar,
> Her petals yellow, delicate. . . .
>
> She has no lovers like the red,
> That dances with the noble corn:
> Her blossoms on the waves are shed,
> Where she stands shivering and forlorn.
>
> ROBERT BRIDGES (1844–1930)

The word *glaucus* is commonly used by botanists to describe the blue-green foliage common to many plants that grow near the seashore. According to Greek mythology Glaucus was a fisherman who sprang into the sea and 'by transmutation strange' became a sea god. The sickle-like pods waving above the yellow petals set in their hoary foliage give this handsome plant its common name.

Superstitious people believed that the horned-poppy had wide powers. Ben Jonson, in 'The Witches' Song', placed it in unusual company:

> Yes, I have brought to help our vows
> Horned Poppy, Cypress boughs,
> The fig tree wild that grows on tombs,
> And juice that from larch tree comes.

The plant was used medicinally in earlier times, although the root, similar in appearance to the **carrot**, was thought to cause madness, if eaten.

Potato
Solanum tuberosum

For the derivation of the common name see **black nightshade**. The plant is a native of the Americas, which was introduced into Spain in the early part of the sixteenth century; Sir Walter Raleigh brought the plant from Virginia to England in 1586. He first planted it on his estate in Ireland, and its food value was not appreciated in England until about ten years later. For some time after its introduction the potato was regarded as a tropical luxury, as Edmund Waller's (1606–87) lines indicate:

> With candy'd Plantains and the juicy Pine,
> On choicest Melons and sweet Grapes they dine,
> And with Potatoes fat their wanton swine.

The name potato comes from Haitian *batata*, which probably belonged to another tuberous plant, the sweet potato (*Ipomoea batatas*). The latter was supposed to have aphrodisiac qualities, which led to a great deal of confusion on the one hand and no doubt disappointment on the other. It is to this plant that Falstaff refers in *The Merry Wives of Windsor*, when he says, 'Let the sky rain potatoes'.

In some areas the planting of potatoes required thought, particularly in coastal regions where a rising tide was said to be essential to ensure a good crop:

> As tides are affected by the moon;
> Go plant the bean when the moon is light,
> And you will find that this is right;
> Plant the potato when the moon is dark
> And to this line you will always hark.
> But if you vary from this rule,
> You will find you are a fool.

Nevertheless the general attitude was philosphical:

> Plant your taturs when you will
> They wont come up before April.

An unusual competitive approach was adopted in Ireland, where a kettle full of boiled potatoes left in a neighbour's field was thought to prevent his crop from growing at all.

Superstition surrounded the vegetable. It was for a long time associated with the forbidden fruit of the Garden of Eden, and until the turn of the present century it was supposed to be planted on Good Friday to ensure a good crop. A stolen potato was thought to be a useful charm against rheumatism, whether carried in the pocket or round the neck: devotees in Yorkshire thought that it was more effective if previously dried in the morning sun. Warts rubbed with the potato would disappear as the vegetable rotted. It is still customary to make a wish when eating the first new potatoes of the season, based on the old belief that anything newly emerged is quite propitious for having one's request granted.

Potato blossom is the birthday flower for 13 June, symbolizing benevolence. In the language of the flowers potato means poverty and sustenance.

Primrose
Primula vulgaris

But sweeter than the lids of Juno's eyes
Or Cytherea's breath; pale primroses,
That die unmarried, ere they can behold
Bright Phoebus in his strength.
WILLIAM SHAKESPEARE (1564–1616)

For the derivation of the generic name see **auricula**. The primorse is also known as Easter rose, darling of April, Lent rose and golden stars.

In mythology the primrose is the metamorphosed Paralisos, son of Priapus and Flora, who died of grief for his lost love. In plant lore the primrose, like several other flowers, was thought to be a magic key for opening treasure caves, but lost the power once it had been used. The flowers were regarded as protection against witches, and on May Day they were hung up in cowsheds for this reason. In some parts of England it was unlucky to bring fewer than thirteen primroses into the house, because a smaller number would indicate how many eggs each hen would hatch out during the year; in some areas this only applied to geese. Children ate the flowers in the delightful expectancy of seeing fairies, while sweethearts used the flower as a love oracle. Robert Herrick wrote:

Ask me why this flower does show
So yellow-green, and sickly too?
Ask me why the stalk so weak,
And bending, (yet it doth break?)
I will answer, these discover
What fainting hopes are in a lover.

A primrose with six petals was of special significance:

The Primrose when with six-leaved gotten grace
Maids as a true love in their bosom place.

A strange contrast is to be found in a Suffolk custom of decorating graves with primroses.

In more recent times it was the favourite flower of Disraeli, the nineteenth-century Prime Minister; Queen Victoria sent a wreath of primroses to his funeral. Later, Primrose Day was celebrated on 19 April, the date of his death. His old supporters wore a buttonhole of the flower and decorated their homes in his memory. The Primrose League song runs:

O come, ye Tories, all unite,
To bear the Primrose badge with might,
And work and hope and strive and fight
And pray may God defend the right.

The primrose is the birthday flower for 7 May, and in the language of the flowers means, 'Believe me'. It is symbolic of inconstancy, sadness, innocence, lovers' doubts and fears, and early youth.

Privet
Ligustrum vulgare

The generic name is Latin for privet. Older writers claim that the name is derived from *ligo*, I bind, from the use made of the twigs in basket making. Alternative common names are prim, primprint, privy and dog drake.

Evergreen, hardy and quick-growing, privet has for hundreds of years been used for hedges. Victoria Sackville-West disliked privet hedges: 'Plant not the vulgar privet, to your shame . . .'.

The use made of the shrub in topiary is referred to by Gerard in writings published in 1649: 'It is carried up with the many slender branches, to a reasonable height and breadth to cover bowers, arbours and banquetting houses and wrought and cut into many forms of men, horses, birdes and as the workmen list, though at first supported, after groweth strong of it self.' Privet berries provide a green dye for woollens; glovemakers used them to give a black colour to kid. The leaves yield a yellow dye.

In medicine an oil extracted from the creamy white flowers by infusion, and set in the sun, was used to treat inflamed wounds and headaches, while a sweet distilled water from the flowers relieved stomach aches, menstruation and women's complaints generally. A lotion was also used as a gargle for sore mouths and open sores.

In the language of the flowers privet symbolizes prohibition. Astrologically it is under the dominion of the moon.

Purple loosestrife   see **Loosestrife**

Purslane
Portulaca oleracea

The generic name is from Latin *porto*, I carry, and *lac*, milk, in reference to the plant's milky juice. Purslane has fleshy green leaves and pinkish-red stems containing mucilage.

Old herbalists used the juice to prevent vomiting, to relieve coughing and shortness of breath, and to fix loose teeth. Bruised, the plant was applied to the forehead and temples to induce a restful state of mind, and to the eyes to reduce inflammation. Placed under the tongue, it was said to quench the thirst. The seeds of the plant, bruised and boiled in wine, were thought to expel worms in children.

Modern herbalists recommend the herb as a salad plant, for which purpose it has been grown for centuries. The famous soup *potage bonne femme* is said to contain equal parts of purslane and **sorrel**.

Astrologically purslane is under the dominion of the moon. Strewn around one's bed, it was said to protect the occupant against magic, lightning, planets and death by gunpowder.

Quince

Common quince
Cydonia oblonga

The generic name is a place in Crete where the edible quince grows. Formerly quinces were known as coynes in England:

> And many homely trees there were
> That Peches, Coynes and Apples here,
> Medlers, Plommes, Perys, Chestyns,
> Cherys, of which many oom fayneis.

In the Christian tradition the quince is an attribute of Jesus Christ, and is sometimes claimed to be the fruit of the Tree of Knowledge. In Norse mythology it is the fruit of the Tree of Redemption. Nevertheless it was among the Greeks and Romans that the quince was held in honour, especially the fruit, which was sacred to Venus. To send quinces as presents, to eat them with other people or throw them at each other, were all gestures of love. To dream of quince was a sign of success in love. Newly married couples traditionally shared the fruit as a symbol of their love. A passage from *In Praise of Musicke*, published in 1586, declares the 'eating of a Quince Peare to be preparative of sweet and delightful dayes between the married persons'. However, the high esteem in which the quince was held must be seen in the climatic conditions in which it grew. Obviously the quince of warmer countries varied considerably from the English one, which, although agreeable in colour and shape, is better cooked, while its foreign counterpart can be eaten raw.

In 'Eros and Psyche', by Robert Bridges, the blossom is used as a funeral flower:

> And next the virgin tribe in white forth sail'd,
> With wreaths of dittany; and 'midst them there
> Went Psyche, all in lily-whiteness veil'd,
> The white Quince blossom chapleting her hair.

Herbalists collected the down of quince as a plaster for plague sores, as a hair restorer, and to prevent hair from falling out. Quince juice was used as an antidote for poison, particularly that of the hellebore (see **Christmas rose**). A syrup with vinegar added was taken to sharpen the appetite, while green quinces were recommended in the treatment of diarrhoea.

Astrologically quince is under the dominion of Saturn, and the plant is the birthday flower for 6 May. It symbolizes love, fruitfulness, disappointment, scornful beauty, bitterness and temptation.

Japanese quince
Chaenomeles lagenaria

The generic name is from Greek *chaino*, split, and *meles*, apple – an allusion to the erroneous belief that the fruit is split. The Japanese quince was until recently known as *Cydonia japonica*, and is still frequently called japonica. This attractive shrub is often grown on walls, and Victoria Sackville-West writes about it in her poem 'The Garden':

> So for your hedges plant the teasing quince,
> Cydonia many coloured as a flag.
> In sentimental Apple-bloom, full blown,
> Or Knaphill Scarlet wrongly named, that rag
> Coral not scarlet, flown
> Startling against a sky as grey as stone;
> Or, deep as a Venetian robe outspread
> Against a cottage wall, the veteran Red.

Japanese quince is the birthday flower for 21 December, and is a symbol of excellence.

Radish
Raphanus sativus

The generic name is the Greek word for the vegetable which has been known from antiquity. The radish was named by the Romans as their root *par excellence* and was used as 'a stimulus before meat, giving an appetite thereunto'. It is eaten as a Jewish side dish, particularly at the Passover feast. The Elizabethans believed that radishes caused 'humours in the stomach and corrupt the blood'. However, if one had a strong constitution they helped in urinary complaints. Although to sleep too soon after eating them caused 'stinking breath'. Thomas Lupton, writing in *Notable Things*, 1586, says, 'If you would kill snakes and adders strike

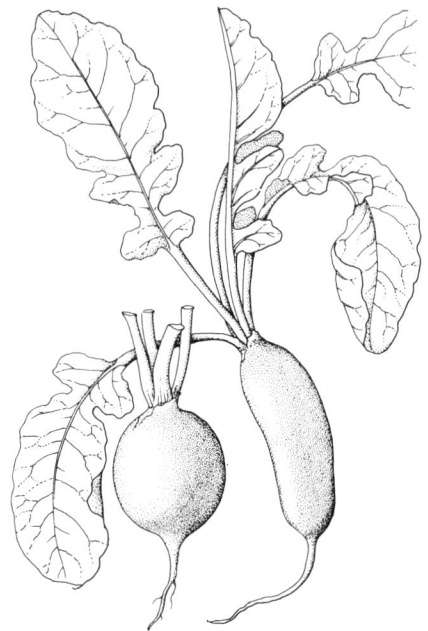

them with a large Radish, and to handle adders and snakes wash your hands in the juice of Radishes and you may do without harm.'

In the early part of the nineteenth century many boys were engaged selling radishes. This is the street cry of the radish boys of Great Yarmouth:

> More disher, more disher, come here, yew raw,
> Spring radish, come two bunch, ee yow-who,
> Come you that got money, whilst I a' got none,
> Buy all my spring radishes, and let me go home.
> Come all yo' pretty maids, that used to buy any,
> For here's your spring radishes, two bunches a penny
> Come all yo' old women, be joyful and sing,
> For here's your old radish boy, now come again
> Here I am both weary and tired;
> For here's my last pennorth, and I don't care who buy it.

Astrologically the radish is under the dominion of Mars. It is symbolic of the coming of spring, suggesting the perpetual renewal of life and ever-sustaining hope of human redemption.

Ragged robin
Lychnis flos-cuculi

The generic name is said to be derived from Greek *lychnos*, lamp, alluding to the flame-coloured flowers. Ragged robin flowers when the cuckoo is in full song, hence the specific name, *flos-cuculi*, flower of the cuckoo. It is the flower of St Barnabas whose feast day falls on 11 June, the traditional time of the hay harvest. An early English calendar of flowers says:

> When Saint Barnabie bright smiles night and daie,
> Poor Ragged Robin blossoms in the haie.

The delightful, tattered-looking bright pink flowers appear in May and June. In his poem, 'Noon' John Clare mourns their passing:

> O to see how flow'rs are took!
> How it grieves me when I look:
> Ragged-robins once so pink
> Now are turn'd as black as ink,
> And their leaves being scorch'd so much
> Even crumble at the touch.

A more permanent passing is lamented by Reginald Arkell, writing about modern farming methods which have done away with the pastures and streamsides where once wild flowers grew in abundance:

> They have cleaned the brook
> Where the ragged robin grew;
> Swilled it and scraped it,
> Till it looks like new
> Cleanly, serenely, the brook flows on –
> But the ragged robins have gone.

In the language of the flowers ragged robin symbolizes ardour and wit.

Ragwort
Senecio jacobaea

The generic name is from Latin *senex*, old man, referring to the plant's characteristic grey seed down. *Jacobaea* equates with James, and St James wort is an old name for the plant. According to Prior, ragwort is derived from German *Ragwurz*, 'a term of indecent meaning expressive of supposed aphrodisiac virtues, and originally assigned to plants of the Orchis tribe'. Another name for the plant, staggerwort, is said to have come into being from the plant's use in treating staggers in horses, a disease of the brain and spinal cord which causes dizziness. In some old works it is spelt staggwort and is thought to be derived from its application to castrated bulls, called seggs or staggs. The connection with animals is interesting, as St James is the patron saint of horses and colts.

In Irish folklore, leprechauns buried their treasure under the ragwort. If one was fortunate enough to keep one's eye on a leprechaun until it had reached the plant, it would be obliged to show you where to dig for treasure. It was generally believed that witches used the plant as a horse for their midnight rides. A similar claim was made for ragweed (*Ambrosia artemisifolia*).

There are several other species of ragwort. Broad-leaved ragwort (*S. fluviatilis*) in particular was well known to our ancestors, and was probably introduced by the Crusaders, who cultivated the plant for healing wounds. Highly valued by the Saracens for the same purpose, it was also known as Saracen's consound and Saracen's comfrey. Old herbalists considered ragwort a valuable remedy for sore throats, quinsy, catarrh and the healing of wounds in humans. Modern herbalists use an infusion of the plant as a gargle for ulcerated throats. A poultice is also made from the plant to treat sciatica.

Astrologically the plant is assigned to Venus. It yields a yellow dye.

Ramsons
Allium ursinum

For the derivation of the generic name see **onion**. The umbels of pure white, starlike flowers make the plant conspicuously beautiful. However, the pungent odour which emanates from it when it is trodden on, or picked, has earned it the name devil's posy. It is also known as wood garlic, broad-leaved garlic, ramsin and ramsey.

Garlic was well known in England centuries ago; its strong antiseptic properties were familiar to the ancients, who also believed it to be excellent against witchcraft and vampires, and to protect children from evil spirits. Roman soldiers thought it gave one courage in battle. The leaves, eaten in butter, were thought to be beneficial to the working man, as an old adage suggests:

Eate Leekes in Lide [March], and Ramsins in May
And all the year after Physitians may play.

The esteem attached to both onion and garlic was perhaps best illustrated by the ancient Egyptians, whose attitude to them was such that Juvenal (69–140), the Roman satarist, wrote:

How Egypt, mad with superstition grown,
Makes gods of monsters, both too well known:
'Tis mortal sin an onion to devour;
Each clove of garlic hath a sacred power –
Religious nation sure, and blest abodes,
Where every garden is o'errun with gods!

Herbalists used garlic to treat worms and dog bites, to bring on menstruation, to ease pains in the ear, to cleanse plague sores and ulcers and to encourage urination. Nevertheless taking too much garlic was thought to give one strange visions. Eating garlic is always obvious to those round about, which caused Evelyn to observe: 'Tis not for ladies' palates nor those who court them.' Popular recipes to relieve such an unfortunate situation were to eat a few cumin seeds on a green bean, or to chew **parsley** and celery simultaneously. Ramsons infused in brandy was used as a tonic.

Raspberry
Rubus idaeus

The generic name is the Latin for brambles, to which the plant is closely related. The specific name refers to Mount Ida where the raspberry was said to be very common and where in classical mythology Paris, son of King Priam of Troy, judged Aphrodite to be the most beautiful of all women. The fruit, which has a delightful flavour, can be used for various desserts, pies, jellies, jams and cordials. It also yields a red dye.

Early herbalists agreed that the fruit made an excellent cordial recommended for stomach disorders, particularly vomiting, as well as for dissolving tartare on the teeth, while modern ones suggest an infusion of the leaves for mild diarrhoea, for promoting sweating in fever, and as a gargle for sore throats. Powdered leaves, in tablet form, are prescribed for relaxation in childbirth, while an infusion of them is said to give relief in cases of painful menstruation.

Raspberry blossom is the birthday flower for 15 October symbolizing envy, remorse and misery. The fruit is symbolic of the human heart. In 'The Cottage of the Kindly Light' Alfred Noyes recalls a charming scene:

> Or little children, with their baskets, trip
> Merrily through the firwoods and the fern,
> And climb the crumbling thistle-empurpled wall
> Around the tangled copse, and laugh to find
> The hardy straggling raspberries all their own.

Redshank
Polygonum persicaria

The generic name is a Greek word derived from *polys*, much and *gony*, knee joint, referring to the characteristics of the plant. It is also known as persicaria. A dark spot marks each leaf, which popular tradition asserts appeared when the plant grew at the foot of the cross – the blood that fell from Christ's wounds marked them for all time. However another source, also with religious significance, says that the Virgin Mary used redshank leaves to make a special ointment. On one occasion she was unable to find it; later, when the need had passed, she found some, and in her annoyance condemned it to the rank of an ordinary weed.

> She could not find in time of need
> And so she pinched it for a weed.

The mark on the leaf is said to be the impress of the Virgin's finger. From that time the plant was said to be the only weed without any use at all. Astrologically redshank is under the dominion of Saturn.

Reed   see **Common reed**

Rhododendron
Rhododendron

The name is derived from two Greek words, *rhodon*, rose, and *dendron*, tree. The earliest hybrids appeared in England about 1825, and many new and exciting species have since been introduced from its natural habitat, China and the eastern Himalayas. It is the birthday flower for 18

October, symbolizing danger and intoxication. In the language of the flowers it means, 'Beware! I am dangerous'. Some species contain a poison which can be harmful to browsing sheep.

Rhubarb
Rheum rhaponticum

The Greek name for rhubarb is *rha*, from which both the generic and common names are derived. For hundreds of years rhubarb has had a reputation as a purgative. In Shakespeare's *Macbeth*, when Macbeth speaks to his doctor about the English army, he says:

> What rhubarb, senna or what purgative drug
> Would scour these English hence?
> Hear'st thou of them?

Other medicinal uses included a preparation of the root to strengthen nails. Distilled water of rhubarb was rcommended to remove scabs, to relieve earache, and as a gargle for sore throats. The seeds were claimed to ease stomach pains. A mixture containing powdered rhubarb in red wine was prescribed for dissolving blood clots and to relieve head swellings, gout and cramp. Modern herbalists use rhubarb in mild cases of diarrhoea. The leaves contain the same properties, but more concentrated, and can be deadly.

During the great trading days with China in the nineteenth century rhubarb was so popular that it was imported from Canton. Nowadays we think of it as a rather less exotic fruit (a vegetable, in fact) that, sweetened, is good in pies, puddings, jams, wines and cordials.

Astrologically it is under the dominion of Mars. It is the birthday flower for 25 May, symbolizing advice.

Rock-rose   see **Common rock-rose**

Rock samphire
Crithmum maritimum

The generic name is from Greek *krithe*, barley, to which grain the fruit bears a similarity. Samphire may be a corruption of the old French name, *herbe de St Pierre*. Crest marine was the original name, that was cried by vendors in the streets of London.

Gathering samphire was a dangerous occupation, as it is frequently found on sea cliffs. In *King Lear* Shakespeare described the hazardous task:

> . . . Halfway down
> Hangs one that gathers samphire, dreadful trade!
> Methinks he seems no bigger than his head.

An old story shows how a little botanical knowledge can serve a useful purpose. Years ago a ship was wrecked on the Sussex coast, and some of the survivors found themselves on a large rock. To their horror the sea began to rise and they debated their chances of swimming ashore before being submerged or swept away. Then one of the ship's officers noticed some samphire growing, and knew that they were safe, because although the plant grows within reach of sea spray it will not grow where the sea can cover it.

This pleasantly aromatic and succulent plant used to be very popular, eaten raw as a salad, boiled as a vegetable, or pickled. It was in reference to the latter that Culpepper wrote: 'If people would have sauce to their meat, they may take some for profit as well as for pleasure.'

Herbalists used the plant in the belief that it was beneficial to the urinary system and the digestion, and dissolved kidney stones. Astrologically samphire is a herb of Jupiter.

Rose

Rose
Rosa

Some sources trace the origin of the name to Celtic *rhos*, and others to Greek *rodon*: both mean, red. The rose has perhaps been written about more than any other flower. Most of our garden roses, which this account mainly concerns, are derived from species native to Asia, from the eastern Mediterranean to China and Japan. The rose is the symbol of the western world and the national flower of England. The hundred-leaf rose is claimed to be the rose of England, though it was not until the Wars of the Roses (1455–85) that it became the emblem of the country. The Lancastrians adopted a red rose; in Shakespeare's words in *Henry VI* part 2:

> Let him that is no coward nor no flatterer,
> But can maintain the party of truth,
> Pluck a red rose from off this thorn with me.

The Yorkists on their part took the white rose as their emblem:

> I love no colours; and without all colour
> Of base insinuating flattery,
> I pluck this white rose with Plantagenet.

The white rose in question was alleged to be a trailing **dog rose**.

A white variety of the cabbage or Provence rose became the emblem of the unfortunate House of Stuart when the Duke of York became James II in 1685. It was said to flower on 10 June, a day regarded by Jacobites with much interest.

> Of all the days in the year,
> The tenth of June I love most dear,
> When sweet white roses to appear
> For the sake of James the rover.

In classical legend, Venus presented the rose to her son Cupid, who in his turn gave it to the god of silence, Harpocrates, to induce him to conceal the weaknesses of the gods. Thus the rose became an emblem of silence. In northern countries it was customary to suspend a rose from the ceiling at meetings where secrecy was enjoined. The saying *sub rosa*, under the rose, was also quoted – people used to have the flower carved in the centre of a dining room or refectory ceiling. Anything spoken there was considered sacrosanct. In 1526 the motif was placed over confessional boxes.

In Greek legend the rose was said to be a beautiful lady from Corinth named Rhodanthe, who was constantly besieged by kings and lords eager to win her love. To escape her lovers she fled to the temple of the goddess of purity, Artemis. Unfortunately her suitors and the people of the town followed, breaking open the temple gates. Artemis, angered by this outrage, changed Rhodanthe into a red rose – the colour represented the blush which spread over her lovely face when she was exposed to the gaze of her suitors.

For centuries roses have been favoured for their fragrance in oils and perfumes:

> O how much doth beauty beauteous seem
> By that sweet ornament which truth doth give!

The rose looks fair, but fairer we it deem
For that sweet odour which doth in it live.

The dew from rose petals was highly prized for making a rare and costly cosmetic for Elizabethan ladies. Rosewater, distilled from the petals, was used for bathing face and hands. In *The Taming of the Shrew* Shakespeare refers to the custom:

Let one attend him with a silver basin,
Full of rose-water and bestrew'd with flowers.

Herbalists used distilled water of roses, vinegar of roses, ointment oil, syrup of roses and dried rose leaves to treat a wide variety of ailments. The red rose was particularly popular for internal complaints, although the white was considered to contain more effective properties.

The rose is the Christian symbol of charity, divine love, forgiveness, martyrdom, mercy and victory; it is an attribute of Christ and signifies heavenly bliss. Carved on the tombs of martyrs, it symbolizes the Resurrection. Being emblematic of a paragon or one without peer, it is assigned to the Virgin Mary, one of whose titles is the Mystical Rose. It is also associated with various saints: Dorothea, Casilda, Elizabeth of Portugal, Thérèse of Lisieux, Rosalie, Angelus, Rose, Ascylus and Victoria. The rose supplies the three chaplets of the rosary (a rosary is made up of 165 beads and each chaplet is fifty-five beads): green for joy, the thorn for sorrow, and the rose itself signifying glory. Originally devotional beads were made from rose leaves.

In the language of the flowers different roses are assigned to different birthdays, each having its own symbolism. Generally speaking the rose signifies beauty, bliss, elegance, flame, fragrance, frailty, joy, life, pleasure, pomp, praise, prayer, pride, secrecy, silence, a star, the sun, wine, wisdom and woman.

The Burgundy rose is the birthday flower for 1 August, symbolizing simplicity and unconscious beauty. The cabbage rose means ambassador of love. The China rose is the birthday flower for 14 October, symbolizing grace, beauty and something that is always new. The damask rose is the birthday flower for 12 August, signifying bashful love. In the language of the flowers it means, 'You are young and brilliant'. The hundred-leaf rose is the birthday flower for 5 August, symbolizing pride and dignity. Lancaster rose is the birthday flower for 5 June, symbolizing marriage and union. A red-leafed rose signifies beauty and prosperity. A red rose is the birthday flower for 13 October, meaning admiration, blushing, death, desire, embarrassment, martyrdom, motherhood and shame. It is a Christian symbol of the vanities of the world, and an emblem of Aphrodite and other love goddesses. A red rosebud is the birthday flower for 7 July, meaning pure, inclined to love, and 'You are young and beautiful'. A white rose is the birthday flower for 8 July, symbolizing abstract thought, purity, silence and virginity. It means, 'I am worthy of you'. A white rosebud is the birthday flower for 6 July, and symbolizes a heart ignorant of love. A white rose dried means death in preference to loss of innocence. A white rose withered signifies a transient impression, and 'I am in despair'. A yellow rose is the birthday flower for 2 February, symbolizing infidelity, and jealousy. It means, 'Let us forget'.

A rosebud of any kind suggests hope, promise and youthful beauty. A rose in full bloom over two buds signifies secrecy. A full-blown rose stands for beauty and engagement. A rose leaf signifies, 'You may hope', and a rose thorn means death and pain; it is a Christian symbol of sin.

Dog rose
Rosa canina

Unkempt about those hedges blows
An English unofficial rose
RUPERT BROOKE (1887–1915)

The specific name *canina*, dog, was occasionally added to a flower to express its worthlessness – another example is dog violet. Some writers believe that the reason why this pretty wild flower was so called was because the Greeks named it *cynorhodon* – the root was supposed to cure the bite of mad dogs. The Romans who concurred, named it *canina*. Canker rose is an old country name for the flower, an unjust expression of contempt because of its small size and delicate perfume compared with those of the garden varieties.

> The rose looks fair, but fairer we it deem
> For that sweet odour which doth in it live;
> The canker blooms have full as deep a dye
> As the perfumed tincture of the roses,
> Hang on such thorns, and play as wantonly,
> When summer's breath their masked buds discloses;
> But (for their virtue only in their show)
> They live unwoo'd and unrespected fade,
> Die to themselves. Sweet roses do not so,
> Of their sweet deaths are sweetest odours made.

Superstitious people believed that if the dog rose was passed close to the eyes in June it would cause blindness, and violent earache if it touched the ears. Stray flowering blossoms appearing in the autumn were taken as a sign of the plague. The rosehips are not only colourful but very rich in vitamin C. Formerly they had an excellent reputation as a remedy for gall bladder and kidney complaints. The dog rose is the birthday flower for 9 July, symbolizing pleasure and pain.

Rosebay willowherb
Epilobium angustifolium

The generic name is from Greek *epi*, upon, and *lobos*, pod; the flowers are at the top of a pod-shaped seed vessel. There are many species of willowherb; the specific name of this one means narrow-leaved. The plant is also known as codlins and cream, flowering willow and fireweed. The last name was given it because it grows up quickly after woodland fires. It was a familiar sight for this reason on bomb sites during and after the Second World War.

Modern herbalists recommend the root, dried and powdered, as a remedy for digestive disorders accompanied by diarrhoea, and an infusion of the dried plant as a treatment for whooping cough and asthma. A tea can also be made from the leaves. Rosebay willowherb is the birthday flower for 11 August, symbolizing celibacy.

Rosemary
Rosmarinus

The generic name means dew of the sea, because the shrub was supposed to thrive best within the sound of the waves. Rosemary is thought to have been introduced to England by the Romans and was certainly known to the Anglo-Saxons, as it is mentioned in the eleventh-century *Leech Book* of Bald (a physician).

In ancient times to wear rosemary at a wedding was as significant as a white flower. On the appearance of the bridegroom the bridesmaids would present him with a bunch of rosemary bound with ribbons. In a quaint marriage sermon preached by Dr Roger Hackett in 1648, entitled 'A Marriage Present', some of the qualities, good or imaginary, are mentioned: 'The Rosemary is for married men, which by name, nature and continual use man challengeth as properly belonging to himself. It toppeth over all the flowers in the garden, boasting man's rule; it helpeth the brain, strengtheneth the memory and is very medicinal for the head. Another property is it affects the heart. Let this *ros-marinus*, this flower of man, ensign of your wisdom, love and loyalty, be carried not only in your hands but in your heads and hearts.' Rosemary also formed part of the wreath which the bride took to her new home in remembrance of 'the dear old roof-tree, which had sheltered her youth and of loving hearts which had cherished her'. After the ceremony, one of the bridesmaids would plant a sprig of rosemary from the bouquet in the garden of the bride's new home, which would in due course be used for her own daughter. An extract from an old ballad, 'The Bride's Good-morrow', describes the customs:

> Young men and maids do ready stand,
> With sweet Rosemary in their hand,
> A perfect token of your virgin's life
> To wait upon you they intend
> Unto the church to make an end,
> And God make thee a joyful wedded wife.

Nevertheless, sprigs of rosemary were also carried at funerals, which may have its origins in the idea that the herb had preservative virtues against 'pestilential distempers'. The smell of the herb would alleviate the odour of a corpse. Herrick refers to the different uses in the lines:

> Grow for two ends, it matter not at all,
> Be't for my bridal or my burial.

Sprigs of rosemary were strewn on the grave by the mourners. John Gay proposed a riddle for naming the plant:

> What flower is that which royal honour craves,
> Adjoin the Virgin, and 'tis strewn on graves?

Naturally the herb was used as a love oracle. To dream of her future husband, a girl would place a sixpence and a sprig of rosemary under her pillow. An alternative custom took place on St Agnes Eve (20 January – St Agnes is the patron saint of young virgins), when a pair of shoes, one holding a sprig of rosemary and the other a sprig of **thyme**, previously sprinkled with water, were positioned either side of the bed and the following words spoken:

> St Agnes, that's to lovers kind,
> Come ease the trouble of my mind.

A vision of her future husband would then appear. On Midsummer Eve, if a bowl of flour was placed under a rosemary bush during the hours of darkness, the initials of her future husband would be found inscribed on the flour.

Rosemary placed under the bed is said to prevent bad dreams. To make a box of rosemary wood and sniff it is claimed to reveal the secret of eternal youth, a quest that has occupied man for centuries. To drink from a spoon carved from rosemary wood prevented one being poisoned, and a comb of the wood was said to cure baldness.

Rosemary is a symbol of the Nativity of Christ, and the herb, along with other plants, was hung in early Christian churches as a sign of welcome to elves and fairies. Traditionally it crowned the wassail bowl, and at Christmas the main course was ceremonially brought in to the accompaniment of the carol beginning:

> The boar's head in hand bring I
> With garlands gay, and rosemary.

It was used with **holly**, **ivy**, **bay** and **mistletoe** as a Christmas decoration. A delightful New Year's gift was a clove orange and a branch of rosemary decorated with silk ribbons.

On Maundy Thursday, when the Queen distributes the Maundy money to elderly people, a nosegay of herbs is presented to her which customarily includes rosemary, **thyme**, **violets**, **primroses**, **daffodils** and white stock. This custom is a reminder of the days when herbs were believed to give protection against infection and plague. Belief in the effectiveness of herbs, particularly in treating plagues, caused their cost to soar during epidemics. Rosemary was also burnt in the sickroom, giving off an odour similar to frankincense. However, the Romans believed the herb stimulated the memory, binding it round their heads when studying.

Because of its carminative qualities, oil of rosemary, distilled from the flowering heads, was used for headaches and stomach upsets, and rosemary tea was prescribed for colds. A wine and a liqueur can be produced from the shrub. For culinary purposes, rosemary gives an excellent flavour to egg and cheese dishes, soups and sauces, fish, poultry and game, veal and lamb. Only a small sprig is necessary. Like **clary** and **sage**, it is reputed to grow well only where the mistress of the house plays the role of master.

Astrologically rosemary is under the dominion of the sun and the sign of Aries. It is the birthday flower for 17 January, symbolizing affectionate remembrance. In Shakespeare's *Hamlet* Ophelia says:

> There's Rosemary for you, that's for remembrance,
> I pray you, love, remember.

Rowan
Sorbus aucuparia

The botanical name derives from the Latin *sorbum*, the fruit, and *aucuparius*, for catching birds. Fowlers used the fruit as a bait (hence one of its country names). The common name, rowan or roan, is probably a corruption of *raun*, old Norse for a charm, from the tree's alleged power to avert the evil eye:

> Roan-tree and red thread
> Haud the witches a' in dread.

The tree is also known as mountain ash, quicken wicken, quick-beam tree and fowler's service. Quicken or quick-beam means a tree ever-moving, from Old English *cwic*, alive, and *beam*, tree. (This name was originally applied to the **aspen**.) In his *Popular Names of British Plants*, Prior suggests it may have been due to the confusion of *cwic* and *wicce*, witch, the rowan being regarded as a preservative against witchcraft.

In Scandinavian mythology it is Thor's helper or Thor's deliverer, because by clutching a rowan branch he was able to cross the flooded River Vimur safely on his way to the Land of the Frost Giants. The rowan is a charm against bewitchment: its protective value against evil spirits and witches was known throughout Britain. The rowan was kindled by druids to summon spirits to take part in battle. It was believed that rowan branches, collected on the Eve of the Invention of the Cross, a church festival held on 3 May to commemorate the discovery of the cross by St Helena, would give protection against the evil influences of witches and others; red thread, as mentioned above, was sometimes bound around the branches, which were placed conspicuously in windows. Similar claims are made for Good Friday and Holy Rood Day (14 September).

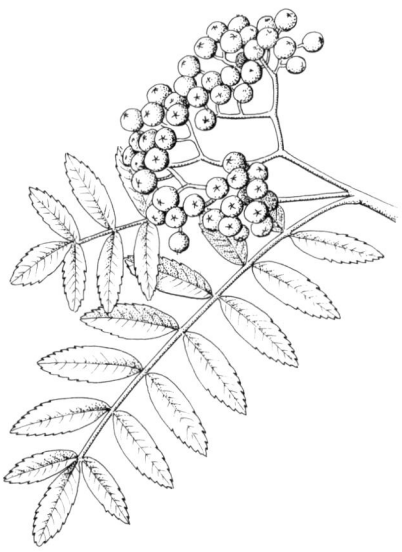

A rowan tree was sometimes planted near a house in the supposed belief that it gave protection to the inhabitants:

> Their spells were vain. The hags returned
> To their queen in sorrowful mood,
> Crying that witches have no power
> Where thrives the Roan-tree wood.

In Scotland, when a house was built, the cross beams of the chimney were often made from the wood for this reason, and on quarter days a rowan stick was laid over the door lintel, both being vulnerable points at which evil spirits or witches could enter or leave. A farmer and his wife would wear rowan necklaces. In some parts of Britain rowan was placed in the roof thatch as a protection against fire. Cradles had rowan rockers to guard the innocence of babies. Not only the home but the livestock and buildings housing them had to be protected. If a cow was thought to have been 'overlooked', a bunch of rowan was hung above the stall and over its horns. A pig was thought to fatten more quickly if a garland of rowan was hung around its neck. A churn staff of the wood prevented the butter from being subjected to evil influences, and plough pins, tethering pegs for cattle and horse whips were all fashioned from the wood.

Too many rowan berries foretold a poor grain harvest. A Scottish saying warns:

> Mony rains, mony Rowans
> Mony Rowans, mony Yewans.

Yewans are light grain.

Rowan berries have an agreeable flavour and were used to garnish dishes. A beer, a fermented liquor similar in flavour to perry (see **pear**) and a spirit can be made from them, and a dye produced. In the language of the flowers the rowan symbolizes beauty, hospitality and protection.

Rue
Ruta graveolens

The botanical name derives from the Latin *ruta*, bitterness or unpleasantness, and the Latin *graveolen*, heavy-scented. The common name also derives from *ruta*. Country names include herb of grace and herb of repentence. Shakespeare mentions both names frequently; Ophelia speaks of the former:

> There's rue for you, and here's some for me,
> We may call it 'herb of grace o' Sundays.'

According to Aristotle, the Greeks suffered from severe indigestion if they ate with strangers; they believed this was due to witchcraft and, finding that rue relieved their complaint, they assumed that the plant had power against evil. Mithridates IV, King of Pontus and Bithynia, is said to have made himself immune to poison by taking a preventative consisting of twenty leaves of rue, two dry **walnut** kernels, two figs and a grain of salt pressed firmly together. Rue was alleged to be the antidote which Mercury gave to Ulysses to counteract the drugged drink offered by Circe, the enchantress.

The herb is an ingredient of the Vinegar of the Four Thieves, drunk by a small band of men who stole from corpses during the Great Plague.

They believed themselves protected from infection by a concoction of
1½ ounces each of the tops of rue, **sage**, mint, sea and Roman
wormwood and **rosemary**, 2 ounces of **lavender** flowers, a quarter of
an ounce each of *Calamus aromaticus*, cinnamon, cloves, nutmeg and
garlic, and half an ounce of camphor to one gallon of red wine vinegar.
The bunch of rue presented to a Judge at the Assizes is an emblem both of
mercy and of an antidote to jail fever (typhus), common in former times.
As an anti-pestilential it was strewn in the Law Courts as late as the
eighteenth century. Tussar wrote:

> What savour is better, if Physicke be true,
> For places infected, than wormwood and rue.

The reputation of rue was so high that it was regarded in Britain as
sacred. Christian missionaries to the Ancient Britons sprinkled holy
water with its branches, and the congregation was showered before and
after a service. The use of rue by witches is a relic of pagan times.
Nevertheless the plant was used as a witch repellent: a popular belief was
that if the floor of a house was rubbed with the herb all witches would fly
from the building.

Several proverbs and beliefs are associated with the plant. For instance,
it is said to thrive best when stolen from a neighbour's garden, and be
most potent when grown under a fig tree. Shot boiled in rue ensured a
direct hit each time. The expression, 'May you rue this day as long as
you live', is alleged to have originated in Herefordshire and been used as
a curse by a girl attending the wedding of a former lover. As he came out
of the church with his bride she threw a handful of rue picked from the
churchyard – an ideal location – and it fell between consecrated and
unconsecrated ground, also a favourable sign from the girl's point of
view. The curse is said to have been an outstanding success.

Rue is one of the few herbs used in heraldry. In Britain it is intertwined
on the collar of the Order of the Thistle.

Medicinally rue was said to be safe if gathered in the morning, but
poisonous later in the day. Rue tea provided a remedy for coughs,
flatulence and convulsions. The leaves were wrapped round a patient's
wounds to cure the bites of mad dogs, and a distillation of the flower
heads was employed as an eye lotion. Modern herbalists use the plant to
treat epilepsy, hysterics and colic.

Animals were also treated with the herb, which was the main
ingredient in an old and popular remedy for croup in poultry and certain
cattle diseases. Rue water was said to kill fleas. Weasels are alleged to eat
the herb before attacking a snake.

The plant is the birthday flower for 18 January, symbolizing grace, pity, mercy, purification, an antidote and bitterness. Astrologically rue is a herb of the sun, under Leo.

Rush

Flowering rush
Butomus umbellatus

> . . . Higher there,
> As conscious of her claims, in beauty rare,
> Her rosy umbels rears the flow'ring rush;
> While with reflected charms the waters blush.
> CHARLOTTE SMITH (1749–1806)

The generic name is from Greek *bous*, ox, and *temmo*, cut. The long, tapering leaves have a sharp edge which if inadvertently eaten by cattle could easily cut their mouths. The flowering rush is a tall, pink-flowered, aquatic plant, now rare because of increased drainage of farmland. A former country name is pride of the Thames.

Herablists claimed that the slightly fragrant seeds had a relaxing effect if taken before going to bed. The root stocks, baked, are said to be edible.

Soft rush
Juncus effusus

The generic name means rush in Latin. In former centuries rushes were plaited into mats and chair seats – these are still popular today – and the pith used as candle wick. Rush Fairs were held. For the most part the rushes were gathered and prepared by women and children, which involved wading in water that was often waist-high.

Rushes were once of great importance in the household because, until carpets came into general use, sleeping apartments, halls and dining rooms were strewn with green rushes to conceal the general dirt. Even in the reign of Queen Elizabeth I they were used on many of the floors in the royal palaces. Wealthier homes changed their rushes daily or at the most weekly; hay was used in winter when there were no rushes. In an account of the household of Thomas à Becket, published in 1528, the writer records that the floors were freshly strewn every day, and that this saved 'the knyghtes clothes that sate on the floor, for defaute of a place to sit'.

The great use made of the plant resulted in festivals called Rush Bearings, which usually ended up as a general drunken party. Some varieties of rushes were used in other ways, as John Clare recalls:

> And on this bank how happy have I felt,
> When here I sat and murmur'd nameless songs
> And, with the shepherd-boy and neat-herd, knelt
> Upon yon rush-beds, plaiting whips and thongs!

Rush candles were a familiar means of lighting in Elizabethan times:

> Be it moon or sun, or what you please,
> And if you please to call it a Rush-candle,
> Henceforth I vow it shall be so for me.

Formerly rings fashioned from rushes were used for betrothals, later to be abused in mock marriage ceremonies. As early as 1217 Richard, Bishop of Salisbury, issued an edict against the use of the '*annulum de junco*'. However Francis Quarles (1592–1644), author of *Emblems*, suggests that such rings were still being used three hundred years later.

> . . . Love-sick swains
> Compose Rush-rings, and Myrtle-berry chains
> And stuck with glorious King-cups in their bonnets,
> Adorned with Laurel slip, chant true love sonnets.

Rush is the birthday flower for 2 April. It symbolizes docility.

Sage
Salvia officinalis

For the derivation of the generic name see **clary**. The plant is said to have been brought to England from the mountain slopes of Southern Europe via the monastery gardens.

The plant was thought to soothe grief. The leaves were strewn on graves as a sign of remembrance, because it withered only slowly. Samuel Pepys (1633–1703), the famous diarist, refers to this custom, mentioning a churchyard where it was customary to sow all the graves with the herb.

Sage leaves were used as love oracles, and the customs vary in different regions. In some parts twelve leaves picked on Christmas Eve would ensure a shadowy vision of one's future husband – great care had to be taken not to damage the plant. Alternatively at midnight on Halloween one leaf gathered on each stroke of the clock produced a similar result.

Faith in the medicinal value of the plant was extremely high. An old Arabic saying asks, 'How shall a man die who has sage in his garden?' The power of the plant was claimed to be more potent at a certain time of the year, and to take full advantage of this:

> He who would live for aye,
> Must eat sage in May.

If a patient was unable to speak, sage juice was put into his mouth 'and by the Grace of God it shall speak'. In *The Englishman's Doctor* published in 1607, it says:

> Sage strengthens the sinews, feavers heat doth swage,
> The palsie helps and rids of mickle woe,
> In Latin takes the name of safety,
> In English Sage, is rather wise than craftie,
> Sith then the name, betokens wise and saving,
> We count it Nature's friend and worth the having.

As a remedy for ague and 'St Anthony's Fire' (erysipelas), seven leaves had to be eaten on seven consecutive mornings before breakfast. The leaves and branches were used for menstrual problems, to expel after-birth, staunch the flow of blood from open wounds, and cleanse ulcers and sores; coughs and sore throats were treated with sage juice in warm water. A twentieth-century remedy for relieving flatulence and nausea consists of an infusion of leaves and tops mixed with honey; mixed with alum, it is a gargle for throat infections.

Since the seventeenth century the herb has been used for cleaning the teeth – every morning the mouth was to be washed with **lemon** juice and the teeth rubbed with sage leaves. It had such a reputation for whitening the teeth and strengthening the gums that it was in use even quite recently. Formerly the leaves were offered to the visitors of Tunbridge Wells after they had taken the medicinal waters, as they were thought to remove the iron stains from teeth.

Sage, which is said to stimulate the growth of **rue** and **rosemary**, is a great asset to any herb garden and can be used fresh or dried with meat, fish, poultry, game, egg and cheese dishes, also in soups, stews and sauces. Both sage ale and sage tea were highly valued in the past. Ideally the leaves should be picked before the herb flowers in May.

Astrologically sage is a herb of Jupiter. It is the birthday flower for 19 January, symbolizing mutual love and domestic virtue. It is alleged to flourish when the wife rules the household. Formerly some husbands, in fear of being ridiculed by their neighbours, would cut down a vigorous sage bush:

> If the sage tree thrives and grows
> The master's not master and he knows.

Sainfoin
Onobrychis viciifolia

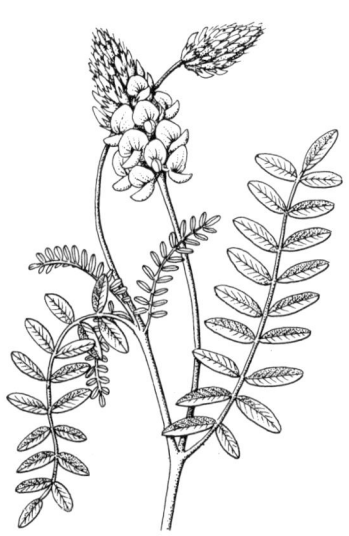

The generic name is from Greek *onos*, ass, and *brycho*, bray, because the smell of the plant was thought to make the animal bray. The common name is derived from the French – the plant was introduced from France – and means holy hay. Other country names are cock's head, red flitching, medick fitch, saint-foin and holy hay. The last name was acquired because in Christian legend it is recorded that when Jesus was sleeping in the manger, on hay, the part on which his head rested began to sprout pink flowers.

Herbalists credited the plant with the 'power to rarify and digest, and therefore the green leaves, bruised and laid as a plaister, disperse swellings'. Gerard, commenting later on this claim, reflects on the standard of medical training of that time: 'Whereof they had those notions I know not; it may be of some doctor who never went to school.'

Sainfoin is the birthday flower for 7 August. The flower symbolizes trust in God and in the language of the flowers means, 'You confuse me'.

St John's wort
Hypericum

The generic name is from the Greek name of the plant – *hyper*, above, and *eikon*, picture; the flowers were placed above images to ward off evil. The plant is dedicated to St John the Baptist, and its reddish sap is known as the blood of the saint. Red spots are said to appear on the leaves on the day of his martyrdom. His feast day falls on 24 June, Midsummer Day, and it is at this time that St John's wort was said to be the most potent when gathered, with the dew still fresh on it, and placed in house windows to keep away the evil eye, the spirits of darkness, ghosts, goblins, elves, fire and thunderbolts. The doorways of houses were decorated with it, together with plants such as **fennel**, **birch**, or **pine** and **lilies**. St John's wort could also be gathered 'upon a Friday, in the hour of Jupiter, when he comes to his operation, so gathered, or borne or hung about the neck, it nightly helps to drive away all phantastical spirits'.

There was at one time a strong belief in the magical properties of the plant. In the Isle of Wight it was considered dangerous to step on the plant as a fairy horse would appear and carry a person away, eventually abandoning the victim a long way from home. Less hazardous was the custom of a girl picking the plant on Midsummer Eve; if it was found to be fresh the following morning her chance of marriage was good.

The herb was also used medicinally; most dramatically it was prescribed for hysteria and manical causes. A decoction of the seed, taken for forty days, was said to relieve sciatica, falling sickness and palsy. Ointments, oils and lotions were made for external complaints and the herb boiled in wine for internal ones, whether it be a snake bite or a wound. A comparatively recent cure for bedsores was an ointment made from St John's wort. The flower heads yield a red dye.

Astrologically St John's wort is under the dominion of the sun and the sign of Leo. It is the birthday flower for 29 June, symbolizing simplicity and animosity. In the language of the flowers it means, 'You are a prophet'.

Salad burnet
Sanguisorba officinalis

Sanguisorba is from the Latin *sanguis*, blood and *sorbes*, to staunch, referring to a supposed virtue of the plant.

Salad burnet is one of the last herbs to die back in winter. Its leaves,

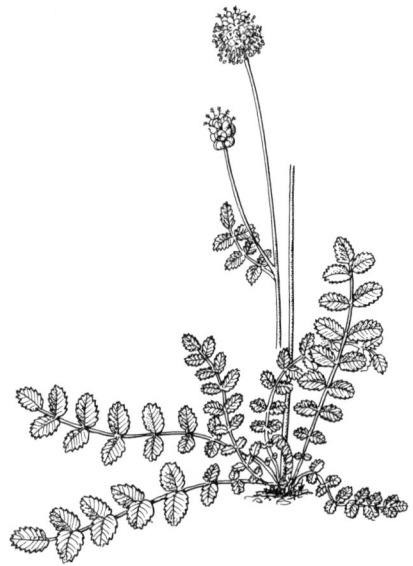

with a pleasant cucumber flavour, are suitable for flavouring soups and salads. A refreshing tea can be made from the leaves.

The plant was in use during the sixteenth century as strewing herb, as Michael Drayton recounts:

> Amongst these strewing kinds some others wild that grow,
> As burnet, all abroad, and meadow-wort they throw.

It is one of the plants that the Pilgrim Fathers took to the New World in the seventeenth century.

Herbalists recommended the juice and seeds of the plant be used as a preventative medicine against the plague and various diseases. It was also used to staunch the flow of blood from open wounds. Culpepper wrote glowingly of the herb: 'It is under the sun, and is a most precious herb, little inferior to betony; the continual use of it preserves the body in health and spirit in vigour; for if the sun be the preserver of life under God, his herbs are the best in the world.'

Sallow   see **Willow**

Samphire   see **Rock samphire**

Savory
Satureja

There are two varieties of this kitchen herb, summer savory (*S. montana*) and winter savory (*S. hortensis*); the latter is a low perennial shrub more popular than the summer variety. Savory is mentioned by Virgil as being one of the most fragrant of herbs. In the *Georgics* he recommends it for bees.

Medicinally the herb was prescribed for colic, particularly in pregnant women. It was also said to ease phlegm in the throat. The juice was used as an eye lotion for improving the eyesight, while mixed with oil of **roses** it was claimed to relieve noises and singing sounds in the ear. A poultice of savory and flour was applied to ease sciatica, while snakebite and wasp and bee stings were dressed with a bruised sprig of the herb.

Both varieties of savory are used in soups, sauces, meat dishes, sausages and salads. Old recipes recommended the herb when dressing trout and as an ingredient of mint sauce. Summer savory gives a pleasant flavour when cooking broad beans. Astrologically savory is under the dominion of Mercury.

Saxifrage   see **Meadow saxifrage**

Scarlet pimpernel
Anagallis arvensis

The generic name is derived from Greek *anagelas*, delight. Pliny said that when it was taken inwardly it promoted mirth, which may explain why it has been referred to as the 'cheerful Pimpernel'.

Scarlet pimpernel is perhaps best known as a weather oracle, because it closes up at the approach of bad weather. John Clare refers to this and other country names by which it was known:

> And scarlet starry points of flowers
> Pimpernel dreading nights and showers
> Oft called 'shepherds weather glass'
> That sleeps till suns have dyed the grass
> Then wakes and spreads its creeping bloom
> Till close it shuts to sleep again
> Which weeders see and talk of rain
> And boys that mark them shut so soon
> Will call them 'John go bed at noon'.

The distinctive scarlet colouring of the petals can only be found in one other British wild flower, the poppy. Superstitious people believed that to hold the flower in one's hand gave one second sight.

The Greeks and Romans used the juice of the plant, mixed with honey, for eye complaints. Early medical writers of good repute recommended the juice of the flower alone in the treatment of brain diseases and liver complaints. The bruised leaves, it was said 'draweth forth thorns and splinters, or other such things gotten in the flesh', arrows in particular, and 'cure the bites of mad dogs' (Culpepper). Nevertheless, old herbals recommended the plant for its cosmetic value in removing freckles. Scarlet pimpernel boiled with hog's lard was said to be an excellent remedy for encouraging hair growth.

Astrologically scarlet pimpernel is assigned to the sun. It is the birthday flower for 19 August, symbolizing assignation, change, childhood and faithfulness. The flower typifies one who functions in the dark.

Scented vernal-grass
Anthoxanthum odoratum

The generic name is from Greek *anthos*, flower, and *xanthos*, yellow. This flowering grass is fragant both fresh and dry; by mid-June the seed head is yellow. The common name was given it because it flowers early, in spring.

During Roman times, when an army was freed from a blockade they gave their deliverer a crown of grass picked from the area of the siege. A crown of grass symbolizes honour.

Scented vernal-grass carries the sentiment poor but happy and is the birthday flower for 30 April, symbolic of submission and usefulness as an old proverb suggests:

> We trample grass, and prize the flowers of May,
> Yet grass is green when flowers do pass away.

However another old saying warns:

> If the grass grow in Janiveer
> It grows the worse for 't all the year.

Scots pine
Pinus sylvestris

The generic name is the Latin word for the tree. The Scots pine, commonly but incorrectly known as the Scotch fir, is the typical pine tree of Northern Europe. Formerly the tree was widely distributed over Britain, although it is only in the Highlands of Scotland that it can now be regarded as truly wild and indigenous. It is an emblem of many Scottish clans, and Sir Walter Scott (1771–1832) refers to it in 'The Boat Song of the Macgregors':

> Hail to the chief who in triumph advances,
> Honour'd and bless'd be the evergreen pine!
> Long may the tree in his banner that glances
> Flourish the shelter and grace of our line!

In classical mythology Attis, a fertility deity, mutilated himself under a pine tree into which his spirit passed and it was bled (cut) for turpentine at the vernal equinox. When the tree was eventually cut down it was adorned with ribbons and carried with pomp to the mother goddess's sanctuary, where it was decorated with fleeces and **violets**. The pine is dedicated to Neptune, Bacchus, Osiris, Poseidon and Pan.

Herbalists used the bark of the tree and the resin for treating urinary complaints, gout and open wounds.

Pine is the birthday flower for 21 March, symbolizing boldness, endurance, fidelity, health and immortality. Twin pine trees signify fidelity and passionate love. The pine cone is sacred to love goddesses and was used as a charm against witchcraft; it symbolizes fecundity, fire, good luck and the phallic principle. Pine pitch signifies philosophy and time, and is the birthday flower for 26 March.

Sea aster
Aster tripolium

The generic name is Greek for a star. *Tripolium* is the old Greek name for the plant, which according to Dioscorides was given it because the flowers change colour three times a day – a statement which later writers refuted. Blue daisy, blue chamomile and starwort are among its other common names. Sea aster is related to the **michaelmas daisy**. The solitariness of the flower, blooming on coastal mudflats, is expressed by P. Merritt (1848–95):

> No sound is heard, save when the sea bird screams
> Its lonely presage of the coming storm
> And the sole blossom which can glad the eye
> Is yon pale starwort nodding to the wind.

The succulent leaves and stems of the plant were sometimes gathered and sold as samphire (see **rock samphire**). Sea aster is the birthday flower for 1 May, signifying afterthought.

Sea holly
Eryngium maritimum

The generic name is a corruption of *eryngion*, the name given to the plant by Dioscorides, who praised its virtues. It is also known as sea eryngo. The plant resembles members of the thistle family, and has bright blue flowers which colour sandy seashores in summer:

> Eryngo to the threat'ning storm,
> With dauntless pride uprears
> His azure crest and warrior form,
> And points his spears.

The roots of the plant were formerly candied and eaten as a sweet. An apothecary Robert Buxton, introduced them into general use, bringing fame to the town of Colchester. It is recorded that when Queen Charlotte, George III's consort, visited the place she was presented with a box of the sweetmeat. Earlier, during the reign of Elizabeth I, the candied root was prepared as a breath-sweetening lozenge known as kissing comfits.

The Elizabethans believed the sea holly to be an aphrodisiac, and thought that it could 'secure a straying lover' (Gerard). However the magic of the plant was said to work in quite a different way on animals. A goat who had eaten this plant could, by standing still, bring the whole flock to a halt.

Herbalists used sea holly in the treatment of jaundice, dropsy, and kidney and bladder ailments. The juice of the leaves was employed as ear drops, and the bruised root was used to treat insect stings and snakebite. Astrologically it is under the sign of Libra.

Self-heal
Prunella vulgaris

Self-heal means that with which one may cure oneself, without the help of a surgeon. An old French proverb states: 'No one wants a surgeon who keeps *Prunelle*.' Another source gives the German *braune*, quinsy, a complaint it was supposed to cure – an old name for the plant is brunella. However many names become confused in translation. It is also known as carpenter's herb, hookweed and sickle-wort, as it was used to treat wounds inflicted as a result of sharp implements.

The juice of self-heal, blended with oil of **roses**, was applied to the temples to relieve headaches. Ulcerated mouths were treated with self-heal, **rue** juice and honey. Herbalists used the plant for many other complaints, such as worms, cramp, convulsions, toothache, and head colds, as well as obstructions of the liver, spleen, kidney and bladder. Astrologically it is under the dominion of Venus.

Shepherd's needle
Scandix pecten-veneris

The generic name is the Greek word for the plant; *pecten* is Latin for comb, and *pecten-veneris* means the comb of Venus. The long, beaklike fruits do suggest a packet of needles or the teeth of a comb. Country names include beggar's needle, crow needle, scandix, Venus comb and devil's darning needle. According to an apothecary, Dodonoeus, writing in 1578, 'Scandix eaten is good and wholesome, and in times past hath beene a common herbe amongst the Greekes, but of small estimation and value, and taken but only for a wild wort or herbs.' Aristophanes, the comic poet of Athens, born in about 444 B.C., 'by occasion of this herbe taunted Euriphides, saying that his mother was not a seller of worts or good potherbes, but only of Scandix.'

Shepherd's purse
Capsella bursa-pastoris

The generic name is derived from Latin *capsa*, seed case; the specific name *bursa-pastoris*, means a shepherd's purse, again a reference to the form of the fruit. The seed pods resemble old-fashioned purses in shape, and open in a similar manner.

The plant has several interesting country names, such as clap-pedepouch: lepers, licensed as beggars, waited at crossroads with a bell or clapper. Alms were usually placed in a brass cup fastened to the end of a long pole. The lepers were named rattle-pouches, which was extended to the plant. Another name for the plant was poor man's pharmacetic – faith in the virtues of the plant in the treatment of external and internal complaints of man and beast was very strong. The name pick-pocket is said by some to have been given because of the amount of space it occupies on valuable land. Children sang a rhyme when picking it:

> Pick pocket, penny nail
> Put the rogue in jail

However John Clare spares a kind thought for the plant:

> Een here my simple feelings nurse
> A love for every simple weed
> And een this little shepherds purse
> Grieves me to cut it up.

Herbalists used the juice to treat earache and noises in the ear. An ointment produced from the plant was considered particularly beneficial in treating head wounds. The soles of the feet and wrists of people suffering from jaundice were bound with the plant in the belief that it gave relief.

Shepherd's purse is under the dominance of Saturn. In the language of the flowers it means, 'I offer you my all'.

Silver birch
Betula pendula

The generic name is the Latin word for birch. It was widely used in the past for a variety of purposes. Birch and **hazel** were used as charcoal in forges. Because of its resinous content the bark not only burned brightly but gave off a delicious smell. Birch wood was used to build houses, for furniture (particularly chairs), ploughs, fences, stakes and barrows. The branches were used in distilling whisky, smoking ham and herrings, and thatching house roofs. The protuberances on the trees, known as witch's knobs, were carved into bowls. From the sap obtained by tapping the tree a pleasant but potent wine can be brewed. The bark is one of the materials on which the ancients wrote. According to Pliny, the celebrated books which Numa Pompilius compiled, seven hundred years before Christ, and burned with him, were written on birch bark. It is alleged that the dwarf birch is stunted because it was used to scourge Christ.

The Romans used birch during the installation of their consuls as a tree of inception. In England, birch rods were used to drive out the spirits of the old year. In many parts of the country, as late as the nineteenth century, it was customary on the Feast of the Holy Innocents (28 December) to beat boys in a ritualistic reminder of the children murdered by Herod so long ago. In *Measure for Measure* Shakespeare wrote of a more practical use:

> Now, as fond fathers,
> Having bound up the threatening twigs of birch,
> Only to stick it in their children's sight
> For terror, not to use, do find in time
> The rod more mock'd than fear'd.

The Scots associated the tree with the dead, particularly with the wraiths of those who appear to the living after death.

As late as the nineteenth century, on Midsummer Day, also the feast day of St John the Baptist, garlands and crosses of birch, **may**, **rowan** and **cowslips** decorated doorways and shop signs. Entries by church-wardens in their parish records during the reign of Edward IV refer to 'various payments for Birch bowes against Midsummer'. Branches were transported to London especially for this festival. However in the country a birch tree was brought into the farmyard, decorated with pieces of white and red cloth, and placed against the stable door to protect the horses from being 'hag-ridden' by witches. A broomstick or besom wedding was once held to be legal. A couple who jumped, separately, over a birch broom held against the doorway of the house were considered married.

Herbalists used the juice of leaves, or the water bored from a tree and later distilled, as a remedy to break stones in the bladder or kidneys, and as a mouthwash. More recently birch leaves were used in the treatment of eczema and other skin complaints, gout, rheumatism, and dropsy. The leaves produce a yellow dye, and the bark a reddish brown one.

Astrologically birch, which is also known as lady of the woods, is under the dominion of Venus. It is the birthday flower for 14 April, with the sentiments of grace and meekness. In the language of the flowers it means, 'You may begin', and it was formerly given by a girl to a young man as a sign of encouragement (see **hazel**).

Silverweed
Potentilla anserina

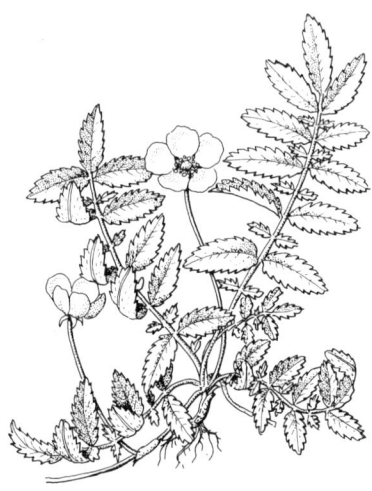

The generic name is derived from Latin *potens*, powerful, an allusion to the medicinal properties of some of the species; *anserina* refers to geese – the plant was common on goose feeding grounds in Sweden when Linnaeus named the plant. However early herbalists long before him were referring to silverweed as goosewort, either because geese ate the silver leaves or because the leaves resembled downy goose feathers, which would also account for one of its many country names, Prince's feathers – the individual leaves were thought to resemble the ostrich feathers of the Prince of Wales' crest. However to John Clare, in 'Eternity of Nature', the plant was simply goosegrass:

> And spreading goosegrass trailing all abroad
> In leaves of silver green about the road
> Five leaves make every blossom all along
> I step for many none are counted wrong.

Other country names are midsummer silver, silver fern, fern buttercup and traveller's ease. Travellers, soldiers and runners believed in silverweed's power to relieve foot complaints and put the leaves in their shoes to ensure comfort when walking.

Silverweed was a favourite flower of the herbarium as it retained its colour and beauty for many years. It was sometimes arranged on paper as a memento, and the silvery leaves and yellow flowers are still popular today for pictures and collage work. The roots were used as a vegetable, either boiled or roasted and taste like parsnip.

The plant has astringent properties, suggesting both medicinal and cosmetic uses. Boiled in salt water, it was used to treat ruptures in children. Boiled in wine, it alleviated griping pains in the bowel, aching joints and sciatica. Boiled in vinegar, alum and honey, it was said to relieve toothache and sore gums, fix loose teeth and heal ulcers of the mouth and genitals. A distillation of the plant was used as a cosmetic preparation for freckles, sunburn, pimples, discoloration of the skin and the pits made by smallpox.

Astrologically the plant is assigned to Venus. In the language of the flowers it means, 'I claim, at least, your esteem'.

Snapdragon
Antirrhinum majus

The generic name is from two Greek words: *anti*, like, and *rhis*, nose or snout, from the masklike appearance of the flowers. Children enjoy pinching the flowers between their thumb and forefingers, causing it to open in imitation of the fabulous monster from which it derives its common name. In the words of D.H. Lawrence:

> 'I like to see', said she
> 'The snap-dragon put out his tongue at me.'

Other country names, all with animal connectins, are toad's mouth, dog's mouth, rabbit's mouth and lion's snap.

> Antirrhinum, more modest, takes the style
> Of Lion's-mouth, sometimes of Calf's-snout vile,
> By us Snapdragon called, to make amends
> But say what this chimera name intends?

wrote Abraham Cowley.

A supernatural influence was one attributed to the snapdragon by people who claimed that it countered the evil eye. It is the birthday flower for 28 June, and in the language of the flowers symbolizes indiscretion, no and presumption.

Snowdrop
Galanthus nivalis

The generic name comes from Greek and means milk flower; *nivalis* is Latin and means associated with snow. Other names for the plant are purification flower, fair maid of February and Candlemas bells, which all relate to an old custom practised on the Feast of the Purification, Candlemas Day, 2 February, when the image of the Virgin Mary, to whom the flower is sacred, was removed from church altars and snowdrops strewn in its place.

Italian monks visiting Britain in the first century are believed to have brought the plant with them. A drift of snowdrops is a beautiful sight in early spring.

> The snow's fair coverlet is spread
> Lightly on lawn and garden bed
> Where the white-wimpled snowdrops blow.

wrote John Gordon. In more recent times, Scottish soldiers returning from the Crimean War (1854–6) in Southern Russia brought back a larger variety, *G. plicatus*, which was introduced to the Isle of Skye off the west coast of Scotland.

In legend it is said that, when Adam and Eve left the Garden of Eden, snow began to fall. An angel, wishing to comfort them with the thought that winter would soon give way to spring, touched some falling snowflakes which changed instantly into snowdrops. To St Francis of Assisi (1182–1226) the flower was an emblem of hope.

Religious connections do not, however, preclude superstitions, of which several are associated with the plant. It was considered unlucky to bring one snowdrop into the house, because of its resemblance to a corpse in a shroud, a death omen. Nevertheless a bunch of flowers was considered quite safe, unless you reared chickens, in which case no snowdrops should be brought into the house at all, otherwise the hens would not hatch their eggs. Formerly it was customary for the first snowdrops of the year to be hung on family graves – almost all spring flowers that hang their heads were associated with death. For girls who intended marrying during the year it was unlucky to pick the flower before St Valentine's Day (14 February).

Herablists used the root of the plant as an emetic and for dressing wounds. The snowdrop is the birthday flower for 20 January, symbolic of friendship in adversity, hope in sorrow, and purity. Tennyson, like other poets, was aware of the symbolism of the flower:

> Make thou my spirit pure and clean,
> As are the frosty skies,
> Or the first snowdrop of the year
> That in my bosom lies.

Soapwort
Saponaria officinalis

The generic name is derived from Latin *sap*, soap, because the plant possesses the soapy principle, particularly in the root. Other common names include soaproot, latherwort and crow soap, as well as bruiswort because the bitter juice was considered a good remedy for bruises. An Elizabethan name for the plant was fuller's herb – presumably they used it in cleaning wool – and Gerard tells us that the plant was used in baths 'to beautifie and cleanse the skin'. Bouncing Bet, wild sweet William and goodbye summer were country names by which soapwort was familiarly known. Some references state that soapwort was introduced during the sixteenth century, although as it was known to the Romans it seems likely that they grew the plant in Britain.

The soapy substance was used as a cleaning agent for tapestries and curtains, and is still used today by some people for cleaning old tapestries and lace, though it is being superceded by a chemical equivalent. Herbalists recommended the plant in the treatment of jaundice and liver complaints, and for long-standing cases of venereal disease where mercury had proved unsuccessful; it was also used as a tonic. The leaves were used as a poultice for minor cuts and wounds.

Astrologically the plant is assigned to Venus.

Solomon's seal   see **Common Solomon's seal**

Sorrel   see **Common sorrel**

Southernwood
Artemisia abrotanum

For the derivation of the generic name see **mugwort**. The specific name derives from the Greek and means life-preserving. Southernwood is a typical cottage garden plant with aromatic foliage whose pouplar names include lad's love, old man, boy's love and maiden's ruin. Lad's love originates from the use young men made of the herb to encourage the growth of their beards so as to appear more mature and attractive to the opposite sex, and later as a pomade to stimulate hair growth and prevent baldness. Placed under a man's pillow it took on a different significance, as it 'provoketh men to multiplyinge of there kind'.

Because of the plant's scent it was a popular choice for nosegays. Apart from being a delightful custom, the practice of carrying sweet-scented flowers had a practical purpose too, in masking unpleasant smells at a time when sanitation was primitive. Southernwood in particular was used to ward off jail fever (typhus), and ladies also carried the herb in church to prevent drowiness. In *The Shepherd's Calendar* John Clare refers to a typical lover's posy:

> And marjoram notts sweet briar and ribbon grass
> And lavender the choice of every lass
> And sprigs of lads love all familiar names
> Which every garden thro the village claims
> These the maids gather wi cosy delight
> And tyes them up in readiness for night
> Giving to every swain tween love and shame
> Her 'clipping posy' as their yearly charm.

Southernwood was also used as a strewing herb and a moth repellent.

The seeds, bruised and heated in water, were used in the treatment of cramp, sciatica and urinary complaints, and for expelling worms. Boiled with **barley** meal they were said to remove pimples and blemishes on the face and body. The whole plant, bruised, was applied 'to draw splinters from the flesh' (Gerard).

Southernwood is the birthday flower for 21 January, symbolizing jest and bantering. Astrologically it is a plant of Mercury.

Sowbread
Cyclamen hederifolium

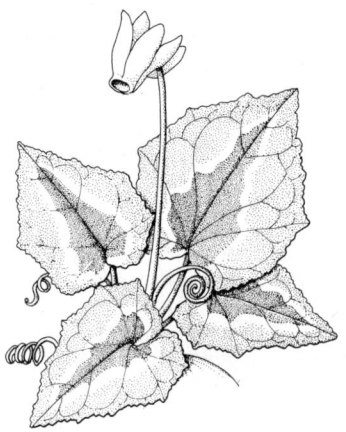

The generic name is from Greek *kyklos*, circular, because the flower stalks of some of the species twist in a spiral after they have flowered. The common name derives from the fact that pigs easily uprooted the plant in the wild and ate it. Another name, bleeding nun, was used by Christians to suggest the sorrow bleeding in Mary's heart. Victoria Sackville-West thought of them differently:

> Only the little frightened cyclamen
> With leveret ears laid back look fresh and young.

Superstition held that a pregnant woman stepping over a cyclamen would suffer a miscarriage. However, in company with **St John's wort** it was used to protect loved ones as in this poem by Michael Drayton.

> St John's Wort and fresh cyclamen she in his chamber kept
> From the power of evils angels to guard him while he slept.

Sowbread was also used as a weather oracle and a love charm. Taken internally, it induced one to fall in love.

Apothecaries used the root of the plant in childbirth. A recipe for curing baldness required the patient to stuff a concoction of the plant up the nostrils – the results of this strange procedure are not recorded.

In the language of the flowers sowbread means 'Goodbye', symbolizing diffidence and voluptuousness. To dream of the flower signifies catastrophe.

Sow-thistle
Sonchus

The generic name is derived from a Greek word meaning hollow. Country names are hare's bush, hare's lettuce, hare's thistle, milkweed and swine's thistle. According to an old writer, the hare 'when fainting with the heat shc recruits her strength with this herb; or if a hare eat of this herb in summer when he is mad, he shall become whole'. The hunted animal is said to rest in peace and safety beneath the plant. Rabbits do enjoy the herb as a welcome addition to their diet.

It is recorded by Pliny that Theseus ate a dish of sow-thistle, because of its nourishing and sustaining qualities, before capturing the bull which was ravaging the plain of Marathon. The earliest traces of the sow-thistle's fruit have been found in excavated Roman settlements. Hundreds of years ago the plant was used as a salad herb – the tender young leaves are particularly tasty.

In the Middle Ages the milk extracted from the stalks was thought helpful to those who suffered from shortage of breath, deafness and wheezing. A decoction of leaves and stalks was alleged to increase the 'milk in nursing mothers and prevented curdling in the breast' (Culpepper). Ladies used a lotion prepared from sow-thistles to improve their complexion.

The plant was used in an unusual form of rustic divination:

> Upon the various earth's embroidered gown,
> There is a weed upon whose head grows down,
> Sow Thistle 'tis clept, whose downy wreath
> If anyone can blow off at a breath
> We deem her for a maid.

wrote William Browne. Sow-thistle is astrologically assigned to the planet Venus.

Spearmint
Mentha spicata

The generic name is the Latin word for the plant, so called from Minthe, a nymph, daughter of the river god, Cocytus, and a favourite of Pluto, who was metamorphosed by his jealous wife, Proserpina, into the herb of that name.

Mint species have been cultivated for hundreds of years and can be found in gardens from cottage to palace. Spearmint is thought to have been introduced by the Romans. Pliny wrote that it 'would not suffer milk to curddle'. In ancient Greece different parts of the body were perfumed with various herbs, mint being assigned to the arms. During this time it was used to scent bathwater, a practice that the British were later to adopt with this and other herbs to 'strengthen the nerves and the sinews' (Culpepper). Mint was also used as a strewing herb for bedchambers and banqueting halls. Other names for spearmint include Our Lady's mint, sprie mint and fish mint.

Today mint sauce is the accepted accompaniment to lamb. Fresh leaves chopped and sprinkled on vegetables, especially new potatoes, salads and soups give an appetizing flavour and sprigs of mint provide a refreshing garnish to cool summer drinks. Formerly mint cordials were very popular. Jean Ingelow, in her 'Supper at the Mill', wrote:

> Playing on the virginals,
> Who but I! Sae glad, sae free,
> Smelling for all cordials,
> The green mint and marjorie.

The culinary value of the plant has been known for a long time, but it was never eaten by wounded men because 'whoever eat mint when wounded will never be cured' (Gerard). Its healing qualities were recorded by Dioscorides. Apart from improving the appetite, the smell of the plant was thought to be good for the memory. Later herbalists applied **rose** petals and mint to the head as a cure for sleeplessness. Powdered mint in wine was recommended for women in labour. A decoction of the herb was used as a gargle and as a remedy for sores and ulcers. Two or three sprigs of the herb, taken with the juice of four **pomegranates**, provided an unusual cure for hiccups. The leaves, sprinkled with salt, were applied as a dressing for the bites of mad dogs – a widespread hazard, if the variety of cures are any guide. Distilled water from the plant was claimed to relieve flatulence and hiccups. A warm infusion of mint was recommended by twentieth-century herbalists to 'produce perspiration while suffering from symptoms of various causes'.

It is the birthday flower for 25 February, symbolizing burning love. In the language of the flowers it means 'Let us be friends again'.

Speedwell   see **Germander speedwell**

Spiderwort
Tradescantia virginiana

The plant was named after John Tradescant, gardener to Henrietta Maria and Charles I. Spiderwort was imported in error from Virginia and given to him by a friend. The English name was mistakenly given because botanists formerly classified the plant as one of the Phalangiums, alleged to cure the bite of the phalangium spider. As this particular insect is quite harmless the success accorded to the plant must have seemed exceptional. It is also known as Trinity flower, because of the three-petal flower head, and Moses in the bulrushes because of the appearance of the flower among rushlike leaves. Lastly it is called by some widow's tears, for when the flower dies it dissolves into inky wet blobs instead of drying up. In the language of the flowers spiderwort means, 'Esteem but not love'.

Spindle-tree
Euonymus europaeus

The generic name is the Latin word for the tree. Older writers claim that *Euonymus* is derived from Euonyme, the mother of the Furies, an allusion to the harmful properties of the berries. The bark and leaves are also poisonous to humans and to many animals. The berries do, however, yield a yellow dye, and the burnt wood produces a good charcoal which was popular with artists. Formerly the wood was used for making spindles, and later for skewers and musical instruments. In Ireland it was known as peg-wood, because shoemakers cut their pegs from its branches. Another country name was prickweed.

The small, pale green flowers appear in June and July; for them to bloom in May was a sign of the plague. In the language of the flowers the spindle signifies, 'Your image is engraved on my heart'.

Spurge   see **Wood spurge**

Star of Bethlehem
Ornithogalum

The generic name is from Greek *ornis*, bird, and *gala*, milk. Other country names are wake-at-noon, sleepy Dick and eleven o'clock lady, referring to the plant's supposed habit of opening its petals at eleven o'clock in the morning and closing them at about three o'clock in the afternoon.

Linnaeus believed that the star of Bethlehem was the 'dove's dung' mentioned in 2 Kings 6:25, which was eaten in time of famine. A variety of the plant certainly grows in Palestine and was dried and stored as part

of the provisions for long journeys. In Europe during times of hardship some of the species were eaten by poor people.

The flower was probably introduced to England during the sixteenth century, although some sources indicate that it was already growing wild at that time. However, by 1597 it was a common garden plant.

Star of Bethlehem is the birthday flower for 12 May, symbolizing purity.

Star thistle
Centaurea calcitrapa

For the derivation of the generic name see **black knapweed**. The specific name, *calcitrapa*, refers to the scales of the plant, whose long, broad, strong spines resemble a caltrop, a weapon used in ancient battles, which consisted of an iron ball covered with spikes which was thrown under the feet of cavalry, cruelly wounding them as they charged forward. Despite its common name the plant is not a true thistle, but a member of the daisy family.

The distilled water of star thistle was recommended as a cure for the French disease (syphilis), liver complaints and fevers. A remedy against the plague consisted of powdered root in wine; the seed, also taken in wine, was said 'to provoke urine' (Culpepper). Astrologically star thistle is under the dominion of the planet Mars.

Stitchwort   see **Greater stitchwort**

Stock
Matthiola

The stock was first known as *Leucoium album* or *viola album*, the white violet. The genus was later renamed after Pierandrea Mattioli (1501–77), an Italian botanist and physician. Most of the garden stocks of today are descended from hoary stock (*M. incana*), which grows wild on the Isle of Wight. The stock was known to the Elizabethans as stock-gilloflower, from the similarity of their scent to the carnation, which was then called gilloflower.

Night-scented stock (*M. bicornis*) is less well known historically. Although not particularly striking in appearance, the plant does smell beautiful, as Victoria Sackville-West recalls in 'The Garden':

> And sow when danger of the frost is past
> Generous sprinklings of night-scented stock,
> Dingy and insignificant and plain,
> But speaking with a quiet voice at dusk.

Stock is the birthday flower for 10 October. It symbolizes lasting beauty and promptness.

Stonecrop   see **Biting stonecrop**

Strawberry tree
Arbutus unedo

The generic name is the Latin word for the plant; *unedo* means 'I eat one.' Pliny maintained that the specific name was given because one was sufficient for most people. A beautiful evergreen with rough reddish bark, the strawberry tree bears clusters of pinkish or creamy white flowers which are at absolute perfection when the fruit of the previous year is ripening, presenting an eye-catching spectacle in early autumn. The fruit, a round, orange-red berry studded with little points, is edible, although less attractive to the taste than to the eye. The tree is often popularly referred to as trailing arbutus.

It was said to be the first flower to greet the Pilgrim Fathers after a severe winter in America. Subsequently it became known as mayflower and was adopted as the emblem of Massachusetts.

> God be praised the Pilgrim said
> Who saw the blossom peer
> Above the brown leaves dry and dead,
> Behold our Mayflower here!

In the language of the flowers the strawberry tree means, 'I love only you'.

Sundew
Drosera

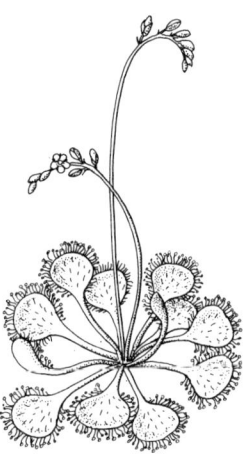

The generic name is from Greek *drosys*, dew. Sundew leaves are covered with fine red hairs, each tipped with fluid and giving the appearance of a dewdrop in the sunlight – a beautiful trap laid by this insectivorous plant.

Formerly herbalists used sundew in the treatment of corns, warts, whooping cough, asthmatic complaints, convulsions, hysteria and trembling of the limbs. A less attractive name for the plant was red–rot, because it was supposed to cause liver rot in sheep. However, there may have been other compensations from the sheep eating the plant, 'because if Sheepe feede thereon they will go to the Ramme'. From this belief came the popular name lustwort.

Astrologically the plant is under the dominion of the sun and the sign of Cancer.

Sunflower
Helianthus annuus

The generic name is derived from two Greek words: *helios*, sun, and *anthos*, flower. The common name is so called from the plant's resemblance to a drawing of the sun, and not, as is frequently supposed, because it follows the course of the sun. The sunflower is a native of the Americas where carvings of it were found in the ancient Inca temples, on gold jewellery and ornaments, and forming the head of ceremonial standards.

The blooming of the sunflower is recorded in *An Early Calendar of English Flowers*:

> And yet anon, the full Sunflower below,
> And became a starre for Bartholomew.

The feast of St Bartholomew is celebrated on 24 August.

The leaves and seeds are an expectorant and a diuretic, and were used as a herbal treatment for pulmonary infections. Sunflowers produce a large quantity of seeds from which an oil, suitable for culinary purposes, is extracted. Modern herbalists prescribe linoleic acid, an extract of the oil, for people suffering from multiple sclerosis, in an attempt to delay its progress.

The sunflower is the birthday flower for 30 June and symbolizes, in the language of the flowers, adoration, affection, constancy, false riches, glory, gratitude, infatuation and the solar wheel. Generally speaking, a tall flower symbolizes haughtiness and lofty thoughts. In the language of the flowers it means, 'You are splendid'. The plant is a Christian symbol of religious obedience, as it faces the sun (Christ) all day. The flower is an attribute of the Virgin Mary, Daphne and Mithra, ancient Persian deity of sunlight and fertility.

Sweet briar
Rosa rubiginosa

For the derivation of the generic name see **rose**. *Rubiginosa* is Latin for rusty – a brownish red tint is frequently found on both stems and foliage. The fragrance of the leaves and flowers have made it a favourite subject of poets, particularly under the older name of eglantine. Sir Walter Scott wrote of a scene where:

> Nature scatter'd free and wild
> Each plant and flower, the mountain's child,
> Here eglantine perfumed the air,
> Hawthorn and hazel mingled there.

Sweet briar is the birthday flower for 29 March, symbolic of poetry, simplicity and talent. In the language of the flowers it signifies, 'I wound to heal'.

Sweet Cicely
Myrrhis odorata

The generic name is from Greek *myrrha*, myrrh, from the fragrance of its leaves. The large, black, clove-scented seeds, ground and mixed with wax, made an excellent furniture polish, imparting a pleasant perfume to the home. In times of plague it was regarded as a protective plant. Herbalists later applied the bruised plant to swellings and prescribed the juice or distilled water from the plant for kidney complaints and pleurisy.

Apart from being a salad herb, the roots, boiled and eaten with oil and vinegar, were regarded as a tonic. It can be chopped up and sprinkled on trifles and sugared strawberries; sweet Cicely is one of the herbs used to flavour Chartreuse liqueur. Astrologically it is under the dominion of the planet Jupiter.

Sweet flag
Acorus calamus

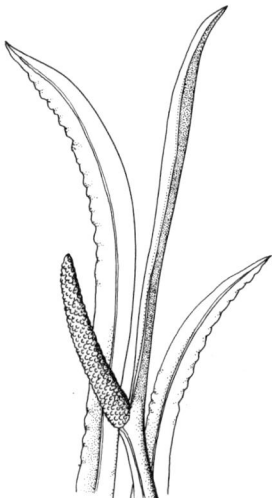

The generic name is the Latin word for the plant; *calamus* comes from Greek *kalamus*, reed, referring to the leaves. Older writers claim that *Acorus* is from Greek *a*, without, and *korion*, the pupil of the eye, because the plant was formerly used to treat diseases of the eye. Former popular names included cegge or wylde gladone, and with common sedge it shared the name of stare or starre.

Because of the plant's pleasant perfume it was used in garlands for churches and homes and strewn with rushes in the houses of the rich. The fragrance increased when the plant was trodden upon. For many years it was used on the floor of Norwich and Ely Cathedrals. In passing it is of interest to note that changing rushes too frequently was considered a grave extravagance, and was listed as one of the many offences committed by Cardinal Wolsey.

Formerly, sweet flag grew on riverbanks in the London area. However the demand created by the perfumers and the makers of hair powder resulted in it being almost totally 'destroyed in that neighbourhood by their continual maraudings'.

The root has been used medicinally since the time of Hippocrates, various cures being attributed to it. Boiled with grass roots and smallage (wild celery) it was used to treat dropsy and ruptures. A syrup consisting of bruised roots steeped in vinegar and boiled until reduced to half the quantity, then reheated with honey added, was taken daily for liver complaints. The root was also used as an antidote for bad breath and poison. Fumes from the plant, taken through a pipe with an optional extra, turpentine, were a recommended cure for a cough. The root was still in use earlier this century as a tonic and as a remedy for colic and dyspepsia.

Sweet flag is the birthday flower for 25 August, symbolizing fitness. Astrologically it is assigned to Venus.

Sweet gale
Myrica gale

The generic name is the Greek word for tamarisk. Country names for the plant include bog myrtle, sweet willow, Dutch myrtle, candleberry myrtle, withy wind and golden withy.

Sweet gale was well known to the Elizabethans. Gerard recorded 'the Gaule groweth plentifully in the Isle of Ely, and in the fenny counties thereabouts, whereof there is such store in that country that they make faggots of it, and sheaves which they call Gaule sheaves, to burn and heat their ovens'. The powerful but pleasant odour of the plant acted as an insect repellent: boughs of sweet gale were hung about beds, sprigs were placed among clothes, and the leaves provided a stuffing for mattresses. The catkins, boiled, yield an inferior tallow from which candles and sealing wax were produced. The economic uses of the plant were many, but it was of particular importance in all northern countries in brewing ale. The berries and bitter leaves have been used since time immemorial, and the dried berries were often added to a broth. In some parts a fine was imposed on any person collecting from 'another man's estate or from any common, before a certain period'.

The practical use of sweet gale far outweighed any superstitious beliefs. It was, however, considered unlucky if used as a cattle switch.

Sweet pea   see **Pea**

Sweet William
Dianthus barbatus

For the derivation of the generic name see **cottage pink**. *Barbatus* comes from the Latin for bearded. In England the botanical name was generally confined to that plant. Cowley commented facetiously:

> Sweet William small has form and aspect bright,
> Like that sweet flower [pink] that yields great Jove delight,
> Had he majestic bulk he'd now be styled
> Jove's flower, and, if my skill is not beguiled,
> He was Jove's flower when Jove was but a child.
> Take him with many flowers in one conferred,
> He's worthy Jove, e'em now he has a beard.

Accounts differ on the origin of the common name, although the Church maintains that the plant was dedicated to St William.

The plant was probably introduced to England by Carthusian monks during the twelfth century. By the reign of Henry VIII the sweet William could be bought quite cheaply; records show they were used in the planting out of a new garden at Hampton Court. Gerard mentions the flower as being 'highly esteemed in Elizabethan times to deck up gardens, the bosoms of the beautiful, garlands and crowns for pleasure'.

An historical link connects the flower with the Battle of Culloden during the Jacobite Rebllion in 1745, when William, Duke of Cumberland, led the English army to victory over the ill-trained remnants of the

Scottish clans. There was general rejoicing in England, and a poet quickly connected the sweet William with the now celebrated Duke:

> The pride of France is lily white
> The rose in June is Jacobite
> The prickly thistle of the Scot
> Is nothern knighthoods badge and lot;
> But since the Duke's victorious blows
> The lily thistle and the rose
> All droop and fade, all die away;
> Sweet William only rules the day.
> No plant with brighter lustre grows,
> Except the laurel on his brow.

When the Scots heard of this floral compliment they named one of the more obnoxious of their weeds stinking Billy.

Sweet William is the birthday flower for 15 May, symbolizing craftiness, gallantry and treachery. In the language of the flowers it means, 'Grant me one smile'.

Sweet woodruff
Asperula odorata

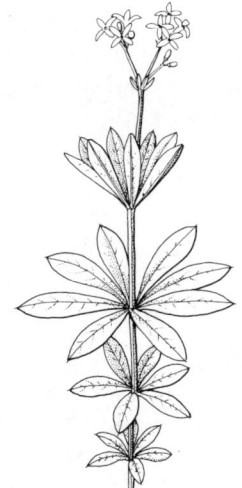

The generic name is from Latin *asper*, rough, referring to the roughness of some of the species. It is the wuderove of the thirteenth century which later became wood-rove. Rove is from French *rouelle*, wheel, from the arrangement of the leaves. An anonymous fourteenth-century poet wrote of the flower:

> When the woderove springeth
> This foules singeth ferly fele
> And wlytheth on huere wynter wele,
> That al the wode ryngeth.

Another more recent, but incorrect, spelling is commemorated in a country rhyme:

> Double U double O double DE
> RO double U double FE.

When dried, the plant imparts an agreeable perfume, and for this reason was a popular strewing herb in bedchambers and provided an excellent mattress stuffing. Placed among linen and clothing it was said to act as a moth repellent. Gerard suggested that it should be made up into garlands and 'hanged up in houses in the heat of summer, as it doth very well attemper the aire and coole and make fresh the place'. The scent of cumin is noticeable when the herb is dry. In the Middle Ages bunches of woodruff were hung up in churches with **lavender**, **rose** and **box**, each giving off a sweet fragrance.

Herbalists recommended woodruff as a preventative against the plague and used it in the treatment of palsy, epilepsy and heart complaints. Mixed with wine, woodruff was said to 'make a man merry' and be good for the liver – an old name for the plant was cordialis. Woodruff tea was a popular treatment for headaches. In the language of the flowers it means 'modest worth'.

Sycamore
Acer pseudoplatanus

The generic name means sharp in Latin, referring to the hardness of the wood which the Romans used for spear shafts. The name sycamore was given by earlier botanists in the mistaken belief that the tree was identical to the sycamore or mulberry-fig of Palestine, which it resembles in size and foliage. It is also known as the great maple or false plane. The sycamore is not a native tree, but appears to have been introduced in the fifteenth century. The scimitar-shaped keys are produced freely after about twenty years' growth. Bishop Mant describes:

The branching sycamore, that veils
His golden sheets in dark-green scales,
While still, as on the fabric goes,
Each pair to each succeeding shows
Its produce in a transverse line,
That step by step they all combine
To frame, by constant interchange,
Of cross like ferns a gradual range.

Old herbalists describe the leaves as being good for the liver and spleen, and recommend the roots, bruised, to alleviate various pains. The milk extracted from the tree was dried and used for treating wounds, and the fruits applied as a plaster.

The tree is the Christian symbol of the cross (Peter of Capua), cupidity (St Malitus), an unbelieving Jew (Rhaban Maur) and wisdom (St Euchre). Astrologically it is under the dominion of Venus. It is the birthday plant for 1 July, symbolizing curiosity, grief and truth.

Tamarisk
Tamarix anglica

This ornamental shrub was named after the Tamarisci, who inhabited the banks of the Tamaris, now known as the Tambra, in Spain, where it grew in abundance. Although some sources suggest that the tamarisk was first introduced to Cornwall, Rev. Thomas Fuller (1608–61) remarks in *Worthies of England*: 'The Tamarisk was brought over by Bishop

Grindal from Switzerland where he was in exile under Queen Mary, and planted in his garden at Fulham where the soil being moist and fenny, well complied with the nature of this plant; yet it groweth not up to be timber, as in Arabia, though often to that substance that cups of great size are made thereof.'

In those days a cup made of the wood was thought to improve the flavour of ale. Physicians further increased the popularity of the wood by advising their patients to eat from dishes carved from tamarisk wood. Similarly a spit on which meat was roasted could only add to the excellence. Browne, in his *Pastorals*, records another domestic use:

> Amongst the rest, Tamarisk there stood,
> For housewives besoms onely knowne most good.

Pliny also mentions the use the Romans made of the tree as a broom. Homer, among others, refers to the tamarisk as the tree by which Achilles laid his spear before he rushed into the Xanthus in pursuit of the fleeing Trojans:

> So plunged in Xanthus, by Achilles force
> Roars the resounding surge with men and horse;
> His bloody lance the hero cast aside,
> Which spreading Tamarisk on the margin hide.

In ancient times the tamarisk was bound round the head of criminals.

Many references are made to the tree in the Bible. Those that grow in the Middle East are a larger variety, highly prized by the Arabs for their medicinal qualities, as fuel, and for drinking vessels.

English herbalists used the root and leaves or young branches of *T. anglica* boiled in wine or vinegar as a poultice in the area of the spleen. The leaves only, boiled in wine, produced a medicine for the treatment of jaundice, colic, snakebite and bleeding haemorrhoids.

Astrologically the tamarisk is under the dominion of Saturn. It is the birthday flower for 8 October, symbolizing crime.

Tansy
Tanacetum vulgare

The generic name is a form of the medieval Latin, *tanazeta*, once regarded as a specific for intestinal worms. Another name for the plant is

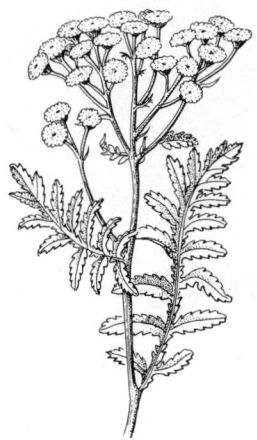

athanasia, signifying something that cannot perish (see below). This bitter, aromatic herb was held in great esteem by monks and medieval herbalists and was dedicated to St Athanasia and later to the Virgin Mary.

Tansy juice was used to flavour what has been described as a nauseating dish, tansy pudding.

> On Easter Sunday, be the pudding seen
> To which the tansy lends her sober green.

Although it was used to flavour other Easter foods, such as cakes and omelettes, it was formerly popular during Lent as a representative bitter herb, taken with the Paschal lamb. Meat was rubbed over with tansy juice, which was said to act as a fly repellent in hot weather – the flavour of the meat was thought not to have been impaired. Bundles of tansy and **elder** were placed on windowsills as fly preventatives. The Elizabethans liked to include tansy in their bedding as a deterrent against vermin. In ancient times the herb was used to preserve corpses, lending credence to the meaning of the old name, athanasia.

Tansy tea was popular for the treatment of worms, ague and kidney complaints. The root, preserved with honey, was used in a remedy for gout. The bruised herb, applied to the navel, was believed to prevent a miscarriage. Fomentations for sprains and rheumatic pains were other healing uses of the plant. Fresh leaves, placed in the shoes, were said to prevent ague.

It is the birthday flower for 23 February, symbolizing courage and resistance. In the language of the flowers it means, 'I declare against you'.

Tarragon
Artemisia dracunculus

For the derivation of the generic name see **mugwort**. The name tarragon comes from French *estragon*, meaning a little dragon, because the plant was thought to cure the bites and stings of venomous creatures. *A. dracunculus* is the French for true tarragon, a native of Southern Europe.

Familiar to the Tudors, it was used by them as a salad plant. Tarragon is known throughout the world for its unusual flavour and is an important culinary herb.

> . . . For few
> Can resist the charm
> Of a sprig of balm
> Or the hope of becoming a paragon
> By the tactful use of tarragon.

wrote Margaret Brownlow. It is an essential ingredient of French mustard, tartare sauce and the classic French chicken dish, *poulet à l'estragon*. Tarragon vinegar is made from the fresh leaves, picked when dry, stripped from their stems, bottled and covered with white wine vinegar. The flavoured vinegar is strained off after several days and rebottled. Tarragon can be used fresh or dried in salads, hors-d'oeuvres, egg and cheese dishes, soups, stews, sauces, fish, meat, poultry, game and vegetable dishes.

Teasel
Dipsacus fullonum

The generic name is from Greek *dipsakos*, thirst: the leaves, which are joined at their base, form a hollow in which rainwater collects. This also explains the country name, Venus's basin. This natural feature of the plant is very useful to other wildlife, as John Clare recalls in 'Noon':

> E'en the dew is parched up
> From the teazle's jointed cup –
> O poor birds where must ye fly,
> Now your water-pots are dry?

The teasel is perhaps best known for its former use by fullers in raising the nap on wollen cloth (hence its specific name); the heads of the plant were fastened around a large wheel which revolved so that the arms 'teased' the nap of the cloth. The plant is also a weather oracle – if the prickles are closed it is a sign of rain.

The root of the plant, bruised and boiled in wine until thick, formed a herbalists' salve for warts and abscesses. Juice extracted from the leaves and dropped in the ears was said to kill worms. Distilled water of the leaves, as well as rainwater caught up in the leaves, was used to improve the eyesight, and applied to the face to remove spots and beautify one generally.

In the language of the flowers, teasel symbolizes importunity and misanthropy. Astrologically it is under the sign of Venus.

Thistle
Onopordum

The generic name is the Greek word for thistle-like plants. It is the emblem of Scotland, adopted during the eighth century to commemorate an unsuccessful attack by the Danes on Stirling Castle. It is alleged that the cries of pain from the barefooted Danish scouts warned the Scots of their presence. With the thistle was adopted the motto, '*Nemo me impune lacessit*' (Nobody provokes me with impunity).

There are many species of thistle, all assigned to Thor, son of Odin, god of war, and sacred in ancient Nordic culture. The brightly coloured flowers are said to come from lightning, and to protect the person or building under their guardianship. In Roman mythology Ceres, goddess of agriculture and of all the fruits of the earth, carried a torch of thistle.

The thistle, like many plants was used as a love oracle. An old custom to discover the identity of one's future husband or wife involved placing a thistle head at each corner of one's pillow before sleeping – each head representing a different lover. The one which represented the most faithful of them would grow a shoot during the night. The head of a thistle was also used as a weather oracle, as it closes up before rain. Cutting down of thistles was most important:

> Cut your thistles before St John,
> You will have two instead of one.

and

> Don't cut your thistles before Midsummer Day
> Or two will grow for every one.

Herbalists used a whole range of thistles to treat various complaints. The juice was used to bathe bald patches in the belief that the hair would grow again. As decoction of the plant was recommended in the treatment of jaundice, liver complaints and melancholy. Milk thistle (*Silybum marianum*), boiled and eaten in the spring, was said to change your blood as the seasons changed.

Astrologically all thistles are assigned to Mars and Saturn. It is the birthday flower for 17 May, symbolizing austerity, defiance, desolation, grief, independence and rejection.

Thorn apple
Datura stramonium

The generic name means angel's trumpet, from an oriental vernacular name. *Stramonium* is a powerful narcotic used in twentieth-century remedies for epilepsy and tetanus, and as a pain reliever generally. Taken in large doses it is a powerful poison. Thorn apple is also known as love apple, and as Jamestown weed or jimson weed, as it grew in abundance in Jamestown, where a number of early settlers in America were poisoned after eating the leaves. Gerard claims that it was introduced from Constantinople in 1597, and that the leaves were used at that time to make a salve for burns. The seeds and leaves were used dried, sometimes with other herbs, and ignited: asmatic patients would inhale the smoke in an effort to seek relief for their complaint. However, certain hazards accompanied this medicinal inhaling of drugs. A recipe popular with medieval witches consisted of a mixture of **deadly nightshade, henbane** and thorn apple. Smeared over the body, it induced strange hallucinations, flying through the air being one of the many extraordinary sensations experienced.

The seeds and leaves are alleged to have been used by the priests of Apollo, in the temple at Delphi, to induce wild and frenzied utterances by the Oracle. Superstitious people believed that to sleep under the shade of the plant would be fatal.

Astrologically, thorn apple is under the sign of Venus. It is the birthday flower for 6 June, meaning deceitful charms.

Thrift
Armeria maritima

The generic name is the Latin word for a type of dianthus: *Flos armeria* was an old name given by monks to one of the sweet William pinks. Thrift is from Middle English *threave* or *thrive*, press close together, because it grows in dense tufts. Another modern name for thrift is sea pink, while the Elizabethans called it ladies' cushion.

Thrift is as familiar on saltmarshes as on the mountainside or in the garden. By the sea it contains iodine and soda; the mountain and garden varieties exchange these two salts for potash.

Gerard did not credit thrift with any particular virtue, although it was used in Elizabethan knot gardens. Thrift is the birthday flower for 14 August, symbolizing sympathy for the fallen.

Thyme
Thymus

The generic name is the Greek word for these shrubs. It is a popular aromatic herb long established in the garden and folklore. When honey was the most important sweetening agent, thyme was a favourite plant near the beehives. During the seventeenth century Gervas Markham instructed English beekeepers to perfume their hives with **fennel**, **hyssop** and 'Time-flowers'! Wild thyme (*T. serpyllum*), also known as shepherd's thyme, was thought to possess similar virtues to the cultivated variety. Alfred Noyes wrote:

> The wild thyme on the mountains knees
> Unrolls its purple market to the bees.

In the Middle Ages the herb was given by a lady to her beloved knight as a farewell gift when he embarked on the Crusades. A scarf embroidered with a sprig of thyme was a popular present, denoting loving remembrance.

Superstition surrounds the herb both as a love oracle and as a plant that foretells death. The ancients believed that thyme harboured the souls of the dead (a belief surrounding many sweet-smelling flowers) and had a particular affinity with murdered people. Stories are told of the sweet smell of thyme lingering in the air after a violent death. This association with death is reflected in the belief that it was unlucky to bring it into the home, because it would cause death or severe illness to a member of the family. In Wales it was often planted on graves.

A concoction of flower buds from thyme, **marigold**, **hollyhock** and **hazel** formed the basis of a seventeenth-century recipe claimed to enable one to see fairies. With **rosemary**, thyme was used as a love oracle. A sprig of rosemary placed in one shoe, and a sprig of thyme in the other, ensured a vision of one's future husband. The ceremony had to take place on St Agnes Eve, 21 January.

The traditional *bouquet garni* consists of two sprigs of thyme, one sprig of **parsley** and a **bay** leaf. Placed in a muslin bag, or tied in a bunch, it is used to flavour soups, stocks and meat dishes, particularly casseroles. The Romans used thyme to flavour cheese and liqueurs. The leaves of thyme placed 'near the resorts of mice are said to drive these animals from the place'.

Herbalists used an ointment produced from thyme blossom for healing wounds, removing warts and relieving gout. The leaves, bruised, were an antidote for bee stings. An infusion of the leaves was claimed to be an excellent remedy for headaches and an 'infallible cure for a nightmare'. The herb was also sometimes used as a cough mixture for children, 'purging the body of phlegm, also for killing worms in the belly'.

Astrologically under the dominion of Mars and Venus, thyme is the birthday flower for 9 June. It symbolizes strength, courage and activity.

Toadflax   see **Common toadflax**

Traveller's joy
Clematis vitalba

The generic name is a Greek word denoting various climbing plants. Gerard claims that the common name was given from the plant 'decking

and adorning waies and hedges where people travel'. Bishop Mant describes the plant in its summer display:

> . . . The traveller's joy!
> Most beauteous when its flowers assume
> Their autumn form of a feathery plume.
> The traveller's joy! name well bestowed
> On that wild plant.

Other names include wild clematis, wild vine, withywind and, certainly the most popular, old man's beard. John Clare recalls:

> And Old Man's Beard, that wreath'd along the hedge
> Its oddly rude misshapen tawney flowers.

Beggars wandering along country lanes used the plant to make wounds, 'in order to excite compassion' in more populated areas. Although the plant was said to be poisonous when fresh, it was used, dried, as cattle fodder. The hollow stem, when old, was cut into small pieces and smoked in pipes – the acrid flavour was thought to resemble tobacco.

Traveller's joy is the birthday flower for 7 October. It symbolizes rest, mental beauty, safety, artfulness and filial love.

Tulip
Tulipa gesneriana

The name *Tulipa* is the Latin version of the Arabic for a turban. It was
the flower of the Turkish court, where it was discovered by a European
diplomat who subsequently took some bulbs to Holland. *T. gesneriana*,
named after the botanist Conrad von Gesner, is a cultivated hybrid, the
principal ancestor of the garden tulips of today. Tulips were introduced
to England in about 1578. Victoria Sackville-West wrote:

> So cosmopolitan, these English tulips,
> To cottager as native as himself!
> Aliens, that Shakespeare neither saw nor sang.
> Alien Asiatics, that have blown
> Between the boulders of the Persian hill
> Long centuries before they reached the dykes
> To charm van Huysum and the curious Brueghel.

Of the hundreds of varieties produced the striped ones were preferred,
and plain coloured ones were not highly regarded. In the 1630s fortunes
were made and lost in the European bulb trade – people called it tulip
mania, and single bulbs changed hands for hundreds of pounds.

Tulip bulbs have been eaten as a sweetmeat, the taste of which was said
to have been 'almost as pleasant as the Eringus rootes, being firme and
sound, fit to be presented to the curious'. The bulbs were believed to be
an aphrodisiac. A writer reporting on the matter commented cautiously,
'I cannot say either from my selfe, not having eaten many . . . if there be
any special properties in the root of the Orchis or some other tending to
that purpose, I think this may as well have it as they.' In the language of
the flowers, tulip symbolizes eloquence, eternal separation, fame, extravagance, oratory and spring.

A red tulip is the birthday flower for 7 June, symbolizing ardent love.
A variegated tulip is the birthday flower for 8 June, and in the language
of the flowers means, 'Your eyes are beautiful'. A yellow tulip signifies
hopeless love. In the Christian tradition, the tulip is an emblem of Christ,
symbolic of the chalice.

Turnip
Brassica rapa

The generic name is Latin for cabbage, of which family the turnip is a
member. The turnips of the Elizabethans were similar to ours, although

their cultivation was chiefly confined to gardens. An abundance of blossom on turnips running to seed is said to indicate a good crop the following season.

An old Halloween custom still popular today, though originally intended to frighten away witches and evil spirits, involved hollowing out a turnip to resemble a sinister face. A lighted candle was then placed inside and it was hung on a gatepost or tree near the house, to protect the occupants.

A country expression for a girl who has given her lover the cold shoulder is 'She has given him turnips'. Another saying is, 'Don't try to squeeze blood out of a turnip', as opposed to a stone, and to someone who looks pale: 'You must have cut a turnip and rubbed the blood on your cheeks.'

Turnip blossom is the birthday flower for 5 October. It symbolizes charity.

Valerian   see **Common valerian**

Venus's looking glass
Legousia hybrida

The small purple-flowering Venus's looking glass was found by Gerard growing wild; he collected seeds from it for his garden. Classified by him originally among the gentians, it became a popular annual. The flower is also known as corn violet.

In classical legend the plant is associated with Venus and her magic mirror, which made everything reflected in it appear beautiful. Unfortunately she lost her treasured looking glass, which was found by a lowly shepherd who, charmed by his own reflection, had no wish to return it to its lovely owner. His stubborn refusal resulted in Cupid being dispatched to collect it. As he struck the mirror from the shepherd's hands it fell to the ground and shattered. The flower sprang up in their place.

In the language of the flowers the plant signifies flattery.

Vervain
Verbena officinalis

The generic name is a corruption of Latin *herba bona*, good plant. *Verbena* is the classical Latin name for this herb especially, and also signified 'altar plants' in general. Country names include frog's foot, which is particularly old:

> Frossie-foot men call it
> For his levys are like frossy's feet.

The Crusaders believed that it sprang up at Calvary when the nails were driven into Christ's hands, from which legend it became known as herb on the cross. For this reason it was used to sprinkle holy water.

Vervain was valued by the druids second only to **mistletoe**. Those who collected 'the plant took care that before they take up the herb, they bistow upon the ground, where it groweth, honey with the combs, in token of satisfaction and amends for the wrong and violence done in depriving her of so holy a herb' (J. Ingram, *Flora Symbolica*). In more recent times it was customary in Lancashire to cross the herb with one's hands before gathering it, saying:

> Hallowed by Thou, Vervain
> As thou growest on the ground.

Many superstitions surrounded the plant. The Romans believed it was a herb of good omen. In medieval times people who bathed in water containing vervain were said to be able to see into the future and have every wish granted. It was used as a charm against possible enchantments, as a love philtre, and to make people laugh. Locks could be opened at will if a leaf was pressed into a small cut on the hand, and to hang the roots around one's neck prevented dreaming.

In the *London Pharmacopaeia*, as late as 1837, a necklace of vervain roots tied with white satin was recommended to ward off the King's evil, or scrofula.

Astrologically vervain is under the sign of Venus. It is the birthday flower for 18 May, symbolizing enchantment, and faithfulness.

Vetch
Vicia

The generic name is the classical Latin name of the plant, which is also known as tare. Formerly vetch was grown extensively for cattle food. The plant was probably introduced by the Romans. Its hardiness is indicated in the old saying:

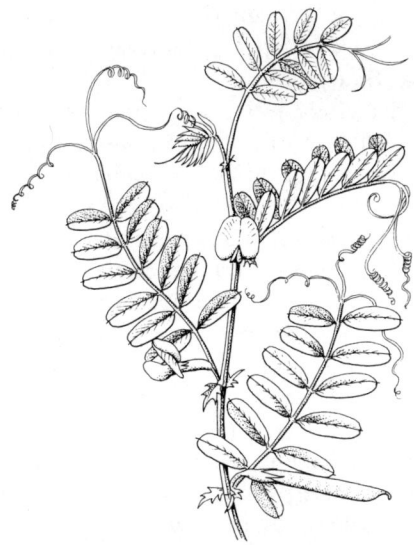

A vetch will grow through
The bottom of an old shoe.

Vetch is the birthday flower for 13 August, symbolizing shyness.

Violet
Viola

The generic name is the Latin word for various sweet-scented flowers, derived from the same source as Greek *ion*. The violet was the plant which the Greeks named *ion* from Io, a daughter of Ianchus, beloved of Zeus, who fed on violets after she had been transformed into a heifer by Jupiter:

> Love's dropped eyelids and a kiss
> Such our breath and blueness is.
> Io, the mild shape,
> Hidden by Jove's fears,
> Found us first i' in the sward, when she
> For hunger stooped in tears;
> Where so'er her lips she sets,
> Said Jove, be breaths called violets.

Greek legend alternatively claims that the violet sprang from the blood of

Ajax, famous hero of the Trojan War. Violets are also alleged to have sprung up from the blood of Attis, a Phrygian vegetation diety who was brutally killed beneath a pine tree.

In earlier times the violet was regarded by troubadours, as was the **wallflower**, as an emblem of constancy. In competitions a prize of a golden violet was awarded to the best versifier, indicating the esteem in which the flower was held. Violets were used in the religious ceremony called Creeping the Cross, which was celebrated on Good Friday: priests in crimson robes, singing mournfully, carried the image of the cross accompanied by another image representing a dead person. In more recent times the flower was a popular choice for Mothering Sunday. On this day young people who worked away from their homes visited their mothers. A posy of violets made a pretty gift and gave rise to the saying: 'Go a-mothering, and find violets in the lane.' Nevertheless some superstition did surround the plant, although in some parts of England people thought they harboured fleas if brought into the house. A wreath of the flowers worn around the neck was said to prevent drunkenness.

In history the flower was associated with Napoleon, who, when banished to Elba, told his friends that he would return with the violets. 'Corporal Violet' became a favourite toast among his faithful followers. The Empress Josephine had thrown him a bunch of violets at their first meeting.

Syrup of violets consists of a quart of freshly picked flowers steeped in a quart of cold water until the colour and flavour are absorbed into the water. The liquid is then strained and 4 pounds of sugar added for each quart of fluid. Gradually the liquid is brought to the boil and simmered until it forms a thick syrup. A violet conserve was made from flower petals beaten to a smooth paste with twice their weight in sugar, and then potted and sealed. Violet vinegar, which is said to lend a special flavour to salad dressing, can be made by filling a jar half full with flower heads then topping it up with boiled white wine vinegar and allowing it to stand for one week. The liquid is then carefully strained, bottled and well corked. Violet honey was also very popular. A handful of petals was mixed with one pound of ordinary honey and heated in a double boiler until the mixture acquired the flavour of violets.

A toilet water, which gives a fragrant scent to the body when applied after bathing, can be made from 2 ounces of violet petals to one pint of wine vinegar. The ingredients should be placed in a container and stood in a warm place, ideally in sunlight, for two weeks, then strained and bottled. Violet-scented toilet waters, soaps and powders are still very popular today.

Pliny referred to the violet's excellent properties, believing that the odour of some species cured headaches, and that healing virtues existed in the leaves and flowers. In the Middle Ages the flower was quite extensively used in medicine. A powder produced from the dried petals and taken in water was used to counteract epilepsy, quinsy, pleurisy, jaundice and sleeplessness. A poultice of flowers and leaves was applied to the forehead to relieve headaches, and the expressed juice, which forms a slightly laxative syrup, was prescribed for children.

Astrologically the violet is under the dominion of Venus and the sign of Aries. However, the various species and colours are associated with different days, each having their own symbolism. A blue violet is the birthday flower for 11 March, symbolizing faithfulness and love. A white violet is the birthday flower for 14 March, symbolizing candour, innocence and modesty. A purple violet signifies, 'You occupy my thoughts'. A yellow violet is the birthday flower for 28 April, signifying rare worth and rural happiness. The wild violet means love in idleness.

Viper's bugloss
Echium vulgare

The generic name is derived from a Greek word for viper, from the resemblance of the spotted stem to the skin of a snake, although other sources claim that it is an excellent antidote for snakebite – the seeds of the plant resembling the head of a viper, and because of this are considered effective against the bite of reptiles. Ideally, it was recommended that the remedy be taken before the snakebite! Bugloss is from Greek *bous*, ox, and Latin *glossa*, tongue, suggested by the shape of the leaves. In legend a variety of bugloss leaf is said to have provided the flannel for the Christ child's clothes.

Herablists recommended the seeds or roots, drunk in wine, to increase milk in nursing mothers. It was also prescribed for backache, kidney complaints, fevers and to 'defend the heart' (Culpepper).

Astrologically bugloss is under the dominion of the sun and the sign of Leo. In the language of the flowers it signifies falsehood.

Wallflower
Cheiranthus cheiri

The generic name is probably derived from Greek *cheir*, hand, and *anthos*, flower, referring to the custom of carrying these sweet-smelling flowers in the hand. *Cheiri* is an adaptation of the Moorish name *keiri*, the plant having originally been introduced from Spain. Earlier names for the plant included wall stock-gillofer, wild cheir, bleeding heart and chevi-saunce – the last was probably a misprint for cherisaunce. It was also known as winter gilly-flower, March gilly-flower, yellow violet and yellow stock gillyflower.

Legend tells how during the fourteenth century it was said to bloom on the walls of a Scottish castle where Elizabeth, daughter of the Earl of March, resided. Although betrothed to Robert III of Scotland, she fell in love with the son of a border chief, who, disguised as a minstrel, sang beneath her window. They agreed to elope – she would drop a sprig of wallflower as a sign. Unfortunately, in her haste to escape, she fell to her death. Her distraught lover travelled through Europe as a minstrel, wearing the flower in his cap in her memory. Other troubadours copied the gesture and the wallflower became a symbol of fidelity in adversity. The story was later retold by Robert Herrick; in his version the dead girl is transformed into a wallflower by Jupiter.

It was a common belief that certain plants could encourage or discourage each other's growth. If wallflowers were planted near **apple** trees, the fruiting of those trees was supposed to benefit.

Herbalists thought the yellow wallflower more effective than others. The flowers were made into a conserve to deal with apoplexy and palsy, and for cleansing the blood and liver. Earlier writers advised that 'It stayeth inflammation and swellings, and comforteth and strengtheneth any weak part.' Culpepper claimed that the wallflowers could be used to cleanse the eyes and 'foul and filthy sores in the mouth'. A plaster consisting of the flowers, oil and wax was applied to chapped areas around the sexual organs. Wallflower seeds were used to bring about an abortion, to encourage menstruation and to expel a stillborn baby.

It is the birthday flower for 20 May and symbolizes fidelity in adversity. Astrologically, the flower is assigned to the moon.

Walnut
Juglans regia

The generic name is derived from Latin Jovis (Jupiter), and *glans*, acorn –
Jupiter's nut. The walnut was introduced to England in the sixteenth
century, and an old saying refers to its slow growth: 'Who plants a
walnut tree expects not to eat the fruit.' The tree was considered an
enemy of the **oak**, and if oak and walnut were planted near each other
one of them would be expected to wither. Similarly an **apple** tree would
not bear fruit if planted in the vicinity of a black walnut. The nuts should
be beaten off the tree, as the old saying advises:

> A woman and a spaniel and a Walnut tree,
> The more you beat them the better they be.

In Greek and Roman antiquity the fruit, a symbol of fertility, was served
at wedding celebrations and feasts.

The Ancient Doctrine of Plant Signatures suggests that the convoluted
surface of the walnut shell made it suitable for the treatment of brain
disorders. Herbalists used the juice of the unripened green husks mixed
with honey as a gargle – the fruit was considered more potent when
green. Bites of mad dogs and venomous creatures were treated with it,
although for this purpose it was mixed with honey, **onion** and salt.
When old and oily the kernels were prescribed for gangrenous wounds
and carbuncles. Ash of the kernels, taken in red wine, was thought to
stop hair from falling out and also colour it blonde. A dark brown dye,
for general use, can be produced from the shells and husks.

Walnut is the birthday plant for 15 March, symbolizing intellect,
longevity, presentiment and stratagem. The white walnut means lack of
dignity, explained by the tree's cragginess and sparse foliage, while the
black walnut symbolizes majesty, strength and tenacity. A walnut
branch signifies contagion. Astrologically the walnut is assigned to the
sun.

Watercress
Nasturtium officinalis

For the derivation of the common name see **nasturtium**. Listed as one of
the Nine Sacred Herbs, it was used by the Hebrews as a side dish at
banquets, particularly the Passover feast. Watercress is symbolic of the
coming of spring, suggesting perpetual life and the renewal of the

sustaining hope of human redemption. The ancient Greeks believed it had special properties, hence the saying: 'Eat cresses and get wit.'

Watercress is a common wild plant which has been cultivated as a salad herb since 1808. Oliver Goldsmith (1728–74) movingly describes an old watercress gatherer in his poem 'The Deserted Village':

> All the bloomy flush of life is fled.
> All but yon widow'd, solitary thing
> That feebly bends beside the plashy spring;
> She, wretched matron, forced in age, for bread,
> To strip the brook with mantling cresses spread.

Herbalists claimed that watercress juice applied to freckles and spots removed them overnight. Mixed with vinegar and placed on the forehead, it was said to revive those who felt 'dull and drowsy'. The plant was thought to be an excellent remedy against scurvy. Revellers suffering from a hangover would relieve their unhappy state by chewing on sprigs of watercress.

Astrologically the plant is assigned to the moon. It is the birthday flower for 24 September, symbolic of power and stability.

Water crowfoot
Ranunculus aquatilis

For the derivation of the generic name see **meadow buttercup**. The name crowfoot comes from the supposed resemblance of the shape of the leaf to a crow's foot. It is probably the same plant as the *coronopus*, the crow's-foot, of Dioscorides. The plant forms a beautiful white and green carpet on ponds and slow-moving streams. Unlike many crowfoot species it does not have an acrid taste and was formerly gathered by boat and used as cattle fodder. In 'The Idle Flowers' Robert Bridges observed the plant's growth:

> . . . along the stream
> My care, hath not forgot
> Crowsfoot's white galaxy
> And love's Forget-me-not.

Crowfoot is the birthday flower for 20 August, symbolizing ingratitude and brilliance.

Water-lily

White water-lily
Nymphaea alba

Older writers claim that *Nymphaea* is so called because the plant grows in the watery haunts of nymphs or naiads. A more modern interpretation is that it was named after Nymphe, one of the water nymphs. The flowers rise above the water under the influence of light and expand only during sunshine. Towards evening they close their petals and sink beneath the surface:

> Asleep upon the stream . . .
> The moonlit stream;
> The water-lilies dream . . .
> Floating they dream
> With cups of purest white
> All folded from the night.

Yellow water-lily
Nuphar lutea

The generic name is a corruption of the Arabic, *neufar* and of the Latin *lutea*, *luteus*, yellow. Old country names include candock, the broad leaves suggesting the dock and the flagon-shaped seed vessel a can, and brandy-bottle from a supposed odour in the flower which is obviously also of similar shape. A third name, water-can, was given it because of the appearance of the half unfolded leaves, rolled into slender, green, vase-like forms. The plant is also known as queen of the river. The heart-shaped leaves rest on the water, although the flowers are raised on their stems above the water.

Wood engravers favoured the flowing lines of lilies, generally in church decoration. They also provided the inspiration for Joseph Paxton when he was working on the plans for the Crystal Palace he designed for the 1851 Exhibition. The various radiating patterns on the underside of the leaves helped to solve the complex problem of a suitable framework capable of supporting hundreds of tons of glass, which was at the same time aesthetically pleasing.

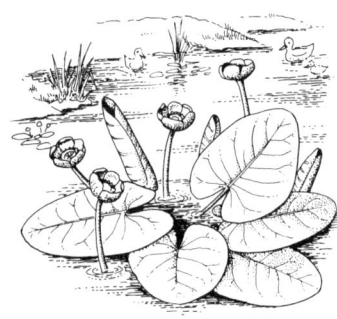

The roots of both the yellow and white species have a bitter and astringent flavour containing a quantity of starch and were toasted and eaten as one would eat potatoes. According to Culpepper the seeds and the root are 'effectual to stay fluxes of blood or humours, either wounds or of the belly: but the roots are most used and more effectual to cool, bind and restrain all fluxes in men or women and passing away of the seed when asleep.' Distilled water of the flowers was 'commended to take away freckles, spots and sunburn from the face.' The Elizabethans were alleged to use the seeds in soup and meat to induce chastity. As recently as the twentieth century a remedy concocted from the root was recommended in the treatment of dysentery, diarrhoea and gonorrhoea. An infusion of the plant was used as a gargle for ulcerations of the mouth and throat, and as an infection in the treatment of leucorrhoea.

Astrologically the water-lily is assigned to the moon and the sign of Pisces. In the language of the flowers it symbolizes purity. It is the Christian symbol of chastity and in the Celtic tradition the five petals of the yellow water-lily signify birth, initiation, marriage, rest from labour and death.

Wayfaring tree
Viburnum lantana

> Wayfaring Tree, what ancient claim
> Hast thou to that right pleasant name?
> Was it that some faint pilgrim came
> Unhopedly to thee,
> In the brown desert's weary way,
> 'Mid toil and thirst's consuming sway,
> And there, as 'neath thy shade he lay,
> Bless'd the Wayfaring Tree?
>
> WILLIAM HOWITT (1792–1879)

For the derivation of the generic name see **guelder rose**, to which it is closely related. Other common names include mealy guelder rose, cobin tree and cotton tree – the last name from the cottonlike appearance of the young shoots. As the foliage unfolds it seems to be covered in dust, and by June the large clusters of white flowers are fully out.

The leaves were used in a number of herbal remedies; combined with those of the olive tree they were mixed with vinegar and water as a mouthwash and gargle, a concoction that was also thought to strengthen loose teeth. The kernels of the unripe fruit, taken in any liquid, were recommended for diarrhoea. Formerly the foliage was used to dye hair black. Astrologically the tree is under the influence of Saturn.

Wheat
Triticum vulgare

The generic name is derived from a Latin word meaning to grind. It is well documented that prehistoric man, using polished stone weapons, grew and ground wheat. There were harvests over fifteen thousand years ago, and the first wheat fields were probably between the Tigris and the Euphrates in present-day Iraq. Harvesting the grain and milling the flour have changed considerably over the centuries, but wheat remains king of the world's food plants.

In former times in England the end of the harvest was steeped in ritual. The last swathe of corn, in which the corn spirits were believed to have hidden, was traditionally made into a corn dolly, decorated with corn marigolds, which are a sun symbol, and coloured ribbons. Customs vary in different parts of the country, but it was usually popular to urinate on the effigy, whatever the ritual – the motivation was fertility. The corn dolly remained in the farmhouse until the following year, to ensure a plentiful harvest.

Modern farming methods have almost destroyed the old custom of taking the last sheaf of corn to decorate the font of a church for the Harvest Festival service. However wheat, with **oats**, is still used on these occasions, particularly in country communities where it is more meaningful. In 'Diary of a Church Mouse' John Betjeman refers to this occasion:

> For me the only feast at all
> Is Autumn's Harvest Festival,
> Where I can satisfy my want
> With ears of corn around the font.

The lore surrounding the sowing of wheat and the abundance of the harvest is explained in various old sayings:

> A wet and windy May
> Fills the barn with corn and hay.

and

> March dry, good rye,
> April wet, good wheat.

also

> Light Christmas, light wheatsheaf,
> Dark Christmas, heavy wheatsheaf.

The ideal conditions for planting seed are reflected in the old adage:

> Sow wheat in dirt
> Rye in dust.

A passage in Brand's *Popular Antiquities* referring to the reign of Henry VIII records that brides wore garlands of corn ears, sometimes finely gilded, and that wheat was sprinkled over their heads. It is recorded that when Henry VIII took one of his brides to Bristol, a baker's wife threw corn, crying, 'Welcome and good luck'.

Herbalists maintained that to eat green wheat caused worms. However, oil pressed from wheat, by heating iron or copper plates, was used to treat ringworm. Slices of wheat bread soaked in red **rose** water were recommended for inflamed eyes. Wheat flour mixed with different herbs to form a poultice was a very popular remedy for a variety of complaints.

Wheat is the birthday plant for 3 October. It symbolizes prosperity, abundance of life and the power of the creator's seed. As an emblem of agriculture and autumn it was worshipped in the west as the staff of life. A bearded wheat ear means faithfulness and rejuvenating fire; a green wheat ear is associated with the Egyptian deity Horus, and a white one with Christ. A wheatsheaf means death, fertility, the harvest and Thanksgiving Day. Wheat is also the Christian emblem of the saints Walburge and Wenceslaus, and an attribute to pagan earth goddesses.

Whitebeam
Sorbus aria

The generic name is from the Latin word for a service tree; *aria* is derived from aries, beam. The Old English word *beam* means tree. This species is known as whitebeam, because of the white down on the young shoots and the undersurface of the leaves. In 'Love in the Valley' George Meredith recalls the sight of the whitebeam among yew trees: 'Flashing as in gusts the sudden-lighted whitebeam.' Other names for the tree are whipcrop, Cumberland hawthorn, henapple, hoar withy and white rice.

The scarlet fruits are known in parts of the Lake District as chess-apples. When over-ripe the fruit is quite pleasant, not unlike the **medlar**.

Whitebeam wood is very hard, and from earliest times has been used to make shafts and axles. Before cast iron was in regular use all machine wheels were cogged with whitebeam.

White bryony
Bryonia dioica

The generic name is derived from Greek *bryo*, sprout; *dioica* refers to the dioecious character of the blossoms – flowers of a different sex appear on different plants. Common names are red-berried bryony, mandragora, devil's turnip, wild vine, wood vine and Our Lady's seal. As Our Lady's seal it has been the emblem of the Nativity of the Virgin as far back as A.D.695. Apart from a common climbing characteristic it is unrelated to black bryony, with which it is often confused.

The Romans had great faith in the protective powers of the plant. Caesar Augustus wore a wreath of bryony around his head as a protection against lightning. The plant has a fleshy forked root which

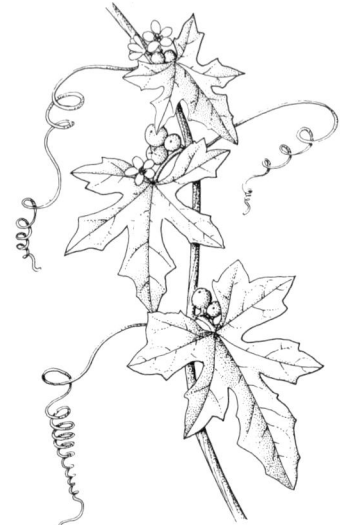

was often substituted for the mandrake (hence the alternative name mandragora) and sold as an aphrodisiac for humans and horses. It is alleged that male plants were taken by women and mares and female ones by men and stallions. Bryony was used as a general horse tonic, and, mixed with corn, to improve the coats of cattle.

Herablists praised the root of the plant as a valuable ingredient in internal and external remedies. The leaves, fruits and roots served a variety of complaints. Taken in wine once a week before going to bed it was said to cleanse the womb; a small quantity of powdered root in wine could bring on menstruation. Leprosy and dropsy were both treated with bryony.

In the language of the flowers, bryony symbolizes prosperity. Astrologically it is assigned to Mars.

White mustard
Sinapis alba

The generic name is from the Greek word for the plant. The white species is particularly large. Although many households grew mustard for their own use it was not until about the fourteenth century that actual crops were cultivated as it was difficult to harvest – the ripe seeds fall at the slightest movement. Women would go out into the fields wearing large aprons or carrying linen bags, and gather it whole, after which it was beaten with a cane to separate the small seeds from the chaff.

> Maids, mustard-seed gather, for being too ripe,
> And weather it well, ere ye give it a stripe;
> Then dress it, and lay it in soller up sweet,
> Lest foistiness make it, for table unmeet.

For several hundred years mustard was traditionally sold in balls. A passage in *Paradise of Plants* by W. Cole, published in 1657, reads: 'In Gloucestershire about Teuxbury they grind Mustard and make it into balls which are brought to London and other remote places as being the best that the world affords.' In Shakespeare's *Henry IV* Falstaff describes Poins thus: 'his wits as thick as Tewkesbury mustard'.

Perhaps the most important uses made of mustard in medicine were as an emetic in cases of poisoning and as a valuable counter-irritant when applied externally. The seeds were recommended as a remedy for constipation, chewed as a cure for toothache, and taken in liquid as a gargle for diseases and swellings of the throat. Formerly a decoction of the seed in wine was used as an antidote for poisonous mushrooms and the bites of 'scorpions or venomous beasts'. A recipe for improving the voice consisted of powdered mustard seed with honey, made into balls.

Mustard is the birthday flower for 18 June, symbolizing growth, fertility, abundance and indifference. In the language of the flowers it signifies, 'I smart'. Astrologically it is a herb of Mars, under the sign of Aries.

Wild asparagus
Asparagus officinalis

The generic word is derived from Greek *asparagos*, from a word meaning to tear, suggesting the prickly nature of some of the species. The plant was formerly known as sporage and sparrow-grass, according to Prior 'an example of the habit of the uneducated to explain an unknown word with a more familiar one'.

Asparagus is one of our oldest and most highly esteemed vegetables. It was a favourite dish of Cato and Pliny, who declared that nature intended it to grow wild so that we all might eat it. In Roman times some of the varieties were said to produce stems 3 pounds in weight – heavy enough, apparently, to knock down a slave! Doctors at that time thought it was injurious to the eyesight; however this could be remedied by taking a slice or two of boiled pumpkin. The Elizabethans believed that asparagus 'increased seed and stirred up lust'.

Earlier herbalists recommended asparagus boiled in white wine for urinary problems, and boiled in broth for the bowels. Modern homoeopaths use it as a diuretic and a laxative, and in the treatment of rheumatism. The seeds used to be removed from the red berries and used as a substitute for coffee.

Astrologically asparagus is under the dominion of Jupiter.

Wild carrot
Daucus carota

> On twigs of hawthorn he regaled,
> On pippens' russet peel,
> And when his juicy salads failed,
> Sliced carrot pleased him well.
> WILLIAM COWPER (1731–1800), 'EPITAPH ON A HARE'

The generic name for the plant has been handed down from the old Greek writers, who valued it for its medicinal properties. During flowering the head of the plant is slightly convex, but as the seeds ripen they assume the shape of curious hollow cups, from which it also became known as bird's nest.

Carrot as a vegetable was familiar to both the Greeks and Romans, although at that time it was used primarily as cattle fodder. During the reign of Elizabeth I Flemish refugees promoted it as an addition to the British diet, though it had been introduced rather earlier. Nevertheless during the reign of James I the plant was rare, and ladies of the court wore the leaves in 'halls and palaces'.

The flowers, boiled in wine, were used as a love philtre in the belief that they helped contraception. The leaves, smeared with honey, were laid on open sores and ulcers, and great faith was placed in the results. The plant was also used to expel wind, to help menstruation, and to 'provoke urine and help stitches in the side'. Astrologically wild carrot is assigned to the planet Mercury.

Wild pansy
Viola tricolor

For the derivation of the generic name see **violet**. *Tricolor* means three-coloured in Latin. The wild pansy has many delightful country names, including three faces in a hood, butterfly flower, herb trinity, kiss behind the garden gate, cull me to you, herb constancy, kiss me quick, heart's-ease, and love in idleness. The garden pansy was not established until the nineteenth century and is a cross between the wild pansy and other species.

In legend, Cupid shot an arrow at the wild pansy, which was originally white. The wound is said to have caused the flower to change colour. The juice was used as a love charm when placed on the eyelids while a person slept, causing them, on awakening, to fall in love with the first person they saw. This was the plant that Shakespeare has Puck apply to Titania's eyelids in *A Midsummer Night's Dream*, causing her subsequently to fall in love with Bottom:

> Yet marked I where the bolt of Cupid fell,
> It fell upon a little Western flower.
> Before milk white, now purple with love's wound;
> The maidens call it Love-in-idleness.
> Fetch me that flower; the herb I show'd thee once;
> The juice of it on sleeping eye-lids laid
> Will make a man or woman madly dote
> Upon the next live creature that it sees.

Superstitious people believed that to pick a pansy with dew on the petals would cause the death of a loved one. The flower was also used as a weather oracle – if picked on a fine day, it was claimed it would rain. Counting the lines on a pansy petal, which should either have been picked or given, not bought, was used to tell one's fortune:

> Four: your wish will come true.
> Five: there's trouble ahead but you will overcome it.
> Six: a surprise is coming to you.
> Seven: you have a faithful sweetheart.
> Eight: your sweetheart may be fickle.
> Nine: you will go over the water to wed.

It is luckier for the lines to incline towards the right, and if the centre line is the longest you should insist that your engagement is announced on a Sunday.

An Elizabethan herbalist recommended the use of the plant in venereal disorders. It was also alleged to cure asthma, convulsions in children, epilepsy and pleurisy. A cordial made from the herb was used for heart complaints: some old writers supposed that that was how it received the name heart's-ease.

Pansy is the birthday flower for 4 February, meaning, in the language of the flowers, 'You occupy my thoughts'. Older writers dedicated the flower to the Trinity because of the three colours found in each flower; many old herbals refer to it as *Herba Trinitatis*.

Wild plum
Prunus domestica

For the derivation of the generic name see **blackthorn**. The garden plum was probably introduced by the Romans. In his *Shepherd's Calendar* John Clare describes the flowering of the tree and a seasonal companion:

> And sloe and wild plum blossom peeping out
> In thickset knotts of flowers preparing gay
> For Aprils reign a mockery of May
> That soon will glisten on the earnest eye
> Like snow white cloaths hung in the sun to drye.

In Wales the flowering of the plum in December foretold a death in the family.

Herbalists recommended the leaves boiled in wine as a gargle and mouthwash, the gum or leaves boiled in vinegar for ringworm, and the oil pressed from the stones for the treatment of inflamed piles, ulcers, sore throats and earache. Culpepper, however, dismissed the fruit with the pronouncement that 'all plumbs are under Venus, and are, like women, some better and some worse'.

Plum blossom symbolizes fidelity and in the language of the flowers means, 'Keep your promises'. Wild plum is the birthday flower for 15 June, meaning independence; a withered plum tree signifies a bastard.

Wild strawberry
Fragaria vesca

The generic name is derived from Latin *fragans*, fragrant, and *vesca*, edible. In Anglo-Saxon times it was *streowberie*, suggesting stray-berry, from the long suckers and its ability to cover a wide area of ground. Some sources, however, suggest that the common name has arisen from the practice of putting straw around the plant to prevent the fruit from becoming soiled. The smallness of the fruit of the wild strawberry makes it difficult to pick; nevertheless it often tastes as sweet as the garden varieties developed from it.

In Browne's *Pastorals* a centuries-old custom is recalled, when the fruit was threaded on stems of grass for one's lover:

> The wood-nymphs often times would busy be,
> And pluck for him the blushing strawberry;
> Making of them a bracelet on a bent
> Which for a favour to this swain they sent.

In the Christian tradition the strawberry plant with both flower and fruit is a symbol of the good fruits of the Holy Spirit; the strawberry leaf stands for the Trinity. The strawberry is an emblem of the Virgin Mary and John the Baptist and, because it is cool and dry when green and moist when ripe, it is an attribute of pagan love goddesses. In Norse mythology Frigga, queen of the gods and principal wife of Odin, concealed dead children in strawberry leaves and smuggled them into heaven. In Britain the strawberry leaf is symbolic of rank – ducal coronets are ornamented with eight such leaves.

Herbalists made a lotion from the roots and leaves for mouth ulcers and to fix loose teeth. The distilled juice of the fruit was recommended for 'purification of the heart', jaundice and ulcers of the skin, and to cool the liver, spleen and blood. Nevertheless eating strawberries during a fever could cause one to have a fit – or so our ancestors would have us believe.

The stawberry plant is the birthday flower for 13 May. In the linguage of the flowers strawberry blossom means, 'Be on the alert' and signifies innocence. The fruit symbolizes esteem, love and perfection. Astrologically it is under the sign of Venus.

Willow
Salix

The generic name, *salix*, is the Latin for willow and is probably derived from two Celtic words, *sal* and *lis*, meaning near water. Willow is derived from the Old English *wilig*, *welige* and *withig*, signifying a plant suitable for withes or ties, and the flexible twigs were widely used in basketwork and finer types of wickerwork. As James Graham recalls:

> To name the uses of the Willow tribe
> Were endless tasks. The baskets various forms
> For various purposes of household thrift,
> The wicker chair, of size and shape antique,
> The rocking couch of sleeping infancy.

The tough white wood was also used to make handles for agricultural implements, hurdles and fences, and when burnt it yields charcoal – used for gunpowder. The silky down on the catkins of some varieties was used to fill cushions and pillows.

Great sallow, *salix caprea*, is a type of willow and *caprea* is the Latin for goat. A 1532 woodcut by the German botanist Tragus (Jerome Boch) shows a goat standing on its hind legs and eating sallow catkins. The tree is also known as goat willow, sally withy, saugh tree palmer and palm.

In mythology, willow is sacred to Circe, Hecate and Persephone, all death aspects of the mother goddess, and it became a symbol of mourning (especially the weeping willow, whose branches droop mournfully to the ground and whose long, narrow leaves resemble tears). In some parts of the country it is thought to be unlucky to bring it into the house.

Willow was used in Palm Sunday processions to represent the palm leaves strewn in the road when Jesus rode into Jerusalem, and in some churches children are still given small 'palm' crosses made of willow. Goethe wrote:

> In Rome upon Palm Sunday
> They bear true palms:
> The Cardinals bow reverently,
> And sing old psalms;
> Elsewhere their psalms are sung
> 'Mid olive branches,
> The holly bough supplies their places
> Among the avalanches:
> More northern climes must be content
> With the sad willow.

Willow might have been chosen because it was one of the plants used by the Israelites to celebrate the Feast of the Tabernacle: 'They were to gather the boughs of goodly trees, branches of palm, and the boughs of thick trees and willow of the brook and to rejoice before the Lord their God seven days.' It was also the willow upon which the Jews hung their harps when they sat down and wept in remembrance of their native land and in Christianity it signifies Christ's gospel.

During the Middle Ages willow was believed to be a giver of eloquence and was sacred to poets. It was also a means of love divination: after running three times round the house carrying a willow wand a girl would see her future husband grasping the end of the stick. However, beating a child with a willow stick was thought to stunt its growth – because the willow decays early.

In the *Brevairie of Health*, published in 1598, the oil of **water-lily**, **rose** and willow is recommended for cramp. Herbalists also used the burnt ashes of willow bark mixed with vinegar to treat warts and a decoction of the leaves or bark in wine could be rinsed through the hair to cure dandruff and scurf. The boughs of the tree were thought to have a cooling effect if placed in the room of a person with fever.

Willow, astrologically assigned to the moon, is the birthday flower for 22 May, and symbolizes celibacy and forsaken love:

> A Willow garland thou didst send
> Perfumed, last day, to me,
> Which did but only this portend
> I was forsook by thee.
>
> ROBERT HERRICK

The weeping willow is the birthday flower for 21 May and signifies sadness and mourning.

Witch hazel
Hamamelis

The generic name is from an old Greek word meaning together and apple. *H. mollis*, the Chinese witch hazel, was introduced to England in 1879 and is the most popular and handsome of all the witch hazels, producing fragrant golden flowers before the leaves:

> And the Witch-hazel, *Hamamelis mollis*,
> That comes before its leaf on naked bough,
> Torn ribbons frayed, of yellow and maroon
> And sharp of scent in frosty English air.

wrote Victoria Sackville-West.

The bark and leaves are tonic, astringent and sedative. Some of the uses made of these properties included treatment for diarrhoea, dysentery, excessive discharges of mucus and bleeding from the lungs and stomach. The witch hazel used commercially today, to treat bruises and swellings, is obtained from *H. virginiana*.

Witch hazel is the birthday flower for 9 August, symbolizing autumn, changeability, consolation, enchantment, inspiration and mysticism. The Red Indians used a variety of witch hazel as divining rods.

Wood anemone
Anemone nemorosa

The generic name is from the Greek word for wind. Country names for the plant include wind flower and granny's nightcap. Some writers claim that it received the name wind flower in Greek because it grew on high places, exposed to Boreas, the mythological Greek god of the north wind:

The wind forbids the flowers to flourish long,
Which owe to winds their name in Grecian song.

In legend Anemone was an attendant in the court of Chloris, the deity of flowers, whose husband Zephyr fell in love with her. Chloris, jealous and angry, caused Anemone to be banished, where she pined away and died of a broken heart. In remorse Zephyr asked Venus to change her body into the anemone flower. However, he soon lost interest and abandoned the beautiful flower to the north wind, who, angry that he was unable to win her love, pulled open her petals, causing them to fade.

Because of its frail and delicate appearance, the flower was thought to be a symbol of ill-omen, 'the flush of pale red which tinges the white delicate glow which lingers on the cheek of the consumptive sufferer, marking to others inward decay, but giving a lustre of beauty which deceives its victim'. Nevertheless, magicians and wise men attributed wonderful powers to the first wood anemones to be gathered in the spring which had to be plucked by someone saying, 'I gather thee for a remedy against disease'. The flower was then placed in a scarlet cloth until required, when it was tied either round the neck or under the arm of the sufferer. An old couplet suggests that it was also carried as a protective plant:

The first spring-bloom anemone she in his doublet wove,
To keep him safe from pestilence where ever he should rove.

In the language of the flowers wood anemone means brevity and expectation. Medicinally a concoction of the leaves was used in the treatment of leprosy. The juice, sniffed up the nostrils, was thought to relieve headaches, and the root of the plant, chewed, to loosen phlegm. An eye ointment was also made from the plant. It is under the astrological dominion of Mars.

Wood sorrel
Oxalis acetosella

The generic name comes from Greek *oxys*, sharp or acid, referring to the acidity of the leaves; *acetosella* is from Latin *acetum*, vinegar. The plant has many country names such as wood-sour, cuckoo bread and cheese, cuckoo-sorrel, alleluia-flower, stubwort and fairy bells. Cuckoo-sorrel originated from the idea that the bird used the plant to clear his voice. The monkish name alleluia may have arisen from the fact that it flowers between Easter and Whitsun, when psalms of rejoicing would be sung. The plant does occur frequently in ecclesiastical decorations. John Ruskin, the nineteenth-century art critic, wrote: 'The triple leaf of this plant and white flower stained purple probably gave it strange typical interest among Christian painters.' Fairy bells is a Welsh name, given in the belief that the merry peal of its bells called the elves to moonlight dancing and revelry.

Older writers claim the wood sorrel is the true shamrock of St Patrick. The plant was an old druidic emblem in Ireland, a lucky symbol associated with the ancient Celtic sun wheel, long before A.D.432 when St Patrick arrived to teach Christianity. According to legend he was trying unsuccessfully to convert his pagan audience when, seeing at his feet the wood sorrel, he used the familiar leaf form to explain the Holy Trinity to them; from that time the plant has been dedicated to him. The plant is usually in full flower on St Patrick's Day, 17 March.

The leaves were formerly eaten as a salad herb. Domestic use was made of the oxalic acid extracted from the leaves in removing iron mould and ink stains. Twenty ounces of wood sorrel leaves yield about 3 ounces of the salt.

Greek and Roman doctors used the plant for kidney complaints. Many herbals recommend recipes containing wood sorrel for drinks, syrups and sauces in the treatment of mouth ulcers and sore throats, and as an appetizer for cleansing the blood:

> Here cooling sorrel, that againe
> We use in hot diseases.

wrote Michael Drayton.

Astrologically, wood sorrel is assigned to Venus. In the language of the flowers it signifies secret sweetness.

Wood spurge
Euphorbia amygdaloides

The generic name comes from Euphorbus, the physician of King Juba II of Numidia and Mauritania (King Juba's wife, Selene, was the daughter of Antony and Cleopatra). The king is said to have written a paper on the medicinal uses of spurge, which he named after him. Older writers claim that the common name, spurge, is from Latin *expurgare*, alluding to the medicinal effects of the plant. Wood spurge has many country names, including Bible leaf, wartweed, devil's milk, devil's cup and saucer, deer's milk, cat's milk, little-good and churn staff. The names in some instances reflect the shape of the plant; Dante Gabriel Rossetti, the nineteenth-century poet and Pre-Raphaelite painter, describes in his poem 'The Woodspurge' a characteristic of the plant:

> My eyes, wide open, had the run
> Of some ten weeds to fix upon;
> Amongst those few, out of the sun
> The woodspurge flowered, three cups in one.

All the spurges contain a large quantity of milky juice, an acid, corrosive character. Parkinson, in his *Theatrum Botanicum*, says: 'All the Spurges are heating and exulcerating the skinne, if they be outwardly applyed, and are vehement and excoriating taken inwardly, for they are offensive to the heart, liver and stomache.' Consequently herbs that were particularly beneficial to these organs were taken at the same time to ensure the success of the treatment. The juice was thought to be the most effective part of the plant, followed by the seeds and leaves and lastly the roots, which were boiled in vinegar as a remedy against toothache. It was thought important that spurge was collected with one's back to the wind, taking care not to touch either one's face or eyes with one's hands. Wood spurge was alleged to be an effective mole repellent.

Wormwood
Artemisia absinthium

For the derivation of the generic name see **mugwort**. The name wormwood is of great antiquity and is probably derived from the legend of the Garden of Eden, when it was alleged to have sprung from the track made by the serpent as it was driven out of the garden. Two country names by which the plant was known were St John's girdle, from the old custom of throwing a wreath of the herb on to the Midsummer Eve fire, to ensure protection against misfortune for the coming year, and green ginger – the taste of the root was said to be similar to the spice.

During the Middle Ages wormwood was a well-known strewing herb. As both the plant and the moth were said to be under the influence of Mars, it was thought that if wormwood was laid among clothes the moths would not touch them. Fleas were thought to be similarly affected by the plant. This belief is confirmed by Tusser, writing in 1557:

> While wormwood hath seed get a handful or twain,
> To save against March, to make flea to refrain,
> Where chamber is sweeped and wormwood is strowne,
> What saw is better if physic be true,
> For places infected with wormwood and rue.

Bunches of wormwood were hung up in the house to act as a fly repellent, and if mixed with ink the plant was said to prevent mice and rats nibbling at paper.

The whole plant is bitter and aromatic, and even as recently as this century it was applied as a tincture or fomentation for bruises, sprains and local inflammations. In earlier times the flowers and leaves were used to treat jaundice and worms, and to restore the appetite by stimulating the digestive system. A draught of wormwood beer taken every morning was said to be a remedy against bad breath and poor eyesight. Formerly, wormwood was steeped in wine, a practice thought to have originated from the ancients who mixed the plant in their wine in order to prevent them getting drunk. The seeds and flowers were favoured by the Scottish whisky distillers. Wormwood was also used in making absinthe and Chartreuse.

Wormwood is the birthday flower for 29 April, symbolizing absence, affection, calamity and false judgement. In the Old Testament the plant symbolized moral bitterness.

Yarrow
Achillea millefolium

The generic name is derived from the Greek hero Achilles. When the Greeks invaded Troy, Telephus, King Priam's son-in-law, tried to prevent them landing; Bacchus caused him to stumble and Achilles wounded him with his spear. Telephus was told by an oracle that Achilles (meaning milfoil or yarrow) would cure the wound. Instead of looking for the plant he promised to conduct Achilles to Troy if he would cure his wound. Achilles scraped some rust from his spear, and as

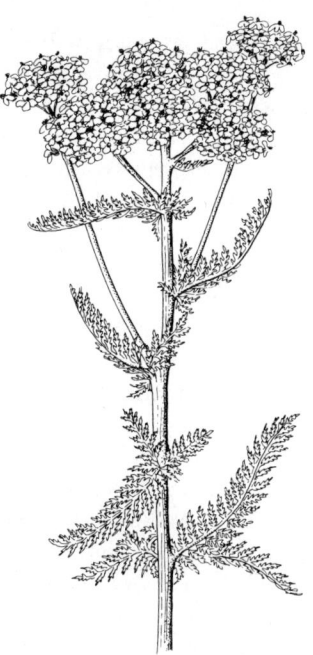

the filings fell to the ground the plant sprang up and Telephus was subsequently cured. The common name yarrow is a corruption of Old English *geavre*. Milfoil is from Norman French *mille-feuille*, from its finely cut leaves. Other names for the plant are thousand-leaf, soldier's woundwort, nosebleed, sneezewort and green arrow. The young shoots, eaten in salads, are said to have the flavour of **tarragon**.

Formerly the plant was regarded as protective, and on Midsummer Eve it was woven into the garlands which decorated homes and churches to ensure protection against evil spirits. Medieval witches favoured the plant for their spells and love potions, although it was later used as a charm against them – yarrow was strewn across thresholds and tied to babies' cradles. An ancient charm for curing a fever involved pulling off a yarrow leaf with the left hand, saying the sick person's name simultaneously, and then eating the leaf. It is said to grow in churchyards as a reproach to the dead for failing to eat their yarrow broth, whereby they would still be alive!

The superstitious had great faith in the plant as a love oracle. If a stem of yarrow was cut crosswise the initials of one's future husband were said to appear. As the plant was used as a means of making one's nose bleed, it was incorporated into a form of love divination:

> Green 'arrow, green 'arrow, you bears a white blow
> If my love loves me my nose will bleed now.

Another old name for the plant was Venus-tree:

> Thou pretty herb of Venus-tree,
> Thy true name it is Yarrow;
> Now who my bosom friends must be,
> Pray tell thou me tomorrow.

This rhyme followed a very simple ritual in which the participant placed an ounce of yarrow in a piece of flannel under a pillow enabling one to dream of one's future spouse. Eaten at a wedding, it was thought to ensure love between the bride and groom for seven years.

Yarrow was used in herbal remedies, either applied as a poultice to wounds or taken orally for internal injuries. Michael Drayton refers to the plants use: 'The yarrow, wherewithall he stops the wound made gore.' The leaves were pushed up the nostrils to cause a nosebleed, which in turn was said to ease the 'pain of megrim'. An ointment compounded from the plant was used to treat ulcers and abscesses; it was also said to stop hair falling out. The leaves, chewed, were a remedy for toothache, while a tea, claimed to be stimulating, healing and astringent, was recommended for kidney disorders. As recently as the twentieth century, yarrow was used to treat bleeding from the lungs, excessive menstruation, colic and chronic dysentery.

Yarrow is the birthday flower for 16 January. It symbolizes heartache and cure.

Yellow archangel
Lamiastrum galeobdolon

The generic name is derived from Latin *lamium*, throat, referring to the long, tubular corolla. *Galeobdolon* is from Greek *to*, meaning with the smell of a weasel. The old names weasel snout and yellow snout are self-explanatory. The name archangel would seem to have been given because the plant blooms at the time of the Feast of St Michael the Archangel, while yellow dead nettle infers that there are no stinging hairs on the plant, differing in that respect from **nettle**, which belongs to a separate family. However it does belong to the same family as white dead-nettle (*Lamium album*) and red dead-nettle (*Lamium purpureum*).

The flowering tips of the plant, cooked with butter and chives, make a tasty vegetable dish. An infusion of tea can be made from the leaves.

Yellow iris

Iris pseudacorus

The generic name is the name of the Greek goddess of the rainbow. This and other species of iris have from early times been known as fleur-de-lis or fleur-de-luce, from their many shades. Old country names include sword flag, dragon flower, daggers, livers and shalders, yellow skeggs, sheggs, fliggers, Jacob's sword, cegg, cucumber and gladyne. Skeggs, sheggs and cegg are of Anglo-Saxon origin from Old English *segg*, a small sword, in reference to the shape of the leaf. The name gladyne dates from Chaucer's day, and cucumber refers to the appearance of the seed vessel.

The iris was the symbol of conquerors. It is alleged that in ancient Egypt, when King Thutmosis III returned home from fighting in Syria, making Egypt the master of the Empire, he held aloft an iris which became a treasured flower in his country. The emblem was carved on temple walls, on the brows of statues, on the Sphinx and on royal sceptres.

During the sixth century the army of King Clovis I of France escaped defeat at the hands of the Goths when it was noticed that the yellow iris was growing far out into the River Rhine, indicating shallow water, which enabled them to ford the river to safety. In gratitude he adopted the iris as his emblem. It is known as the lily of France – this is because both irises and **daffodils** were often referred to as lilies in earlier times. In the twelfth century Louis VII of France adopted the flower as the emblem of his shield during the Crusades.

The very fragrant roots of some iris species were used for tooth and hair powder and laid among clothes as a moth repellent. An ointment and a distillation of yellow iris were prescribed for infections of the eyes and lids. Distilled water from the plant was recommended for inflammation of the breasts and ulcers on the sexual organs, both male and female. A mixture of the root with other ingredients, taken in wine, cleansed the face of 'freckles, pockye and whelkye'.

The flowers yield a yellow dye, and the roots a black one. The black dye was in demand in the woollen trade for 'Sabbath black' clothing, which everybody wore on Sundays and other important occasions.

The iris is the birthday flower for 6 September and is symbolic of eloquence, hope, light, power, primeval fire and royalty. In the language of the flowers it means, 'I have a message from you' or 'My compliments'. The petals signify faith, wisdom and valour. It is an emblem of Christ and St Barbara, to indicate her royal birth.

Yellow rattle
Rhinanthus minor

The generic name is derived from two Greek words meaning nose and flower – the projecting upper portion of the corolla suggests the name, which in other members of the genus is more pronounced. Rattle was known as pennygrass in Elizabethan times – the capsules, flat and almost circular, vaguely resemble a coin. The natural habitat of the plant is pasture – hence another popular name, hayrattle – and as the seeds rattle when they are dry this was taken as a sign that the hay was ready for cutting. It is also known as yellow rattle and yellow cockscombe, from a resemblance to the head of the domestic bird, rattle box and shackle caps.

Herbalists recommended yellow rattle boiled with beans and honey for coughs and poor eyesight. For either complaint the liquid could be drunk or dropped in the eye. The seed could also be placed in the eye removing any film or dimness without 'trouble or pain'.

Rattle is the birthday flower for 14 December symbolizing singularity. The Church dedicated the flower to St Peter (29 June).

Yew
Taxus baccata

The generic name is the Latin word for the tree. The common name is derived from Old English *iw*, signifying its evergreen character. Yew, native to England, has dark green foliage which, if eaten by animals in quantity, is poisonous; although the berries contain poisonous properties they are less dangerous. According to Greek legend the yew was formerly the nymph Smilax (see **crocus**).

When Augustine came to Britain to preach Christianity he was instructed to purify but not destroy temples of pagan worship. These sites were often surrounded by trees, and places that once gave shade and shelter to our pagan ancestors were often gradually integrated into the new religion. An ancient custom was to decorate graves with evergreens; this tradition probably dates from the occupation by the Romans who used it as a substitute for **cypress**. Later, unhappy lovers were to be remembered with garlands of yew, **willow** and **rosemary** which were placed on their coffins. *The Maid's Tragedy* by Beaumont and Fletcher, published in 1619, contains a reference to the custom:

> Lay a garland on my hearse
> Of the dismal yew;
> Maidens, willow branches bear . . . .
> Say I died true.
> My love was false, but I was firm,
> From my hour of birth.

Practically every churchyard has its yew tree. The branches were once used in Palm Sunday celebrations instead of palm branches, and in some parts of England as a Whitsuntide decoration. A pair of yew trees can sometimes be seen at the entrance to a churchyard; in Greek antiquity, these were used as a representation of the celestial twins. Nevertheless the ancients would not sit in the shade of the tree or place their beehives nearby in case the bees sucked its poison, nor would they drink wine from a bowl carved from the wood. Pliny wrote, 'It is unpleasant and fearful to look upon, as a cursed tree, without any liquid substance at all.'

Trees planted at the south-west corner of houses and in churchyards were regarded as potent protection against evil spirits. A sprig of yew stolen from a churchyard was considered an excellent ingredient for a magic potion. Cutting down and burning a tree was believed to be unlucky. In the North of England a yew branch was used as a divination rod in seeking lost property. The fiery cross which was used to summon the clans in Scotland was of yew.

The famous English longbows were fashioned from the trees, suggesting its deadliness; ones made from a consecrated yew from a churchyard were considered to be of higher value. During the reign of Edward IV every Englishman and Irishman living in England was commanded to have 'a bow of his height made of Yew, Wych-hazel or Awburne'. Several English kings have died by the bow, including Harold, William Rufus and Richard Coeur-de-Lion.

Yew is the birthday flower for 20 February, symbolizing faith, death, sadness, immortality and resurrection.

Bibliography

Arkell, Reginald, *Green Fingers*, Herbert Jenkins, 1934
    Green Fingers Again, Herbert Jenkins, 1942
Bailey, L.H. *How Plants Get Their Names*, Macmillan Co., New York, 1933
    Manual of Cultivated Plants, Macmillan Co., New York, 1924
Bateson, Frederick N.W. (ed), *Cambridge Bibliography of English Literature*,
    University Press, Cambridge, 1940
Betjeman, John and Taylor, Geoffrey, *English, Scottish and Welsh Landscape
    1700–1860*, Frederick Muller, 1944
Brewer's Dictionary of Phrase and Fable, Cassels
Bridges, Robert, *The Poetical Works*, Oxford University Press, 1914
Brimble, L.J.F., *Flowers in Britain*, Macmillan, 1944
Britton, Nathaniel and Brown, Addison, *The Illustrated Flora of the North-eastern
    United States and Canada*, Hafner Publishing, New York and London, 1963
Brownlow, M., *Herbs and the Fragrant Garden*, Darton, Longman & Todd, 1963
Church, Richard, *The Collected Poems*, J.M. Dent, 1935
Clare, John, *Selected Poems and Prose*, (ed. Eric Robinson and Geoffrey
    Summerfield), Oxford University Press, 1967
    The Shepherd's Calendar, Oxford University Press, 1964
Coats, Alice, *Flowers and their Histories*, Adam & Charles Black, 1968
Coats, Peter, *Flowers in History*, Weidenfeld & Nicolson, 1970
Condon, Edith J., *Virtue's Family Physician*, Virtue & Co, 1964
Cowper, William, *The Poetical Works*, Frederick Warne, 1872
Culpepper, Nicholas, *Culpepper's Complete Herbal*, W. Foulsham, 1923
    Culpepper's English Physician and Complete Herbal, (arranged by Mrs C.F.
    Leyel), Arco Publications, 1961
Davies, Roger (ed), *The Practical Gardening Encyclopaedia*, Ward Lock, 1977
De La Mare, Walter, *Collected Poems*, Faber & Faber, 1979
Ellacombe, Henry, *The Plant-lore and Garden-craft of Shakespeare*, E. Arnold, 1896
Fitter, A., Fitter, R. and Blamey, M., *The Wild Flowers of Britain and Northern
    Europe*, Collins, 1977
Friend, Hilderic, *Flowers and Flower-Lore*, Sonnenschein & Co., London, 1892
Gerard, John, *Leaves from Gerard's Herbal*, (arranged by Marcus Woodward),
    Dover Publications, 1969
Grigson, Geoffrey, *A Dictionary of English Plant Names*, Allen Lane, 1974
    An Englishman's Flora, Phoenix House, 1955
Hardy, Thomas, *Poems of the Past and the Present*, Macmillan, 1902
Hillier's Manual of Trees & Shrubs, David & Charles, 1981
Hulme, F., *Bards and Blossoms*, London, 1877
Ingelow, Jean, *Poems*, London, 1866
Ingram, J.H., *Flora Symbolica*, London 1870
Ingwersen, Will, *Classic Garden Plants*, Hamlyn, 1975
Jacob, Dorothy, *A Witch's Guide to Gardening*, Elek Books, 1964
Jobes, Gertrude, *Dictionary of Mythology, Folklore and Symbols*, Scarecrow Press,
    New York, 1962

Johnson, A.T., *Plant Names Simplified*, W.H. & L. Collingridge, 1931
Keble, Martin, W., *The Concise British Flora in Colour*, Ebury Press & Michael
    Joseph, 1976
Lehane, Brendan, *The Power of Plants*, J. Murray, 1977
Le Strange, Richard, *A History of Herbal Plants*, Angus & Robertson, 1977
MacLeod, Dawn, *A Book of Herbs*, Duckworth, 1968
Noyes, Alfred, *Collected Poems*, William Blackwood, 1910
Osgood, Irene and Wyndham, Horace, *Garden Anthology*, John Richmond, 1914
The Oxford Book of Garden Flowers, Oxford University Press, 1963
Poets of our Time, (compiled by F.E.S. Finn), J. Murray, 1975
Pratt, Anne, *The Flowering Plants and Ferns of Great Britain*, London 1855
Prior, R.C.A., *On the Popular Names of British Plants*, London, 1863
Sackville-West, Victoria, *The Garden*, Michael Joseph, 1946
Smith, A.W., *A Gardener's Book of Plant Names*, Harper & Row, New York, 1963
Tennyson, Alfred Lord, *The Works*, Macmillan, 1902
Thurstan, Violetta, *The Use of Vegetable Dies*, Dryad Press, 1975
Whittier, John Greenleaf, *The Poetical Works* (ed W.G. Horder), Oxford
    University Press, 1904
Wordsworth, William, *Poetical Works*, (ed Thomas Hutchinson), Oxford
    University Press, 1895
Young, Andrew, *A Prospect of Flowers*, Jonathan Cape, 1945

Index